Web of Memory

The Promise Me Series #15

Tara Fox Hall

Published by
Melange Books, LLC
White Bear Lake, MN 55110
www.melange-books.com

Web of Memory ~ Copyright © 2016 by Tara Fox Hall

ISBN: 978-1-68046-331-6

Cover Design by Caroline Andrus

To Eric...Now and Forever

Much love, T

Chapter One

I walked through the front door of Hayden the second week of September, a little over twenty-four hours after being liberated from Michael's fortress. Two seconds later, V grabbed hold of me around my waist, sobbing. I hugged her, dissolving into tears as Elle and T threw their arms around me too. Their love enveloped me, washing away the horror of the last four months of captivity, making it seem like a bad dream. Even my parents were there to hug me, my mom's eyes bright with unshed tears.

God, it is good to be home.

* * * *

After showering quickly, I went to Lash's room where Titus had carried his prone body. He had still not responded to the blood infusions Devlin had given him on our trip home. I lay down near him and slept. By morning, he had still not regained consciousness. I squeezed his hand, wanting to shake him but worried I'd somehow make his condition worse.

"Give it time," Titus rumbled comfortingly as he entered. "His wounds were mortal, Sar. It's only with luck we saved his life. He's got a strong will to life, that snake has."

"And two small incentives," Devlin added meaningfully from behind him. "He'll awaken soon."

He came over to me. "Love, I've made you an appointment with Stephen for two days from now to check on your twins. Titus said Lash should wait that long before moving around. I'm betting he'll want to go with you."

"Thank you," I said gratefully.

1

"I must go over some things with Titus," Devlin said, giving me a quick kiss. "Please, would you remain here with Lash?"

"Don't worry," I said, giving him a weary look. "I've no plans to go anywhere without a full platoon with me for quite a while."

I spent the better part of that day at Lash's bedside, sometimes dozing, sometimes reading. Everyone stayed away, even my kids. Now they were young adults with their own lives; Elle was just starting a new semester, T had a business to run, and even V had her lessons. That was what I told myself, anyway.

But all this solitude gave me too much time to think on all that had happened. The last five years had been filled with so much heartache along with the happiness of becoming a mother and a partner. *Maybe if it hadn't been multiple times with potential deadly consequences, sigh.* My latest disaster, becoming Michael's prisoner for months as he tried to force me to have his child had been terrible. Almost losing Lash had been horrific, both to his degeneration and then when he had taken a sorcerer's killing blow meant for me. But I was home now and everything would go back to normal. Or what had passed for normal for me for the last few years: being Oathed–read, partnered–to Devlin, the blond vampire golden-eyed who Ruled the North American Continent, and also his co-Ruling brother Danial, who was the matching shadow of Devlin, albeit with dark hair and dark eyes. The comatose weresnake in front of me, Lash, was part of that Oath, as vampire law called it. I was pregnant with his twins, something that had made the captivity bearable, and all of our failed attempts at escape. *We made it, we're free. Thanks to Shaker…*

At once I heard the demon's voice in my head. *You called mistress?* he said in my mind in teasing tones.

Michael and his sorcerer, Cyrus, had foiled all our escape attempts. It had only been my agreeing to become Shaker's Mistress–read, his human anchor in the mortal world, to keep him out of Hell–that had let Devlin and his own demon, Titus, find Lash and I in the nick of time. The ramifications of my Hellish pact were sure to cause ripples in my life, something I hadn't had time to think about until now. *But what choice did I have? None.*

Mistress, Shaker said again in my mind.

I'm okay, I thought back to him. *Just thinking.*

If the touch of my hands would help you to ponder the benefits of our alliance…

No! I interrupted, blushing. *Leave me.*

As you wish.

I breathed a sigh of relief, then told myself not to think about any of it. There would be time enough for that in the days ahead. *You dealt with everything you went through so far okay. You can deal with this too, you just have to be strong.*

* * * *

Lash finally awakened near dusk. "Sar," he said weakly, reaching for me. "Are they okay?"

I hugged him. "They're fine," I said, patting my stomach. "I didn't miscarry. I have an appointment with Stephen the day after tomorrow."

"Come lay next to me," he said with effort. "I'm feeling like I got the tar beat out of me. But I want to hold you."

I lay down beside him and held him gently.

"I should've given you my gift sooner," Lash said bitterly, kissing my brow. "But I was worried that it might not work unless you got beyond the perimeter of Cyrus's magic, and it took me until that last day to finally find a weak spot to slip through. If that fucking Michael hadn't moved us so many Goddamned times—!"

"You shouldn't have gotten in front of me. Cyrus meant to kill me. He nearly killed you."

"Why?" Lash hissed thoughtfully. "Does Dev know why he tried to?"

"No one knows why. He said some stuff about how I was causing trouble between Rulers and vampire hunters. He went crazy and attacked Michael."

"He was crazy, just like most fucking wizards. And what the hell was I supposed to do, let him hurt you or our babies?" Lash hissed, his eyes going flat as he partially turned to snake in his annoyance. "I'd give my life for them or you, Love. I did the right thing, protecting you. And I'd do it again, even if I didn't wake up."

"I'm grateful," I said quickly, not wanting him to talk any more about dying. "I was just worried for you."

"I'll be fine in a few days," Lash groaned. "Go ahead, leave me here, Love. You've spent enough time trapped in a room with me. Go and see everybody. I'm sure they want to see you."

"Do you need anything?" I said, getting to my feet.

"You're safe, they're safe, and I'm going to live," he hissed with a crooked smile. "I'd say I'd be an idiot to ask for anything more about now."

* * * *

After I knew Lash was okay, I went looking for the next man on my list: Terian. He had something to answer for, and it was going to be the end of our long friendship. Cyrus's magic had uncovered a glamour that Terian had used on me, to visit me in dreams guised as my heart's desire, something he had sworn to me he would never do. He had done a lot of questionable things in our friendship over the years, not that I had been the best friend to him that I could have been, either.

When Terian saw me standing in the doorway of his lab, he didn't look surprised. He just put down the book he was reading and faced me. "I'm sorry."

"Why did you do it?" I said wearily, sitting down across from him. "I was in the worst possible position, with Lash in jail, Theo being with Jenny, and Devon dying. You took advantage of that, when you invaded my dream. Worse, it was something you promised never to do."

"I did it because I could, Sar. I wanted that with you so badly," Terian said, rubbing his eyes. "I think even then, I knew things weren't going to work out with Sundown like I hoped."

"You're still married." At least, no one had told me they'd split up yet. "And that doesn't make what you did right, not at all."

"Sure, but most nights I sleep on the couch," he said sadly. "Or in the nursery with Sunrise. I'm the one who cares for our baby, Sar. Sun hates getting up."

"That doesn't mean she doesn't love you or the baby."

"I know," he sighed. "I just thought that she'd become more mothering, more like a wife, and she hasn't." His eyes filled up. "She's not like you, Sar. She doesn't love like you do." He swallowed. "In

4

everything, she's just a shadow of you."

God, this was all I needed. This is not my problem, none of it. "She's your wife. Try harder with her. She is trying; she's just trying to find out who she can be. I wasn't the greatest mother, even though I tried."

"Maybe," he said, his eyes of that rich cherrywood color fastened on me. "Or maybe I just should have tried harder with someone else."

I thought about leaving. I didn't want to discuss this with him. But this conversation was long, long overdue. *It's time we have it out, once and for all.* "Tears, even if it had worked between us, which it probably wouldn't, that doesn't mean it would be as great as you think it would've been. Look at Theo and me. We tried so long to make it work. It didn't, because we'd made a mistake."

"You didn't make a mistake," Terian interjected. "Theo and you had the purest form of love there is. That shared dream doesn't lie. You can't dream with just anyone, the chances are something like one in a million—"

I don't care, I don't want to hear it. "Maybe he and I did have something once," I interrupted. "But what I have now with Lash and Dev is better. And you're way off subject here, Tears."

Terian's eyes flashed red. "So you're saying I should cut her loose?"

"No. I'm not your marriage counselor. But I can tell you to stop comparing her to me. I'm just a woman who makes mistakes like everyone else."

"You're the reason I fell for her," he said abruptly. "Because she looked like you and she wanted me, where you didn't no matter what I did for you."

For all Terian had done for me over the years, I made myself stay there and not tell him he was full of shit, though I thought I was going to drown in his BS and self-pity. "That wasn't all there was to it. You stayed faithful to her since you met her, even years after you broke up. There was more than just her looking like me. What is wrong with you that you can't see that?"

"She was funny and sarcastic, like you, but she didn't have your hope. I wanted to give her hope, because I wanted her to be happy. Because with her, I first felt like I had a chance to be happy."

Okay, that's it, I'm leaving. "Then go home to her and tell her you

5

want to try again, that you love her. Tell her you want to make her happy. Start treating her as if she was me, if that's a more of a clear goal for you. If you do that, consider yourself forgiven."

"Okay," Terian said, nodding. "I'll try, Sar. And I am sorry."

You had fucking better be. "Don't do it again, Tears. I ever find you in my dreams again and someone is going to come looking for you as soon as I wake up. Maybe several someones."

Terian's eyes flashed red briefly and then resumed their normal cherrywood color. "Are you going to tell Lash about what we shared?"

"What you *did*, NOT what we 'shared'. No, I don't need him fighting with you. Just leave it in the past where it belongs."

"So you forgive me?"

"Not completely. I thought you were my friend. I forgave you for what you did when you became demon. But this, this you did all on your own. Too many times I trusted you and you let me down."

"You let me down too, Sar," Terian said angrily. "You let us all down, when you traded Theo in for Devlin."

"Then why did you help save me?" I said, folding my arms across my chest, anger flooding my voice. "You had other important things to do, I'm sure."

"Titus asked me to. I can't refuse him anything after all he did for me."

Bad as that may have sounded, it made me feel better to hear that Terian had not done it for me. "I appreciate what you did to find Lash and I. But I can't trust you, and I don't want to be your friend anymore."

"Love spells are more resilient than real love," Terian said evocatively. "If you'd gone back to Theo, you'd never have been with Lash again. Devlin and Danial would also have taken a backseat—"

I let all my anger flood my tone, making my words sharp and cruel. "Why are you telling me this? Do you think I care? I wouldn't have wanted it to turn out any other way." I let my eyes look him up and down. "Any other way, Tears."

"You're right, it doesn't matter," Terian said abruptly. "Get going back to your thugs—"

"My Oathed one and my Mate, you mean," I stated harshly, putting emphasis on the proper titles. "The fathers of my children."

"It doesn't take much to father a child," Terian sneered, his eyes completely red. "Both of your lovers had enough practice in their long lives to manage that well enough. But it takes far more to *be* a father to a child. Think Lash will be good at that? Do you think Devlin has been?"

"Yes," I said confidently. "Devlin has done great so far, much better than I hoped. Lash will be good, too."

"Let's hope so, with you for a mother," Terian said with an arch of his brows. "I'm sure you'll be onto other men by that time. That is your MO, isn't it?"

I wanted to kill him or better yet, summon Shaker to beat him into silence.

Mistress, Shaker said in my mind. *You're angry. What's the matter?*

Terian was still going on. "God knows what will happen to those twins of yours. Did you know sometimes male snakes in the wild eat their young as soon as they're born?"

I want him to fucking shut up! I thought. *Make him shut up, Shaker!*

Say these words as I say them, Shaker said quickly, and began making sounds.

I repeated them aloud quickly. Abruptly, Terian's voice choked off and he looked at me with shock and confusion.

He'll stay quiet now, so you can say all you want, Shaker said, laughing evilly. *And he won't be able to leave either, not until he figures out a counter spell, or it wears off in an hour, or you release him by saying 'Release'. Call if you need me.* Then he was gone.

I looked at Terian, savoring him being stuck there for just a moment. He was fuming now, steam rising off his skin, his eyes glowing red as hot coals.

"Lash would never hurt me. He would never change me against my will or do anything to hurt me like you did so casually. You're wrong about him. But that's okay, Tears. I'm going to take pride in him proving you wrong."

Terian struggled, snarled, and went nowhere.

"I didn't come here to fight with you or hear you say nasty things to me. Our friendship is over. But I wish you well and I hope things work out with Sun and you. I know you love her, even if you've forgotten. Be a good father to your daughter. Take care of yourself." I stepped closer and touched him gently on his shoulder. "You're a good man inside. It wasn't your fault I didn't fall in love with you. Please take good care of Theoron and even Theo, for that matter. If he and Jenny succeed in having a baby together, that child is going to need their father."

Terian had stopped struggling. When I said "Release," he fell forward a little, before he caught himself. "That was black magic," he whispered in horror. "And it was powerful, to be able to hold a faire-demon. Who taught you that? It wasn't Titus!"

"Rene did," I lied as I walked out. "And watch your words from now on, Tears. That's not all she taught me."

* * * *

When I teleported back to Hayden, I discovered a three-year old child in the kitchen, eating ice cream. It was such a shock, I had to stand there and look for a while to make sure I was really seeing him. He had dark hair and grey-blue eyes that watched me, unafraid. The boy was dressed in a small pair of jeans, a red shirt of cotton and white sneakers. Ice cream drips dotted his shirt.

I was still taking him in when he said, "Hi. Who're you?"

"I'm Sarelle," I said, coming into the room and sitting down at the table beside him. "Who might you be?"

"Petey," he said, his face breaking into a smile.

"What's your last name?"

"Torrance."

My mouth dropped open. This was a relative of Cushing's, the vampire hunter whose attack had led to my captivity!

"Good evening, Love," Devlin purred from the doorway. He stood there in an electric blue sweater, his face beaming. In his arms, he held another child, a girl. She was dark haired also and related to Petey by the shape of her face.

"This is Sar," Devlin said to the little girl, his golden eyes gleaming with utter joy. "Can you say 'Sar'?"

"Sar," the girl said, and then she gave Devlin a smile.

"Very good!" He beamed back at her, and then turned to me. "This is Patricia, Sar. She and her brother have been staying with me."

"Why?" I managed finally.

"To get these fine children an education in all things vampire," Devlin said, as if it were obvious. "They were not learning it at home."

I felt a cold chill. "Do their parents know they're here?"

Devlin nodded. "Of course. There are some hunters outside the walls of Hayden standing guard, in addition to my own guards, just as there have been for months now." He patted the little girl's head. "Have to keep you safe, my dear, don't we?"

"And they're okay with it?" I asked. "Their parents?"

"They didn't have much choice," Devlin said, baring his sharp double set of fangs in a wide sadistic grin. "Did you, Peter?"

A medium size man with brown hair turning grey and brown eyes walked in. His skin was weathered and rough. He looked tired, but also unrelenting. "Not much after what you did," he said in a lisping voice.

I looked at Peter closer and realized he had fangs. "He turned you?"

"It was Kyle's idea," Devlin said, bouncing the girl a little on his hip, so she shrieked in joy. "I have to say, it worked out much better than mass genocide."

I looked over at Peter with apprehension. This was the man who'd threatened to kill me, my child, Devlin, Lash, and everyone else I loved. This was the man who'd masterminded the attack on Hayden and burnt part of it, who'd driven us from our home in the dead of night. God, he looked so…so nondescript.

He looked back at me with eyes both sad and resigned. "Hello, Sarelle."

"Don't be afraid, Love," Devlin said silkily. "Peter's on our side now, aren't you, Peter?"

"Not by choice," Peter said bitterly. "But you are right; I'm your ally now."

"How is that going to work?" I said incredulously. "Isn't your family out to kill you?"

"No," Peter said, kicking out a chair and sitting down at the table. "They've been supportive. Some of that is that in the beginning, Devlin made it a condition of the children's safety that they let me work with them in my changed state. So they did it, though many of them made it clear they thought I should kill myself—"

"Shh, there are children present," Devlin said chidingly. "Watch your words, Young One. There's no call to scare anyone at the moment."

"—but now that three months have gone by, I've come to an understanding with them. Some have even agreed to feed me—"

"Amazing what you can adapt to when you've been made to try," Devlin said nastily. "And Peter is also subsisting on animal blood a great deal—"

"Stop harping on that," Peter said, annoyed. "I told you that you were right. Without some human blood it does get harder to have clear thoughts or remember memories."

"It will work for you now, the animal with a dash of human now and again," Devlin said, cautionary. "But not forever, Peter. The older you get, the more you'll need human blood. But by then, I'm sure you'll have more of your family willing to let you have a bit." He beamed again at the little girl on his hip, and jostled her, making her shriek again in happiness. "I've done what I could to finesse that upcoming problem a little for you."

"They probably will," Peter said roughly, getting to his feet. "We need to be going."

"At least you'll have more years to hunt down vampire troublemakers," I offered hesitantly. "And you must be stronger than you were, and faster."

"But now I've got the same weaknesses of my prey," Peter said bitingly. "I can't go out in daylight. And I don't regenerate as fast as I'd hoped to—"

"Drink some more of your family's blood," Devlin offered with a shrug. "The better you nourish your changed body, the more it will be able to adapt and heal."

"Enough being helpful," Peter said roughly. "I came for the twins, Devlin. You promised me you'd let me take them home tonight."

"And I shall," Devlin said, handing the little girl to Peter. Then he went to the boy, and helped him stand up.

"You are going home, Peter," Devlin said melodiously. "But don't forget your time here. And remember what you learned, all of it."

"I'll remember," Peter said, nodding as he hugged Devlin.

Devlin hugged him back, as the elder Peter shifted uncomfortably. "Go now," Devlin said, smoothing Petey's hair. "Have a good life,

Petey. And remember there is more to life than video games."

Petey nodded, then went to elder Peter and took his hand. With a nod to Devlin and me, they left.

Devlin sat down beside me. "You should get some sleep, Love."

I didn't move. "Tell me what happened, Dev."

"Lash was not here to deal with the problem of Peter or Hector. Kyle beat up Hector, and Hector admitted that the plan was all Peter's, as we'd thought it was. So Kyle suggested turning Peter, as he balked at killing the whole family. It worked. Peter's family donates blood to him, though as you just heard, he subsists mostly on animal blood." Devlin smiled contentedly. "But that will change. He has seen firsthand that human blood is necessary."

"So he's working for you?"

"Not any more than he did before. The big difference is that although he's still hunting my kind, now he is willing to take on vampires that want to hunt other vampires. And that's good, as most hunters, no matter how well they train, are no match for a vampire over ten years old. And it is also not good for hunters to be going out in platoons, using numbers against the older vampires, as then even very old ones like I am in danger." He paused, his golden eyes fastened on me. "This compromise was the best solution for all. Revenge killing begets more killing, and there has been enough blood shed already for no good purpose."

"Have you turned over a new leaf?" I said, hopeful.

Devlin laughed long and richly. "A kinder, gentler Dalcon, indeed! Perhaps, Love."

"How did you manage it without scaring the kids?"

"I went with a group of state Rulers I trusted and took Peter's family's children the night that I turned him, all of them. I made it an adventure for them, with Titus's help in teleportation."

That was a relief. Despite that he was a demon, Titus would never have stood for seeing children hurt. "How many?"

"About ten children in all, though each month I've given a few back to him. The twins were the last to go. V has had fun playing with them."

"Why did you keep them so long? Leverage?"

"Yes, but with a greater goal. They needed to see I was not the evil their parents thought me to be, just as their parents were learning the same thing from the changed Peter. They needed to see that a vampire could hold a child and see it for a child, and not as food." He paused again. "They needed to understand that a child could be half vampire and still as human as one of their own children."

"It worked out well," Kyle said from behind me. I turned and gave him a smile, and he patted my hand a little awkwardly.

"Thanks for taking care of my family." My words came out emotional and warbling.

"No problem," Kyle said, giving me a smile. "Hey, I'll be at the gatehouse if you need me."

"Go upstairs to Lash," Devlin said, giving me a quick kiss on my cheek. "He needs you tonight, Love."

I thought his words odd, but I gave him a kiss and walked upstairs. Lash was waiting for me in bed, his look expectant.

I took one look at him and grinned. "I take it you're all healed?"

"Why don't you come over here and find out?" he offered, looking me up and down. "Without the clothes."

"Always to the point," I said shaking my head, even as I couldn't resist grinning. I shed my clothes, then slipped into bed beside him.

I wasn't sure what I expected. But instead of initiating sex, Lash just held me close to him. I hugged him, not speaking. Then when he didn't speak, I began running my hands over him, caressing his skin.

"I love you," I said softly. "Please touch me."

Lash ran his callused hands over my shoulders, then stopped suddenly and hugged me close. "I love you," he whispered.

He's thinking how we almost died. I hugged Lash close to me, not speaking. For a long time, we just held each other, until I finally dropped off to sleep.

* * * *

The very next day, Tuesday, Lash and I went to see Dr. Camlyn promptly at ten a.m. As soon as I saw his look of concern as he listened to my stomach I knew it was going to be bad. But I had no idea just how bad.

My doctor put away his stethoscope, then laid one hand on my shoulder. "There are no heartbeats, Sar," Steven said very gently. "I'm sorry."

I managed one gasp and then I was sobbing, Lash holding me tightly, hissing that he was there, it was going to be okay, I was going to be okay.

I cried, not listening. *Everything I did was for nothing. I'm not ever going to be okay again.*

"What do we do?" Lash hissed at Camlyn. "Can you take them out of her?"

"Yes," Stephen said gently. "Just wait here and I'll go prep the room."

He returned a moment later and gave me a sedative, knocking me out within seconds. The procedure was done while I was asleep, and when I woke up I wasn't pregnant anymore. When it was over, I couldn't make myself get up from the table.

Lash came in sometime later with Devlin. His face was shut down, though Devlin's face showed he'd been crying. As Devlin picked me up, I felt familiar demon blackness envelop me as I was teleported. In a second, we were back at Hayden at the foot of the first floor stairs.

Lash immediately turned to Devlin. "Will you stay with her?"

Devlin nodded. Lash turned away abruptly, stalking off.

"Don't kill any guards, please," Devlin called after him wearily. "Come, Love."

For the next few hours, we lay in Lash's bed, just holding each other tightly. Bitterly I was reminded of the scene from the night before when Lash had been in my arms, and I'd felt so triumphant. *At least we got to enjoy the one night.* I blinked, realization dawning. "Did you know this was going to happen?" I asked Devlin finally. "Did Rene see this?"

"She said you would need me," he said in raspy words filled with tears. "She said to keep my distance from you, Love, until you did. But she told me nothing more."

I began to cry again. Devlin held me tightly to him, murmuring words of comfort.

Some time later, I slept. And I dreamed something that was more than a dream.

Chapter Two

I'd woken up in Shaker's arms in the dream. "Hello, Mistress," he'd rumbled. "Why are you so sad? I can feel your pain like an ache within me."

I told him of my loss as he held me. He'd said gruffly that he was sorry.

I'd looked at him then, and said bluntly. "Make me forget."

"What do you wish of me, Mistress?" he asked eagerly.

"Worship me," I said, burrowing into him. "Embrace me. Love me. Make me forget everything but you."

Shaker gently reached down and tilted my chin up. He kissed me tenderly, his lips seeking mine as his arms cradled my body to his. He gently kissed me for a long time, his massive body heating up more and more, my skin beading sweat beneath his hot fingers. Soon, I felt his furry lower body settling gently on mine, and his hard, hot throbbing erection pressing against me.

I jerked beneath him, suddenly afraid. "Please, last time—"

"I apologize for that," Shaker said quickly. "It had been a long time since I was with a human. I will wait until you climax to enter you fully. And this being a dream, I can finesse things a little, in terms of size." He smiled down at me. "Tell me what you desire, Mistress."

"You once told me that demons were legendary lovers, Shaker. Do your best to make this dream unforgettable. I want to forget everything else just for a while. I want to not be me. I want to not be anything."

"Your wish is my command, Mistress," he'd said with ardor. He'd bent his head to my breast, slipped inside me, and begun moving.

That night, Shaker had loved me until I'd felt I was going to die. He'd done what I'd asked: I'd been nothing but sensation. In that brief

14

time, I'd forgotten everything I'd gone through and been. It was relief in its purest form.

But no dream lasts forever. My pain hit me like a fist in the gut as soon as I took my first waking breath. My guilt hit me a second later.

* * * *

When I awoke, Devlin drew me a bath. I relaxed in it quietly, trying not to think about my dream.

I told myself it wasn't important, that it had only been a dream that didn't matter. My choker was still around my throat and had not unclasped. If what I'd done in my dreams didn't bother it, I wasn't going to let it bother me. Shit, for all I knew, the dream had been my own fantasy and nothing else. *Even if it wasn't, I'm going to pretend it was.*

When I came out of Lash's bedroom hours later, Lash and Devlin were sitting out on his deck in the moonlight. A breeze was ruffling Devlin's hair. They were drinking some Laphroig, though neither of them was drunk.

"We did it all for nothing!" Lash hissed, almost spitting the words. "Motherfuck! All that time we stayed put, because I was afraid Sar might lose them if I tried fighting our way out—!"

"How are you feeling, Love?" Devlin interrupted smoothly.

Lash glanced at me too, his flat snake eyes immediately changing back to dark human eyes full of mourning. Then they slipped back to snake eyes again, before he looked away.

"I'm okay." I went over to Lash. "Are you?"

"I'm sorry, Love," he hissed gently. "I'm sorry for putting you through this again."

"It's not your fault," Devlin said angrily. "Stephen said you're healthy, Lash. It was that bastard Cyrus's fault."

"It has to be me. There's something wrong, because of all the years of potions," Lash hissed bitterly. "Sar's had healthy children, Dev. So what if Stephen said I was fine? He's clearly wrong!"

"Lash, I want to try again with you," I said softly.

Both of them looked at me in shock.

"No," Lash said miserably. "I can't watch you lose another of our children, Sar. It hurts too much, and it's bad for you, for your body—"

15

"The first time I got pregnant, there was most likely some problem with one of us. This time with all the stress and trouble Michael caused, I'm not surprised that…what happened, happened. But I want a child with you. Please say you'll try with me again, Tristan."

Lash shook his head and downed his scotch in one swallow. "No, Mate."

I went over to Devlin, who sat me on his lap. "Talk to him, Oathed One."

Devlin looked at Lash like he badly wanted to say something, but then shook his head. "He's given you his answer, Sar—"

"Say it, Dev," Lash hissed, staring out into the black night. "I see you've got something you're just dying to let out."

"If she were offering to have another of my children, I'd be grateful and ecstatic. So would Danial, even though he doesn't know her as Sar. Don't be an idiot, and throw away what she's offering you."

Lash looked at me emotionally for a long moment, and then nodded. "We'll try once more," he hissed softly. "But I'm getting myself cut after your pregnant, so I won't be able to give you any children after that. If it doesn't work this time, if there's some problem, I want you to let it go. It's enough for me that I have you, and we made it through that hell Michael put us through."

"I agree," I said. "But there is something else. I want you to drink from me tonight. And not only a few swallows. You are going to take enough to make me swoon, enough to make you as you were—"

"Sar, he shouldn't—" Devlin started.

"He is going to do it, because I'm asking him to do it."

"I gave him my blood. That was enough."

"And I am going to give him mine!" I said loudly. "Michael almost killed him. My blood can change him again! Now that I'm not pregnant, there isn't any reason not to!"

"Listen to you two!" Lash shouted suddenly, startling us both. "I'm right here! Don't you think you should be asking me what I want?"

I whirled on him. *It's time you and I had this out, too.* "Do you want a child, a child who is part mine and part yours? Yes or no?"

"Yes," Lash said, deeply emotional. "You know I do."

"Do you want to look as you do now, so the next time you're

16

arrested again I'll have to teleport you out of jail if I ever want to see you again? Yes or no?"

"No," he whispered.

"Would you rather drink from me a little every week and have no side effects, at least while it will work, or start taking another potion, knowing what you might have to do?"

"Stop, please," Lash hissed brokenly. "Please, don't say another word, please, Sar, I'll do it, just please don't mention that."

"I'm sorry," I said. "But I want a life with you, to not have to be afraid you aren't coming home to me. This is the best way I can think of to have that happen."

"I don't want to hurt you like last time," Lash said desperately. "Why couldn't I have met you when I was really young, when none of this would have mattered? Why couldn't you have been born a hundred years ago? Eighty years ago even!"

"You don't need to take as much as you did back when you were dying," Devlin broke in. "I am here this time to help. I'll pry you off her as soon as you're altered enough, or if I think she is in any danger."

I turned to Devlin. "Dev, before we start, you'll need to take my blood and give me yours, enough so I start turning—"

"Sar, I'm not going to drink from you, you're weak, you just had surgery—"

"Listen to me both of you, damn it! When Lash was about to die and he drank my blood, it had a lot of the vampire virus in it, a lot of regenerative power, as I'd just given birth! I have maybe half of that now, Dev. I need my blood to be the strongest it can be! Maybe if it's strong enough, he won't have to take as much!"

"I see your point," Devlin said grudgingly. "But I still think this is not a good idea."

I narrowed my eyes and stared meaningfully at them both. "What other ideas are there? Does either of you really want to trust Rosalyn enough to risk Lash's life on some unknown drug? Well? I'm listening!"

Devlin looked at Lash. Lash shrugged. Then the three of us went about preparing, this time with no amorous intent, only business as we brought an unwilling Titus in on the plan. Close to an hour later, Devlin let me drink enough of his blood that I felt myself begin to turn before

Lash and he pried me away from his wrist, the sweet taste of his blood making me lick my lips. Soon after, I was lying back on the bed, my teeth sharp, and Lash began to drink from me.

This time there was no pain, thanks to a spell from Titus. Another spell took the place of the blood replenishing packets, keeping my blood flowing, and my heart beating, even as my blood levels decreased. Titus had explained that it was something like adding in more blood, something that acted in my body as blood, but something that Lash couldn't remove from my body, no matter how much blood he took.

"It won't work, if he takes a lot," Titus rumbled as I drank the potion, his eyes worried. "You'd better watch him carefully, Devlin. And Sar will need a transfusion of blood within a few hours, no matter how little he takes."

Lash hissed something nasty, but Titus ignored him, Devlin already having given him his assent to watch over me.

Thirty minutes later, Devlin stopped Lash, pushing him back from me and inspecting him. "Go check yourself In the bathroom mirror. I believe you are pretty close to how you were after she changed you the first time. I'll wait with her."

Lash got to his feet. Through bleary eyes, I saw he was young again, his features once more altered, looking about twenty-five or so. Yet he looked an emotional wreck and went into the bathroom on unsteady feet, gripping the doorframe as he staggered.

"Lie still, Love," Devlin said. He bent to my neck and kissed the marks, healing them.

In a moment, he drew back. "You taste of summer still," he said with a sigh. "The trick will be how to give you a transfusion without altering your blood again."

Just like that, it clicked together. "Dev!" I shouted, "That's it!"

Lash burst back in immediately, his knife and gun drawn. "What the fuck, Sar?"

"My blood is the key to everything," I said excitedly. "Find a way to use a little of my blood to make more of it out of normal blood. We have Monica's notes that Cyrus stole, and I think they hold the secret to the means. Then we're home free, Dev. Then any woman only needs to have a transfusion and she'll be able to give a dhamphir life—!"

"Yes!" Devlin said, shouting himself. "You're right! Stay right there and rest, I am going to get Titus."

Devlin ran out the door, slamming it behind him. Lash rolled his eyes then eased down beside me, putting a cool washcloth on my forehead.

"I love you," Lash hissed tenderly. "I'm sorry you had to do this for me, Mate."

"I would do it and more for you," I said tiredly, hugging him. "But you've got to do one more thing."

Lash drew back with a sigh. "What now?"

"Call and arrange to see Stephen," I said, caressing his face. "Get tested daily. When he says you are okay for us to start trying to conceive, I want to start trying right away."

Lash gave me a part eager, part worried look. "Don't you think we should wait?"

"For what?" I said with a shrug. "I'm not getting any younger. Neither are you."

"All right," Lash said, nodding. "I'll call him tomorrow. Should I get Titus to make the kind of potion he made for Dev and you for us? A fertility potion would bring your body into readiness, so it will happen as soon as is possible."

"Let's ask Stephen. He'll know if it's safe." Then I grinned. "Maybe we should let conception happen on its own this time. I thought you'd enjoy trying with me, Tryst, especially if it took a few months?"

"That's going to be the best part of all," Lash said as he kissed me.

A moment later, Devlin strode in, Titus in tow. Both of them looked annoyed.

"If it were that easy to duplicate Sar's blood, don't you think I would have?" Titus roared.

Devlin closed his eyes. "Fine. Look over the notes of Monica's and report to me when you find anything we don't already know. As for Sar, check her over, now that Lash is changed again. There must be something you can do to hasten her healing the blood loss."

"It would be best to give her human blood," Titus said. "Lash didn't take near the amount he did the first time, so Sar won't need anything but that. We'll teleport to Steven's now—"

Devlin grimaced. "You know he won't let you in, after what you did to his memories—"

"He found out?" I exclaimed. "When? How?"

"Tatiana's work," my demon kin grumbled, referring to a white witch who I had once considered an ally. "You remember, Steven knows a little magic himself. They are in the same coven."

"It doesn't matter now anyway, with Michael letting the cat out of the bag about Sar not being barren," Devlin said grumpily. "But Samuel has not contacted me about that, nor have any of the others, though they likely know of everything that happened."

"I'll go with her," Lash interjected. "I need to anyway, to get tested." He gave Titus a grin. "Then you can brew my Sweetness up a little something to get her ripe for our progeny. Bet you can't wait, Demon. You're going to be a grandfather again, at least according to demon law."

"All we need is another one of you walking around," Titus said with a roll of his eyes. "Hopefully, Sar's personality and looks will win out over yours."

Lash hissed at him angrily, his eyes going flat, but Titus just smirked. "I'll begin making it tomorrow, I said I would, but I had to say it."

"Just teleport Sar to Camlyn's already!" Devlin growled at Titus. "She's weak and needs blood now, not later."

In a blink, we were there. After a short lecture on the dangers of risky behavior, Stephen gave me a transfusion of human blood mixed with a little of Devlin's blood and a little of Titus's. A half hour later, I was feeling much better. After a taste test by Devlin a little while after that, he confirmed that my blood was very close to summer again, which was music to my ears. I hadn't been afraid for my life like last time, but it still had been a little scary to feel so much of my blood being drained out of me.

Better news was that Lash was fertile, almost hyper-fertile. Steven said that was normal for weres. But all the news wasn't good.

"I'd wait for at least a month or two before trying to get pregnant," Steven cautioned us. "You don't and you might miscarry again. Let your body go through a few cycles. Don't push it."

"Titus can bring her into season right away," Devlin interrupted. "What will waiting help?"

"Maybe nothing," Steven said. "But we don't know what went wrong before for sure, and it's odd that she's miscarried twice with Lash's child. So it pays to be careful."

"I'll wear protection for the next two months," Lash said with a grimace. "I want to give it our best shot."

"Good," Steven said, nodding, then he turned to Titus and Devlin. "Now you two please leave. I don't want you darkening my door ever again, Devlin. Titus, I see you here ever again, and I'll put something in place so that when you teleport in you are forwarded straight on to Hell. Tatiana's already offered to set something up."

Blackness came out of Titus in a cold wave, as he bared his teeth, all of them, but Devlin tried to be pleasant. "I need you to help Sar, Camlyn—"

"I will help Sar and Lash," Steven said angrily. "But not you, no matter what the reason is. You are forbidden from ever coming here again, and your demon, too. Now get out, Dalcon."

Devlin snarled, but he and Titus disappeared in the next moment.

Steven turned to Lash and I. "I have something to tell you both, too."

"I'm sorry," I said quietly. "You have to be mad from having that spell done on you. And it was because of me."

"I'd be dead if it wasn't for you," Steven said grimly. "I'm sure Lash doesn't care if I live or die, so you are the only reason Devlin didn't just arrange for me to have an accident. I'll treat you now and I'll help you have this baby with Lash. But after you deliver, I'm retiring for good."

"What?" Lash hissed, shooting me a worried look. "We need a doctor, what if something happens to Elle, or to my future son? You're the best; in fact, you're the only doctor for a thousand miles that even agrees to treat weresnakes."

"I'll begin training a replacement in a few months," Steven said smoothly. "I've already worked longer than my wife wanted me to, Lash. I'm getting out before I get in any deeper."

"Good luck," I said, touching his hand lightly. "I wish you the best."

Stephen gave me a smile. "I wish you well too. But let's not say goodbye just yet, Sar. There's a lot still ahead. I'm very glad to have been part of your two pregnancies. I'll look forward to being part of this one, too."

* * * *

I headed downstairs with a basket of Dev's, V's, and Lash's laundry the next morning, mulling over a few worries.

Elle had been distant after her emotional outpouring at my homecoming, and excused herself a little while after. Since then, I'd learned from Devlin that she was indeed still at college, but that she wasn't taking classes at a university, she was taking them from home. She'd apparently moved back in to my old homestead and was living there alone.

Part of me was so proud of her for being brave enough to live by herself, for wanting to be where she and I'd spent time when she was young. But the other part was scared to death something would happen to her, especially as the anniversary of her rape approached.

What should I do? Give her a long talk about being careful and protecting herself, or tell myself she was doing fine on her own and that this wasn't the time to lecture, but instead to let her spread her wings a little? The intellect said the latter, but the mother in me said the former. Talking to Danial was out of the question. Calling up Theo and chatting about what he thought of Elle's new direction made me want to barf. Even though he'd saved me, I doubted he liked that Elle had moved out of Danial's old place to be where she and I had lived together when he'd been gone. From what I could tell, Elle was closer to Lash now than she was to either one of her fathers.

I decided to mention it to Lash later, to get his opinion. He was out training with the bears. He—like Theo—believed in daily target practice, as well as sparring practice. I'd come to see in the months I'd lived with him at Hayden that a large part of his usual day was taken up with that. That explained the calluses he'd always had on his hands.

But Elle wasn't the only one I was worried about. I was concerned for T, too: Theo and Tears were spending a lot of time with him on business calls. So who was making sure his guards were practicing their "gun control"? Brian? *Maybe I should talk to him…*

"Lady, do you have a moment?"

I looked up, my concentration broken, to see Danial directly in front of me.

Just great. I had known that Danial still lived here at Hayden, that he'd shared his blood with Dev to replenish the amount given to Lash to save his life. But I hadn't seen him since that night he'd helped with Dev's little fantasy. And that had been just fine with me.

"What is it?" I said brusquely. "I need to get these washing, before the stains set."

"Dev showed Venus how to bite her first human last night, I know. I assisted him in teaching her. But I must speak with you."

Nope. Not today. "The quicker blood is washed out, the better. Let me by."

"It's regarding Elle." Danial took the basket from me and headed downstairs to the laundry room. I followed, not wanting to, but also not wanting to put off whatever it was he felt he had to tell me, especially if it was about Elle.

He started the laundry and then led me into a basement room that I guessed was his. There were easels set up, and canvas, and all kinds of art supplies on the large table and on shelves, as well as a long couch which was obviously being used as a makeshift bed. "I thought you stayed in the green spare bedroom." I'd been avoiding the wrong place.

"I haven't since the night we were attacked," Danial said. "As it was, I barely escaped into the forest and made my way to the cemetery. Several crypts there that Devlin made are false, in case Hayden was ever attacked. I used one, spending the night and next day there. When I emerged the following night, I tried my cell first and found I had a message from Devlin, saying everyone else was safe and to come back if I had made it out alive. After that, Devlin agreed I needed a safer room, one with direct access to a tunnel in case of attack."

I nodded, surprised he'd given me such a detailed explanation. In the horror of that night, I'd not given a thought to how he'd escaped, just that he had.

I caught sight of his latest work. It was a portrait, done in oils. The woman was, at least to my eyes, most likely Monica. But Danial had made her even more beautiful than she'd been in real life, if that were possible. I felt my jealousy rear up, and pushed it back down. There was no point getting upset.

"It's still not finished," Danial said, sad and also shy. "I'm trying to get the eyes right."

He'd made her eyes a blue green color, not the deep rich blue I remembered. But I didn't want to start in on that. "It's well done. But why did you ask me here?"

"To apologize," he said, taking my hand gently. He took a breath. "I'm sorry for what happened between us months ago."

A little late, Danny. I wasn't going to make this easy for him. "Are you?"

"I shouldn't have given in to Dev's request." His voice was heavy with regret. "I was angry because he was happy with you and I thought he had no right to be. But he's right: life is for living. Sarelle would not have wanted me to grieve for the rest of my days, or to lie down and die. And she would have been appalled to know what I did with you."

To me, you mean. I watched him in silence.

"Please forgive me, Lady. Know the disrespect I showed you won't happen again."

"Why the change of heart?" I asked sarcastically.

"I know that you miscarried. I know that you are planning to try again with Lash, on Devlin's wishes. I think that is brave of you. Devlin tells me you care for each other a great deal."

"We do," I said a little less frostily.

"I am happy for you, Lady. I want to end the animosity between us, feelings I fostered and caused."

"Fine," I said abruptly. "Consider it closed." I got to my feet. "I should go."

"I'll let you go," Danial said, sounding sad again. He took his hand off mine. "I know you have much to do. But please know if you need help with anything—"

"I have Lash for that," I said meaningfully. "But I do thank you for your concern."

"Lash is often away, either on jobs or guarding Devlin," Danial said delicately. "And you will be ungainly, Lady, when you are far along.

Please lean on me, if you need to." He paused. "I often had to help Sar when she was pregnant with our son."

I wanted to say something cutting about The Lust he'd had to help me with back then. Instead, I just nodded. "Thanks."

"I also want you to know, I've been sharing blood with Devlin," Danial said forcefully. "I am stronger than I was, Lady, should you need protection."

My curiosity got the better of me. "Why now? You refused before."

"Devlin has been near crazy, these months you and Lash were gone. He fell apart, blaming himself for foolishly trusting Michael. He needed my help and I gave it." He was looking at me, but not seeing me. "It was past time I did."

Danial took my hand and kissed it. "I knew sooner or later he would regain you. It's my place to protect you as well. He loved only two other women in his long life, as you no doubt know. This time, I want to be the brother to him I should've been back then. This is a chance to redeem myself."

I took my hand gently back. "So you're my protector now?"

"Yes," Danial said, biting his lip as he was trying not to smile. "If you want to put it that way, Lady." He paused. "Not that you don't have others."

"None so eloquent," I said, finally giving in and smiling.

Danial gave me a relieved smile back. "Untrue," he said sorrowfully. "Devlin is renowned for his way with words—"

"So *true*," a rich voice said from behind me, as I was enfolded in a cool embrace. "I have been looking for you, Love," Dev said, irritated.

"Sorry," I said, pushing my head into his throat. "I got waylaid on the way to the washer."

Devlin looked over at Danial. "Have you two made your peace?"

"Yes," Danial said.

"Then you must excuse us," Devlin said. "I need some time alone with my Oathed One."

Danial nodded, but there was something in his eyes that was asking to be included. I paused a moment looking at him.

Danial looked back at me. Devlin also paused, looking at us intently.

"Would you paint my picture someday, when this one is finished?" I

25

finally uttered shyly. It was ridiculous that I could be shy around this man I'd known for years, lived with and had a son with. Yet there it was.

When Danial spoke, he was shy, too. "Of course, Lady. Though my skill is only amateurish—"

"You are too modest," Devlin said, surprisingly patient for being delayed. "You've sold your paintings for thousands of dollars over the years, Danial. There is nothing amateurish about them. I would appreciate it very much, brother."

"Come back next week, Lady," Danial said. "I'll be done with this then."

"Promise?" I said, trying hard to make the word sound meaningful, not desperate.

Danial again gave me an odd look, tilting his head. "Yes, I promise," he said, his voice cracking. Then he blinked his eyes a few times. "Come back next week."

Devlin and I left, after thanking him again, and Danial closed the door behind us.

We walked to our bedroom, hand in hand. I said "hi" to a few of the bears we passed, though they just nodded to Devlin and dropped their eyes.

"They are still a little ashamed they let you be taken and my home invaded," Devlin said as we ascended the stairs. "As they should be. But Lash and Titus have been brainstorming with Kyle, and they have plugged all the holes in our defenses. We had to execute a few bears, as some were feeding information to others outside Hayden. But I raised the salary of the rest, and gave them some other perks. No one is complaining now."

I smirked slightly. "Always my ruthless love," I teased. "Taking care of business."

"And you are glad of it," Devlin answered arrogantly, as he pushed open his door, and led me inside. I let my mouth fall open. I'd not been in here for four months. His bedroom had changed in the time I'd been away. There was a woodstove now in the corner, where the fireplace had once been, burning merrily. If I hadn't known better, I'd have guessed it was the one from my house. It was identical, down to the gold trim. Ghost lay in front of it, his massive form outstretched, soaking up the heat. Jessica and Cavity lay beside him, snoozing. Ghost put his head up, saw it was me, and gave a single tail wag. Then he gave a big sigh and relaxed again.

"I had them put it in as I remembered yours was," Devlin said quietly. "Did I get it right?"

"Exactly," I whispered. "It's the same."

"Your things are where they always were," Devlin continued. "Some needed to be washed from smoke contamination. But nothing was damaged."

"Thank you," I said hugging him. "I'm glad you took care of them for me."

"I had to," Devlin said, suddenly choked up. "They and V were all I had left of us."

I looked at my pets there sleeping, and felt a pang for Darkness. I'd known she wouldn't be here to welcome me home, but I'd wished her here just the same. But there was still one pet missing, even given that Briar had been downstairs with Danial. "Where is Phantom?"

Dev gave me a smile. "Outside hunting. There are not enough rats in the dungeon to satisfy him. I may have to stock some soon for him."

For some reason I found that uproariously funny, and I sat down on the floor, laughing so hard I began crying. Devlin eased down to the floor beside me.

"How is the white dog?" I asked him finally, not wanting to say Ghost's name and disturb him.

"His legs are worse. The vet said there was nothing they could do. That was part of what prompted me to get the woodstove. He likes the heat on his feet, where the arthritis is worst."

"How long?" My voice cracked and broke.

"A year at most, the vet said. And that was a few months ago, Love."

I clung to Devlin, swallowing hard. My other hand reached out and stroked Ghost, who moaned a little in doggy happiness as he stretched out a little more in front of the flames.

I'd lost Darkness only six months ago. Now Dev was telling me I was going to lose my other dog within the year. On top of what I'd already lost, the blow staggered me. "Thank you for this," I managed finally.

"I'm so glad to have you home," he said into my hair, tears slurring his words. "Every day I woke up, I'd forget that you weren't beside me, and I'd reach out for you and find you not there and remember—"

"Shh," I said, kissing him. "I'm home, and I'm not leaving again, ever. Okay?"

"Promise?" Devlin said as sexily as he could manage, as I was wiping away his tears.

"Yes," I said seriously, unbuttoning his shirt. "Now show me how much you missed me, Love."

Devlin moved away from me, pulling off his jeans. "That's going to take the rest of the day and night, easy," he said, desire threaded through his words. "Maybe more."

"Good," I said, as I yanked off my own clothes. "I want that. And for no one to disturb us."

"Others will want to see you," Devlin said reticently, even as he pulled my naked form against himself. "Lash may need me or you. Our daughter will need—"

I pushed him to the floor and straddled him. "I need you, Dev. I need this time with you, for it to be just us without any interruptions. Now shut up and kiss me."

Devlin shuddered and slipped inside me with a cry. I'd like to say that that first time with him was moving or sweet or loving, but the truth was we'd been apart for too long to want that. It was over in minutes, and we lay panting together, still joined.

"You'll have to be patient with me," Devlin said apologetically. "I'm out of practice. But I've not made love since you, other than just for release."

I eased back and gave him a long meaningful look. "Spill it."

"It was good for Serena," Devlin said defensively, half embarrassed and half irked. "I made sure it was. But I didn't want to be with her what I am with you. It was just good sex, nothing extraordinary—"

TMI, Dev. But this was just how he was. "Don't worry about it. Or tell me any more about it either, ever."

He kissed my throat. "It's too soon after healing Lash to really drink much from you, Love. But I'll bite you shallowly, if you don't mind. Just a few licks."

Popsicle time. OIY. "Sure, go ahead."

"God, I've dreamed of sinking my fangs into you so often, Love," Devlin said, lust pouring from him, as he moved into position. "I'd awaken starving, and it was a hunger that none of my donors could fill, no matter how much I took from them—"

Devlin pushed inside me, and began moving expertly. I arched my back under him, letting out a sigh.

"There's a sigh for yes, and a sigh for no, and a sigh for I can't bear it," he whispered lovingly, his beautiful voice stirring memories which fanned my desire. "Sigh for me, Love. Give me what I was denied so cruelly for so long."

I let out a passionate gratified sigh, and Devlin chuckled. I grabbed his face in my hands and kissed him. He flattened me to the bed, driving into me, kissing me desperately, and I kissed him back just as desperately.

Part of me had been certain that no matter what else happened, I was never going to make it out of Michael's clutches and back to Dev's arms. By the way he touched me, despite all his reassurances, Dev had thought that, too. His cry of release as he drank from me that first time was so full of happiness and pleasure it made me shudder in his arms.

That day with him was almost as good as our first day together had been. He sang to me, quoted my favorite verses, and called down for some food to be sent up to us. I ate, we drank, and we made love until we fell asleep in each other's arms. And when we awoke, we showered, made love again, ate again, and fell asleep again.

No one disturbed us. We turned off our cell phones and unplugged the bedside phone. We let our pets in and out and back in. Someone, I was guessing Serena, came to get our trays, and cooked my food, and brought us fresh wine and glasses. But no one interrupted.

About thirty-six hours later, I was laying in Devlin's arms feeling supremely comfortable when I decided that soon we'd have to get back to our usual lives. Devlin had been right: we had responsibilities.

But Devlin awoke soon after and began touching me again. And I told myself that Lash and Titus were around, that I'd earned a little break from my responsibilities. We both had.

29

Chapter Three

Yet Devlin himself was no evader of duty. Around six p.m., he told me reluctantly that he would have to leave. "I need to feed. My efforts with you have exhausted me, Love. There is no doubt a list of persons I need to return calls to, to say nothing of V." His voice dropped an octave. "And Rene expects you tomorrow to come to her, according to her."

"I'll go to her." I ran my hand over his arm that was wrapped around me. "I should go and see V, too. Lash will need to see me; he may even need me as snake. And the pets need attention—"

"There is also some filing and email work for you to do for T," Devlin added.

This was news to me. "T told me months ago he didn't want me to do it anymore."

"Jenny did some of it for a while, but then she got fed up and quit. Sundown has helped, according to T, but she also said that it's 'not her thing.' Besides, she has her hands full with Sunrise, who's still an infant. So I've done what I could alone for the last week or so. It's a mess, Sar. I'd be grateful for your help."

"I'll sort it out," I said, feeling a lot less cheery about it than I made myself sound.

"There's no rush," he added lovingly. "You've been through a lot. Don't push yourself."

"Is Danial better?" I asked, changing the subject. "He seems much better."

"Some," he said finally. "He's really helped me in the past months." He paused. "He is back to the strength he once was. He's even been working out occasionally, which is something he never did before. He is no longer grieving, though he has yet to find someone new."

"You'll have to import a dark haired woman with blue eyes for him," I joked.

"There is a new donor coming tonight who fits that description," Devlin said evenly, as I let out a little gasp. "Her name is Danielle, if you can believe the coincidence. But her middle name is Emma, and I have asked that I be allowed to call her that here. I want this to work out."

"What to work out?" I echoed, knowing full well what he was going to say and wanting him not to say it.

"Danial needs a woman of his own," Devlin said, hugging me. "I want him to have days like the ones we just spent together. I want him to be happy."

I sighed. "I want that, too. But it'll be hard to watch, Dev."

"I know. I knew if you made up, it would be. But Danial is right, Sar. I would never have turned to Michael so readily if I'd had my brother there beside me, helping me as he is now. Now that he is acting like a Ruler again, if a slightly distracted one, I want him to keep getting better, so you and V can remain safe."

"Are you saying he's sort of partnering with you in Ruling Canada and the US?"

"Yes, just unofficially for now. He's been a big help, actually. But you know he can be diplomatic even when he's very angry, where I am usually not. Ruling often calls for ruthlessness and cruelty, there are better ways to make warring parties get along. At least, until blood needs to be spilled."

It was definitely time to change the subject. "From now on, I want time with you like this every month," I said seriously. "Time for just us."

Pleasure radiated off Devlin, yet he gave me an odd look. "We have always made time to be together, Sar."

"Not like this we haven't," I replied. "We've both got responsibilities. But what's the point of living a long time, if we're always so busy we don't have time to really enjoy each other?"

"A woman after my own heart," Devlin purred. "I agree, Love. And so it will be this way, from now on." He walked to the door, putting on his jeans, and tossing on a shirt. "Come out when you're ready. I'll be with my donors, but back in your arms by dawn."

* * * *

When I left the bedroom a half hour later, Lash was there waiting for me. He gave me a hug and grinned. "I wondered if you two were ever coming out," he said gruffly. "Because otherwise pretty soon, I was coming in."

"How is everything?" I said, as we walked downstairs.

"Dev's women are coming in an hour or so. V's practicing her piano and wants to see you. The guards are all doing well, but Kyle's got that handled. And I'm starving for some home cooking." The last was said in a very meaningful fashion.

All predictable. "What do you want to eat?"

"Cornbread, regular bread, liquefied steak, pasta, some chocolate cake, and some gingerbread cookies," Lash said, still grinning. "Though you can wait until tomorrow for the apple pie."

Right. I began getting out ingredients. "Pasta and cornbread coming up, Mate. The others will have to wait until tomorrow, though I'll make some of the doughs tonight."

"Tired out?" he asked gently, hugging me from behind.

"Sated. But I feel renewed, too."

"Good," Lash said, relieved. "From what Kyle's told me, Dev needed this very much. He…um…missed you."

That sounded ominous. I let it go, deciding it was better not to ask what he meant.

"I heard you made up with Danial," Lash said casually.

I knew what that casual note in his voice meant; he was at the edge of being pissed off and only needed a quick nudge to get there. *Sorry, I'm not going to lie.* "I did. We're something like friends again."

His tone turned scathing. "I hear Dev's got a Monica look-alike coming tonight—"

"Stop it," I murmured coldly. "I don't want to fight."

Lash abruptly changed the subject. "Are you going to spend the evening with V? Dev's going to feed and then he'll be up all night dealing with his shitload of messages and returning calls."

Sounded bad. But maybe it was nothing. "Yes, probably, if she wants to—"

"I want to!" V said stridently, coming in to grab me around the waist so hard I let out an "Oof!"

"Good," I said, giving her forehead a kiss and marveling how tall she was. "You can help me make the doughs. Later we'll watch a movie."

"Can I pick the movie?" she asked.

Groan. "Sure, Daughter Dear. We'll have a girls' night—"

"I'll be with Kyle until ten," Lash proclaimed loudly from the doorway. "I'll come up to bed after that. Wait up for me."

"Of course," I assured him. "You aren't forgotten."

"I'd better not be," he hissed meaningfully as he swaggered out.

* * * *

I teleported to the convent at first light the next morning. I'd thought Rene would be waiting for me, she'd been so eager to get home to Devlin. Instead, the sister who answered the door told me she would take me to Rene's room.

I followed her for a few minutes. Then we arrived at a plain wooden door with a simple metal cross affixed to it. With a nod to me, the sister left me there.

I knocked and went in. There was a light-blonde-haired woman sitting there on a rough metal frame bed, her head in her hands. She was sobbing,

I went over to her and hugged her. "Rene, what is it?"

"Can you forgive me?" she said brokenly.

"Forgive you for not coming to meet me?"

"For not being able to foresee what was going to happen!" she cried loudly. She looked up from her hands.

I blinked in surprise. Rene was no longer the duplicate of me she had been months ago. She was almost ethereal now in her loveliness, her blue-green eyes large and liquid, her cheekbones high, her face now oval instead of square, and her lips full and undeniably kissable.

I reined in my jealousy with difficulty. "You...look different."

Rene gave a slight smile that made her beauty almost triple. "Yes. The reason the spell said nothing about how to modify a new body was

33

because there was no need to. Apparently, the soul has enough power to modify a new body once inserted; at least, that's what I'm guessing. I wouldn't think it would be true for a stolen body, or else why have a new spell?"

Forget that! "What were you asking forgiveness for?"

A large tear rolled out of her left eye and she wiped it away. "For not being able to see what was going to happen to you with Michael, or find you, or even see of the impending attack on Hayden. I used to be able to see so much, Sar. I was sure I'd be able to have the gift again of precognition once I got my own body. But so far it's just insignificant things!"

"You saw my babies had died within me," I said, trying to keep my hurt and anger out of my voice. "I wouldn't call that insignificant."

"I'm sorry," she said, breaking into sobbing again. "I didn't mean to say it that way! I feel awful that happened to you!"

"It wasn't your fault," I said gruffly. "Please stop crying. Your tears aren't going to help what's happened to me anymore than my own did."

"I know that," Rene said bitterly. "But I owe you so much, Sister. My Goddess, it's the least I could do to warn you of impending disaster. Instead of being there to help defend you, I was here with nuns hiding!"

Sister? Must be from being here with the nuns. "Not anymore," I said, grasping her by the arm and pulling her up. "You're coming home, 'Sister.' It's safe now for you to."

"I know what you did for me," Rene said in a small voice. "That's another reason I feel guilty. You not only gave me a little of your soul, you also helped buy mine back."

"You'll get to return me some big favor yet!" I reassured brightly, uncomfortable and trying to make light of the somberness as I went out the rough door. "You can start by giving me some demon lore right now. Shaker alluded that he would be satisfied with just some blood now and then to satisfy the agreement I made with him. But indubitably there's more to it than that?"

"There is," Rene said, walking beside me. "He'll need to eat flesh and blood every month if he wants to stay at full strength. But likely Devlin will be happy to provide Shaker with that."

"I'd rather not ask him," I said quickly. "So please don't mention it, not to anyone."

Rene stopped walking. "Why not?" She eyed me carefully. "It'd be easy for Dev to—"

"Don't ask me about it," I interrupted darkly. "You said you owe me favors in spades, well here's one you can repay: leave this topic alone, Rene. Don't bring it up unless we're alone."

She nodded, still staring at me. "Shaker may ask you for the sustenance he requires. He'll likely wait to do something in your service before he asks. When he does, let me know. I can get what he needs in a way that will make sure your soul stays more or less as white as it is now."

Now I stared at her. "Why do you say it like that? Is my soul in danger just by being bound to a demon, even if I never ask him to do anything for me?"

"Being bound to a demon is supposed to corrupt. That's the whole point of Hell lending them out." She began to walk again and I fell in step beside her. "Demons don't necessarily do much evil at their owner's bidding. Most other non-human beings, like Devlin, get them for protection. Most humans get them seeking power or wealth. But always, over time, demons need bodies, blood, sometimes even souls or a person's life force if they are badly wounded, or have to expend a lot of energy. It is giving them those things that stains a person's soul, makes it blacker and blacker as the years go by, so that by the time they die they're headed for the Pit, even if they have never done any evil in their life other than sustaining the demon. Though of course, some say once you're bound to a demon you're responsible in terms of evil done for everything the demon does while out of Hell, whether or not you know of it or approve—"

My flesh was beginning to crawl, imagining how dark my soul must already be with what Shaker'd probably done just in the few weeks he'd been in my service. "But if you do this, you'll be corrupted, right? Aren't you worried about your own soul?"

"Mine was never that clean to start with," Rene said ominously. "But that's not an issue, as I don't intend to ever die again. If it looks like that might happen, I'll have to think of something to avert it."

Maybe she just knew Dev was headed via superhighway Downtown, and wanted to join him for the ride. I'd miss him and Lash myself, if somehow I made it to Heaven.

"But enough talk of bad things, Sar. Please tell me that you are well?"

"I am," I said. I told her briefly of how I'd transformed Lash's appearance again, and of making up with Danial, which Rene grimaced at, and of spending the last few days with Devlin in blissful seclusion.

"I'm looking forward to time with him myself," Rene said lustily. She looked out of the corner of her eye at me. "Are you going to be jealous, sharing him with me?"

"Probably, to be honest," I said through gritted teeth, taking in her new gorgeous appearance. "But what's there to do? You were Oathed to him before I was. And like you said, you can make your body strong enough to withstand his great strength. Hell, Rene, I'm already sharing him with Hillary and Tiffany, what's another—"

"Not for much longer," Rene said with a sultry grin. "I am well aware of what they do for him. I'm prepared to handle that rather large aspect of his needs, too. They are, as you say in this time, being 'kicked to the curb'."

I felt appalled and also like bursting out laughing, so I settled for a bright expression that had to look at least a little fake. "Then I'll be sharing him with one less person."

"You know it's not the same as sharing him with whores," Rene said flatly, looking into my eyes. "He doesn't love them. He does love me now, or will in time. And I want you to know I'm not here to get in the way of what you and he have. I've not come back here to wrest him away from you. I just want to be in his life and in yours."

"If we're going to be really honest here, answer me why that is," I said bluntly. "Why would you not want him for yourself? Why wouldn't you want me out of the way, so he would just be yours? If I were in your shoes and had loved him for eons, I would." I felt a momentary flash of jealousy remembering Catherine, and squashed it down.

"I could give you reasons," Rene said after a moment. "But the real reason is not emotional at all: it's that I care very much that he remains in power. Before he came to power there was a lot of unnecessary bloodshed, and many creatures were killed of all kinds. He helped create law from the shouting confusion, and order out of the melee. If he ever falls it will be a short matter of time before this country collapses back into a pattern of the strongest killing whomever they want to as much as they want to and then outright exposure of all those not human—"

"Why?" I interrupted. "No one's ever 'broken cover' in the history as I know it. So why would it happen now, Rene?"

"Because this age is not superstition, it's reason, and proof, and streaming video on the internet 24/7. We are more in danger of exposure than we ever have been, Sar. And I don't just mean vampires, I mean all supernatural beings. As soon as humans found out how weak some of us were, and how evil some of the old beings really are, there would be war: a long bloody war with humans on one side, and nonhumans on the other. And if one didn't go extinct, they both would." Her tone was dismal. "That I did foresee long ago, if Devlin did not succeed in assuming the throne. Much of what I did for Devlin was because of that vision."

"I thought you did it out of love for Devlin."

"Make no mistake that I love him more than my life, Cherie," Rene said kindly. "But my head has always ruled my actions, with my heart second. It is what kept me from seducing Devlin by magical means away from Anna. Things had to play out just as they did." She gave me an unreadable look. "And I would never have gone to my death so willingly those years ago if I didn't believe it was what was fated to happen."

"What if—instead of that—you had foreseen yourself killing him?"

She never paused. "I'd have killed myself as soon as I could've. I could never have hurt him any more than I could now."

"Then that's not your head talking," I said a little triumphantly.

Rene gave me a grin. "You're right. When it comes to Devlin, I do not have the will to fight my heart, even if I know I should. But it's true that in regards to the rest of the world I do. I care about what is best for him, always, even at the expense of myself. You are good for him, Sar. You bring balance to his darkness."

We were at the gates now. Rene took a breath and stepped off holy ground. Like magic, Shaker appeared in front of her, his red eyes full of burning flames. "Decided to make things easy for me?" he rumbled. "Just give me your soul already. If you come along nicely, Witch, I'll put in a good word with Satan for you."

"As if you knew Satan!" Rene scoffed. "You might be powerful, Shaker, but you are no ranked demon."

"Always a bitch," Shaker said almost amicably, then turned to me. "And how are you, Mistress?"

"Good," I said. "Thanks for meeting me...us here."

"You commanded me to," Shaker said, giving me a licentious grin. "I'm always eager to do whatever my Mistress asks of me—"

"Give me back my soul," Rene said forcefully. "I stand before you and ask for it, Shaker."

"Then I release you from your pact," Shaker said grumpily, making some sign of pulling something from Rene. She jerked a little, and grabbed a stone column for support, crying out in pain. "I relinquish all claim to your soul, sorceress."

Rene clung onto the column for support. "Goddess, that hurt!"

"My marker had been on your soul a long time," Shaker said, looking happy. "Your soul had grown over it. Tearing it free was going to hurt. But at least it didn't hurt like *Hell*..."

"Ha ha," Rene said nastily, standing back up. "I thought demons were supposed to be original."

"I am an original," Shaker said, folding his arms across his chest. "That's why I look as I do, Witch-bitch. You on the other hand are just a copy and not a very good one at that—"

"Enough sniping," I said loudly. "Shaker, we need to get back." I paused, seeing his attention shift to me. "Um, by the way...do you need anything?"

"I do not, Mistress," Shaker said, tilting his head and looking at me. "But I must ask if you need anything of me. I like to *provide* for you, my Mistress—"

"Not right now," I said, blushing at the way he said it. "I'll call you if I do."

"As you wish." Shaker shimmered and then he was gone.

I grabbed hold of Rene and teleported her home before she could say anything. We appeared before Devlin who was sitting in his bed, reading.

"You're home!" he said joyously. Then he really looked at Rene and his eyes seemed to drink her in as he looked at her. "God, were you always this beautiful?"

Rene blushed a little and he kissed her hand, murmuring something in French.

I was already jealous, and he hadn't even kissed her for real yet. Not a good start. "I'm going to go," I said quickly. "I have a lot to do today."

"Put it on hold," Rene said, not taking her eyes from Devlin. "Go into Lash's room, Sar."

I gave her a look, but there was something in her voice that told me that I should do it. So I went into Lash's room and lay down.

This is great, being here by myself with nothing to read or occupy my mind. I can lay here and imagine what he's doing to her... Suddenly, I was not in my body anymore. I was in Devlin's room.

What the fuck?

Shh, Rene said to me mentally. *You are with me, in my body.*

"Why? Why do you—?"

"Shh. Wait and watch."

Devlin came in naked from the bathroom, and paused in the doorway. "God, you are a vision," he murmured. "I want to just look at you, Rene. I had remembered you being beautiful, but the memory I have does not do you justice."

"You have eternity to look at me," Rene said jokingly. "Come over here and touch me, Dev. I didn't wait months to be looked at!"

Devlin stalked over to the bed, and crawled to Rene/me on all fours. Then he was holding her/me down as he got into position above us.

He made as if to penetrate us, and she grabbed hold of him. "Stop," she said, splaying our hands across his chest. "Wait."

Devlin gave her/me a look like she was insane. "Are you sure you're well, Love? You have never once stopped me, not in anything I did with you, no matter how deviant—"

Whoa—!

"I am ready," Rene said throatily. "And I want you very much. But you have to be gentle with me the first time, Dev."

"You've made your body resilient, or you couldn't be strong enough to hold me back as you are doing," Devlin almost growled. "So what's the problem, Love?"

39

"There's no problem, idiot," Rene said kindly. "But it's the *first time*. Get it?"

Devlin gave her a puzzled look. Then his expression turned to one of amazement, as he moved off of us, and slid his hand down to touch her intimately. I felt his middle and index fingers slip inside us, and then he shuddered. "You're intact, Love."

Now she'd gotten a new body, Rene was a virgin again? I was speechless.

She was not. "Not for long, Lover," Rene said with a sigh of longing. "But I want to be with you more than once. So you'll have to ease me back into the game gently, unless you want to play most of the night by yourself."

"This seems a little unfair," Devlin said, giving us a grin. "You are way too experienced a lover to be a virgin, My Sweet."

"Be that as it may, I have it only to give away once," Rene said solemnly. "And that is why Sar is with us now, that she can share in this with you and me."

Devlin gave Rene a weird look. "Sar is in you, listening to this? Why?"

Rene smiled. "With men it is easy to do what is expected of you: you are supposed to be adept when you meet your great love, so you don't hurt her, so she gets the most pleasure. So it's accepted by both sexes that men have lots of lovers before they settle down with one woman. But women have it hard, if you'll excuse the pun: we are supposed to be pure until you touch us, and then immediately after we are supposed to be as knowledgeable and comfortable as old whores at pleasuring the male body and ourselves. Women cannot do that so they have to choose between being pure and as useless in bed as a piece of meat, or knowledgeable and thought to be soiled or used because of it—"

"Given the choice, I have always preferred my women knowledgeable," Devlin interrupted lovingly. "Unless I was acting out a fantasy of stealing away a young girl and defiling her—" He abruptly cut off and looked away, coloring.

"He defiled young girls?" I said in horror in Rene's mind. "*How young is 'young'—?*"

You know of how he used to be, Rene said mentally. *Drop it, Sar, or*

40

leave us. I am not going to ruin this night with either his feeling self-conscious or you being judgmental.

I nodded assent.

"That was a long time ago I did that, Sar," Devlin, both upset and embarrassed. "I didn't mean what I said to come out like it sounded—"

"Forget the past," Rene said forcefully, taking his face in her hands. "Be with us, Dev. And let us both be virgin for you, as every girl dreams of being for their soul mate."

Devlin didn't reply, he just kissed us. His hands roamed our body, caressing and squeezing. When he took our left breast in his mouth and bit it gently, grazing it with his fangs, I was already ready for him to make love to us, and by her moans, so was Rene. But Devlin held us down and suckled from us gently for a long while, even as Rene's moments became more frantic and she struggled to get him to enter her.

"Please!" she said urgently. "Please, Lover, take me!"

"Non, mon Coeur," Devlin purred as he licked us, biting gently. "I want you to be writhing beneath me, utterly undeniable! I want you to be flowing with your need to have me within you!"

"I am already a veritable fucking font of desire!" Rene panted, her usual delicate voice coarse. "Stop teasing!"

"Then you go first, Love. Take me," Devlin said lustily, rolling onto his back. "I remember well how good you were."

Rene crawled onto him quickly, and without a word, she swallowed his organ completely. I tried to push back, remembering how scary that could be, but Rene was already moving purposefully on him and he was groaning, jerking as he held her head in his hands.

Devlin began to thrust hard into her mouth, rocking the bed. I felt Rene register a slight pain, but she ignored it, her mouth clamped around his rapidly moving manhood as she manipulated him.

Devlin began to growl and thrash and then he was thrusting so hard the bed seemed sure to break apart. Rene was registering more than mild pain now but she renewed her efforts, her hands gripping Devlin's buttocks as she matched him thrust for thrust.

Devlin screamed loudly, convulsing, and I felt him come in great spurts, almost choking Rene with his seed as he pushed himself as deep inside her as he could. Rene couldn't breathe, but I felt her begin to count, trying to calm herself. When she reached ten, Devlin gave a last shudder and withdrew from her most of the way.

Rene kissed the tip of him, drawing another gasp from his parted lips. "How was that?" she said hoarsely.

"It was the best oral sex I've had in two centuries," Devlin said in a relaxed and sated voice. "But are you okay, Love? I did not hold back at all, as you had asked me not to." He pulled her up into his arms, cuddling her. "Are you bruised?"

Rene was still getting her breath. "I'm okay," she said after a minute. "I need to put up my resilience a notch, but that's all. But other than I'm sure to be sore, I'm fine."

"Good!" Devlin said, biting her gently along her throat. "I want you to know you've been had, Love, and that it was good enough sex to make you remember with soft sighs of bliss long after the deed was done." He bit her earlobe gently. "I want you to feel you've been had by me, Oathed One, me and no other—"

"Will you want others to join us?" Rene asked suddenly.

Devlin drew back and considered her. "Is there someone you had in mind?" he asked neutrally. "A fantasy that kept you sane all those lonely nights we were apart?"

"No. But Sarelle has others listed in her Oath contract with you. I want to know if you are going to ask me to be with them, too, or even others besides them. I know you enjoy watching."

"Lash will not want you to be with him under any circumstances," Devlin said, grinning a little. "For a snake who's spent most of his life being with most anyone, he's turned completely monogamous. So if you were hoping for a foursome—"

"I was not talking of him, Devlin. Do not act dense."

"You do not want to be with Danial," Devlin said, after a moment. "Do not worry, Love. He is most likely not going to ask, not ever."

"Good. But I believe that our contract should be like yours and Sarelle's, Devlin."

Devlin drew back from her and looked at her. "Why are you bringing this up now, in front of Sarelle? There is some purpose. What is it, Rene?"

"I want there to be no jealousy," Rene said flatly. "There are two of us Oathed to you, Devlin. There are questions that need to be answered." She gave a small sigh, running her hands over his manhood. "There are rights that must be spelled out."

Devlin considered her. "Do you want part of my fortune if something happens to me? Part of what I have already promised to Sarelle? By vampire law you as an Oathed One have a right to some of what is

mine—"

Rene shook her head. "If something happens to you I'm following you into death. I came back to this world to be with you. Leave your written contract with her as it stands."

"Then say plainly what it is you mean!" Devlin said, his voice a growl and his eyes tinged red as his little patience abruptly left him. "I want to make love, Oathed One, not spend the night discussing terms!"

"We must discuss them before our Oath is re-consummated," Rene said sharply. "And so I will say it plainly: I wish to be bound by the same Oath Sarelle is. The exact same one. And to receive the same Oath you gave her. That is fair."

"Sarelle tells me you saw Theo," Devlin said, rolling his eyes. "I didn't know you had a taste for werecougar, Love. Because that's got to be it, though I'm surprised—"

Rene wanted to be with Theo? Theo? *You are not missing anything,* I said mentally to her.

She ignored me. "I like all well-built men equally," Rene said, not sounding embarrassed at all. "But you are above all the rest. Now say the words that you agree that Sarelle's Oath she took is mine as well. And then say that the Oath you swore to her stands fair for me too."

Devlin shrugged. "Very well. As Sarelle swore, the same holds for you as my Oathed One: You are to be only with myself or men of my choosing, or Theo, or Lash, or Danial, as they are or were lovers of Sar's. And I swear to be with no other women save you and Sarelle, save women you and she give permission for. Agreed?"

"Agreed. And I will live with you here at Hayden. I promise to do all I can to protect both you and Sarelle, and your children—"

"Agreed, Oathed One," Devlin said impatiently. "Now may we get back to the consummation?"

43

"Of course," Rene said, lying back. "Come and get me, My Lord Vampire."

Devlin grinned as he laid his hips over hers. "You've never called me that before, Rene."

"I intend to do many things with you I never got the chance to," Rene said meaningfully. "But I've waited long enough to feel you within me, Dev."

Devlin took hold of her gently, and slipped the great swollen head of his hard cock inside. Her flesh gave slowly under his pressure, as he eased himself in. "God, I forgot how small virgins are," he murmured, pressing as he shifted his hips back and forth. "But it's been at least fifty years or so since my last one. Please stop me if I hurt you, Love."

"You feel wonderful," Rene moaned, clasping him to her. "No one feels like you do, Dev."

"I'm glad of that," Devlin said rakishly, pushing deeper. Abruptly, he ran into her maidenhead. "Hold onto me, Love. I'll be as quick as I can."

Rene gripped him, and Devlin bore down with a sharp thrust. I felt our flesh part before him, and Rene and I let out a jagged cry.

Devlin was completely motionless, his body still not completely inside us. "Hold onto me, Love," he said gently. "Just hold onto me. I'll not move until the pain ebbs, I promise."

Rene just nodded, her chest falling and rising in rapid movement as she let out soft whimpers. But I understood why: Rene's womanhood was throbbing, and it took many minutes before it subsided to the point where I could think about more than getting from one moment to the next one.

"Why was it so painful?" I asked her finally. "I don't remember it hurting me so much, though I admit it was a long time ago I lost my virginity."

My body is more resilient, Rene said mentally to me with something like a groan. *Harder to hurt. Harder to tear, Sar. It was a tradeoff.*

After some time, Devlin began kissing Rene again, though he still didn't move at all. After a few minutes, she responded to his kisses. With a slow movement, Devlin slipped the rest of himself inside her.

I felt with something like shock that he was completely inside, but he wasn't touching her cervix. How was that possible?

"No one feels like you, Love," Devlin murmured gently to her as he kissed her. "You are the only woman I ever met who took all of me easily, yet still gripped me so tightly. God, you feel so deliciously warm!"

"I'm your soul mate," Rene said, kissing him passionately. "I was made for you, Dev."

"You were," Devlin purred, and he began to thrust into her in earnest, bringing cries of pleasure from Rene. "You are mine, Love."

"I'm yours," she said. Then to my shock, she bit him hard, drawing a tiny bit of blood.

Devlin let out a cry, but it was lust, not pain. "God, your teeth feel so good in my flesh! Bite me again, Love! Bite me hard!"

Rene bit him hard, and he moaned, thrusting into her with abandon. As before the bed began to rock, and Rene suddenly orgasmed, screaming out loudly as Devlin hammered himself into her. She clutched him to her, pushing her hips to his, her movements so frantic with need. Then she sagged beneath him, weak with sated pleasure.

"My little fanged sprite," Devlin said amorously, kissing her gently. "And how was your first orgasm in the flesh?"

"Wonderful," she said, a wide grin on her face. "But I'd like another."

"Then come with me, Faerie-child," Devlin purred, and he began to move again. Rene moaned, arching her back. Devlin reared back, baring his fangs, and sank them into her jugular. Rene jerked, her eyes going wide, but then I felt the pleasure hit her, God it was so wonderful, like the best orgasm ever—!

Rene came loudly, screaming, Devlin convulsed on her, still drinking, and then he gave a muffled shout of pleasure. His orgasm seemed to last for minutes, and then he sagged on her, his back rising and falling rapidly.

Devlin snuggled close to Rene, resting his head on her chest. "I love you," he said with a sated sigh. "Tell me you love me, Rene."

"I love you, Devlin," she whispered. "I have since I first dreamed of you. And I will love you forever."

Chapter Four

I abruptly found myself back in my own body. I lay there for a moment, reliving the experience.

Why had Rene been so adamant about the Oathing being the same for her and me, especially if she didn't want either money or Theo? Could I trust her, knowing how much she loved Devlin? *I mean, c'mon, she loves him that much and she isn't going to want to sleep with him every night—*

I felt a cold shudder. What if she *did* want to sleep with him every night? Could I sleep with another woman in bed with him and me? I already knew Lash wouldn't sleep in the same room as her. But would Rene be content to be with Devlin just when I was with Lash? But that would be more like half the time, right? Maybe Dev wouldn't care who was with him so long as he wasn't alone in bed. How was I supposed to feel about that?

I got up and took a shower. I did have other things to do with my day besides sex. The more I thought about this the less I was feeling good about any of it.

* * * *

Just before the first snow, the bulbs I'd ordered a month in advance arrived. Devlin joined Lash and I the next night in planting them around Darkness's grave. "There's something disquieting about me planting flowers called 'I Love the Sun'," Devlin said in a lilting voice, as we worked. Lash burst out laughing.

I stopped digging and gave him an exasperated look. "I told you, I ordered 'Harvest of Memories,' Dev. They sent me the others because they were out, and this kind is yellow, too."

"Whatever you say," Devlin said, obviously trying not to laugh. "I'm just saying—"

"Shh, Oathed One." I planted my last bulb, then patted the ground. "Rest easy, good dog. You are loved and remembered."

After we came in, Devlin and Lash excused themselves to take a conference call. Telling them I was heading to bed, I headed up to Devlin's bedroom, peering inside first to make sure Rene was not there waiting for him.

There's nothing for it. I'm going to have to start knocking first. Another peculiarity in my life is nothing new at this point.

I'd no sooner taken off my clothes than I felt a soft touch of hot skin as a large hand caressed my naked back. I let out a yelp, and darted away, looking back to see Shaker standing there behind me.

"What are you doing here?" I exclaimed, grabbing a robe, and slipping it on.

"You didn't call for me," Shaker said, giving me a faint grin. "Not that you said you would. But I expected you wanted to see me, after our dream together. So here I am, in case you did, and were too shy to ask me to come. And in the flesh too, so you'll get the full experience this time."

Time to say it. "I'm sorry. I don't."

Shaker looked dumbfounded, then chuckled. "My bad, then. But are you sure? I can whisk us away to Maui, where we can lie on hot sand and make love in the waves." He gave me a look with enough intent and cunning glee to make me freeze. "We'll make them steam, Mistress. No one here will be the wiser, I guarantee it. Just say the word, and you can have your heart's desire—"

I thanked God in that moment for all the guilt I was feeling, because it was helping me do what I knew was right. "I'm sorry," I said. "I made a mistake, asking you to do what you did."

"What, Terian?" Shaker said, advancing languorously. "That whelp needed a little quiet time. I heard what you said to him. Most of it made him feel better. So it was a good thing." He reached out for me. "Come to me, Mistress. I wish to worship you again. And this time I'll use a spell to make our night together seem to last days instead of only hours—"

47

"Stop," I said loudly, and Shaker stopped, looking disgruntled.

"Sar?" Seth said from the other side of the door. "Are you alright?"

"Fine," I called back loudly, then turned to my demon, who had taken my distraction as an opportunity to move closer.

"Leave," I said adamantly to Shaker. "I'll call you if I need you. But you have to go. You can't be here, not like this!"

"I'll settle for another dream," Shaker said, sliding closer. "Let me touch you gently, as I did before and kiss away your pain. You have only to ask. I'll give you anything you want—"

"There aren't going to be any more shared dreams. I want you to go," I said stridently. "Who is Mistress here? Go!"

"I must be losing my touch," Shaker said humorously. "It's the hooves and horns, isn't it?"

In spite of myself, I began to grin at his humor, then pushed it down. "Go or I'll start quoting Scripture! I mean it!"

"Quote me some of Solomon," Shaker said, grinning widely. "Or I will quote some to you, my Valkyrie goddess—"

"Glory be to the Father, to the Son, and to the Holy Ghost—"

"You're supposed to sing that, not say it," Shaker said, grimacing. "But I will go, Mistress. I must tell you I'll need sustenance soon, in the next six months or so. Just enough to sustain my full strength. Liquid is fine."

He must mean blood? God, I hoped so. "Fine. Give me a week's notice."

"Agreed," he blew me a kiss. "Until my hips rest over yours again, Mistress."

He disappeared, and I lay down on the bed, feeling spent, even as I let myself smirk at his sense of humor. Before I thought anything more that might make Shaker think I wanted him to come back, I took two valium and went to bed, relaxing into nothingness.

* * * *

Life went back to normal for the next week. I did email, and took short walks with V and Ghost. We watched movies together, and I taught her basic sewing, though unlike Elle, she showed no interest in learning to craft things. Her mind was on clothes, music, TV, and on her friend

48

Sharon, Samuel's daughter, who she talked to on email. But she did enjoy baking, so at least we had one thing to share.

V also enjoyed her schoolwork and reading, more so even than I. She loved history, and she would spend hours reading of long ago battles. I came to see a lot of the time Devlin spent with her was of him telling her tales of his life, things he'd seen centuries ago and lived through. I only listened a few moments, until some of what he said began to make me emotional, before I left, not wanting to distract V.

All was well until I walked upstairs from exercising one day and caught the sound of Elle speaking. It wasn't her normal voice. This one was upset, almost despairing, with a good deal of resentment mixed in. "Where's mom?"

"She's busy." *Venus's voice.*

"Where is Mom?" Elle repeated, exasperated. "I know she's busy, she's always busy—"

"She's not really your mom, she's mine," V said snottily. "Why don't you get going? I'll tell her you came by."

"I've come by three times before, and she hasn't called me," Elle growled. "That means you didn't tell her I was here."

My mild annoyance was fast turning to fierce rage. I stalked toward the door, livid.

"I can't help if my Mom doesn't want to see you," V sang. "Why don't you go home to your jock father and his new female? She's your own kind, so I'm sure you can call her Mom—"

Don't hit her, Sar. Remember, she's your daughter. I stalked into the room, and grabbed hold of V. "Shut your mouth!" I shouted. "How dare you talk to your sister like that?"

"She's not my sister," V hissed, her fangs elongating, her eyes turning blood red. "She's not my blood! She's were, they're no better than animals—!"

I lost it and slapped her hard. V's head rocked back. She looked at me with shock, holding her face, and then she let out a scream of absolute rage.

"Mom, get behind me," Elle growled, moving in front of me, her eyes yellowing. "She's out of control and she might hurt you!"

"You were-bitch," V hissed at Elle, her nails lengthened to claws. "This is your fault!"

"Stop it!" I screamed. "Both of you, stop fighting!"

Both of them braced themselves to attack. Then like an answer to a prayer, Devlin was suddenly there. He picked up Elle and V by their throats and squeezed. Elle went limp, her human features forming again, and Devlin abruptly let her go. But V fought, snarling, sinking in her talons. Devlin snarled a little, but he didn't slacken his grip.

"Calm down and change back," he said to V. "Stop fighting, daughter."

"Let me go!" V hissed. "You have no right to grab me! She started it, they both did!"

"Don't lie to me," Devlin hissed coldly, squeezing tighter. "Don't think I won't snap your neck, daughter. Perhaps you need some time out cold to think about the rashness of your actions."

V hissed at him, baring her fangs, and he hissed back at her, his eyes bleeding to red. V cast down her eyes, and began to change back.

I turned to Elle. "I'm sorry she said that to you."

Elle gave me a weary look. "I'm just glad someone finally heard her other than Lash."

"Lash knew she spoke to you like this, and said nothing to either of us?" I said, my anger building all over again. "Why—?"

"He talked to her," Elle said, looking over at V balefully. "It just didn't take."

"My talking to *will*," Devlin said stonily. "And if something else ever happens like this, you are to tell me, Elle." He glared down at V. "I will not have you two fighting. Family is too important for you to be at each other's throats."

"Didn't you spend most of your centuries fighting with Dad?" Elle said sarcastically, casting a look at Devlin. "That's what Theo tells me. And that's what I remember."

"I did, and I'm not proud of it," Devlin said flatly, still gripping V, though he'd relaxed his forceful grip substantially. "But I want better for you and V, Elle, especially as you will likely have a new sibling soon—"

Both V and Elle gave me horrified looks. I felt like the worst mother of the year, that the thought of me having another baby was so awful to them both. Jesus, had I been that bad of a mother?

"Whose is it?" Elle whispered.

"Lash's," I said quietly. "We have lost children twice now. We're trying once more, Elle, before we give up for good."

"I'm not going to have a Goddamned snake for a—urk!" V's words cut off as Devlin tightened his grip, grating his fangs together so loud I could hear the crunching sound.

"Do not dare speak a word," he growled, the rage in his voice thick as rock. "Do not dare, daughter. My temper is near the breaking point."

"Why, Mom?" Elle said skeptically. "Why have another child?"

"Because I want to share that with him," I said, feeling both emotional and lame, and hating it. "You know we are mated. It's something he's wanted for a while. It's something I want very much."

"He loves you," Elle said, coming to me reluctantly. "If you both want a baby, I'm not going to say anything. Theo and Jenny are trying for one."

I felt cold water hit me, and made myself focus. Theo was not my business anymore, but Elle was. "Are you okay with that, Elle?"

"I wasn't at first," Elle said reluctantly. "But I'm okay with it now, Mom." She hugged me, and leaned back. "I'm not a child anymore and I'm off to live my own life. I want you to be happy, just like you always wanted me to be." She hugged me. "I hope it works."

How had my daughter become so wise? It wasn't my bad behavior; it must be Danial's influence and guidance. "Please come back and visit or I'll come and see you, if you tell me what day is good."

Elle looked uncomfortable. "My place is messy. But I'll call you soon, ok?"

I nodded, and then with another hug, she left.

By now, V was on the floor, glaring at her father.

"What brought you to say such things to Elle?" Devlin said seriously. "It was Sharon, wasn't it?"

V didn't answer him, looking instead at the floor.

"Samuel is known for his dated views of werecreatures," Devlin said scornfully. "And Sharon has no doubt learned well at his knee. Elijah is likely much the same—"

"Would that he was!" V said in a biting voice. She glared at her father. "But he's more liberal in all his views, as you know."

"There is nothing wrong in being willing to change your views," I interjected, sitting down next to her. "The world changes very fast, Venus—"

"Really Mom? I hadn't noticed in the one year I've been alive!"

"Do not sass your mother," Devlin said sternly. "She and I want what is best for you. And you are too young to know what that is yet, so you will do as I tell you. Now answer me, did you hear your racist views from Sharon or not?"

Venus nodded without looking up.

"Do you really believe that you and I are any less animal than Lash is?" Devlin said, sitting down on the floor next to us. He reached out and took V's hand in his own. "We have fangs and claws like Elle, even if yours are all retractable."

"I'm better than she is." V said confidently.

"You are not better," I said in a tightly controlled voice. "What gives you the right to think you are better?"

"I'm a vampire's child," V said, as if it was obvious. "I'm going to live forever."

I thought of Elle's mortality, and couldn't say anything. I could already see she was getting older, though her rate of growth had slowed considerably. *What will I do when we look the same age? Worse, when she is old and I remain young?* The knowledge that I would live to find out crashed into me, making me speechless.

"We do not know that you will be immortal," Devlin said, bringing V into his arms. "Not for certain, daughter. You may have your mother's lifespan and not mine."

V looked terrified. "Are you saying I'm going to die?"

"Not anytime soon," Devlin said gently. "But everyone can die, even me. Even Titus can, though it is hard to kill a demon. Always remember, those that think something is impossible, and flaunt that, usually witness the impossible come to pass."

I nodded. "Exactly, V. Don't hoard the years you have like a pile of money. Years of living will mean nothing unless you spend them being happy, loving yourself and others."

Devlin's eyes met mine. "Listen to your mother. She said it all right there—"

"I'm still better because I'm Sar's real daughter," V said stubbornly. "And you're my father, and everyone does what you tell them!"

I gave Devlin a meaningful look telling him to speak up.

"It's true I favor you, V," Devlin said, hugging her tight. "I waited for you a long, long time. But that doesn't make you better than Elle."

"I'm a princess," V said contemptuously. "Like Sharon is! And Elle's a peasant!"

"I am a peasant then, too," I said coolly. "I'm not vampire, V."

"But you're Dad's Oathed One," V said in a reassuring tone, taking my hand. "You're a queen, I heard Samuel refer to you as one—"

Fucking Samuel, I was going to knee him in the balls the next time I saw him, for screwing V's values up. Then I kicked myself, because if I'd spent more time talking to V about the stuff that mattered, things wouldn't have got this bad.

"—and we're all rich, and Elle's not—" Venus went on.

"Being rich doesn't make us better," I interrupted, appalled.

"All my clothes and Sharon's are designer," V said nastily. "Elle's probably came from Wal-Mart."

Okay, that was it. I got to my feet, and went up to V's room, Devlin trailing me with V still in his arms. I looked around, and began pulling out clothes, checking labels, but I was at a loss. I'd never owned designer clothes in my life, so I didn't know if these names were designer or not. These clothes were faded and worn out looking. Shouldn't designer clothes be better made?

In a few moments, I was overwhelmed. By the pile on the floor, V owned about fifty pairs of jeans, and at least that many pairs of pants, and that was just from the smaller dresser. I hadn't even gotten to the walk-in closet, the bigger dresser, or to her shoes.

"What are you doing?" Devlin said curiously.

I turned to face him. "V, you are saving out ten pairs of pants and jeans, and twenty tops. And the rest you are to fold up and we are donating them to charity."

V looked at me aghast, and Devlin did too.

"I bought them for her when you were gone," Devlin said gruffly. "It wasn't an easy time for her or me. Her love of clothes matches my own—"

"I understand that," I said gently. "But no one, um...younger than twenty needs this many expensive clothes, especially not a young girl who is using them as a basis to look down on others. Besides, V and I will go shopping after we drop off the clothes and get her some new ones."

V looked overjoyed, and began picking through the mess. And Devlin gave me a quizzical look that said he didn't understand my reasoning, but he left to get some boxes, when I told him to trust me.

The next morning saw us dropping off close to ten boxes of clothes at a local church's clothing bank. After we dropped them off, I took V across town to shop.

"Where are we going?" she said expectantly. "And don't you dare say Wal-Mart, Mom!"

"It's not Wal-Mart," I said, giving her a smile, and she beamed at me.

She was horrified when I pulled up in front of the Salvation Army. "What are we doing here? This place is for poor people!"

"Clothes shopping," I said self-righteously. "Now come on."

"I'm not going in!" she spat at me, her eyes turning red. "You can't make me!"

"Suit yourself," I said, flipping open my phone. "I'll call Titus, and he can teleport you home. But if you don't come in, and pick out a few things, you won't be seeing or talking to or texting Sharon for the next week. Now what's your decision?"

V looked at me, then looked away and didn't move. But when I dialed the phone and began talking to Titus, she relented.

That first hour with her in the store was agony. She sighed, moaned, and complained so much we got stares from all the other customers. But after a while, her female genes got the better of her, and she began to pick through the clothes.

Before long, she had a few and then a few more. Another hour later, we went into the dressing rooms with an armload at a time to try some of them on.

By the time she emerged, she was in a much better mood.

When we got to the checkout, she got nervous. "I don't have my credit card," she whispered to me. "Do you have yours? How are we going to pay for this?"

"I brought cash," I assured her. "I've got it covered."

"It's going to be over a hundred," she said skeptically. "You can't have a hundred thou on you in cash, Mom."

It was then I realized that she'd mistaken the hand writing on the labels, thinking 499 was four hundred ninety-nine dollars, not four dollars and change. My God, how expensive were designer jeans?

"These are on sale," I said, pointing to the sign. "There are the rules, V. Today's family day, besides, so we're in luck. I have enough money. Just watch, and listen."

We put our armfuls of clothes on the table, and the women behind the counter folded them and rang them up. When they said the damage was seventy-eight dollars and thirty-seven cents, I handed them a hundred, and told them to give me the balance in gift certificates. They were a little dubious, but did it.

When we got outside, V put her clothes in the back, and I asked her if she wanted to go get lunch. She nodded.

She was silent through most of lunch. Over dessert, she finally asked, "Why were those clothes so cheap?"

"They're used, most of them," I said flatly. "This way, they don't get thrown away in the landfill after whomever bought them gets tired of them."

V looked ill. "Used? By other people?"

"They are no different than the designer clothes you bought," I said, starting the car. "The labels are different, sure. But I saw what you picked out, and you found some good brands, brands that I'll wager will last you much longer than those designer clothes."

"We could've spent a hundred thousand on what we got today for under a hundred dollars," V said slowly. "Why is there such a difference, if it doesn't matter that much?"

I stopped the car, and turned to face her. "Because some people think it matters. Some people think that is all that does matter, V, that and being seen in the right places, and knowing the right people, and having the best that money can buy."

"And you're saying it doesn't?"

"It's fun," I said, giving her a smile. "And I'm not saying it's not okay to have some expensive clothes, or to spend some money on those you love. But that isn't what matters most."

"So what matters, O Wise One?" V said sarcastically. "Getting what you buy on sale?"

I eyed her carefully. "You say you think we saved a hundred grand today?"

V looked thoughtful, and then nodded.

I drove to the bank, and took out a thousand dollars. And then I handed it to her.

She got a big smile on her face. "Are we going to another store?"

"Yes," I said in a low voice.

I drove across town, and pulled up before a building.

"What is this?" V asked, peering out. "This doesn't look like a store."

"It's a food store," I said, getting out. "Some people would call it a food bank."

"Do we need to get baking supplies? Why haven't we come here before for them—?"

"No, we aren't buying food for us here. Just come with me."

V followed me in, mystified. I went to the counter, and a friendly rumpled looking woman came up to me. "Yes?"

"We want to make a donation," I said firmly. "V, give her half of the money."

"What is she going to do with it?" V said curiously. "What are we buying?"

"Please tell her," I said, smiling and nodding to the woman.

"We have food here for people who are hungry," the woman said kindly. "We give it to families that need it and can't afford to pay for food. We use donated money to buy food to stock our shelves."

V snorted. "Who couldn't afford food?"

"See the line of people behind us?" the woman said gently. "They are in line to get groceries. Some have been there for hours, waiting. And I guarantee you, the workers in back will run out of food before those at the end of the line have any."

V looked incredulous, and then she looked like she was going to cry. She threw the woman the sheaf of bills and ran out.

"Do you want a receipt?" the woman called.

I shook my head, already going after V. I found her by the car, crying.

"Tell me it's not true," V said, sniffling. "What she said can't be true, can it, Mom?"

"It's true," I said, hugging her tight. "If you want, you can ask Elle. There was a time, after she was first born, that I was considering going to stand in line for food, because we were poor, she was a baby, and I didn't have the money to feed us." I took a tissue out of my purse, and wiped away her tears. "But then I went back to Danial, and he took care of us, when Theo went missing. But I remember how I felt, knowing that I couldn't afford enough food for her and I. It's a feeling I hope you never have to feel, V. But it's something you need to be aware of, that not everyone is as fortunate as you are."

"Danial told me once he'd been hungry as a young man, that his family had no bread," she whispered. "I thought he was just saying they'd run out of bread, and eaten something else. So I told him that was too bad, but everyone had to get used to not having fresh bread at some time in his or her lives. I remember him giving me a stricken look and changing the subject. I feel awful!"

"It's okay," I said, taking her into my arms. "You were a child. I'm sure he understood that."

V hugged me tightly. "Can we go home now?"

"Almost," I said. "We have one more stop."

"Where?"

"Well, two more. First, I have to get some more money."

We went again to the bank, and got out another five hundred dollars. Then I drove us to the local Humane Society.

It took me a while to muster up the courage to go inside. I felt embarrassed about that, that I could face hungry humans easily, but not homeless cats and dogs. Then I reminded myself of the difference between them: just being hungry versus possibly being put to death for not being lovable enough.

"What's in there?" V said as she clutched me, scared. "Why are you so upset?"

"Animals are in there. Pets who have no place to go, no homes," I said, staring at the dashboard. "They stay here for a while, but if no one wants them, they get euthanized."

"What's euthanized?"

"Killed."

V let out a gasp. "Why?"

"Because there are too many, V, and not enough homes. Many people don't fix their pets. And seeing them upsets me the way just knowing it happens doesn't—"

"Do we fix our pets?" she interrupted.

"Yes, we do. Come on."

We walked in and I handed the money to the woman at the desk. She got tears in her eyes, thanked me, and practically ordered me to fill out a form so I could claim a tax deduction. It was when I was handing the paperwork back to her that I noticed V was missing. I went looking for her, and found her in front of a cage with a small black cat in it.

"I like him Mom," V said firmly. "I want to take him home."

Oh shit. "V, we have four cats already, and—"

"You said these animals need homes," V said stridently. "It would seem like the better thing to help would be to give one a home, not just hand over some money. Right?"

I knew right then I'd been outmaneuvered. I turned to the woman. "Can you get us the paperwork please?"

After an hour's worth of paperwork, V, Valentino the cat, and I were on our way home.

We got back just as the sun was setting. Devlin met us at the door, and it was evident by his face he'd been awake all day and worried. He gave me a smile of relief to see me home with V, neither of us bleeding.

He was shocked at Valentino. "What made you think we needed another cat?" he said, peering into the cage.

V led him into the kitchen, and proceeded to tell him about what we had done that day in a blast of a few minutes. To say he got emotional wouldn't have been pushing it. I held it together myself just because I concentrated hard on making a quick dinner of soup and salad.

"So what are we going to name him?" Devlin said, when V had finished. "Valentino is a bit much."

"Let him out," I offered, pouring myself some wine. "I didn't get a good look at him. Maybe he has some quirky ways or some odd coloring."

V opened the cage door and Valentino walked out. He was fluffier than I'd thought, and a nice blackish grey color.

Devlin froze looking at him, and before I could blink, he was holding him, murmuring some French to him.

"I see you're already attached," I said jokingly.

"Attached to what?" Lash said loudly from the doorway. Valentino shrieked, and began to claw Devlin, who tried to quiet him.

"Shh!" V hissed at Lash, who held up his hands and nodded.

"A new member of the family, I see," he said more softly. "Where did you get him?"

"An animal shelter," I said, handing him a glass of wine. "His name's Valentino."

"Dev, you must love that!" Lash snickered.

Devlin ignored him.

"We're trying to think up a new name," V said sternly. "Help or be quiet!"

Lash gave her a grumpy look, but then he considered Valentino. "He's fluffy for a guy." When he put out a hand, the cat rubbed against it, purring.

"Another black cat," Devlin said to Lash with a grin. "This is number four. Good thing we aren't superstitious."

"Everyone usually wants cats that aren't black. There are always too many black cats in shelters," I began, and then brought my mind back to the present. This was a happy time, and not one to spend thinking sad thoughts. Instead I fastened on the thought that tonight there was one less black cat who needed a home.

"How about 'Shadow'?" Lash offered. "He is black."

"And part Persian, with those orange eyes," Devlin said affectionately. "But Shadow's not very pretty. How about 'Nightshadow'?"

"There are no shadows at night," V said flatly. "There's no light, because there's no sun."

"Not true. There's the light of the moon," Seth said, as he passed by in the hall. "Good night, all. I'm off duty, Lash."

We all looked at each other. "Moonshadow," Devlin said lovingly, petting our new cat. "Welcome home."

Chapter Five

Later that night, Lash was out making the last check of the guards, and I was reading in bed. Devlin was tucking V in, as he did most nights.

When he came in, he did not look happy. "Sar, what possessed you to take V shopping for clothes at a thrift store?"

He must not have heard all V had said. "We've already discussed this," I said distantly, wanting very much to finish the chapter I was on before Lash came back and told me the reading room was closed for the night.

Devlin snatched my book out of my hands and placed it on the end table. "I need your attention, Sar. All of it."

So much for finding out the killer's identity. *Sigh.* "You have it. Now what's the problem?"

"The problem is that those stores are there for poorer people to procure clothes," Devlin lectured. "They are not there for people who can afford to buy new clothes."

"Don't tell me you're concerned that V's purchases robbed some young teen of a pair of jeans," I said firmly. "You're upset that she's wearing used stuff, aren't you?"

"She is a princess, as she says she is," Devlin said sternly. "She should dress as such, as should you. And no, that does not include used clothes." He gave me a thorough look over. "Or anything that is worn or faded, unless it is supposed to look that way."

I suppressed a snarl at his scrutiny. "There something wrong with the way I dress?"

"As a rule, no," Devlin said in a conciliatory tone. "But I've noticed that you seem like you're afraid to spend my money. I want to know why."

"I was always like this," I said, uncomfortable and more than a little embarrassed.

"You were not when you lived at Danial's," he countered. "I know for a fact you never took Theoron shopping to a thrift store. Danial would have told me. Despite that he's not much for fashion sense, my brother would also have told you what I'm telling you now: this is odd behavior from you."

"I never cared about anything material," I said, shrugging. "Elle didn't either, other than to have elegant dresses for special occasions. That's all a person needs, Devlin: nice things for special occasions, and regular things for everyday life. I don't need to dress in velvet to file paperwork, or wear designer jeans to garden."

"But I get enjoyment out of buying V whatever she wants, as I do with you," Devlin said, his eyes tingeing a little red. "Why should I give that up?"

"Because we don't need it," I said, wanting badly to leave and wondering to myself exactly why this conversation was bothering me so much. "So you don't have to give it—"

"Really? Does this sense of frugality extend to food as well? Are you aware that we have been going through a hundred dollars, if not two, of Godiva chocolate products a month? Rene has also developed a taste for it now."

"I had no idea it was so much," I said guiltily. "We can cut back."

Devlin came to me, and hugged me. "I don't want to cut back, Love. And this is what I want to know: why you feel that you can't enjoy everything you want to." He studied me. "Is there some reason you're afraid to indulge?"

"Because it won't make me happy, getting everything," I said flatly. "It will make me bored, fat, and resentful."

"You are not any of those things," Devlin said, kissing me lightly on my cheek. "So why do you fear them?"

"Because it would be easy to become one of those people who think they need designer jeans, or vacations in Spain, or ten thousand dollar birthday cakes to feel happy. And I know I don't."

"Why not have them, and see if they do?" Devlin said temptingly. "If they make you unhappy, that would be one thing, but—"

The man was part demon, more demon than Titus was by far. "Look, all I see when I see a ten thousand dollar dress is that someone is paying a ton of money for, just to show off to their friends, trying to impress people. Does anyone need a dress that costs that much?"

"I have suits that cost that much," Devlin said, after a moment. "I like the way they fit me, Love. Being tall as I am, most suits that are of a regular man's size do not flatter me."

I found that unbelievable but didn't want to argue. "Look, there is nothing wrong with having some nice things, Dev. But—"

"But nothing, Love. I am a king and must look the part. V should also look her part."

"She's a child and she should look like a child, Love."

"I do not want her to be thought of as anything other than a princess."

"Royal bearing doesn't come from clothes, it comes from behavior and breeding," I said, looking directly at him. "She has enough of both from you to be dressed in rags, and still everyone would know her for what she was."

"You are assimilating my way with words," Devlin purred. "You have a point." He gave me a gentle kiss. "But I will not back down from this, Oathed One. You are not to make V shop at thrift stores from now on. I would encourage you to buy some new clothes as well. It has been at least a year since you did."

An inner wall went up inside me, as words formed that I didn't speak: that wasn't true.

I experienced a fleeting memory of picking out clothes in catalogs while in captivity, and getting the piles of boxes. Looking at all the expensive shirts, jeans, and dresses, and hating having to wear them, because they'd come from Michael…

Cool arms embraced me. "Love, what is it?" Dev whispered. "Please tell me. You look like you're going to be sick or maybe cry."

I'd sent most of them back. But I'd had to keep some, even though I'd hated it. I'd had to do a lot of things I hated because I'd had no choice…

"Sar, say something!" Devlin said worriedly.

I didn't respond, but hearing his worried voice did snap me out of memory. Dev wasn't to blame. I'd trusted Michael too, back almost a year ago, at the...

"Is the Hallows party coming up?" I rasped.

Devlin gave a relieved smile. "Yes. T is holding it this year with Terian and Theo. Danial said he will not attend, but I know T is trying to get him to come, hoping if Danial sees some of his old clients he'll be moved to come back to work."

I clutched the new subject like a life raft. "Why, Dev? Danial has his hands full painting and helping you. He seems better."

"He is, but Solutions, Inc. is not," Devlin said ominously. "Some of that is the fault of Sundown and Jenny, that a few important clients were not handled as they were used to being handled. But a good deal of it is the recession and that the company has changed hands, among other things."

"What other things?" I said, turning my head to look at him.

"Danial's business grew since he moved here and joined up with Theo. But after he met you, there were a lot of changes. He stopped doing hits, then for a while, I took over the vigilante end of things, and he went it alone. Theo and Terian helped him, and then T. And there were those months when he shut down the business, something he'd never done before—"

"Devlin, I know all this! Say plainly what you're trying to say!"

"Solutions, Inc. has changed a lot in the last five years, Sar. But what was the only thing that hadn't changed in that time? Danial. He was always there, running it."

"He wasn't, he was in a coma for most of last fall—!"

"But it's known now he's well and that he's not back to work. This is not a month or two; we are approaching a year now that Danial's not had the reins. T's great at the programming, sure, but he's still very young, despite his adult body and advanced state of learning. He doesn't have Danial's hundred years of experience. Even though Terian's old, he doesn't, either. And Theo might kill and do security work very skillfully, but he's muscle, plain and simple."

Theo was more than muscle: he'd masterminded many of Danial's jobs over the years, and to hear Devlin dismiss him so casually rubbed me wrong in a big way. "Like Lash is?"

"Ooh, a little defensive of your old flame?" Devlin said coolly. "And no, Lash has a hundred times the brains of Theo, and a hundred times the experience. If Lash were to sign on to Solutions, Inc., business would come roaring back!"

"So why hasn't T asked him for help?" I said nastily. "They're good friends."

"Because he knows of Danial's hatred for Lash, despite his politeness to Lash now that they both live here," Devlin said scathingly. "If T asks Lash to help, he knows Danial will never come back. T's a good son; he remembers how much his father enjoyed the work, and he wants that back. He wants his father back."

"We all do," I said, letting out a sigh. "But wanting and getting are two different things."

"Not to mention Theo would leave, and Terian might, too," Devlin said less abrasively. "But that will not happen in any case. Lash has his own business to run, plus his work helping me here. His days are full already."

I nodded, thinking there were a lot of days I didn't see Lash until bedtime. I suspected he was also scheduling more 'demolitions,' though no one had said anything to me on the subject of his assassin work.

"You know Kyle is talking of leaving," Devlin said gently. "He's had a restless spirit his whole life. Now that the demon that was hunting him is neutralized—"

"When did that happen?" I exclaimed. "My God, I was only gone four months!"

"Lash took care of it last week," Devlin said, looking at me steadily out of the corner of his eye. "As a favor for Kyle taking care of things here this summer with Peter and Hector."

"What happened to Hector? I thought Kyle beat him up, and that was it. What else did you do to him?"

"Nothing," Devlin said, baring his fangs in a large toothy grin. "But his daughter who is twenty-two is vampire now. Since she was turned this past spring, he's been a lot more…open minded, shall we say?"

God, he was malevolent. "Did you do it, turn her?"

"Nate did it," Devlin said, lying back expectantly as if waiting for me to start a fight. "He's in change of TN, as you know. Hector lives just outside of Nashville."

"I'm surprised you didn't turn his wife, too."

"Nate, Sweet Sar," Devlin purred dangerously. "It was his prerogative. I just told him to do something to make Hector think twice about any more attacks. Nate's a good Ruler, he knows what to do, and isn't squeamish about doing whatever he must to whomever he has to—"

I repressed a shudder, remembering my one experience with Nate. "Won't this trigger more attacks?"

"No, not by Hector," Devlin said flatly. "Nate reports he's broken, that he may be resigning his position. But as with Peter, he is also allowing vampires who want to hunt into his ranks. So we may in fact be at a turning point in hunter/vampire relations."

I had to admit, it did make me feel better to hear that the two men who'd masterminded the attack on Hayden were neutralized now.

"But we are off topic," Devlin said smoothly. "You were agreeing to buy some newer clothes and go through yours to throw out some of the older things."

I glowered at him. "I'll throw out some worn nightclothes. But most of what I have that's worn I'll save for work clothes, such as when I'm painting. Deal?"

"And no more trips to thrift stores?"

"I'm not promising that," I said loftily. "But I'll promise to buy something new for the Hallows party or have something made, and spend your money to do it. And it'll be expensive. Fair?"

"Fair enough," Devlin said, baring his upper fangs in a grin. "It's a beginning."

Devlin had undressed by now, and was inclining his head, asking me to come into his arms. I snuggled into him, and for the first time since coming home, I really felt safe.

* * * *

Everything went well for the next week. I'd been home now close to a month and a half. Slowly. I was relaxing back into some of my old comforting routines, albeit with a few new twists.

Lash slept with me every night, if he was home. He no longer had the fear of sleeping without his weapons after having had to go without them for so long. His knife, gun and whip were beside the bed but not within reach. When he thrashed or began hissing in nightmares, as he began to in those later weeks, Devlin or I just shook him and he awoke. He never spoke of what he'd nightmared about, but from what he said in his sleep, I guessed most were of his sisters, and of people he'd fought whom he'd killed.

Rene had taken Titus's old room at the end of the hall. Kyle had used it in the months he'd been staying at Hayden, but he said with a smile that now that Lash was back, he would be happy to go back to his old guest room until he left next spring. With Danial moved to the basement, there was plenty of room to spare.

Oddly, Rene never asked that Devlin come to her room. But she spent about half of the nights with him in his room, always when I was with Lash in his room. The other nights she slept alone. I wondered at that, but didn't ask her or Devlin about it, in case my questioning her actions prompted some change.

Devlin seemed happy with the arrangement and weird as it may sound, I was, too. With Rene around, a lot of the pressure I'd always felt with having two lovers was off. It was nice to be alone with Lash, and know that Devlin wasn't lonely, because Rene was with him.

Lash was also relieved at the arrangement. "I can hear them," he said to me one night quietly. "Some of what they do is…well, the kind of thing you don't especially care for, Sweetness. With her living out those fantasies of his for him, I won't worry about him wanting you to." He patted my bottom.

"You and me both," I muttered, thanking God again for Rene.

"Plus she can protect him, like his other lovers over the years usually couldn't," Lash hissed softly. "She's no lightweight, from what I know of her. When we are attacked again—"

"Don't you mean 'if'?" I said in foreboding and fear.

Lash hugged me tightly. "Shh, Love. I'll be here to protect you. But we will be attacked again in our lifetimes. Forever is a long time."

"We aren't going to live forever," I said, trying to smile and feeling just plain scared.

"We may," he said thoughtfully. "Who can say, with all the knowledge and power we have access to now?" He kissed me and nestled in close. "I was saying that Rene can get Devlin and you out of here in an attack, or at the least, hold them off long enough for you to teleport, if I was away when it happened. Best-case scenario would be me being here. Then between Rene and me, most likely we could handle anything that came at us."

"You sound like you are starting to like her," I teased.

"I am," he said, giving me an odd look. "She's made an effort to fit in here. And she respects and likes me, which always puts a being on my good side."

I was grumpy suddenly. "You know she's included in our Oath, Mate. So if you get the urge to taste faerie, you'll be able to just go ahead and indulge it."

Lash let out a loud hiss and thrashed, pulling me up to look at him. "What did you say?"

"Devlin gave permission, but it was she that insisted." I felt a nasty urge and indulged it. "She must have done it for you, Sweetness. She dislikes Danial, and doesn't know Theo at all."

Lash looked panicked. "That can't be it, Sar. She's never been anything but a coworker and friend to me."

"Remember that time she was with us as snake?" I said wickedly. "She said she thought you were amazing, with all you knew. She said she'd never been with a snake that knew as much as you did." I paused for effect. "She said you were talented and it was just wonderful."

Pride came off Lash like heat. "It's true, I'm good," he said, dripping smugness. "But I didn't expect her to ask for that. I didn't expect her to want more of me." He turned musing. "Faeries were some of my best lovers over the years. They were always accommodating, changing form to snake when I asked them to."

I didn't know if I liked where this seemed to be going. Teasing time was over. "Are you going to bed her, Tryst?"

Lash snapped out of his reminiscing. "No, Love. I said no other women and I meant it."

"So you don't have a fantasy of her and me as snakes coiling around you, both of us at once?"

Lash let out a sharp hiss of pleasure, stiffening immediately. "That's not fair. Fantasy is one thing, life is another."

"So you don't want us both there together, squeezing you in our coils as we caressed you with our tongues?"

Lash gave me a passionate kiss, and then he was shoving down my underwear and shoving himself in. He stroked me only a few times before he came, his screams loud and ragged.

"Of *course* I'd like that," he panted, moving off me. "Any male snake would, it'd be like a fucking wet dream come true! But I'm not going to do that." He gave me an apologetic look suddenly. "Shit, I forgot to use anything, Mate, I'm sorry."

"It's okay. It's been a month and a half," I said, kissing him. "I think we might as well go ahead and stop using the condoms, Sweetness."

"You're sure?" he hissed hesitantly. "You're sure it's okay? I'll understand, if you've reconsidered."

"I haven't," I said, kissing him again. "But what will I do if you want me to be snake for you? Can you tell somehow when I'm pregnant and stop me from changing? You...um, said you could...before." I was not going to mention Michael, not here, not ever.

Lash nodded confidently. "Wait to be snake for me until I ask you from now on, Sweetness. If I feel the urge for it, I'll know you aren't pregnant. Even then, we'll have Titus do a quick check to make sure that you aren't. But hopefully after tonight I won't have the urge to have you as snake for the next nine months."

He kissed me again and began moving. I forgot all about being jealous of Rene.

Chapter Six

Danial did indeed finish his painting of Monica, and began to make a few sketches of me two weeks after he'd agreed to. But we had delays from the first, as he said he was unsure of how to pose me.

"You're always in motion. Having you pose makes you seem unnatural."

"Draw me doing something then."

"What do you most like to do, Lady?" he said, and then he blushed.

It was the second time I'd ever seen him blush in my life. He looked so sweet, endearing, and innocent that I fought down the desire to kiss him and looked away. "I like to bake," I said softly. "Sit at the table. When you see me in a flattering pose, have me stop, and take a picture or two on your camera to paint from."

"Drawing from life is better than a picture," he said sadly. "Or a memory."

My heart twisted, hearing that old pain. Why was I doing this? I cursed myself for even asking him. "Take it or leave it."

"My brother wants this, so I will take it," he said evenly, getting to his feet. "Please, let's do it now, as I can see whatever appeal this had for you didn't last."

The rest of the day was spent baking, V helping me. Danial said nothing at all, though I was conscious of him watching me. At the end of the day, he said as he walked away that he had enough for a portrait, and that it should be done in a few weeks. After, I had a large glass of wine and told myself to leave it alone.

Emma had been a moderate success. Danial had asked her to come back after that first night, and I could see he was "fond" of her, as he'd described it. Maybe in time, he'd love her. I had my own life without him, with Lash and the baby we were hoping to have. It was time to move on. *Way past time.*

* * * *

I got my period on schedule. So that day, October 14, I checked with Stephen as an afterthought, and he agreed that it was safe to try for a pregnancy. Lash gave a sigh of relief when he heard the news, saying he was sick of wearing "gloves" and he thought we should maybe try for the rest of that night as he hadn't gotten the job done the week before with three times. I not so gently reminded him it was my time right then, but that it would be over soon.

"No problem," he grumbled. "I'm going to be away, anyway. I've got business for the next few nights with Dev. And Saturday, we've got a boys' night out planned."

Great: drugs and drinking. Shaker would probably be going along, too, like last time…

Shit, don't think about him. I said the Lord's Prayer in my mind quickly, and then looked for Venus, as it was time for lunch.

Because of my search for her, I finally got an answer to a question I had wondered about for years: where Danial's fox head ring had come from. It was a fluke; V had asked him, and if I hadn't had the luck to walk by right at that moment, I would not have overheard. I'd asked him myself before many times in the years I'd known him, but he'd always refused to talk about it.

"My father gave this to my mother for me, when I was born," Danial said to my daughter reluctantly. "He was not a good man, but he did believe in doing his duty."

"Did you not like him? Was he mean?" Venus asked.

"He could be mean, yes. I didn't like him very much."

"Then why keep the ring?" she asked.

Good question, Venus.

"The fox was my family's symbol, and my mother had one she had found orphaned, and nursed back to health. It used to follow her around, like a dog."

Was he remembering what had really happened, or was he mixing up my compassion for animals with his mother's? *Hard to say.*

71

"So he gave it to her because she liked foxes?"

"Yes, Venus. And because he had a ring similar to it; a wolf's head with ruby eyes. It was important to him that I knew where I came from." Danial paused. "But these are not things to concern yourself with, child."

"Ok. Want to color with me?"

"I cannot, princess. I have a portrait I need to finish. But we'll go find your mother. She can make you lunch—"

My cue to exit. I discreetly closed the ballroom door, then took the long way around to the kitchen. When I arrived in the kitchen, V was by herself waiting. I breathed a sigh of relief, and made her lunch.

Later that night, I went to Devlin, who was sitting on Lash's balcony, reading by candlelight.

"Doesn't that bother your eyes?" I asked curiously.

"A little," he admitted, putting aside his young adult paranormal romance. "But I like to experience reading like this sometimes, to remember. With my enhanced sight, it doesn't strain my eyes that much." He smiled slightly. "And this reading is not too taxing."

I smiled in reply, then sat beside him. "Danial mentioned that his ring had come from his father, your father. That your father had one with a wolf's head. So why don't you have a ring, Dev?"

He took my hand in his. "I did, Love, when I was mortal. But sometime through the years, I lost it. I can't remember where." He gave a sad smile. "I have so many memories, Sar. The oldest ones I remember fairly well. My first two hundred years as vampire are…muddy would be the best word. Somewhere before I met Anna, I lost it."

"I'm sorry."

"Don't be." He kissed my hand, closing his left hand over mine. "I have another ring I cherish more."

"You always know what to say," I teased.

"It's the truth," he said primly, then grinned. "Come inside, it's time for bed."

* * * *

The next afternoon, Rene came to see me bearing more than a few catalogs. "Sar, Dev told me of the upcoming Hallow's party. He asked that we wear the same color, or at the least, complimentary colors, and also to let him know which colors we chose."

Dev, always making a big production of everything. I went to say some derogatory comment, then changed my mind. *You're being a curmudgeon.* I deserved to have some fun. Dev was right, it was okay to enjoy myself, and to spend some money to look good at the party that was the highlight of the vampires' social year. "Did you have a particular style of dress in mind? I have no idea if it is going to be a costume party this year, or not."

Rene shook her head. "Devlin said it was not. He also said we were not to pick black, as that is what Lash and the rest of the guards will be wearing."

I gave a mental sigh. Theo was sure to be there. But likely, he'd leave Jenny at home, so at least I wouldn't have to deal with her glaring at me all night. With Lash 'working' and Rene to keep Devlin in hand, he'd likely have nothing to glare about, another good point.

"Devlin also said that Samuel would be attending, and the rest of the Rulers, save Asia's new heir apparent. Several have been fighting over Michael's throne, but it's down to two contenders. Until one wins, neither will be recognized."

I did not want to talk about Michael. "What color would you like, Sister?"

The corners of Rene's mouth curved up in a large grin at the nickname I'd begun using for her and her for me. "I've always liked purple. But I'm partial to most colors, except maybe orange and yellow. They make me look sickly."

I laughed. "Me, too! I'm okay with purple, so long as it's not pastel. I'd rather not look like a Disney Princess."

"We'll leave the light purple to V. Devlin said you were to choose a dress for her, too, something 'modest', though she has final approval. Something of the final color of our dresses, or again complimentary."

I took the catalogs from her. "Do you really want to look through these? It's been weeks now, and you haven't left the grounds. Wouldn't you like to go out and do some hands-on shopping with me?"

"Sure, but first I thought we should go over the styles, and see if we can't agree on one."

I gave her a sideways look and curbed my tongue a little, so that what came out was, "I don't think we should necessarily wear the same dress. You're thinner than I am, Rene. Something that looks good on one of us isn't going to look good on the other."

Rene blushed. "I know that. I don't want to get something too different from yours, that's all."

We had a lot to do, so it was best to get started. I forced a smile and tried to make it real. "Let's see what they have. We're wearing the same color and will have similar chokers. Wearing the exact same dress might be overload, Sister."

Rene nodded. "You're right, Sister."

An hour later, we'd narrowed the choice down to a halter-type dress with a tie around the neck, a plunging neckline, and a long flared skirt with inserts of material, and scalloped edges. The difference between Rene's dress and mine was that hers was fitted over her hips before it belled out to the floor, and mine had princess seaming, with the customary V in the front, and was fitted only throughout the waist. And we'd chosen purple velvet for the dresses, the rich dark purple of an indigo iris in fresh dewy bloom. The bodices were ornate metallic gold cloth, with many cut glass beads and elaborate embroidery.

"Can they have this ready in time?" I said in disbelief. "This disclaimer says at least a month is needed for all dresses ordered that need to be altered or modified. And they've only got one material listed, a satin—"

Rene smiled. "I'll take care of it, Cherie. And I'll order a smaller version of your dress for V in lighter violet velvet." She paused. "Dev said you had a lot to do on email today."

Groan. "Sounds good."

Rene left, and I went down to the basement, and got to work. My computer was as I'd left it almost a year before, though some nice person had covered it with a fabric drop cloth. Devlin had left me a note in his elegant hand that password had been changed on the Solution's Inc. email account to "Tomb Raider 4," so that was first on my list. After logging in, I changed it back to "My Darkness" and got to work. Handling the incoming emails was old hat to me after all these years. As far as Dev had told me, the only thing different now was we no longer had paper copies to file, as Solutions, Inc. had gone paperless as of last

New Year.

Things weren't too bad, in spite of Devlin's warnings. Jenny and Sun hadn't been thorough in their electronic filing, or with emptying the trash or sent mail, which each had 900 emails in them, but nothing looked too bad. I felt evil for wanting it to be massively screwed up, and pushed that thought aside.

In two hours I'd forwarded on some emails to T that looked good, and deleted the rest, most of which were too weird or sketchy on details to likely result in any payday for the company. Then I got into the deleted stuff to make sure it had been handled, checking it against the closed files of the last year. There were about ten emails that I didn't have any confirmation in terms of them being handled or completed, so I forwarded those onto Devlin. Then I spent another two hours e-filing the finished jobs on the hard drive in respective folders, and deleting the junk. When I was done, I had empty inbox, trash, and sent mail.

But I also had something else: a stack of three "thank-you" e-notes written almost a year ago to Danial to thank him for the great work he'd done. I'd printed them before thinking, as I'd always done for Danial. Part of me wanted to give them to him. Before I could talk myself out of it, I turned off the computer and went down the hall to his room.

Danial was there, his back to me, putting finishing touches on my portrait. I leaned against the doorway and watched him paint for a while, liking the seriousness of his expression as he concentrated on making my eyes seem to come to life with a deft touch of his brush.

"It's in acrylic, not oil," he said without turning to me. "But I can finish faster, without having to wait for it to dry."

"It's very good."

"You can take it with you," Danial said neutrally. "I was just finishing a few final touches."

He'd painted me in casual clothes leaning against a tree with a backdrop of more trees, most of them pine. For a moment, I thought he'd painted me at Anna's grave or at the cemetery on his land, as the scenery looked similar. But I noticed what looked like a puddle at the edge of the picture's corner and the edge of a path behind leading away through the trees, and knew at once where this scene was from.

Danial had painted me as he remembered me, that night we'd gone out after I'd come to live with him. We'd had dinner in Alan's Creek, and gone for a walk in a nearby state park. It had been winter, but there hadn't been any snow. The scene he'd painted was of spring, not winter. But the place was the same.

That lake's edge likely still looked exactly as it had been then that long ago night. But Danial had been irreparably changed. I had, too.

"Do you like it?" he said, his back to me as he rinsed out his brushes. "You aren't saying anything."

"I like it," I got out with difficulty. "You've captured me perfectly."

"It did come out well," Danial said, finally turning and giving me a small smile. "I think it was having a deadline. I'd forgotten what it was like to work under pressure."

It wasn't going to get any more promising than this moment. I handed him the three notes. "Please consider going back to Solutions. Your son needs you. Your company needs you."

"My company can get along without me," Danial said dismissively, yet without malice. "It was my life for the last seventy odd years. It's time for a change from me hiding here in shadows, I agree. But I'm not going to backtrack. I have to decide on some new path."

I swallowed hard. "Like what?"

"Devlin said that there may be an opening in Illinois for state ruler. I may take that. I've never been there except on jobs, or travelling through on my way to see Devlin. I'd still be close enough to get back to Dev in a day or so if he needed my help, or if T needed some advice, without needing Hellish travel help."

Get the words out. "Are you going alone?"

"I haven't decided," Danial said, drying his hands. "Part of me thinks I should. But most of me doesn't want to be alone."

I wanted to beg him not to go, or to scream at him for being a jerk. But I did neither, because neither would get him to do what I wanted him to do. But one thing was sure to. "Would you consider waiting until I've had my child? I'd feel much safer knowing you were nearby."

He regarded me seriously. "Are you worried, Lady? We are safe enough now, with the hunters back in subjugation. And I'd not heard you were pregnant yet."

"I'm not yet, though I will be very soon. But I'm scared about being

76

pregnant and having an enemy attack. There is always another enemy to worry about," I said truthfully, locking him with my eyes. "I'd feel better knowing you were here."

Danial nodded. "I can stay until you've given birth, Lady. I'm not in any rush to begin something new when I'm still so uncommitted to a certain path."

"Thank you." Putting down the papers gently on his nearby chair, I walked upstairs.

I'd gotten myself under control and was yelling for Ghost to come inside when I noticed Danial standing there in the kitchen doorway, the painting in his hands. He'd put it in a simple wooden frame. "You forgot this."

"Thanks. Would you bring it upstairs to Dev's room?"

Danial nodded and followed me upstairs. We walked into the bedroom to find a dead-to-the-world Dev, who was snoring loudly.

"Wake up," I said, shaking his shoulder. "Danial finished the painting."

Devlin stretched and opened his eyes. Then he sat up. "Ah! Let me see it, brother."

Danial held it up.

"It's very good," Devlin said, his eyes feasting on it. "But where is Sar, this place you have her standing? It is not Hayden."

"I'm not sure," Danial confessed with embarrassment. "It seemed right to put her in some trees."

Devlin looked over at me and then back to Danial. "Thank you, brother. Please leave us."

Danial leaned the picture up against the wall and left, closing the door behind him.

"This is of you somewhere he remembers you?" Devlin asked me gently.

I nodded. "A local park near his house."

"I'm not sure what to say," Devlin said after a pause. "I'd like to hang this in here, near the door. But will you mind seeing it daily? It has clearly affected you."

"No," I said, taking a breath. "I'd like to remember. Danial said he's going to be leaving before too long."

Devlin brought me into his arms. "I was loathe to tell you, Love. But it does seem a good fit, at least for now."

"Solutions, Inc. needs him," I said petulantly. "T needs him. I feel terrible saying this, but I noticed that there weren't any thank you letters to T, not in all the mail I sifted through."

Devlin grated his fangs a little. "I knew you'd see that, just as I have," he said gruffly. "T is just not Danial. It's not his fault, he's had too much to master in too short a time. He's trying hard and he is getting the jobs done. But it's not the same, and the clients are seeing that."

"Is business affected?"

"Times have been rocky lately with the economic downturn, as we discussed earlier," Devlin replied. "But yes, I think there is a difference in workload. Brian has reported that he spends most days guarding the house, as only Theo and Terian are usually needed to accompany T on his meetings. And Rip being absent has not caused any issues, and it should have, if business was where it should be."

"Convince Danial to go back," I said firmly. "You've got everything you've ever wanted, Dev. Do this for me, and for T. Please."

"I've already done my best," Devlin said gently. "But I'll keep trying, Love. And remember, if Danial were to leave, I'd send Rip with him. He could still run Solutions from Illinois, or another state, if he prefers. Distance does not matter when you have a demon."

Part of me wanted to say it did matter, but that was just me being selfish, wanting Danial around because I'd miss him if he were states away. I only saw him as much as I did because he lived here. Once he left, I'd likely only see him at parties, and only then a few times a year.

"Shh," Devlin said gently. "Remember, you have forever, which means time to let Danial go for a year or ten, Sar. Reunions with old lovers are all the more flavorful when time has passed. Look at Rene and me."

I didn't answer.

"We have not spoken of this," Devlin began suddenly. "But I want to know if you need to see Rosalyn. I'd be happy to go with you if you wanted, even though I know she detests me—"

I started, surprised at his change of topic. "Why?"

"You know why, Love. You've gone through a lot. Lash reports that

Elle is much improved from her time in therapy."

I whipped my head around, struggling to move. "What the hell does that mean, Dev? When has Lash had time to spend with Elle?"

"He took her to dinner one night, on the way back from a job. He said she's a lot more confident than she used to be, and that living at your place agrees with her."

That was mollifying. "Good. Every time I talk of going to see her, she tells me she's busy. I was beginning to worry."

"Her being occupied is a good thing. But we were talking of you, Love. Would you like me to make you an appointment?"

"No," I said slowly. "There really isn't anything to talk about, Dev. The best therapy would be to have an easy winter and a not too difficult pregnancy."

"I can't do much about the latter," Devlin said after a moment. "But the former can be managed. Rene showed me your dress choices. I think they'll be very flattering on you both. V also loved the design. Rene ordered them today, I believe."

I didn't answer.

"Where are you standing, in the painting?"

"A local park we went to when we were first dating. It was a good night."

"Ah." Devlin took the picture, and set it in the corner. Then he went out the door, and appeared a moment later with a hammer and nail. With a few taps, he pounded them in and hung the picture so it was facing us from the wall at the right side of the bed. "How's that? Straight?"

I nodded, amazed he'd found a stud without a big production. "Looks good."

He took the tool back to wherever he'd gotten it from, and reappeared at the door. "Love, I need to work on a few projects. Are you okay to be alone?"

"Sure," I said. A minute after he left, I took a valium and went to a peaceful and dreamless sleep.

* * * *

That next week passed quickly, cumulating with the highlight of the week, Saturday night. I was waiting in bed with my leather bondage wear, wondering where the hell Lash and Devlin were, when I heard the garage door opening. Throwing on a robe, I was just in time to get downstairs to see Lash's Avalanche truck racing toward the gates.

"Devlin said to remind you he'd be out tonight," Seth intoned from behind me, his eyes averted. "Lash said he'd call if they were going to be later than two."

Fuck. My fault. Lash had told me about this boys' night out a few days ago, I'd just forgotten. *So much for my dominatrix get-up.*

Seth had already walked off, so I went upstairs and took off my leather gear, feeling silly. Then I went in search of V. I found her playing in the ballroom alone, practicing the dance steps she'd been learning from Caitlyn in preparation for the party. Watching her, I thought she was rather good for such a young girl.

At ten, I made her stop. A half hour later, I had her in bed in her nightclothes.

"Read to me, Mom?"

She'd not asked me that for a long time. The thought of her needing me filled me with relieved happiness. "Sure."

I spent the next hour reading some of *Little Town on the Prairie* to her. Apparently, the Wilder book set had been a gift from Danial for her last birthday. Sometime around eleven, I looked over and noticed she was asleep. I turned off the light, and decided to turn in myself.

I was hesitant to take anything to help me sleep, worried Lash might call and I'd miss it. So I just got into my nightgown, and lay down. I was asleep in moments.

I dreamed I was walking in a field. Then I heard a bark, and turned. Ghost was there. Darkness, my Darkness, was with him!

I threw myself at her, hugging her as she licked my tears. But when I began to walk with her at my side, as we always had before, she nipped me, not enough to draw blood, but enough I yelped.

I looked down at her in shock. She wagged her tail at me, and gave me an uncertain look.

"It's okay," I said gently. "Come on, let's go look for a mouse."

We'd gone only another few steps when I felt her nip me again. And this time, she growled a little.

I spanked her, and said "no" loudly. With a final growl, she turned

80

and ran, disappearing into the woods in seconds.

I looked around, but Ghost was gone, too. What had happened?

Feeling awful, I woke up at Hayden. As I wiped away a tear, something nuzzled my leg.

Darkness was lying at the bottom of the bed near my legs. She was looking up at me, her tail wagging a little.

Part of me wanted to hug her. But what if she bit me?

What if this somehow wasn't Darkness?

Chapter Seven

I grabbed my courage with both hands, and reached down and touched her. Her soft fur was thick and familiar under my fingers. She let out a gratified sigh.

"Is it you?" I whispered, tears threatening again. "Darkness?"

"Yyyyeeeesssss," a dry voice rasped.

I looked down with horror. The words had come from Darkness's mouth, which was lolling open near my bare legs.

With a shriek, I began flailing and screaming. Suddenly Shaker was there, pushing me back as he grabbed hold of what had been Darkness. It was molting and melting into something with shiny black skin. Shaker dug his talons in and ripped it in two. With a supernatural shriek of grinding metal, grey-black smoke, and splintered bone, the thing vanished.

I was in the throes of hysterics, sobbing, flailing, and screaming. Shaker turned to me, and grabbed hold of me. "Calm down, Mistress."

"Don't tell me to calm down! What the fuck was that thing?"

"A Taker, a low level demon. They are attracted to loss, and can invade dreams, turning them sour. They feed on pain, especially emotional pain."

"Why did it come to me? How did it get in here?"

"That is my fault," Shaker rumbled. "You are bound to me, and your dreams are fair game because of that. Do you have a symbol of your faith?"

"I have a cross."

"Wear it to bed. And it wouldn't hurt to put a cross over your bed, or under it. That will keep any scavengers away."

"I should've taken the drugs," I whispered. "This is the first night I haven't."

"Take one, and go back to sleep," Shaker rumbled. "I can come to you at once, Mistress. Don't fear to call for me if you need me. There is little I can't either kill or send back to Hell."

"Okay. Thanks."

"I could stay, if you wanted me to," he rumbled, pulling me closer. "There is nothing better to soothe a bad dream than good hearty demon sex—"

I rolled my eyes. "Get back to your drinking before you're missed."

"I won't be missed. Devlin and Lash are talking and a shell of me is there, pretending to listen." He concentrated. "All I have to do is nod once in a while, and speak assent if they ask me a question. Then my real body can be here with you, bringing us both pleasure—"

I glared at him as if this new horror had been all his fault, which to my thinking a good portion of it had been. "Leave, Shaker. Now."

"Very well." He disappeared.

I popped a valium and went back to sleep. This time, I dreamed no dreams.

* * * *

Soon, it was the morning of October 31. A blustery day, one I was glad to spend indoors. After doing my morning treadmill run, I settled down to work on email.

Rene came in, and abruptly pulled the computer plug. "Forget work, Sister. Today we're going to have some fun!"

I gave her an annoyed look, not at the nickname, which I liked very much, but at the thought of my planned day being pillaged. "What are you talking about? The party isn't until tonight."

She offered her hand. "Come and see!"

I took it and followed her upstairs. Venus was there, bouncing around already in her coat. A long white Hummer limo parked outside the front door. *What the hell?*

"Come on!" Venus shouted. "I want to go now!"

"Hush," Rene said crossly. "Go tell your father we are leaving, while your mother and I get our coats on."

Venus bounded upstairs. Soon we were in the limo's backseat, sipping some excellent wine. Venus was included, though I gave her just a tablespoonful.

"Where are we going?" I said.

Venus giggled, as Rene produced a clipboard with a day planner on it. "I've not yet gotten the hang of using some of your newfangled gadgets, Sister. But paper serves well enough." She cleared her throat. "We are going to the spa for beauty treatments, and then to get our hair done. After that are the dressmakers for a final fitting, and then the jewelers for accessories. We'll arrive at the party on time, in about twelve hours or so."

Twelve HOURS! "I don't need all this. Just have them send me my dress—"

"No, Sister. You are having fun, if I have to hold you in place with a spell," Rene said, her mouth smiling but her eyes serious. "Like you said, I have not been out since you brought me home. So do this for me, ok?"

I sipped my wine, and then downed the whole glass. *Hell, why not?*

The spa was amazing. I was bathed in mud and baked, and my skin massaged. I had a facial and my hands and toes polished and perfected. And when we left at noon, I was very relaxed.

Lunch was light, as we all wanted to fit into our dresses. But we managed to scarf down a massive peanut butter cup with ice cream and toppings that we split three ways with our salads.

Next, we got our hair done. I knew Dev and Danial preferred mine down, so I had the stylist do the normal highlight to refresh my color, and then trim the ends. A ring of fresh large violets was pinned in my hair to crown my head, and then my hair was pulled back and pinned up, to cascade down my back. Rene had her blond hair shaped and feathered back, so it was layered and windswept, showing off her beauty to the max. When V asked that she be allowed to get that style too, I agreed, knowing it would show off her good looks. Rene and V elected to get just a smattering of violets placed here and there in their hair. Then out came the makeup, though none of us got very much.

By that time, it was four-thirty, and I figured we had plenty of time to finish and get home. It couldn't take six more hours to put on a dress, right?

Wrong. Besides travel time, I was inserted into my dress, and then fussed over, the hem gathered up and sewn by hand there and then, as it'd been made too long, and the sleeves let out, as they were a tad too short. Rene and V fared the same, as their dresses were a little too short. Finally, by seven-thirty, we were dressed, and gave an inward sigh of relief, until I saw several salespeople heading our way with shoeboxes.

We tried on every purple shoe in the place. I finally settled on embroidered moccasin-style flats, as they were comfortable. Rene chose some low heels and V opted for the same.

By this time, it was eight-thirty. Rene had the limo driver gun the engine for the last stop on our list, the jewelry store. We had just enough time to each choose an amethyst necklace and matching earrings, and then Rene was hurrying us back into the limo. We got to the convention center at exactly six minutes after ten.

"You look fucking great," Lash hissed appreciatively as he opened the door to let us inside. "You're in time; most of the guests aren't here yet."

"Where's my dad?" V said imperiously.

"We'll find him," Rene said, taking her hand. "Come with me." They walked down the hallway.

Lash hugged me carefully. "Did you have a good time? I don't want to touch you too much; you look like a big frosted cake I'm afraid to get too close to."

I hugged him back. "I had a great time. I don't know why I balked at going."

"Doesn't matter. Just come with me." Lash took my hand, and led me to the doors. When we got near them, he stopped, and pulled me tight against him.

I looked up at him in shock. "What?"

"Slap me," he whispered quickly, and then he shoved me against the wall and made as if to push up my dress.

I hauled off and slapped him hard. He backed off, hissing.

"Knock it off," I said nastily, half meaning it.

"You'll put out for me later," Lash hissed, baring his snake fangs. "You know you'll have to later on. I can wait. And you're going to love every minute of feeling me wriggling in you!"

I gave him a look of disgust and walked into the main party room.

He didn't follow, not that I expected him to. Someone had been nearby, someone who he'd wanted me to help him lie to, and put on that show for. *Who?*

I scanned the crowd, wondering whom that display had been for. No guests I recognized were here yet. Danial and T were standing near a crowd of guests, Danial expounding on something that had everyone around him nodding. The usual band was just beginning the light classical music I was accustomed to at these parties. The two bartenders were in their usual places, doing moderate business. Over near the tables, I saw Devlin, Rene, and Venus standing. Rene and Dev were sipping some wine, and Venus was eating some food daintily from a plate.

I walked toward them in time to see Tony and Thane arrive with their guards, looking their normal gangster selves. They made a beeline for Devlin.

"Sarelle, you look lovely," Tony said admiringly. "You get lovelier every year. And your child with her is extraordinary, Dalcon."

Red crept up my neck, as it was Rene's hand he had taken hold of and kissed. She was flushing, too.

"This is Rene," Devlin said stonily. "But you are right to compliment her, as she's lovely. She's become mine just as Sarelle is." He beckoned to me, and I strode closer, shame still suffusing my face. "Sar, I believe you remember Tony and Thane?"

I greeted them, and they told me I was beautiful, too. A moment later, I excused myself to get some food, Rene trailing behind me to the tables.

"Sorry," she said. "I should've asked V to get another hairstyle, so she didn't look like a miniature of me. This will probably happen again, Sister."

I swallowed my bitterness, jealousy, and what was left of my pride. It had been those idiots' fault, not hers. "It's okay. It's not a big deal. Let's just enjoy the party."

Rene nodded, and got herself a plate. We didn't speak further.

The night wore on. I was glad to see Tatiana there, though her comments to Devlin were cold, and her only real affection seemed to be for Danial and T. Rene she ignored utterly, until Rene finally stuck out her tongue at her turned back. Tatiana whipped around with a glare as if she'd seen it, but Rene just gave her a blank look. Tatiana walked away in a huff, while Rene shot me a smile.

Terian arrived just as the final guests were walking in, his hair newly trimmed in a much shorter style than I was used to. Theo was with him, dressed in black with a blue shirt and tie, but for the first time I could remember not in guard uniform—instead, he was in a suit himself. His hair was cut short also, surprisingly in that feathered style I'd always preferred it.

"Theo's looking good," Rene whispered. "Blue suits him. Dare me to go up to him and tell him I'm open to a threesome with him and Dev?"

I choked on my wine so much I sputtered. Theo, Terian, and everyone in the immediate vicinity looked over at me. I put up my palm, saying sorry, and got a napkin, still coughing. Rene was laughing her ass off. As I cleaned up Lash sauntered up to Theo, who gave him a look like he was curdled cheese.

"Everything is fine, so far," Lash hissed. "But the Rulers have not arrived. I'll notify you the moment they do, in case you somehow don't notice."

Theo nodded. "Watch the vampires, their children, and their women, as usual. We can take care of ourselves."

Lash nodded. "Not a problem," he hissed. "Anything I should be watching for, like loose morals?"

Theo gave him a growl. "Just do your fucking job, Snake."

Lash nodded, smirking. Theo and Terian moved off, and began greeting guests. Lash himself went back to his position outside the main door.

"So what do we do now?" Rene said, eating a deviled egg. "Is there dancing?"

"Yes, but don't get your hopes up," I said, eating a cracker. "Mostly it's greeting people, and smiling a lot. When the vampires get here, it's the same thing."

"When does the good music begin? I much prefer your modern music to the classical music the band is playing."

"This is it, honey," I said, downing my drink and pouring another. "All there is."

"This sounds dreadful," Rene said grumpily. "I assumed I'd be dancing the night away."

I was tempted to dance with her, but the music was all wrong. "You still might, if you want to. Devlin loves to dance. As long as one of us watches over Venus, there won't be a problem."

"Where is Venus?" Rene said suddenly, looking around worriedly.

"With Devlin." Venus was standing near her father, looking regal and aloof. "She's a handful, but she knows better than to make her father worried here. She's enjoying being princess to his king."

Abruptly my eyes fastened on Emma, who'd just come through the doors and was scanning the crowd with her liquid blue eyes. Seeing Danial, she gave him a wide smile and started toward him in her sequined blue evening gown, her long blue-black hair wound up in a French twist. He motioned her to come closer, giving her a smile back.

"What's she doing here?" I growled out.

"You know," Rene said gently. "That collar she's wearing is just for tonight. It's real, but it's not more than a necklace to her or to Danial."

Protection. I got it. "It doesn't matter," I said, filling my wine glass. "Maybe soon it will be a permanent thing. It's not any of my business."

Rene sipped her wine and didn't say anything. I concentrated on looking everywhere but at Danial and Emma.

The night wore on. I smiled, ate a little, and had a few more glasses of wine. Rene matched me glass for glass, and for the most part, we watched Venus, and talked a little to each other and to Devlin. As it had been for every other Hallows party, Danial was the center of attention. From the few glances I cast his way, T was always near him, looking his twin in their matching suits and shirts. And so was Emma.

Hell, probably more than a few clients are thinking she is his mother...

I finished my glass, poured another, and told myself it didn't matter.

The human party finally ended at midnight. A few moments later, the vampire one began.

The first vampire to approach us was Akira. I was dismayed to see Chi was not with him, but didn't know how to mention that. So I just said hello.

He gave me a sad look. "I am alone now, yes. Chi has gone back to

Japan. She did not agree with Michael's ruling of our country, as he was not native to it, as many Asian vampires did not. But now that one of native descent is sure to rule, many are returning."

That was better than to hear she was dust. "Why did you not go with her?"

"My place is here. I worked many years to get into this position of power, and back home I'd be just another vampire." He smiled without baring his fangs. "Sixty is not very old in my native land. I can't go back to being a pawn now that I've had a taste of being a duke."

"I'm sorry for your loss," Rene interjected. "I'm Rene. And you are?"

"This is Akira," I said formally. "Ruler of New York."

"Pleased to meet you," Akira said, kissing her hand formally. "Devlin chose wisely for an Oathed One both times."

At this point I'd run out of things to say, but Rene took up the slack, asking of the local business economy, and Akira told her some of how the state was faring, most of which I tuned out with a smile pasted on my face. When he left ten minutes later, I breathed a sigh of relief. I turned to say something funny to Rene when a hand tapped my shoulder.

I turned to find Erik and Van, both of them looking dashing as always. "Good to see you, Sar," Erik said, giving me a smile with just a hint of fang.

It was good to be back to feeling appreciated. Shoot, it was good to be back to just being called by my correct name. "This is Van and Erik," I said, "Rulers of PA. This is Rene, Devlin's other Oathed One."

"Good to meet you," Van said, "And good to see you, Sar. We'd heard of your troubled summer. We hope you enjoyed the Godiva basket we sent to welcome you back. Devlin said you liked that brand."

I thanked them, casting my mind back frantically to remember any kind of gift basket coming from them, and failing miserably. But maybe Rene had eaten it, if it was small? "How is your adjustment? You're managing a state now, where before you used to do bounty hunting."

"A little boring, but a lot less hassle," Van said, putting his hands in his pockets. "For the most part we're ruling a vampire-empty state, save for the big cities. We've got many weres though, so that's an issue. But so far we love it."

Erik nodded his agreement. "Come down some evening," he said cordially. "We'd love a visit. We have a nice country home in Montrose, or if you prefer the city scene, we can visit at our penthouse apartment in Pittsburg."

I said that I'd happily mention a visit to Dev, and they moved away.

"Are they gay?" Rene whispered telepathically. "I thought they might be related, they look so much alike."

"No one knows, or if they do, they didn't tell me," I said back to her in my mind. "But I suspect—"

We were cut short as Samuel walked in, his children at his side. I'd been expecting children Venus's age, even knowing the reports that the late Harriet's children had a fast growth rate. But Elijah and Sharon were at least sixteen, Elijah looking almost eighteen. Where Sharon looked much like Harriet, with a demure expression, Elijah was almost a copy of Samuel, except he was taller. But he had the same dense muscle mass, blue eyes, and brown hair.

Samuel said hello to Danial, and then looked for me. He got to Rene and I just as Devlin made it to our side with Venus.

"Dalcon, how good to see you. Your daughter is lovely."

"As is yours," Devlin said formally. "And such a strapping son. Elijah, you look already a man!"

Elijah blushed. His eyes were red, just as they had been reported to be, and his fangs were also present. But his words were easily spoken in a clear voice. "Thank you, Sir. It's been hard to adjust fast enough, but I'm learning quickly."

"How are you, Sharon?" Venus interjected. "I've missed you."

Sharon glanced at Venus, who still looked at most eight or nine, clearly torn on what to say. "I've been mostly studying, V. And I—"

"Sharon is learning how to be a lady, which fills her days," Samuel said sternly. "But you are welcome to visit her, Venus. Now if you ladies will give us a moment to discuss business?"

Sharon came to stand with us, while Dev, Samuel and Elijah walked away to join Danial and T.

"I think he wouldn't notice if I screamed sometimes," Sharon said softly. "I'm always second to Elijah, no matter how much they fight about things. And I'm never supposed to interrupt him when he's speaking."

"Tell him to fuck off," I said bluntly, then blushed because everyone was giving me shocked looks. "Sorry," I said quickly. "It's the wine."

"I do not dare say something like that," Sharon said, laughing nervously. "Samuel has exacting rules for women, Lady Dalcon. I know better than to break them."

"What are your plans?" Rene asked. "College? Do you have someone?"

"Who?" Sharon said bitterly. "My father keeps all men away from me. I've never been alone with any man not a relative, except Harp and Song. But college will be a chance for me to get some space, if my father agrees to let me attend one."

I looked over to the door to see two demons standing there. Lash was watching them discreetly from a few feet away, but they were just watching the party with red eyes, Samuel's children in particular. Demons with the name 'Harp' and 'Song'? They sounded more like angels. Then it hit me that they *were* angels, fallen angels, and I shivered, averting my eyes.

"I want more than to sit and watch my life pass," Sharon continued yearningly. "I want to have a life of my own. But I don't know what to do. I can't fight my father, he's too strong willed. I don't want to be a prisoner the rest of my life—"

Prisoner. The room seemed to close in on me suddenly, my heart pounding. I had to do something or I was going to lose it.

"Be strong," I said determinedly, grabbing her hand. "You can do anything your brother can do, remember that. Don't let your domineering father beat you down."

"I think of running away sometimes," Sharon said quietly. "But I have nowhere to go."

"You must have friends. Dev tells me you visited with Elle," I said hesitantly.

Sharon's face broke into a smile. "I have. She's been a good friend to me. We kind of got off to a bad start, but I've talked to her a little on the phone. She offered to let me stay with her."

This was odd. I thought Sharon had already stayed with Elle. Before I could ask about that, Venus walked off in a huff and Rene went after her, giving me a look to say don't worry.

"I'm too old for her now," Sharon said apologetically. "I reply to her emails, but we aren't interested in the same things anymore. She's angry about it and I feel like a freak."

"You're who you are," I said flatly. "Just be yourself. Everything else will work out okay." I downed the rest of my wine. "Get away from your father for a while. Go spend some time with Elle. Everyone needs to spread their wings."

"I'm going to try to," Sharon whispered. "But Song will have to come, too. Think she'll mind if he does?"

"Ask her." I filled my glass again. "The most my daughter can say is 'no,' right?"

"Yes," Sharon said politely. Then she added quickly, "You're just as nice as Elle said you were."

I watched her walk to her beckoning father, and then downed my glass. I put it down, thinking lazily that this had to be glass four. Or was it five?

"You've had enough," a voice growled in my ear. I looked up to see Theo, his blue eyes stony, his mouth a grim line. "Go sit down, before you fall down and embarrass yourself."

"It's not your call," I said nastily. "The time you could tell me what to do is over. And really, there was never a time you could. The most you ever could do is ask, and hope for me to agree." I reached for the wine to refill my glass.

Theo stopped me. "Enough, Sarelle. Go and sit down."

"Why don't you fucking make me," I hissed at him. "That's all you're good for, isn't it, forcing people to do what they don't want to—"

"Get her out of here before she makes a scene."

I opened my mouth to protest, and suddenly Lash was there. Before I knew it, he had hold of me, and was guiding me toward the door.

He settled me in a chair outside, and handed me a glass of water. "Drink this."

I drank it gratefully, and then ran to the bathroom. When I emerged a few moments later, I was feeling better, though still very drunk.

"What is the matter?" Lash hissed, his human eyes worried. "You never get like this, not purposely."

92

I almost told him about Shaker, how I was upset my soul was already getting black, how I was afraid to sleep without drugs. About how everyone seemed to have their own place and I felt like I didn't have one anymore. Then the urgent need to share my pain passed, as I told myself to be strong and handle this.

I rubbed my eyes instead. "I just wanted to not care for once," I said tiredly. "I'm always doing...um, I always try to do what's right, and I'm sick of it. I wanted a break."

"I understand that," Lash hissed gently, hugging me. "But you can't have one tonight. You have to get back out there. Perseus is going to show up soon, and Zane, too. They aren't going to be satisfied with Rene, or with just seeing Venus. Be tough. And know that if it comes to you needing me, I'll be right there, fuck what anyone thinks."

I nodded, and got to my feet.

When we got back, Lash brought me to Devlin, and then resumed his post by the door. A second later, Perseus walked in, followed by Zane.

They greeted us, both of them looking as evil as ever. But they were polite, and soon were talking to Devlin, with Rene and me listening, Venus hugging me around my waist. I made myself pay attention, at least when Perseus brought up the subject of demons.

"I've gotten another demon," Perseus was saying to Devlin. "The one your man killed wasn't great, but this one's better. He's almost as old as Titus is, though I admit, not as well known. But so far, it's working out. It's only been a year now."

"That's a good thing. It takes a while to break in a demon, and get it used to your habits." Devlin sipped his wine. "Titus and I have had our moments. But he's very good. I don't know what I'd do without him."

"Does he give you trouble? Mine sometimes refuses me, and I have to punish him to make him obey."

"Titus still defies me, when he thinks he should. But I call the shots always, and he knows that. So threat of punishment is usually enough, once a harsh toll for disobedience has been inflicted once or twice. Give it time."

"Perhaps."

"It is good to see you, Sarelle," Zane said respectfully. "We've all heard about what you went through. I hope you've recovered and are well, even with Michael still unaccounted for—"

I looked up at him watching me so earnestly and lost it. I dashed from the room, and made it to the bathroom just in time to throw up everything I'd eaten that day, and then some.

I sat there, and wiped away tears, looking at the smears of makeup on my toilet paper and feeling pitiful, aged, and brittle as old dried tape.

"Sister?" Rene said softly. "Are you well? Everyone is worried."

I would hold it together. I would. *Hold it together.*

"Do something to make me sober quick," I said, ashamed but determined. "I need to not act like a fool. Please, Rene."

She murmured something and my head cleared. I stood up, feeling much better.

"Be warned," she said apologetically as she fixed my makeup as best she could. "You'll feel worse tomorrow than you just did. But this will stave off the effects tonight."

I nodded, and we went back out. I apologized for my abrupt leaving, saying I'd eaten something that didn't agree with me. I'm not sure I was believed, but I quickly asked Zane how Africa was doing in terms of its native endangered animals, and when he answered, the conversation again became something of a normal one.

The rest of the party went smoothly. Rene and Devlin danced a few times, though I declined when he asked me. I noticed with evil delight that Emma was annoyed, as Danial had danced with her only once, and mostly ignored her the rest of the night. There were no fights, and the ritual part went quickly, especially as Devlin just drank from Rene and me in a chaste kiss that lasted no more than a few seconds. By now it was almost an hour until dawn, and everyone was winding down. I breathed a sigh of relief when the Rulers made their exit.

That's when the real trouble started.

Chapter Eight

I don't know how it started. But within a moment, Samuel had grabbed hold of Elijah, and they were fighting, as all the guests around them shrank back, some fleeing in fear.

Lash was there in a half second, pushing Samuel off Elijah with uncharacteristic restraint. Samuel shoved him, and he went flying into a wall, taking some of the werefoxes with him. But only a few seconds later, the demons went in, Harp pulling a bloodied Elijah back, as Song pulled Samuel off him with great effort, his huge muscles straining.

"You dare to go against my wishes! I forbade you, Elijah! You're no better than an animal—!"

"I am an animal," Elijah hissed, baring his fangs. "I've got needs and desires, and I'm going to do what I feel is right to meet them, all of them! But I'm human, too, Father. I've got emotions and I'm not afraid to show them, like you've always been!"

"A man acts like a man! He does not act like a woman! Your place is not on your knees, not to some undeserving peasant!"

"There was a time I looked up to you," Elijah said softly. "But if you break with me over this, you never loved me, Father. And if you never loved me, you aren't my father." He shook off the demon, and walked away, Harp following at a distance. Samuel cursed, and shook off Song, who released him while putting up his hands in a submissive gesture.

Samuel strode out with his guards. Song and Sharon followed with a last look back at us.

"What was that about?" I asked Devlin.

"A disagreement over a choice of Elijah's, no doubt," Devlin said thoughtfully. He was cradling a sleeping Venus. "But it's late for talking

95

of such things. Let's go home."

Danial and Emma had disappeared. T was talking to Theo and Terian, as the last vampires left. Lash was with the guards, both bears and foxes, directing them to check the building for "stragglers" and to report if they found anything out of the ordinary. I followed Devlin with a sigh, glad it was over for another year.

When I got back, I tucked in a still-sleeping Venus, took a quick shower in Lash's room, and then got into his bed. Devlin was with Rene in his room, and they were hot and heavy by the sounds I could hear through the door.

Lash came in just when I was dozing off, looking tired. He came to me as soon as he'd taken his weapons off.

"Tell me what's wrong," he hissed. "Please, Sweetness. I was worried about you all night, so worried I'm glad nothing else happened or I'd probably not handled it well. Talk to me."

I told him of the dream about Darkness, leaving out Shaker, and he hugged me. Then he handed me a vial of valium from his bedside drawer. "Take it for now," he hissed. "And consider going to Rosalyn."

"Are you going to go with me?" I said bluntly.

"No," he said, shedding his clothes as he walked to the bathroom. "I'm not having bad dreams, or at least, no more than usual. You are."

I heard the shower start as I took one of the pills, and slipped off to sleep.

I woke up in the early afternoon, and abruptly ran for the bathroom. Again, I puked, though there was nothing more than bile to come up this time. The pain was awful. *God, my head feels like it's cracking open!*

"Sar?" Lash said from the other side of the door. "Sweetness?"

"I'm okay," I said in a rough voice. "Go away."

I cleaned myself up, washed my face, and then went back out to him. "Why are you dressed?" He was ready to go; he even had his weapons on.

"I thought you might need me to take you to Camlyn," he said hopefully. "I thought it might be morning sickness."

"No," I said, getting slowly back into bed. "Rene said this would happen. I drank too much last night, and I'm paying the price."

Lash took off his clothes and his weapons, and got back into bed.

"I'm sorry for jumping the gun. I was just hopeful, Love."

I heard that same old longing in his voice and burst into tears.

He hugged me. "Don't cry. It's okay if it takes a while," he hissed in my ear. "I don't mind, Sar. The only thing I mind is having to be shitty or uncaring towards you in public. But it's safest for you."

I wanted to say something nasty, in that he never cared about being shitty to me when we were arguing. Then I told myself not to be so petty and mean. "Don't worry about it. But tell me, who was the one scene for? I didn't see anyone around."

"A vampire was nearby. I scented blood. It was a young one, too young to be Danial or Devlin. So I thought it best to give whomever it was a show."

Made sense. "Did the slap hurt? I tried to make it real."

"No more than the other time you slapped me," Lash teased. "Though that time I deserved it." He nuzzled closer. "I have something to tell you, Sar."

What now? "What?"

"I got a letter from that woman, the one we met at Diane's funeral. She wanted to know if I was related to Trystan Valeras—"

"How did she get our address?"

"You signed the book, remember?"

Shit, I had. In my nervousness, I'd forgotten and put down Hayden's real address. "Sorry."

"Let me finish. Anyway, she wanted to know if I'd heard of a Trystan Valeras, her Great Aunt's brother, since we had the same name, save that mine is now spelled with an "i," not a "y"."

"What did you write back?"

"Nothing yet. I'm wondering if I should. The letter is a long one, and it talks a good deal about how there was an old story passed down about how Trystan didn't die in a fire, like he was supposed to, how instead he got out, saving some kids. One of those kids, the eldest, spilled the beans on his deathbed, and the others who'd been saved with him that night agreed that it was true. So a lot of the descendants did research, looking for this long lost relative. But no one can find a trace of him." He paused. "Diana asked if I knew who my grandfather was, as she thought it might be this Trystan."

"Why don't they know that you're you? Your sisters knew you as Lash, didn't they? They knew you were still alive, that you went to work for Dev, right?"

"I was a kind of outcast," Lash said in a low voice. "They did know me as Lash, but they kept it from their children. I let them believe I died back in the late 30's, except for Diane. I never contacted anyone but her, though I made sure they had enough money. They never knew about Dev, or any of that. So it's a buried secret."

"It needs to stay buried," I whispered. "Don't you think?"

"I do," Lash hissed sadly. "I just wish it were otherwise."

"You got them out. They went on to have kids, and create this big loving family, and pass on your legend. Doesn't that make you happy?"

"I'd rather not be a legend, and be a favorite uncle, or great-uncle," Lash hissed very softly. "I'd rather be around my family than be remembered as a legend by family I'll never get to know."

"We're going to have a family," I whispered back. "Can being a dad be enough?"

Lash squeezed me so tight I let out a grunt. "Yes, Sweetness. I'm just being melancholy. I'll write back in the morning, telling her that my grandfather was some other snake. I can forge a believable history. That'll be the end of it."

He kissed me, and then he was easing me back, pulling up my nightgown.

There was an insistent knock at the door.

"What the hell is it?" Lash yelled. "We're trying to fuck in here, for God's sake!"

Jazz's voice was reluctant. "Peter for you, Lash."

"Tell him I'll call him back. Now go the fuck away, Jazz!"

"He's here. He's been injured, Lash. There's trouble. Devlin wants you."

Lash swore, threw off the covers, and pulled on his jeans. I grabbed some clothes, and hurriedly began dressing. Lash was already buckling his belt with his weapons, and I went out the door after him buttoning one of his shirts over me, forgoing a bra because this was too important.

We hurried downstairs, and into the dining room. Peter was in the kitchen, gray as paste. But he was healing, the new skin forming over his bare shoulder and left arm. He'd been sliced deep by something, turning his shirt to ribbons. That whole side of him was soaked in blood.

"What happened?"

"I tracked a vampire just over the Canadian border. He'd been staying in Niagara Falls, and he was headed this way. Mad said she needed my help—"

"Mad?" I said questioningly.

"She'll need help for a while, until she settles into Hector's position," Devlin said coolly. "But Madeline is a good fit for the job; she's just as capable as Rene and Sarelle are. And I do not want to hear more protests from you that she is not fit to lead because she's a woman. Now continue."

Peter glared at Devlin. "I tracked him here to this county and lost the trail. Knowing your party was last night, I watched to see who arrived and left. I caught sight of him again lurking nearby. Figuring that he was attending, I waited for him to leave, and when he did, I followed him—"

"What did he look like?" Lash interjected. "You know the Rulers, and the big names, Cushing. So—"

"Don't call me Cushing."

"Stop fighting and remember you're on the same side," Devlin growled. "Peter, what did he look like?"

"He was tall like you, Dalcon, but not so broad shouldered. He moved fast, but seemed very young, as in newly made. But when he hit me, he hit me with the force of an old vampire—"

"How old?" Lash interjected.

"At least a hundred, maybe two. Not more than that." Peter groaned. "If I'd been human, I'd be dead. My neck was broken, and so was my shoulder, not to mention torn to shreds. It was only because my hunters drove him off that I'm not dust."

"Any men with him? Did he smell of any weres at any time?"

"No. He's working alone, at least from what I saw."

"What are you chasing him for?" I interjected.

"He killed a ten-year-old girl in Canada who was vacationing with her parents. He drained her and threw her into the Falls. It was ruled an accident, but I examined the body. It was his work, his scent."

"Did he assault her?" Devlin said.

"No," Peter said scathingly. "But that doesn't mean he won't next time."

"He was after blood, not sex," Lash hissed flatly. "Some vampires prefer young blood. He shouldn't be a problem to take out. Give me an hour to plan, and I'll go with you and some of the bears and your hunters. We'll finish this before the sun sets."

"I'm in no condition—"

"Call your family, and tell them you need a donation," Devlin said, offering him the phone. "We will teleport them here for your convenience. Do it now."

Peter took the phone and began dialing.

Lash took my hand and led me into the hallway. "Go do some sewing, or take a walk," he said gently. "I'll be gone at least a day on this. You need to keep your mind on better things."

"Be careful," I murmured, knowing there wasn't anything else to say.

"I'll be fine," Lash hissed. "Um, I'll need you as snake when I get back. I was going to mention it earlier, but I wanted to ask Titus about checking you first."

"I can do that. Just go kill that son of a bitch."

Lash gave me a grin. "You got it, Sweetness. I'll call when it's done, like usual."

He gave me a kiss on the cheek, and walked off, already dialing his cell phone. I decided to look for Rene, and found her dancing with Venus in the ballroom.

"How are you feeling?" she said, eyeing me. "You look better than I expected."

"I'm better. But I need to ask you, can you make me a potion to be snake for Lash?"

"I could," Rene said, after a moment. "But we'd need demon blood. Demons usually don't like to part with that, unless you've got something worth trading for."

"Can I command it from Shaker?" I said delicately. "I feel odd asking for that."

"No," Rene said with a grin. "Blood is currency to them. Cash or other valuables are all demons will take in return, Sister. Going to Titus

100

for that is better, as otherwise he'll wonder where you got the blood and from whom. He'll know it wasn't Terian or Rip."

Duh, Sar. "Sorry, I didn't think." I gave her a weak smile. "I seem to be doing a lot of that lately."

"That's because you have a secret," Rene said, holding my gaze with her own. "You're thinking of that all the time and everything else is in the noise. And it'll be like that until the secret is told, or gets discovered."

That was a big help. "I have more than one, Rene," I said bitingly.

I opened the door to leave and felt her hand on my arm. "Don't be mad at me," she said. "I'll help you, if you ask me to. It's not a question of that, Sister. It never will be."

"I'm not angry," I said, taking her hand off me. "I'm just burn out. And the more I rest, the more burned out I feel. We had a wonderful day yesterday, and I should feel refreshed and ready to go. I don't."

"One day of fun isn't going to erase months of things that were awful. Give it time. Take some time for yourself, Sar. Venus is content to have her lessons, and when she asks for you, I'll come and get you—"

"I don't need you replacing me as her mom!" I shouted.

Rene looked stricken. "I didn't mean that."

I muttered an apology and left, hearing Venus ask as I fled what was wrong with me.

I woke up Ghost, and we went for a walk. The day was nice, in the high fifties, and the sun was out. *This will probably be one of the last nice days...*

I heard shots and followed them. Kyle was doing some target practice with a sniper type semiautomatic rifle. I watched him silently until his clip was empty, and then yelled hello.

He gave me a smile, and beckoned me over. "Want to try a few shots?"

I hadn't handled many rifles over the years, but I knew enough to locate the clip release, loaded some bullets, and took a few shots. The rifle was an older make, some kind of German by the writing on the stock. It was dead-on accurate.

"Nice," I said, handing it to him. "I've never shot one of these before."

"Want to try some others?" he offered. "I'm practicing, as I've not shot anything but handguns and shotguns since I began living here. But I need to get back into handling these, if I'm going to continue the good fight."

"So you're still planning on leaving?" I said, trying not to sound sad.

Kyle wasn't fooled. "I'll come back and visit, Sarelle. But I've got my own life to live."

"I understand. But I don't have to like it."

We shot several other types of rifle, one of which was mounted on a tripod, and had ammo so large it made a crater in the rock behind the row of targets.

"Why are you using guns, if your targets are demons?"

Kyle gave me a sideways look. "I don't go after the demons anymore, not directly. I target the humans bound to the demons. They are usually easier to kill than the demons themselves. The result is the same as destroying the demon's body; the demon gets sent back to hell."

I felt for the trunk of the tree behind me and latched onto it tightly to support my wobbling legs. "You kill humans, not just demons."

"I'm not proud of it," Kyle said with a shrug. "But it's good business sense. Humans get attached to having a demon within a few months, if not less. So most are like Devlin; when one is destroyed, it's only a short time before they summon another out of Hell. You don't stop a vampire by shooting it in its heart over and over with regular bullets, and letting it heal in-between. You kill it by normal means; taking the heart and the head, and burning the rest, to make sure."

"Are the humans all like that, addicted?"

Kyle gave me a strange look. "I'd not thought of it like that. But yes, most of them are. Experience tells me this addiction isn't one that most humans, if any, can break."

"Do others who target demons go after the human who summoned them?"

"Most of them do."

God, another thing to worry about. "I didn't know that," I mumbled.

Kyle gave me another strange look. "Is something wrong?"

"Lash is going out hunting with Peter. They were going to leave at dusk. There's a vampire killing children in the area who crossed in from

Canada."

"Don't worry about him. That snake has a hundred lives." Kyle beamed at me. "I don't suppose you'd like to help me clean these?"

I hated cleaning guns. But it would take my mind off what a mess I'd made of the day. So I helped him load them into his pack, and carry them back to Hayden, wishing all the while for my tractor so I didn't have to haul their weight through the forest. *God, why did everything have to be so hard all the time! Couldn't I catch a break?*

Out of nowhere, a flare of pride washed away my self-pity. *What was wrong with me?* It was a nice day, and the scenery was beautiful. I was with a friend and safe, as was everyone I cared about. Screw that I was tired; I was a strong woman and I should be proud I had the strength to do this, that I was the kind of woman Sharon someday wanted to be, the kind of woman Elle was trying to be. I didn't need my tractor. I didn't need a break. I just needed to believe in myself.

Feeling better than I had in days, I arrived at Hayden, and spent the rest of the evening helping Kyle clean his guns, and pack most of them away. Then I went to find Venus.

She was alone in her room, reading. I noticed with sadness she was already looking eleven. But she was taking blood from Devlin's donors now too, so that was to be expected.

"Hi," I said, coming and sitting on her bed. "Want me to read to you?"

"No," she said giving me a smile. "But I'll read to you, okay?"

"Sure." I lay down next to her. Before she'd gone more than a few paragraphs, I was asleep.

I woke up with a gentle nudge to see Devlin peering down at me. "Wake up, Love. It's morning."

"Is Lash back?" I said, yawning.

Devlin shook his head. "They stopped for the night, but plan to attack at full dark. Some vampires are with them, lending assistance." He gave me a soft look. "You looked so sweet lying there with Venus, Love. I'm glad I got a few pictures before I woke you."

"How is Rene?" I said tentatively. "I was kind of mean to her yesterday."

Devlin's demeanor changed instantly. "She didn't mention anything to me," he said coldly. "What did you say to her, Sar?"

I walked out into the hallway, closing the door behind me. Venus didn't need to hear us fight. "Something I didn't mean. I apologized, but I still feel bad—"

"She's in the living room watching TV. Go down to her and apologize again." His tone was still cold. "Now."

My hackles rose at his commanding manner. "Don't tell me what to do, Devlin. I didn't see you ask one person at that party to apologize to me for what was said."

"I hardly expected you to fall apart at the seams like you did, Sar," he replied. "You'd met and handled far worse in the past capably."

Fear and self-doubt stuck me like a stiletto's blade, making me lash out. "How are Danial and Emma? She seemed quite annoyed when he did his usual 'business comes before anything else' bullshit at the party."

"Emma fed Danial last night," Devlin said smugly. "She was here for three hours. From the pleased expressions on their faces afterwards, I'm guessing he finally released some of his tension—"

"Fuck you!" I screamed at him.

Devlin's eyes widened with shock. Before he could reply, I stalked down the stairs. He was after me in a moment. As he reached to grab me, I teleported, his yell at me to get back here this instant cut off in mid-screech. A split second later, I arrived in Wyoming, at that house I'd shared with Theo for that brief time we were married and happy.

It was still vacant, though it had been cleaned recently. It was very cold, enough so my breath came out in puffs. I made a fire in the small woodstove and sat before it, thinking. I cried for a while, too. Why not? I'd become a bitch of the first degree, and been shitty to everyone that mattered. My moods were like a rollercoaster, and I felt ready to snap all the time. I needed some time away from everyone, before I hurt anyone else I cared about.

It wasn't long afterward that I felt Shaker's presence in my mind. *Mistress?*

What? I thought to him.

Titus is looking for you. He's contacted me, asking me to help. Come back, please. Devlin is frantic, and he's got Rip looking, too.

"I don't want to come back, Shaker. I want to be alone."

But no one is guarding you, Mistress. Permit me to join you, to make sure you're safe.

"Sure. I'm cold. But you mention sex once and I'm going to start singing hymns, understand?"

Shaker appeared a moment later. With an interesting movement of his beast legs, he settled himself at my feet on the floor.

I basked in his heat, feeling it warming me more than the fire. "Come closer."

Shaker leaned up against me, his warmth radiating into me. *Ahh.*

"Are you still cold?" he rumbled. "Usually feet are coldest, which is why I'm here, and didn't put you on my lap."

I let out a brittle laugh. "I'm okay, thanks."

"You'll have to go back," he rumbled regretfully. "I've blocked Titus from seeing you're here, but it won't last long. Be warned, he'll put a tracking spell back on you as soon as he sees you, Mistress."

"I guess there's no point in asking you to block that," I whispered. "Or he'd know it was your work."

"Correct. But is there nothing else I can offer you?" Shaker turned to me, and put his clawed hands on either chair arm, resting his massive chest against my knees. "Your will is paramount, Mistress. Much as you make it easy for me, I'd feel better about our arrangement if you asked something significant of me once in a while."

"Sit here with me a while and don't talk. Just be near me, and don't tell me I have to be anything, or do anything, or feel anything. Do that for me, because that's what I need most."

"As you wish." Shaker leaned against me, laying his head on my lap. For a long time, I watched the fire, and before I realized it, I was running my fingers through his black hair, ruffling it, touching his short horns casually, liking the way they seemed to be smooth yet still warm. Though Shaker rumbled occasionally in what I guessed was pleasure, he didn't speak, and neither did I. Before long, I was asleep.

Chapter Nine

Suddenly ice water bathed me, abruptly waking me. Shaker had set me down in a drift of snow. "What the hell are you doing?" I sputtered.

"Titus was going to find us," Shaker replied. "As it is, he nearly did. So we are in Canada near the tundra, but you can't stay here. It is only my heat that is keeping you from frostbite."

"I'll go home," I said, sighing. "Thanks. I feel better."

Our surroundings shimmered, and suddenly, we were in the cemetery at Hayden.

"Think up something believable," Shaker rumbled. "And remember, Titus checked all of North America for you. So you were somewhere else and I wasn't with you." He disappeared.

A second later, Titus appeared. "Where were you, Kin-daughter?" he said in exasperation. "I've been looking for you for hours!" Before I could reply, I saw him mouth a few words, the glowing shimmer of a tracking spell sinking into me.

"I went to Europe, to that hotel I stayed in with Danial years ago," I lied. "I sat in the lobby for a while."

Titus gave me an odd look. "You're sure?"

Shit, he must smell Shaker on me. "There was a demon there; at least I think that's what he was. So I stayed in public, but he kept getting closer to me slowly. When he got close enough to talk to me, I ran for the bathroom, and teleported home."

Titus nodded. "Likely he scented the demon blood in you and was just curious. The levels in you are strong enough you smell a little demon-like. Don't be alarmed."

Why hell no, that sure shouldn't make one alarmed, to know they smelled like a demon. I rolled my eyes. "I'm not."

106

"Come inside," Titus said. "A snowstorm is nearly here. You look like you're wet?"

I teleported without answering, ending up in my bedroom. I was just changing my clothes when Devlin appeared.

His first look was one of abject relief, and then his eyes narrowed. "You are not ever to leave, Sar, not without telling me where you are going. I thought I made that clear to you once, but you must need a reminder."

I ignored him, finishing dressing.

"Where have you been?"

I ignored him, went into the bathroom, and began brushing out my hair.

"I scent demon on you."

I put the brush down guiltily, and repeated the lie of being in Europe, ending with saying I was sorry for worrying him.

Devlin's arms went around me, hugging me gently. "This behavior must stop, Love. Lash and I love you. You must let Danial go, or you'll destroy yourself."

I opened my mouth to say this hadn't been about Danial, and then wondered if deep down it had been. Then I decided it didn't matter; it was better to make him believe that. "I know, you're right. It's best for everyone if he leaves, the sooner the better."

"He's said he'd leave in the spring after you've given birth. But with you not pregnant yet, he'll likely delay."

"I'll talk to him, tell him I've reconsidered." I swallowed. "I'll tell him he should go be with Emma, and that he should leave as soon as possible."

Devlin hugged me, and then let me go. "As you wish."

I turned to face him. "Any news from Lash?"

"Nothing. If you're asking if I told him you've been AWOL the last five hours, the answer is no. I didn't want to jeopardize him, even though he'll be livid when he learns what you did—"

"Look, I needed some time. You take time to go out with Lash, and never tell me where you go, or what you do while you're gone. I've needed the same thing lately. What's so hard for you to understand about that?"

"Take some additional time then," he said stiffly. "I'll be downstairs." He left before I could reply.

Deciding there was no point in going to bed possibly smelling of demon, I took off my clothes, and had myself a long shower. Then I got dressed in nightclothes, grabbed the basket of demon-smelling clothes, and took it downstairs to the washer. There was already a load of wet clean clothes in there of Venus's, so with a sigh I loaded the dryer, too. I got the loads going, and turned around, and there was Danial, blocking the door.

"Did you disappear because of me?" he said softly. "Because you were jealous?"

"No. Let me by, I want to go to bed."

"Not until you answer me."

I thought about lying, but I knew he'd see through it like he always did. "Maybe. I don't know why you'd care about my reasons. Devlin said you'd bedded your woman—"

"That is no one's business but mine and hers," Danial said neutrally.

"Just fucking let me past!" I said harshly.

Danial moved over. As I pushed past him, he grabbed one arm, making me face him. "Where does this jealousy come from? How can it matter to you what I do, when you are Oathed to my brother, a veritable God among lovers? I'm like your brother-in-law, Lady!"

Get out the words and make them count. "It shouldn't. It's my problem, Danial, and I'll handle it. I shouldn't have asked you to stay in the first place. I can take care of myself. So it would be better for all of us if you left as soon as you could for your new life."

"I already promised you to stay—"

"Fuck you and your promises," I said in a hitching tone. "Go be with your new dark-haired blue-eyed woman. Go give her your Oath. I hope it lasts fucking forever."

Danial loosened his grip. "What do you mean?" he said, unnerved. "I sense you meant something more than your words."

"Fucking let me go!" I shouted. "You don't have any rights to me, none!"

Danial looked at me oddly, and slowly released me. "You believe I do have a right to you," he whispered. "I can hear the lie in your voice."

"Do you love her?" I said harshly. "Do you?"

"Not yet," Danial said, his dark eyes confused. "I barely know her, Lady. Real love takes time."

I turned and walked away, and this time, he let me.

I got upstairs, and ran into Kyle, who was putting on a coat.

"Are you leaving?" I said in alarm. "It's winter, not even Christmas—?" My eyes widened with sudden panic. "Is Lash okay?"

"He's not the reason I've got to leave for a few days, Sar. A friend who said a demon had been sighted killing men in Toronto has called me. I'm heading there tonight. The human can't be far, at least, that's usually the case."

Shit. Shaker had taken me to the tundra. What if he was the demon Kyle was after? Shit! He'd kill Kyle like it was nothing! "Lash isn't back yet."

"He called an hour ago. They located and killed the vampire. Lash should be back within the hour." He gave me a smile. "You'll be fine."

He walked outside with a final wave. A moment later, one of the Hummers drove off.

"Kin daughter," Titus rumbled from behind me. "I must talk to you. Come."

What now? I can't handle anything else right now! God! I followed him to his old basement study, where he placed a potion in my hands. "Lash said to get that ready for him yesterday."

I sagged in relief. *The potion to become snake.* "Thanks. I forgot to ask you for it."

Titus looked at me for a moment, almost as if he was working up to something. God, did he know about Shaker and me?

"Why do you and Kyle get along?" I blurted out. "You should be enemies, right?"

"As a favor to Devlin," Titus said, grinning like a shark. "I leave Kyle alone, and he does the same for me. He knows what I must eat is dead when I eat it, Kin daughter, and that I protect Devlin, killing only on his orders. And that is enough for you to know."

Hell, yes, that was more than enough info.

"But enough of my delaying. I wanted to speak to you in private to ask if you wanted a fertility potion," Titus continued uncomfortably.

"Lash mentioned wanting one, but no more was said to me about it. I didn't know if that was from your shyness, so I wanted to offer."

"No, not yet," I said, after a moment. "I'd rather not unless I have to, Titus."

"Let me know if you change your mind, Kin daughter. That is all." He paused. "If you are looking for Rene, she is in Devlin's office, perusing some notes of Cyrus's on Monica's plans for how to alter her blood. As you know, she was faerie, too, like Rene. I gave her the notes this morning." It was clear he was unsure how I would take the news.

Best to get my apology to her over with. I thanked him, and went to Rene.

She turned when she saw me coming, and gave me a smile. "I'm glad you're safe."

"I'm sorry for what I said."

"Don't mention it," she said, shrugging. "I'm not angry."

"Devlin was."

"He forgets I'm well able to stick up for myself," Rene said loftily. "You know he loves to come to the rescue of a damsel in distress."

I smiled back at her, and then looked at her screen. Most was in English.

"Do you need some of my blood? If I'm reading this right, you do."

"Would you mind?" she said, giving me a lopsided smile. "I could understand this process she devised a little better if I had a sample to work with. None of Cyrus's 'wet' work was recovered, just these notes."

"Sure." I let her prick my finger and draw out a small sample. Then she healed it with a little magic.

"Would you teach me some simple spells?" I said shyly. "I'd like to know how to zap people with lightning."

Rene laughed. "I'm not going to teach you black magic, Sister. You're too at risk already from being bound to a demon. But would you like to learn healing? Most is white magic, and although it's not easy to learn, it wouldn't be nearly as risky."

I grimaced, but decided that was a good thing. We had enough fights and bloodshed around here that knowing how to heal would come in handy. "Sure."

"Then let's start tomorrow. Come down when you're ready, I'll be here."

I went upstairs, and bumped into Lash, who was just coming in from the garage. He took one look at me and grabbed me up in his arms. He walked me upstairs, kissing me so passionately I couldn't get out any words. Then he took me into the bedroom, locked the door, and told me to get ready as he headed into the bathroom. Five minutes later, he slithered out in snake form, still wet from the shower, and onto the bed, where I waited for him curled in the most seductive pile I could manage. I reminded myself again to thank Rene for the spell she'd done to make me able to understand him, as I hissed to him to come and get me.

A second later, he was coiling around me, hissing he fucking had me now and he knew just what to do with me. I gave myself up to sensation, losing myself in him.

Chapter Ten

A sharp pain lanced though my side, waking me gasping for air. I screamed, waking Lash as I writhed in his arms, the pain like fire burning me. Lash shouted for Titus as the pain suddenly passed and I went limp.

Titus appeared at the foot of the bed, blue fireballs in each hand. "What happened?"

"She's hurt! Sweetness! What's wrong?"

"A bad dream, I think," I said, wincing. "I needed a moment to tell reality from dreams. It was agony."

Titus nodded, and disappeared.

"Rest," Lash hissed. "I'll be right here—"

The rest of his words were cut off by Shaker's rumble in my head. *Mistress, I need you.*

What is it? I thought back at him.

I've been injured. What you felt was a wound I took. I need healing.

Blood? I thought.

Maybe more. The wound is a bad one. If I succumb, you'll be dragged down with me to Hell. That's not going to happen if I can heal myself.

Shit, I needed Rene—!

"Mate?" Lash hissed. "What is it?"

"Is Rene next door? Can you hear her?" I asked him.

"Why do you need her? Are you hurt?" Lash said worriedly. "I thought it was just a dream?"

"It was," I said, thinking frantically. "Let me get a drink of water. I'm rattled."

"I'll get it. Stay here." Lash got up.

112

The moment he was gone, I cast my mind out for Rene. *"Sister?"*

Sar? she answered. *What is it?*

Shaker's injured, I thought to her. *He needs blood, and maybe more. I felt a sharp pain.*

Damned demon, Rene cursed. *Shaker, can you hear me? Where are you?*

In Toronto, near the Holiday Inn on the far side of the city, on its outskirts, came his mental rumbling voice

Is Kyle still after you? I thought.

I struck him a solid blow. He's dead, or close to it, Shaker thought back. *But it was him or me.* He paused. *You should've warned me, Mistress.*

"I didn't know you were killing people," I whispered aloud.

"Sweetness, why are you bringing that up now?" Lash hissed, handing me my water. "And really, you did know. So why are you—?"

I'm a demon, and that's what I do, Shaker rumbled over Lash, irritated. *Who'd have thought a couple dismembered drug dealers would be enough to set off alarms with demon hunters?*

I'll be there in a little while, Rene thought back. *Stay hidden, Shaker. Luckily, Devlin is on some conference call and not with me tonight. But it may take me some time to get to you—*

"Mate?" Lash hissed. "What's wrong? You have this odd look on your face."

Save Kyle, Rene! I thought frantically. *Please don't let him die.*

I'll do what I can, Rene said flatly. *Shaker, where did you two fight?*

Shaker groaned. *Near—*

"Sweetness, ANSWER ME!" Lash shouted, dissolving the telepathic connection completely. I cast a terrified look at him, leapt out of bed, and ran to Rene's room. I tried to open the door but it was locked. Shit, what if she needed me to hold the mental connection to Shaker? I had to find her! Kyle would die!

Sar, I've got a connection, Rene broke in. *Don't—*

Lash abruptly grabbed hold of me, yelled my name, and shook me hard. Again, the telepathic connection dissolved. I sank to my knees limp with relief. Lash picked me up easily, brought me back to our bed, and got me under the covers. I whimpered a little, as he tried to soothe me

113

with words, telling me it was just a dream and not to worry, that we were all okay and everything was going to be fine. When he handed me the bottle of valium, I took three instead of one, and drifted off.

I didn't awake until almost four the next afternoon. Once I showered and dressed, I felt much better. A large part of that was upon waking, I'd quickly made a mind connection to Rene, who assured me she'd found Kyle, and healed him.

He was near death, Rene said in my mind. *Shaker hit him with Hellfire and he was badly burnt. But he's mostly healed now, though he'll need to spend some time regaining the use of his limbs.*

"This is my fault," I whispered. "I was going to warn Shaker and I forgot—"

This is Kyle's fault, for going after Shaker, and Shaker's fault, for not covering his tracks better. It isn't your fault, Sister.

"I should've told Dev, given Shaker bodies like you said to—"

I'm setting something up, Rene said roughly. *Shaker won't need to haunt any more alleys. He'll be at full strength again soon. But I'll be gone for a few days.*

How did you make a mind connection to Shaker without me?

I was bound to him once, remember? It was brief and a long time ago, but it's not something you forget how to do. He also contacted me mentally when he first told me of how you'd become his Mistress. So it was easy to make the link.

Do you need me to do anything? I asked.

Keep Devlin warm for me, Rene said, smiling by her tone. *And stay out of trouble.*

I thanked her, and she severed the connection.

Lash came to find me around dinnertime. I was on the treadmill, trying to walk off my celebratory binge lunch of chocolate.

"Want to go to dinner with me?" he said hopefully.

"Why today?" I shut off the machine and stepped down, glad the torture was over for another day.

"We haven't gone out for a long time," he said, putting his hand over mine. "I thought you could use some attention."

"Sure," I said easily. "Sushi?"

"Of course," he said, laughing. "Give me a few minutes to change."

"Meet you in the hall?"

He nodded. Ten minutes later, we met there. An hour later, we were enjoying some eel and salmon respectively, and talking.

"Are you okay?" Lash hissed, when we were almost done. "Your dreams seem to be getting worse, even on the drugs. Last night you scared me when you wouldn't snap out of it."

"I'm okay," I said, sipping my wine. "I just need more time."

"I'm not going to push," he hissed. "Just tell me if you need anything, Love."

"Tell me something: did you see a Godiva gift basket arrive from Van and Erik? They said they sent one. But I didn't see one arrive from them."

Lash looked at the wall. "They did. I had Titus melt it, in case it was poisoned."

I gave him a look. "It wasn't poisoned. Tell me the truth."

Lash looked over at me, his eyes flat. "I don't know they're gay for sure. No mate of mine's going to be eating another straight man's chocolate, unless it's from Dev."

I cracked a smile. "It's was just chocolate, Tryst. They were just being nice."

"Yeah, right." He checked his watch. "We should get back."

"Wait, Tryst. I need to know about the work you've been doing."

Lash looked over at me again, irritated and defensive. "What about it?"

"Devlin's mentioned you've got a bunch to do. I've noticed you've been gone a lot. I wanted to know why there were so many jobs in such a short time?" I paused. "I'm worried about getting pregnant, and something happening to you."

"Nothing's going to happen to me, Sweetness," Lash hissed easily. "I told you, no one bothers me. As for the work, I'm doing that because you'll be pregnant soon. Once you are, I'm not going out on jobs for a while, until our young is old enough to defend both itself and you if I was to not be nearby."

The relief was like the cool water of a quiet lake on a sweltering hot day. All my tension seeped out of me. "Okay. I just wanted to ask."

"Not a problem. Let's go."

We got up to leave, and suddenly, Devlin was there.

Lash gave him a look. "What are you doing here? It's day."

"Rip brought me. Kyle's hurt bad, Lash. Titus's got him at Hayden now." Devlin paused. "He tangled with a high level demon and got hit with Hellfire."

Lash swore. "Damn it. I'll have to hunt that son of a bitch down."

"Kyle says he killed him, sent him back to Hell. But he's going to be laid up for a while. I've got to go via Titus to an emergency meeting to meet with Nate regarding Hector's daughter. I need you to go home, so Venus is protected with more than just Rip."

"Let's go," Lash said, throwing some cash on the table. Devlin nodded, and headed back the way he'd come, presumably to be teleported by Titus directly to Nate's home.

As soon as Lash drove us to a secluded place, I teleported us to Hayden. We went directly to the grey guest room Kyle had been using. Devlin was already there when we arrived; standing near the bed and looking worried. It was easy to see why. Kyle looked awful, his color as grey as the surrounding walls, his lips bloodless. His entire right side was a mass of healed skin. His right eye had a patch over it. The left side had also burned and been healed, the skin dark pink and red in places, most of his body hair missing.

He opened his one good eye when he heard us come in. "Come to see me?"

"Rest and don't talk," Devlin said gently. "You were hurt bad, friend."

"But the son of a bitch is dead," Kyle said with pride. "He was old, five hundred at least."

"You're lucky you may get older," Lash hissed. "Don't be going after old demons, Kyle. Stick to the young ones, like Rip. I don't want to have to go avenge you, I'm going to be a father, and I can't be risking my life."

Kyle smiled, making it look painful. "Agreed."

"Do you want some cookies?" I whispered, wanting to offer him some comfort. "I could make you some."

"Yes. Chocolate chip?"

I nodded, and Devlin excused us all to let Kyle get some sleep.

Devlin left with Titus for his meeting. When Lash went to man the gatehouse, his form vibrating with anger, I let him go without protest. I had enough to wonder about, like why didn't Kyle have memories of Rene healing him, or Shaker escaping?

Venus found me just as I began making cookies. For the next two hours, I relaxed, letting her mix the cookies and shape them. When they were done, I sent her with a small tray to Kyle. I was putting the rest in bags to keep them soft when Rip came in.

"Do you want some?" I offered. "I know Titus can make you a spell."

"I can make my own," Rip said with a grin. "I'm just as good at that spell as he is. Would you mind?"

I handed him a small bag, and he thanked me. Then he looked at me uneasily.

"What?"

"Would you mind if I took some to my brother?" he said, his stony voice unusually hesitant. "He's…not feeling well. Shaker likes cookies."

I bit my lip hard, then forced a smile. "Tell him I hope he feels better," I said, handing him another small bag.

He gave me a large happy grin, thanked me profusely, and walked out.

That night, Lash was still on duty. Devlin came in to find me reading.

"That was nice of you to make the cookies. They were good."

I gave him a small smile, knowing he had to have asked Titus for a spell to eat solid food. "How many did you eat?"

"Seven," he said with a chuckle. "I can't get enough of chocolate. I can't believe I got along without it for centuries." He began to take off his suit.

"I'm glad you liked them. I hope you saved some for Lash."

"He sent Seth to bring him some at the gatehouse. He said they were good, too."

Devlin crawled in beside me, and began to bite me lightly. When he did, I moved suddenly, impaling myself on his fangs. He let out a moan as the blood hit him, and bit deeper, moving me under him so he could push inside me with a thrust of his hips.

117

We didn't last long. After, we lay holding each other, panting hard.

"I love that you desired me so much," he whispered seductively. "We have not been together since before the Hallows party. I was worried you were still angry with me." He lightly kissed my cheek. "I worried you were jealous of Rene, that you had words with her over me."

I wondered what he was talking about, and then realized he meant the night I'd teleported to escape his ordering me around. "I'm not angry or jealous. There's just a lot going on."

"I know. Despite Lash killing that vampire, other children have been reported missing across the country, and in a number abnormally high. Some are likely usual victims of evil men, or splitting parents, nothing to do with vampires. But three were in Pennsylvania, near Pittsburg, all in one week. So we suspect we missed another vampire or were. Van and Erik are looking into it. Akira has volunteered to help, as he thinks it is possible that this being originally came from New York, and not Pennsylvania. Nate said he will also report any missing children."

I felt my old friend panic rise in me. "Will Lash go?"

"Not unless they have trouble. As you know, he's got quite a few jobs lined up for himself before the end of the year, and a couple will be tricky."

I got more panicked, if that were possible. "Are you saying that he might get hurt?"

Devlin kissed me gently. "He'll be fine, Sar. Really, everything is fairly calm right now, knock on wood." Devlin rapped gently on the headboard of the bed. "Rene has even taken a little time to travel, saying she wished to visit some places of her youth. I cleared it with Samuel, and he gave her a pass. So she'll be away for a few days overseas."

"When did she ask you to set this up? She didn't mention anything to me."

"A few weeks ago."

Uneasiness became anxiety. Rene had known what would happen to Shaker and Kyle, and not warned them or me. *Why?*

"Would you mind another bout?" Devlin said, breaking into my thoughts. "I've recovered some of my stamina, Love, and it's been a long time since I loved you for hours."

I seized on his words like an inflatable raft in a shipwreck. "Make love to me as long as you can," I said tenderly, my eyes misting. "You once threatened to love me until I lost consciousness. Tonight, I dare you to make good on that threat."

Devlin let out a rich low laugh that caressed me just as utterly as it had the first time I'd heard it. "Remember, you asked."

* * * *

The next morning, I woke up to find Devlin nestled on my chest, his arms wrapped around me. I stretched, and felt so sore it was like a gentle ache all through me.

I'd not taken any drugs last night at all, and had no bad dreams. I let loose a long sigh of relief, and Devlin opened his melting golden eyes.

"I won," he said, pride dripping from his arrogant words. "You lasted until two a.m."

I grinned. "I was happy to lose, Love."

"Would you mind if Lash and I went out this weekend?" he said, gently inquisitive. "We'd like to one last time before it gets too cold for us to ride our motorcycles. You can come if you want to."

"Will Rene go?"

"She won't return until at least Sunday," Devlin said longingly. "But we'd be happy for you to join us."

"No," I said, yawning. "I'm happy to stay home, and be warm."

"Suit yourself. It's only Wednesday." He grinned at me. "You may change your mind."

Chapter Eleven

The rest of that week passed quickly, and soon it was Friday night.

After a long successful day of working outdoors in Hayden's gardens, I was looking forward to a long soak in Lash's tub. Venus was at Samuel's estate in Europe, visiting Sharon, with Titus as escort. Kyle was on the mend, though Leri had said it would be some time before he was up and around again.

I took off my clothes, started running the bathwater, and then heard a hard knock at the bedroom door.

Who could that be? Devlin and Lash were out riding on their motorcycles. They'd asked me several times to come, saying they would drop me off before they went "cruising." I'd told them no way in hell. My memories of crashing over a year ago with Devlin while riding on his motorcycle were still too strong, so what that I hadn't broken any bones?

I pulled on my bathrobe, and went to the door. By the time I reached it, I had a sinking idea of who it could be. Sure enough, I opened it to find Danial.

"Is something wrong?" I said coolly.

"No, Lady," Danial replied neutrally. "Devlin said you would be here alone for a few hours, and I wanted to let you know that I would be in my room. My cell will be on. I'm working on a new drawing, but feel free to call if you need something."

For Danial to be "on call" was a usual thing now on the nights Dev and Lash went off to do male bonding. As much as they liked to hellraise together, they worried about leaving me, and told Danial to leave his cell on, as a backup for Titus and for Kyle. Since Danial rarely went anywhere, he always agreed. But Danial had never come to my room

120

before to speak to me. *It must be because Kyle is hurt, and Titus is off with V...*

I gritted my teeth as the rest of Danial's words sank in. The "new" drawing was likely of Emma, who'd come to Danial last night for more than triple the total time Devlin took with his normal three donors. *Slut.*

"Lady?"

"Sounds fine, Danial," I said, giving him a frosty smile. "I'll be here in Lash's room—"

Shit! I forgot Frank! I ran quickly to the bathroom, shut off the tub, and began looking into the water for any dark specks. *Ah ha!* I finally saw the black speck at the far side of the tub, the rapidly drowning spider that Lash and I had nicknamed Frank. I fished him out, put him to the side, and he crawled off stalwartly to hide under the lip of the tub, dragging his waterlogged back legs and body with his front four legs.

"You never learn," I said tenderly, watching him crawl off to hide. "One of these days I'm not going to remember in time, and you're going to drown, Frank—"

"What are you doing?" Danial said curiously from the doorway. "Who are you talking to?"

"Saving a spider," I explained, blushing. "He's in there most times because we don't use this tub too often anymore, and he'll die if I don't scoop him out—"

Danial had become still as a statue, watching me. "Why did you save him, Lady?" he said raggedly. "Why?"

It suddenly hit me: he remembered that other night with me years ago. *The spider in my old house whom I'd saved in front of him, the night Danial had asked me to give him my Oath. Oh shit.* "Because I can't watch him struggle to live without helping him," I said, tense as a coiled spring.

"Why not just move him somewhere else?" Danial whispered. "He would be safe, if you moved him."

His old but still familiar words made my heart race. I took a deep breath and tried to slow it. "He might not be able to survive where I put him. Outside right now, it's too cold. Winter is coming—"

"Why do you bother to save him, knowing you will only have to save him again?" Every one of his words echoing down from years past was raw agony, tortured.

I took another deep breath and faced him. "Because I can't let him die, not when I know I can save him."

Danial came to me hesitantly. He almost reached out for me, but then he drew his hand back. I held his gaze with my eyes, but didn't reach out for him.

My reason said to break the moment, to stop what was happening with a few cruel words. But I felt the same for him as I had that long ago night I'd first saved him. I just couldn't leave him in his grief, because it was so much easier for me to let him think I was dead, not if there was a chance that he would remember me. He'd done so much for me, to save me, to make me happy, and he was the father of my firstborn child, and my Oathed One. Even if he didn't remember that any more, I did.

I owed him this. And God damn it, whatever else I was, I always paid my debts.

"I remember a night, years ago," Danial said hoarsely, his expression fearful and also hopeful. "A night I never told anyone about, not Theo, not my brother, no one. I remember another place, another woman, and another bathtub that held a drowning spider."

I thought frantically. *What did I say to him that night?* I needed the exact words. *What were they?*

"She saved its life in front of my eyes, even though she was embarrassed after. I told her that she wasn't crazy for saving a spider. I compared it to her saving me, when an attacker was trying to kill me."

Danial had said that and more, the night he'd asked me for my Oath.

"She said to me a single phrase," he whispered. "But it was enough for me to know that she was the one I wanted. I asked her to promise herself to me that very night."

There was so much hope in his voice, so much pain and fear that he might be wrong, that I wouldn't know the words, or even what he was talking about. Reliving the memory, my words of that long ago night suddenly came back to me. "I told you I couldn't let you die, not if I could save you."

Tears spilled out of Danial's eyes as he reached for me, embracing me as if he would never let me go. "You are her," he rasped, shaking with joy and realized hope. "You are my Sar. God, it's true."

"Yes, I'm her," I whispered.

He sank to his knees, still holding me, and I eased down to the floor with him, unwilling to let him go. For a long time, Danial just cried in my arms, his tears soaking the front and shoulders of my bathrobe. I stroked his hair and told him not to cry, that he was loved and I was here, in his arms.

He pulled back from me finally, and looked at me for several moments, studying my face. "Why do you not look as I remember you?" he said softly. "Your hair, your face, even your voice, it's completely different."

"It was the injury you took at the hands of Ulysses," I said carefully. "My choker with your symbol fell off. Dev and I got to you as soon as we could. You almost died, your heart was stopped for minutes, and it affected some of your memories."

"Why could it not be of my youth!" he said angrily. "Or of all the years I spent alone! I have spent almost a year without you! Months thinking you were dead, and grieving for you!"

I felt myself wanting to give in to the moment. Hadn't this been what I'd hoped for? *And now it's finally happening.* "I'm not dead, Danial," I said, taking his face in my hands. "I'm here with you."

Danial leaned forward, and kissed me. I slid my fingers into his hair, caressing him as I kissed him back. He picked me up in his arms, still kissing me, and carried me in, to Lash's bed. He left me for a moment to shut and lock the door, and then he was back, easing down beside me. Danial kissed me gently at first, but soon he was crushing my body against his, his hands sliding over my feverishly hot body, caressing and squeezing me through my robe as he kissed me. I pushed him back gently, and pulled off my bathrobe, revealing my nakedness. Danial looked at me darkly, and then he was pulling off his shirt and jeans, tearing the black cloth in his haste. He crawled to me eagerly, his erection standing proudly at attention. He eased down on me, but he didn't slide into me, he just held his body to mine.

"Are you sure this is what you want?" Danial asked tenderly. "I have treated you as another woman these past months, Sar. Even now that I know you are my Oathed One, my Love, I look at you and I see Lady, a woman I liked a great deal though I didn't love her. I may call you Lady when I make love to you." He paused. "It may not be the same with me now as it was between us once."

His words brought back painful memories of the last time we'd been together. I went still beneath him, drawing back my hand that had been reaching for his face.

He grasped it quickly, putting it to his cheek. "I know I hurt you with some of the things I said in my grief," Danial said unevenly, his dark eyes looking down at me in shame. "I am sorry for that, Darling, and I don't want to hurt you more than I have already. I'm sorry for what happened between us, that time with Devlin and you, that I acted so atrociously, that I…" He trailed off, tears again falling from his eyes. "I'm so sorry, Sar. Please forgive me. Please, please forgive me."

I pushed him back and sat up, my romantic notions fading. "I forgive you." I rubbed my eyes. "We both said and did things that we shouldn't have."

"And?" he added expectantly.

I looked at him, surprised.

"You were leading into something," Danial continued, reaching for his shirt, and slipping it back on.

You always knew me, best of all. My heart I'd been working so hard to keep rational softened. I touched his hand with my fingers gently, and shook my head.

"I love you enough that I can wait to be intimate with you again, until I can look at you and only see you as Lady—" He stopped immediately. "I'm sorry." He moved to get up from the bed.

I took his face in my hands, stopping him. "Don't be. I am your Lady, Danial, your Lady in Red. I have been your lady since that night you had Tatiana play us that song, and we danced together, me in my red dress that I wore for you, the one you keep in your memory boxes."

"My Lady in Red," Danial whispered tenderly, and then he kissed me with a groan, moving his body close to mine.

I reached down for him and took his hard cock in my hand. He gasped, and I slipped my tongue into his mouth eagerly as my hand caressed his throbbing erection. Danial pulled me tight against him, licking me with his tongue, and then he was kissing down my neck, sucking gently. He ran his fangs over my breasts and I let out a little cry,

124

as he took my right breast in his mouth, caressing the other with his hand. I writhed beneath him eagerly, but he didn't penetrate me yet, though I wanted him more and more with each passing second.

Danial released my breast, and looked up at me, his eyes hot with lust and love. "Does it still hurt you, if you are bitten outside of climax?" he whispered gently.

I grimaced, and nodded yes.

"Then I will wait," Danial said, kissing me again deeply.

I'd had enough of waiting. I began to slide my hand up and down his hard penis, my hand slick with his need so long denied. Danial moaned into my mouth, his hips quickly pushing closer. I maneuvered beneath him and pushed the tip of him against my swollen clit, rubbing slightly so he could feel how much I wanted him inside me, sliding in my warm wetness.

Danial twitched, but he didn't move to take me. So I did it for him, putting the head of him against my opening and thrusting up with my hips, impaling myself on him.

Danial cried out as I pushed him inside me, and his hands slid down to my hips, reaching around to hold my buttocks. Then he bore down hard, sliding himself all the way in with a loud sigh of pleasure. "You feel the same, Sar," he said, his words overflowing with love and absolute joy as he moved in me. "Just as I remember you, my Love."

Danial kissed me on my throat as he loved me. I kissed him back on his neck and broad shoulders, sliding my hands down his lean, hard body, to finally rest on his rear. I pushed down hard, wanting to feel him all the way in me, loving the sensation of his muscles contracting under my hands as he pleasured me.

Danial began to jerk. *He's close, he'll only last a few more seconds.* I disengaged, then rolled him over, moving atop him to straddle him. He held my breasts as I moved on him rhythmically, until I lay my body down on his.

I wanted to draw this out, to see him beneath me, his body slack with need, his eyes closed as he focused all of his being on the rapture he was feeling at my body's motion on his. But I couldn't hold back any longer, and I came hard, crying out his name, "Danial! Oh, Danial!"

Before the orgasm ebbed, he rolled me beneath him, sinking his fangs into the side of my neck. Danial spilled his seed into my body in the next second, convulsing hard against me, and I heard him crying out his joy into my throat as he climaxed. He was moaning loudly as he drank from me, his hands trembling as they caressed me. I held him close to me, tears streaming from my eyes, because I'd thought never to feel him again this way, and I still loved him, no matter how we had hurt one another over the years.

Danial jerked one final time, and then went still. He quickly healed my neck bite, and then gave my neck a gentle kiss. He eased off me to lie beside me, and pulled me close to him, cuddling me. "You taste like the Sar I remember now." Danial sighed, completely happy. "That day I tasted you, you didn't. I'd forgotten I only ever bit you this way, and some of it was I was looking for the 'high' of the orgasm in your blood. You weren't climaxing when I tasted you, so it makes sense, that you didn't have it."

"It doesn't matter," I murmured. "You know who I am now."

"I'm sorry I could not last longer," he replied, clearly embarrassed. "I have not been with a woman since…since that night with you and Devlin, all those months ago. I am sorry again for that night, that I acted so deplorably with you. Again, please forgive me."

"I forgive you," I said, stroking his dark hair with my hands. "We both have said and done some terrible things. Let it go. It's enough to just be here with you like this again." I let out a long breath. "I just want to forget." I glanced over at him meaningfully. "And no more dark haired, blue-eyed bimbos, please."

Danial had the good grace to look ashamed. "I was not with Emma. I want you to know that. I admit to wanting to be, but I—"

"Please do not mention her or any of the other past loves of yours," I interrupted bitterly. "You can find some blonde donors."

"Do not envy Emma," Danial said tenderly, hugging me tight. "I love you and only you, Sar. Now that I have you back, I'll tell her that she and I are finished. I'll not see her as a donor again, Love. And yes, I will do as you ask; only blonde donors from now on."

Damn straight. I let out a soft sigh, mollified.

We held each other for a while, just liking the feeling of shared intimacy after so long apart. But after an hour had passed, I reluctantly began to get up.

"Stay here with me," Danial said softly, pulling me back down. "I haven't held you in so long. I want to sleep with you in my arms, to hold you close. I've missed you so much."

"I can't," I said gently, disentangling myself from him. "Lash and Dev will be coming back soon. As much as they'll be happy that you know who I am again, it would be best that they didn't find us here naked in Lash's bed." *And Lash is likely going to be pissed, to put it mildly.*

"We are Oathed," Danial said in a tone that said he didn't understand at all what I was saying. "They both know this. Devlin has repeatedly asked me to join you and he in bed, telling me that he wanted to share you, though I refused. It is not as if I am an interloper here..." Danial's eyes narrowed as he stared at me. "You already know Devlin wouldn't mind to find us this way, that he would just climb in beside us with a smile. It is Lash you are worried about."

"Yes," I said curtly, getting up. "I don't know how Lash will react." *Total lie.* Lash was going to be very jealous and upset to see Danial was my lover again, no matter that he had agreed to it under Oath to Devlin. Almost a year had passed since then.

"Then we'll go to Devlin's bed." He took my hand. "Come."

I let him take it, but forced myself to keep talking as he led me towards the door. "I'm talking about more than whose bed we're in. Dev may want you to sleep with us instead of Lash, but—"

"And I shall," Danial interrupted, embracing me suddenly. "You no longer need to be with Lash, Sar. As much as Devlin might consider him a friend, you and I are Oathed." He hugged me to him. "You don't have to worry, Love. Lash will accept that he is no longer needed, just as he did after you no longer needed him before. Devlin will get a female of his own kind to keep him happy and to bear him a child, if he still desires one."

How can you know me so well and still not see me? "Danial, listen to me. I was pregnant and I lost—"

Danial held me tighter. "I know, Love. I know you had to do it. It was very brave of you to get yourself pregnant with Lash's children, knowing what he is. But now there's no need—"

I tried again. "I'm trying to tell you that it wasn't just a ploy, I wanted another—"

"Then I'll give you another, Love," Danial said with pleasure, as he stroked my fingers with his cool hands. "Dev will likely wish to try, also. He and I will both begin taking the potion as soon as it can be made for us, though this time I'll make sure he takes the same one I—"

Time to be blunt. "Danial, listen to me! I am not going to banish Lash from my arms because you are yourself again. I want him beside me." I took a deep breath, bracing myself. "I want to have a child with him. Do you understand? Not with anyone else." I paused for emphasis. "With him."

Danial looked at me in confusion, which quickly turned to horror. "You can't...you can't want him more than me?"

Chapter Twelve

Heat suffused my face, as the months of guilt crashed down on me. Danial's look of confusion turned to one of deep hurt the instant he saw my flush. "You do," he said in disbelief, his voice trembling a little. "You want him, not me."

I can't lie, he'll know. "I don't want there to be a fight, or to hurt either of you," I said weakly. "I love you both."

I reached out for Danial, but he evaded me, returning to the bed. He picked up his shirt in a graceful motion, looking at me coldly. Then he began to put on his clothes. I grabbed my robe and belted it tightly around myself, then sat on the bed.

"You are indeed my long-lost Sar," Danial said, angry and hurt. "Always with her, it was the same thing; from the moment she began to love Theo. She was all too willing to hurt me, and so unwilling to hurt him."

"That's not true, it never was! Lash is not just my lover, he's my mate. Our bond is part of the Oath, Danial."

Danial recoiled, disgust in his eyes. "You are not weresnake," he said, studying me. "You can't be mated if you aren't weresnake, because you can't be with him as a snake."

"I am his mate," I assured firmly. "I have been with him as a snake, Danial."

The shock and revulsion on Danial's face was horrible. "You took a potion to be with him like that?" he said, wrinkling his nose in disgust. "Ugh! Why would you want to?"

"Because I love him," I said simply. "I want him to be happy. I enjoy his caresses as a snake."

Danial sank to the bed, put his head in his hands, and didn't look at me. "Why couldn't you have left me alone?" he whispered. "It would have been better to let me think you were dead, Sar, than to hear you say these words, to know you really love that gutter trash—"

"How can you say that?" I gasped out, deeply hurt. "I love you! Do you know how much it tore me up to see you in so much pain and not be able to stop it? To know I was right here and you thought I was dead, that I had to let you keep grieving and suffering alone? To finally let you go because you couldn't remember us and you were happier loving one of your cookie-cutter bimbos instead of me, because I wasn't fucking blue-eyed or dark-haired!" All my frustration and anger was flooding back in a tidal wave, washing away my guilt.

Danial's anger was also mounting. "If you had come to me, and only told me of our early days together, I'd have known it was you," he said coolly. "Don't lie and tell me that you didn't think of that! You thought of it all right, you were just happy to shed a few tears, to make it look good for my brother, when all along you were happy to let me go!" He turned menacing. "I remember well Sar defending Lash to me one night in bed. I'd thought it had to be a false memory." He gave me a scathing look. "But your words prove it true." He bared his upper fangs. "I told you that night, you need to remember who you're Oathed to, Sarelle! Because I'll make good on my word to kill that filth, if I place my choker on your neck and it refuses to fasten!"

I looked at him in contempt. "You are unbelievable! Can't you for once love me without judging me, or telling me what to do, or who I can and can't love?"

Danial went from anger to utter rage in the space of a few seconds. He lunged off the bed and turned to me, his eyes red, his fangs bared, his fingernails grown to talons. I backed away from him instinctively. Danial had hit me once, years ago, when he had been in the same kind of rage he was in now. He'd gone to therapy, but who knew if he'd forgotten all that as well?

"I can tell you whatever I want, Sarelle! You are Oathed to me or have you forgotten, in all those months spent on your back with my brother and Lash? Did you ever once grieve for me, for what we had? For what we lost?" His tone was sharp as razors. "Or did you not want me to remember you, so you could forget your promise to me?"

Danial knew me best of all. He hit me hardest where I was weakest, his accusation like a sharp knife in my guilty heart. Tears came immediately, coursing down my face. "Danial, all I did was grieve for you, when you were in your trancelike state—"

"And after?" he said, filled with pain. "Don't lie, sweetheart! Did you even miss me; after all we once were to each other?"

I glared at him. "Don't blame this all on me, you ass! You couldn't stand to be with me! You hated me! And when I told you I loved you, you used that to try to hurt Devlin, because you didn't give a fuck about me!"

"So you turned to Lash for some consolation?" he said bitterly. "Did you not have Devlin for that? Was one man not enough?" He snorted. "Why should I be surprised? One has never been enough for you, has it?"

My guilt shifted to anger in a split second. "You bastard, I was in love with him. You knew that, you saw it before I realized it myself."

Danial gave me a scathing look. "You love him? Do you even know who and what Lash has been, for all of his life? You balked at my killings for the mob when we first met, so much that it was a condition of you being with me that I never killed again for money, no matter that they were all evil men! Yet you love a fiend that has made it his life's work to be a paid assassin, who kills whomever he is told to kill, no matter if they are evil or innocent!" He'd gotten louder with every word and now was shouting. "And you married him! You fucking married him, after you refused to marry me or Oath to me, even after we lived together for years, and had a child together! My God, have you changed!"

"Danial, please!"

"You love a monster who has kills in the triple digits, Sar!" Danial shouted. "And that is from this decade alone! Do you know all of what he did, these past hundred years? Do you know how he got that scar he had? Who it was who gave him that wound, and why?" He took a step towards me.

I took a step back. "Danial, please don't—!"

"Shut your fucking mouth before I shut it for you!"

I turned to see Lash in the doorway, his face furious. He didn't look at me; his flat snake eyes were all for Danial as he got between us. "Back off, Vampire. Now."

Danial bared his fangs, a smile of absolute maliciousness that I had rarely seen gracing his features, one I hadn't seen since the night I'd told him I was leaving him for Theo. "So you didn't tell her the sordid details? About how you and Dev—?"

"ENOUGH!" Devlin walked in, slamming the door behind him. "All of you, enough!"

Danial faced him. "You are hardly the one to tell me what is enough." Yet a little of the red left his eyes and his taloned fingers reformed into hands.

"Lash, back off," Devlin said, not taking his eyes off Danial.

Lash moved back from Danial, putting his arms around me as he led me behind Devlin.

I embraced him with relief, that he was here, and I didn't have to face Danial's rage alone.

"Danial," Devlin said gently. "I'm glad to see you know who Sar is now, and that you were intimate with her again. She has missed you this past year."

"She's got you and that abomination to keep her sated," Danial spat. "She certainly has not missed me."

"Shut up, before I let Lash kick your ass," Devlin growled, his eyes red. "I know he wants to, and if you don't shut up this second, I'm going to forget I should be stopping him, and decide to help him do it instead."

Danial glowered, but he shut up.

"They are in love, as you can see," Devlin said. "You are not going to change Sar's heart by telling her things it's not your place to tell her, or that she can't really love Lash. Theo tried that, and all it got him was divorced."

"How could you pick Lash over Theo?" Danial said to me in disbelief. "He loved you so much. You loved him more than anything. What the hell happened?"

"A great deal of that was the binding spell," I said tiredly. "Terian did something wrong, that first time. While my affection for Theo was real, just as his was for me, Terian's spell enhanced it, made it much more powerful than it really was. Once Titus broke the spell, Theo no longer loved me as he had. It was easy for him to fall in love with Jenny, after she turned and became cougar like him. I don't love him now, if I ever really did." I paused. "And I'm sorry for what I did to you when I was under the influence of that spell." I let out a breath, and faced him. "Maybe I would have Oathed to you when we'd had Theoron, if I hadn't been bespelled. But all I could think of was Theo. I didn't know magic was dictating my decisions."

"Why didn't you turn for him?" Danial said abruptly. "I know he asked you to, from what I've overheard. He would have stayed with you and not gone to her. He loved you before the spell was cast. You were his wife. And if you were bespelled to love him above everything else, why not turn? I'll ask you again, what happened?"

Because I don't want to be a were-anything. But I can't say that. The silence stretched.

"Answer him, Sar," Lash hissed softly. "My feelings for you won't change, no matter what words you say."

"Because I didn't love Theo enough to be a werecougar."

"That is not the whole reason," Lash hissed. "You aren't saying it all. Say the rest."

Well, I'd held this secret long enough. Lash by his prodding was telling me it was time to come clean. I took a deep breath, and let it out. "I didn't love Theo enough to give up being with Devlin, or Lash, or you, Danial. Not once the spell was broken. That's what turning would have meant."

"We could have still been together," Devlin said. "I don't mind the taste of were blood, though I would have missed your blood tasting like summer. But if it had been your choice, I would have understood. I would still have wanted to be Oathed with you, to be with you as we are now—"

"Don't you see, if I was turned, I wouldn't need it!" I shouted, losing my composure. "That was why Theo wanted me to be werecougar, why he almost turned me against my will! Theo thought he had solved the problem of having to share me. I was mortal again, or close enough that I didn't need vampire blood to keep living. He would turn me, and my blood would become werecougar; it would be bitter. The other Rulers would no longer be able to use me for breeding purposes, so I'd be useless to them. Then we wouldn't need you or Danial to protect me, or give me your blood to keep me alive. With my immortality a thing of the past, Theo and I could live out our lives together. It was the surest way to keep you from me, Dev! It also assured him I'd never touch Lash again, that I'd find him repellent once I was cat and could smell him as snake." I snorted bitterly. "That's not loving someone. It's pure control."

"That plotting son of a bitch!" Devlin snarled, his eyes red glowing orbs. "I'll kill him! I'll fucking kill him!"

That's rich, coming from you, after all your plots. I turned to Lash. "Theo couldn't believe when he gave me the choice of him or you, and I chose you. He almost did turn me that night against my will, like you heard Elle say. It was the end of what we had when he tried to do that. I had to shoot him in the heart to stop him."

Lash held me tightly. "Shh. You are here with me, and no one is turning you into anything, Sweetness. You are safe and loved, and I'll kick whomever's ass I have to in order to keep it that way. So will Dev."

"I didn't know that," Danial said slowly. "No one ever said Theo attacked you. I'm sorry, Sarelle."

"I didn't know, either," Devlin growled. "Don't feel as if you're the only one in the dark, brother."

"It happened after you were already injured, Danial. Theo left me for Jenny the next day. We were divorced months ago and they were mated the day after." I turned to Devlin. "And no one told you because killing Theo would only hurt Elle, not help anything."

"He is lucky, very lucky, that you refused to turn," Devlin said in his voice of death and pain. "He is very lucky that he didn't succeed. Because I would have killed him the very next day. I see the ramifications now, all of them, as Theo saw them." He ratcheted up in volume. "But I tell you right now, Sarelle McGarran, it would have been for nothing! It wouldn't have mattered to me if your humanity had been lost! It would not have kept you from me! Nothing is keeping you from me, not ever!" He let out an explosive breath. "I would have killed him, and brought you back here, and gotten your Oath anyway, even as a werecougar."

Danial watched me; his eyes still red-cast, but thoughtful and calculating now. "We all know of your protectiveness, brother," he said wearily. "The question now is how we are going to fairly share time with Sar. I do not want her to feel overwhelmed as she did last time."

"What nights would you prefer?" Devlin said, facing his brother, a serious expression on his face. "You two are still Oathed. You have rights, Brother, and no one here will deny that."

Danial looked at Lash holding me, then back to Devlin. "I want Sar beside me every other night," he said, his eyes glowing faintly red. "I want her to live with me part of the time. I'll share her with you, but not with Lash—"

"You are going to have to share her with Lash," Devlin interrupted firmly. "She's his mate, Danial. I'm not separating them, nor will I stand for you trying to separate them. Lash was part of the deal, just like Theo was when I got her Oath the first time."

"Is Theo still part of it?" Danial asked mildly.

The look in his eyes made me shiver. "No, Danial. If you love me at all, don't go there."

Devlin narrowed his eyes at Danial. "Don't be thinking what I know you're thinking," he growled low and dangerously. "Everyone is happy. Sar lives here with Lash and I. Theo is off with his cougar woman."

"I am not happy!" Danial snarled. "Sar is mine."

"You have been happy these past months doing your drawings of Monica, Gabriella, Angelica, or whichever woman it was that you thought Sar looked like. She has endured all of your slights, your painful dalliances with her, your moralistic bullshit, your being with another woman, and your looking down on her for being with Lash. While you have rights to her for sure, she is not yours, Danial. She is ours."

"Exactly, brother! You chose to ask Lash to your bed, to let her be with him, under vampire law," Danial said forcefully. "I have the same right! I intend to exercise that right, to ask Theo to my bed with Sar."

"Don't you dare, Danial," I said, appalled. "It will only cause trouble. Moreover, I won't do it!"

"I wanted to be with you and him together more than anything, last fall," Danial retorted. "I am going to have my night with the both of you, no matter what I have to do to get it."

"He's not going to agree," I said flatly. "Theo wants nothing to do with me, it's like he was when I first knew him, and he barely tolerated me. I feel the same way."

"Theo loves you still," Lash hissed, upset. "He may be an idiot, but he won't pass at the chance to have you again for a night. He'll take it just to fuck with me, just as I would in his shoes."

"And what about Jenny in all this?" I said angrily to Danial. "Why hurt her, just so you can have your fantasy, Danial? She's not going to want her husband to spend the night with his ex-wife."

"I am no longer Jenny's employer, or any kind of guardian of hers," Danial said simply. "I owe her nothing. She can adjust for one night."

"Theo's not going to agree," Devlin said with a sneer. "He's way too straight-laced to consider it, Danial. To him, it would be like cheating on Jenny—"

"It IS cheating on Jenny," I corrected, shooting Devlin a nasty look. "Theo would never do that. I won't be a part of asking him to, either, not for any reason."

"You let me worry about that," Danial said with a curled lip. "I just expect you to do as you're told, Sar. You are my Oathed One, and you will do as I tell you."

"Watch your mouth, Vampire," Lash hissed. "Sar's my mate, and no one tells her what to do when it's against her will. She doesn't want to be with that stupid fuck again."

"You sure about that, Lash?" Danial purred nastily. "She loved him enough to marry him, and she's still wearing his ring."

"That's my ring she's wearing, you fuck." Lash drew his knife and went for Danial.

Devlin got between them quickly.

"Move, Dev," Lash hissed angrily. "He's had this coming for a while now."

"Stop it, both of you," Devlin said, holding them apart with his hands. Then he looked at me. "Explain to Danial, Sarelle."

"It's Lash's ring, not Theo's. The design is similar, but it is not Theo's, Danial. And for the record, I don't want to be intimate with Theo ever again. Not. Ever. You understand! NOT EVER! Not after what he tried! What is wrong with you that you'd even ask me to?"

There was silence for a few moments after my outburst.

"Sar, will you do it, if he can get Theo to agree?" Devlin said, as if I hadn't spoken.

He, Lash, and Danial looked at me, waiting. I knew right then that Dev was going to go along with Danial, and try to make me do it. But I'd be damned if I would. *Fuck, if I have to I'll use Shaker, even if I have to give him my soul to do it!*

Mistress? Shaker said in my mind. *Do you need me?*

I'll talk to you after, I shot back mentally. *Leave.*

Shaker vanished from my mind, as Lash hissed, "Mate?"

Buy some time for now, time to make a plan. "I'll do it if I have to, according to vampire law," I said grudgingly. "I don't want to do it—I will not do it, otherwise."

"I have the right," Danial said, folding his arms across his chest. "Go ahead and check it, Dev."

Devlin shot him a nasty look, but he just nodded to me. "Danial and I will check. Lash, stay here with Sar."

"I want to see the applicable law, when you find it," I said firmly. "With my own eyes."

Devlin nodded, and then he and Danial left.

Lash came to me and hugged me. "Jacuzzi?" he hissed. "I smell that the tub's full. We can add some warm water."

I nodded. We took off our clothes, stepped in, and sat for a few moments, letting the hot water relax us. Lash had put his gun on the side of the tub, as he usually did, though we weren't expecting any problems. "It's okay if you are with him," Lash hissed, after a while. "I can deal with it, if it's just the once."

I looked over at him, appalled afresh. "You didn't want me to eat a gifted basket of chocolate, and you're saying this?"

"What?" he hissed, leaning back in the water. "I'm being honest."

"You hate him. How can you be willing to share with him, especially your mate?"

"Because I'm not sharing!" Lash hissed with anger. "Danial is being a prick, hoping that you spending a night with Theo and he is going to give you some kind of wake up call, and get me out of your bed. That's not going to happen. When the night is over, you won't have to go to Theo again. But most of all it matters that you don't want to go, that you're being made to go, Sar." He paused. "I'll probably have to go out that night and brawl a little," he hissed, his anger evident. "I'm already pissed off thinking of him being with you. But I won't take it out on you. This isn't your fault, Love. We need to enlist Titus, too. I don't want Danial to put a love spell on you or Theo, or cause you to dream together again, as you once did. There had to be something that will block that kind of spell. Titus can give it to you before you leave."

"I just never would have thought of this kind of thing coming from Danial," I said with a grimace. "Dev, sure. But never Danial. He never pressed his rights with me those years we were together, and he could have. He could have sent Theo to drag me back to him when I left him that first time."

"I'm sure over the years since then, he regretted that he didn't do exactly that," Lash said darkly. "If he had, he wouldn't be sharing you now with anyone. But he has always been full of himself, sure that his elegant words, charming manner, and good looks would win him whatever woman he wanted. They won you for him, Sweetness, both when you first met, and later, as soon as you were alone. He was right there at your side, as soon as Theo was thought dead, wasn't he? Right back in your bed?"

I looked at him, aghast. "Danial wanted to find Theo as much as I did, if not more. He searched for months."

"Don't forget Danial was the one who started all the trouble with Annabelle. Dev is more in your face, but Danial is the same kind of man, he's just sneakier about it. I always wondered that I found Theo so quickly, when his months of searching more than a year earlier didn't."

"Danial would never have used Theo's disappearance to get me back, never."

"But you appreciated that he went to look himself, didn't you? Made you feel almost indebted to him, right? Him, a powerful Vampire Ruler, so selflessly searching—"

"Stop it, Lash!" He shut up, glaring at me a little. "Besides, maybe there won't be a law."

"I know Danial, so I know there's a law," Lash hissed in resignation. "He fucking knows the almighty vampire lawbook better than any vampire I ever knew." He became determined. "But the one night won't change anything between you and me. I won't let it."

I pulled back, curious.

Lash's eyes were full of love, brimming with raw emotion. "You did it for me," he whispered, his voice cracking. "I heard it in your words. That was the real reason you didn't change for Theo. It wasn't because of Devlin or of Danial. It was because of me. Because you loved me, and wanted to be with me, not him."

My eyes were moist and my voice when I spoke cracked and warbled, too. "He said you wouldn't want me ever again if I was cougar. That I wouldn't be able to stand the smell of you."

"I would have wanted you anyway," Lash said fiercely, hugging me tightly, trying to wrap his body as closely around mine as he could. "I would have gotten something from Titus to mask my scent, anything it took to be with you, so you'd still want me! I love you, Sar. I'm going to be your mate until I'm dead. I'm not giving you up any other way, not ever. I'm going to be your lover forever, if I have to come back from the dead to do you!"

I burst out laughing at the last line, then pulled him to me, kissing him hard. Lash reacted at once, his arms going around me to pull my body close to his, slipping his tongue between my lips. I ran my hands over his body, and stroked his chest scales, and he groaned at my touch. Then he was standing, lifting me dripping from the water to stand me beside the tub.

"You sure you're up to go again?" he hissed lustily, even as he *wrapped me in a towel and moved us from the bathroom to the bed. "You were just with Danial."*

"I need more, Mate," I breathed seductively. "I need you."

Lash's eyes went black, and he didn't waste any more time, covering my lips with his.

Chapter Thirteen

After, we lay tangled together in the sheets, our bodies entwined. Lash kissed me down one arm, and sighed in content. "It's good to be your mate. Want to go out and get dinner?" he said with a grin. "Not much is open this time of night, but we could get steaks at Davy's."

"It's too cold," I said, snuggling next to him. "I'm much happier here with you, under the covers."

"I'm happy here, too, but I'm starving," Lash said, grinning wider. "And Dev'll be pissed if we eat in front of him in bed. You remember how he got last week when he found a few chocolate smears from that body frosting—"

Devlin had been pissed off in the extreme. *Sigh.* "Then sure, Davy's it is."

Just then, Devlin came in with Danial in tow. Devlin rolled his eyes to see us together, though he grinned, but Danial bared his fangs so they showed completely. His eyes were glowing red, to see what had happened while he'd been away. "I'll get her away from you if it's the last thing I ever do," he hissed.

"Knock off your shit, or it will be the last thing you ever do," Lash hissed back, his arms tightening around me. "She is my mate, and I love her. You try to stop me laying her, you're going to end up on your ass, Vampire, with my knife in your heart."

Devlin walked to me and handed me a heavy tome that had to be a thousand pages thick. I read the paragraph he indicated, and sure enough, it said that unless otherwise specified by the vampire, that any person, woman or man, who was Oathed to a vampire was required to give both their blood, or their "favor" to said vampire, or additional person(s) of the vampire's choosing, if said vampire ever asked that "favor(s)" be bestowed upon any other person(s). The only exemption was if the Oath taken specifically stipulated that the vampire waived that right. Refusal was grounds for Oath-breaking.

Son of a bitch. I'd been Oathed twice before, and never even known of this clause!

"Well?" Devlin said to me.

"Why not break it, then?" I said coldly. "I'll re-Oath just to you, Dev, since you're the only one here who can be trusted!"

Danial hissed in fury, and started for me, but Devlin grabbed him.

"You cannot break it without your life as payment," Danial said sinisterly. "I read your Oath contract to Dev, Sarelle, when I was studying up for creating my own with Emma. Devlin can—"

Devlin bared his fangs. "I'll not force her into this against her will, Danial."

Danial bared his right back. "I can, and I will, brother. The contract is binding and valid, and I am entitled to my rights under it! The other Rulers will back me up, if I but petition them! And you can do nothing! Nothing!"

Motherfucker. "I'll not be forced into anything I don't want ever again, not for any reason or by anyone! I am not your slave! I don't belong to you, Danial! Do you hear me?"

"You are my Oathed one, Darling," Danial hissed silkily. "You do indeed belong to me! And you will act accordingly, even if I must lead you around on a leash!" He gave me a malicious smile. "There is a good reason vampires call the choker a collar—"

"Danial, shut up! Sar, will you not consider this?" Devlin said, pleading. "Danial has agreed to give you right of refusal for all men ever after this, if you but give him the one night."

"No," I said between clenched teeth. "You want to go ahead and drain me, go ahead. But I. Will. Not. Do. It."

I waited for Lash to attack Danial, to get him to back off, but he just stayed where he was, shaking slightly in anger.

"Did you ever really love me?" Danial yelled at me, his eyes ablaze. "Ever? Was there ever a time I meant anything to you?"

"This isn't about you, can't you get that straight!" I yelled at him. "This is about me, about my rights, about what I want. That matters enough to me to die for." I faced him. "Does what you want matter enough that it's worth killing me for?"

"Enough yelling, both of you! Will you do it, Sarelle?" Devlin said flatly. "Yes or no?"

"I told you, no!" I screamed.

"She'll do it," Lash said loudly, talking over me. "She said she would, if you found the law. But there are rules you will follow, Racklan. No spells; Titus will check her for them. No dreaming with Theo and rebinding them. No sex without protection. And not until Theo swears on his life not to hurt her, or try to turn her, if she comes into reach of his fangs. You break any of my conditions by a hair's breadth, and your life will be forfeit, Vampire. And so will his."

I looked at Lash in absolute fury, vibrating in my anger but too pissed off to speak.

"Good," Danial said, nodding. "Perhaps it is good she's spent some time with you, serpent. You seem to have succeeded in taming her where Dev and I failed."

He left, and Devlin followed, with a surprised look at Lash.

"How dare you answer for me?" I shouted at Lash when they had gone. "How dare you!"

"Because it was easier than hearing any more of your bitching," Lash hissed. "I have set parameters so you'll be safe. Soon enough it will be all over with."

"You had no right!"

"I'm your mate, and I have every right to do anything I feel is right to protect you. You had already agreed anyway. This is the best course of action."

"You don't own me either, you asshole!"

"I am the male here," Lash hissed with authority as if that meant something, folding his hands back under his head. "Not you, despite how you often seem to forget your place."

"Please spare me your bullshit, you fucking chauvinist!" I laughed in his face, which seemed to enrage him, because he bared his fangs at me, venom glistening on the tips. But I wasn't afraid of him, not anymore. "You have no right to tell me who I must give myself to! I'm not a whore!"

Lash gave me a nasty smile. "You said the words, Sweetness, not me. But you're right, you've never cared about money, or other returns on your favors to me, so I guess you must not be. Or maybe you're just one who's bad at her finances."

I opened my mouth, but nothing came out; I was too shocked and revolted.

His next words were worse. "But you've always been hot to trot, and it's been what, almost a year with no new dick? Well, that you wanted anyway. Old Mike was gay, and you didn't get to enjoy that, being asleep when he stole in to put it to you. But you clearly hadn't lost your lust for Danial, so maybe there's another old lover's body you're jonesing for too! Being with Theo again might float your boat! Maybe part of me wants to know if you'll change your mind about me, once you're under him again for a night. You do seem to go from one mate to another like it was changing a pair of shoes."

Son of a bitch bastard! I got out of the bed, too enraged to speak, and left the room, grabbing a pair of my jeans and his shirt on the way out, and my sneakers. Lash came after me in his birthday suit, still yelling. "Sar, you know it's true! You were Oathed to Danial, married to Theo, Oathed to Dev and Danial again, and now you're mated to me and Oathed to them both again!"

I slammed the door to the garage, locking it, and got into my truck. My keys were under the visor, and I started it. I put the truck in drive just as Lash kicked in the door to the garage.

I backed out, and he was still yelling something, but I couldn't hear it.

I drove down one of the access roads to the cemetery, and parked the truck. *Screw all men.* I'd go see Anna. She'd heard me bitch often enough about Devlin. Besides, a long walk would calm me down.

I pulled on a spare jacket from behind my seat, grabbed a flashlight from the glove compartment, and walked in my sockless sneakered feet, glad it was in the fifties tonight. I'd only gone about ten feet when I heard a truck screech to a stop, a door slam, and Lash calling my name. *God, it is easier to shake a bloodhound.*

"Sar, answer me!" Lash called. "I'm sorry! Please answer me, so I know you're all right."

143

He knew I was all right, just as I knew he'd find me before long by sound and smell. I kept walking fast toward the stone tomb on the hill, using the full moon instead of my flashlight to light my path through the many grave markers. While I walked, I telepathically contacted Shaker, and told him what had happened.

Devlin is right, this is the best way to handle Danial, he rumbled. *Vampire law is tricky to navigate, and it favors the Oathed vampire, not the Oathed human. It's worth a night's fucking to get his word that you'd never have to do this again for him with any other male, Mistress. I could kill Danial and Theo if that would help, but I'm afraid I can't offer much else.*

"There's been enough killing," I said aloud bitterly. "Could you make Danial forget me?"

Devlin and Lash would need to be bespelled and Titus would know, Shaker said apologetically. *And there is Terian to consider, who would likely find traces of the forgetting spell over time. Besides, I thought you wanted Danial to remember and want you? I know you were giving him blood before the attack on Hayden.*

"I did," I said brokenly. "I loved him and wanted him to love me again. I should have lied somehow to him, when he found me rescuing the spider. There's no one to blame but myself."

Lash was still yelling for me and his voice was getting closer. I walked faster.

Thank you for the sustenance, both the flesh and the cookies, Shaker rumbled. *I'm almost well.*

Rene, at least you come through for me. "Rest and get better," I said aloud. "I may need your help before too long."

Just call, Shaker rumbled, and then he was gone.

Lash's calls were very close now. About two minutes later, when I was almost to Anna's grave, strong arms enveloped me from behind.

"Please forgive me, Sweetness, I'm sorry," Lash hissed quickly. "I didn't mean what I said."

"Then why'd you say it?" I said, turning to him. "I always thought I'd heard harsh words before from the other guys. But you take the prize for being the shittiest at the drop of a hat with no provoking from me at all."

"You did provoke me! I was hurt that you'd break our mating so casually," Lash said furiously. "You said you'd re-Oath just to Dev, because you could trust only him!"

"Asshole! You had to know I still wanted to be with you, I was suggesting excluding Danial! Anyway, I'm your mate apart from that Oath to him, remember?"

Lash looked away, embarrassed. "I'm sorry, Sweetness," he said heavily with remorse. "But I'd just told you how much you meant to me and it felt like a slap in the face."

"Are you ever going to believe I love you?" I turned and shouted at him. "How long is it going to take?"

"Years," Lash said, his eyes moist. "Years of you telling me that you love me, and waking up with you, and reaching out for you, and you not recoiling from me. Years of you welcoming me into your body, feeling I'm different from you and not seeing fear in your eyes. Years of us coiling together, and you helping me shed, and you not...not coming at me with a knife...trying to sever my head from my body as I change form. Not wanting...to hurt...me..."

The pain in Lash's tone was monumental. In his agony he had changed too much, his words degenerating into garbled hissing as he shifted.

I went to my knees. Lash was thrashing in his clothes, his head covered, hissing curses in snake language fiercely. "Tryst, be still," I said quietly.

His thrashing stopped. "I'm sorry," he hissed in snake.

"I'll set you free, just hold still." I reached out, and uncovered his head. Lash flicked his tongue at me. I motioned to him, and he came into my lap, still hissing he was sorry.

"I'm here with you, and I'm not leaving you," I said, hugging him as best I could. "I'd never try to really hurt you, though I really do feel like kicking your ass on occasion." I stroked him gently. "Besides, who else is going to laugh at the same things I laugh at? Who else is going to write 'help me find my loving mate' on post it notes and stick them on errant socks from the dryer, or write 'penis oil' instead of 'peanut oil' on my shopping lists?" I kissed his head gently. "I love you. You just need to learn to curb what you say. Some of the things you say make me feel terrible."

"I'm sorry," he apologized. "I'll try not to, from now on."

Lash snuggled into me, and then began to change back. Soon he was naked and human in my arms again. But he didn't say anything, and neither did I. *Because nothing is solved. I'm not going along with him and Dev and Danial about spending a night with Theo. But there's no point fighting about it, either.*

When it began to get light, I helped him up, and he got dressed. I walked back to my truck, and saw his beside it.

"If you want, we can ride back in one if you'll teleport the other," he offered.

"I'll drive it back, it's only a few minutes," I said.

After parking the vehicles back in the garage, we headed into the house. No one was around, which I thought was a blessing, especially with what I was going to ask him.

"What did Danial mean about the scar?" I said innocuously, as we walked into the kitchen. "You got that in Rio, right? He made it sound like there was more to it."

"There was a woman long ago who gave me a similar wound," Lash hissed. "Danial is remembering that, not the scar you saw when we met. That was made by a demon attacking Dev and I got it defending him."

That cold feeling returned. "Who was the woman Danial meant to mention? And why did she hurt you?"

"I want you not to ask this," Lash said desperately, beginning to pace. "You are happier not knowing. Please drop it, especially after we just made up. I want to go to bed and hold you."

"Tell me, Mate. Right now."

"Her name I can't remember, if I ever knew it," Lash said flatly. "She was human, and we'd had sex, and she hadn't...she didn't..."

"Come?"

"Want to," Lash whispered. "She didn't want to."

I turned to him, horrified. "I don't believe that of you, that you would do that," I said finally. "Not with how you've asked me every time we've been together."

"I thought she did," Lash admitted. "Devlin had given her a drug and she'd acted like she did, so I had her. But when she woke up after and saw me next to her, she hit me with a lamp. It caught me by surprise and cut me. Danial saw that happen."

"That wasn't your fault then," I said, sickened at Devlin. Every time I started to think I'd been wrong about him, I'd hear something like this. "Why would Danial act as though it was?"

"He thought I should have known, because of how I looked and what I was. He thought I should have known that it had to be rape, because she was human and pretty, and I was snake and…and ugly."

Danial, you are one vindictive son of a bitch. "Then Danial's an ass. But I understand now why he is so outraged that I love you. Some of it is that he's pissed off that I do when other human women didn't."

"Some of it is that he's plain jealous," Lash said, opening a bottle of Groom wine. "It's a new feeling, to have him jealous of me. I thought I'd enjoy it more, after envying him for so many years, but I spent too many years in his shoes. I pity him instead."

I took the offered glass and sat down. Lash sat down as well.

"Can we not fight anymore?" Lash asked. "We seem to fight a lot, Sar."

"Why are you asking me, like it's my fault?" I said wearily. "I didn't start this one, Lash."

"I'm sorry, again, for what I said," Lash hissed, taking my hand. "I didn't mean it."

"Then don't say it."

He slammed his hand down on the table. "Can't you just accept a fucking apology from me? Jesus Christ!"

"I'm sorry," I said quickly, squeezing his hand. "I'd like to say some of is me being pregnant. But we don't know if I am yet. It's driving me crazy not knowing, and we keep trying and failing…" I sighed. "Maybe this is all a mistake. Maybe we should give up."

"Sar, it's okay," Lash soothed, scooting his chair closer. "I haven't had the operation yet. We can try again next month if you aren't. But I'm sure that you are, with what Stephen said and how much sex we've had lately."

I rubbed my temple, and looked at him. "Do you still even want one with me? You're right; we have been fighting a lot. Is some of it because you feel like you're trapped, and you don't want—"

"Come here," he said, pulling me onto his lap. "Of course I do. You know I do. We've been mated a year now, and with all the times I've slipped and said things, you know I want young…um, a baby. Some of my upset is that we're trying, and I'm scared," he said finally. "But not scared like you might think. I'm not scared it might happen; I'm scared that it's happened, and you'll miscarry again, like you did before. God, I'm scared of that."

I held onto him tightly. "I'm scared of that, too," I whispered.

"I wish our others had made it into the world, and were here with us," Lash hissed in sadness. "The first would be ten months old now, or close to it. And the twins would be getting ready to be born."

"Don't think about it," I said, pushing down my own despair. "We can't bring them back. We only have the future, and the hope it will work this time."

"It should," Lash hissed with confidence. "We are doing everything we can."

Would it be enough, though? Scared to say that, I asked instead, "Are you hungry?"

"Come upstairs," he hissed gently, getting to his feet. "It's already morning. You need your sleep. We'll have a big lunch later."

"Why did you come home so early?" I asked, following him upstairs. "I didn't expect you until dawn."

"Seth went past your door and heard sobbing. He looked in to see Danial hugging you, crying. He called Devlin to report, asking if he should do something, and we started for home immediately."

"Why not call Titus, and teleport?"

"Devlin said he thought you were in no danger, and refused to call Titus, saying you could teleport yourself if there was trouble. It was easy to see he was hoping to come back, and find that Danial'd fucked you."

"Please don't say it like that," I said a little stiffly. "It's not just sex to me with him, just like it's not with you and Dev."

Lash cast me a disgruntled look. "You've never cared before how I talked."

"You're going to be a father, sooner or later," I countered. "Want him to be quoting you, telling people how his parents fuck?"

Lash rolled his eyes, but also looked embarrassed. "Ok, point taken.

Dev thought the two of you would be intimate. From the first, he delayed, because he knew if I got here, I'd have stopped it. I beat him here by a few minutes, as you saw, but we were an hour away."

"You got here just in time."

Lash squeezed me gently. "You could have teleported, Sweetness. Just rest, please."

Lash and I held each other for a long time. I was still wound up, but took comfort from his presence. It was almost nine a.m. by now, and Devlin had still not returned.

"Sar?" Lash said, just as I was finally falling asleep.

"What?" I said groggily.

"I have to tell you something," he said in that same awful voice, part despair, part hopeless and part emptiness. It woke me up at once.

"What?" I said, turning to face him.

"I have forced women before." He wouldn't meet my eyes.

"When?" I said, my throat dry as a desert.

He swallowed hard. "It wasn't often. There were women that attacked Dev through the years. These weren't helpless maidens, they were warriors who knew what would happen if they failed. Before I killed them, I often had them, if...if they were human, or faerie."

I said nothing. I wanted to run from him, but couldn't make myself move.

"I knew it wasn't right to do," he hissed softly, then swallowed hard again. "But for the most part, human and faerie women never wanted me, not even when I could hide my fangs. And the truth is I have always liked human women best. I'm ashamed to say it, being what I am. I was born snake and it's wrong that I always wanted something not of my own kind. But there it is."

"Why?" I said again, trying hard to get my mind around this. "Devlin asked you to, didn't he?"

"Devlin encouraged it as a form of punishment, but I can't blame this on him. It was my fault. I had a choice and I chose to do it."

"But your sisters," I choked out "You said they were—"

"They were," Lash said, raw. "And that haunted me for a long, long time. I didn't have sex as human, not for years afterward. But one night, the opportunity presented itself, and I took it." He took a breath. "I'm not

149

asking for absolution, just for your acceptance of that as a part of someone I used to be, and aren't any longer."

"Why are you telling me this now? Do you think I want to know this about you, Lash? I don't! I don't want to know!"

"I'm sorry," he said, gripping me tight. "What I said earlier seemed like a lie. And I don't want to lie to you." He took a breath. "You accepted it about Dev, so—"

Bile rose in my throat and I swallowed it down, sickened. "What?"

"You know what kind of things he's capable of. He's done most anything and everything to a woman that can be done. I've been there and seen him do it. Yet you love him." He paused. "I'm coming to you, admitting this willingly, and asking you: Can you still love me?"

I would not think about Devlin. I would not. "Will you ever do it again, hurt a woman like that?"

"No, not even if Devlin asks me to as part of my job. You are my Mate and your wants come first."

"Even if I wasn't giving you enough sex? Even if you and I never had sex again as human, and there was a young and beautiful female vampire hunter alive in the dungeon, locked in a cell?"

Lash went motionless. "Do you not want me anymore, after telling you what I did?"

"Answer the question. Answer it honestly, because a lot depends on your answer, Trystan Jared Valeras. And I'll know if you're lying."

"You never made Devlin promise not to hurt—"

"Answer me, Tryst. Or get out of this bed and leave me now, and we're done."

"No," he hissed. "I give you my word, Mate. You are more important to me than anything. I told you I'd be a better man for you. I meant what I said." He sighed. "I would go to Titus, and ask him to give me something to take away my desire, or subvert it, so I only wanted you as snake, or not at all." He shivered a little. "It wouldn't be easy, and the thought terrifies me, because since I was sixteen, I have always felt desire for females, and loved sex. But I'd do it for you if you asked me to, provided you had good reason."

"Such as?"

"Such as if you couldn't have sex, for some medical reason, or you were somehow hurt in a way that made you not want sex anymore, or made it painful for you."

"Why?"

"Because you're more to me than sex," he said simply. "A lot more. You're worth it. After being with you, I don't really want anyone else, no matter how beautiful they are or sexy. But I am animal, at least half of me, and I would need help to fight the animal side of me." He paused. "It's common knowledge in were circles, that matings most often don't last because the two partners cannot be faithful when faced with others of their kind who offer sex, especially if they are younger or more fertile. That is why you see very few mated pairs that have been together longer than a few years."

"Most of Devlin's bears are mated."

"The larger animals, those who are more powerful, they are the one exception. There are fewer bears than werefoxes, or werecoyotes, or other types of weres that are more numerous, because as animal they can hide easier in plain sight. But the more there are of your kind around, the more the urge for sex takes control of you. The bears' numbers have been dwindling for years, just as the werewolves did years ago. So it's difficult to find a sex partner, and as soon as they do, they're so happy they pair up, live together, and say they are mated. But I know well what goes on weekends with more than a few of the so-called mated bears, and their spouses."

"What goes on?"

"Trading of partners. Sometimes many males on one female, one after the other. Sometimes orgies, when it is spring. But everyone knows, and for them it works."

"No one ever said anything remotely—"

"Serena cannot be bear, save by potion, as you do," Lash interrupted sharply. "She cannot take it every day! The males who come to her for sex need that part of them sated as well. Nick had Klara, and it was true she sometimes did others, but that leaves at least twenty unpaired males as of my last hiring. What did you think was going on?"

God, why had I never seen that? Why hadn't I asked? Serena had been busy for most of the time since I'd been home, with me seeing her only fleetingly at breakfast sometimes. Why hadn't I asked her why she was so tired looking? Probably because subconsciously, I hadn't wanted to know. *God, I should go to her, ask her if she was okay...*

I was quiet for a while, thinking of what I could do to help her, and coming up with nothing. *Well, nothing that I would ever want to do...*

Lash couldn't stand it any longer. "Sar, say something. Either tell me you can accept this, or that we're done. I can't lay here anymore, and—"

"I'll need time to work through this," I said, turning to look him in the eyes. "You might want to consider that even if it's okay with me, it doesn't make what you did okay with the universe. You'll have to answer to someone when you die, or maybe stay in purgatory for a while."

"Shaker says no one goes there," Lash said sarcastically. "You either go to Heaven or Hell. I already know where I'm headed."

"Maybe you are headed to Hell," I said seriously. "But maybe not. It makes sense to me that you need to finish with things in this life before you move on to the next. People that got hurt because of what you did, or people who hurt you, I think they do come to settle up with you, when it's all over with. There's always a reckoning."

"Great," Lash said more sarcastically. "Even seeing twenty a day, I'll be doing that for a hundred years, dealing with all of that shit, if I've got to see every Goddamn person I hurt, or who hurt me—"

"I'll wait for you to come to me," I said, touching his cheek gently. "It's okay if it takes you a while. I'm going to be dealing with a lot myself. I've hurt people too, maybe not as many as you, but everyone does things they shouldn't. It's not my place to judge. That's God's department."

"What are you saying?" he asked, suddenly hopeful.

"That it isn't okay, what you did. But I believe you're sorry for it, and you said you won't do it again, no matter what. And if God and Jesus say that's enough for them to know to forgive you, and they can still love you, then it's enough for me, too."

Lash hugged me tightly. "Thank you."

A few minutes later, he said, "Just so we're clear, we're still going to be having sex?"

"Yes," I replied, rolling my eyes.

"In both forms?"

"Yes."

"Every day? As human, I mean? Well, unless you're pregnant—"

"Lash..."

"Sorry. Being cut off...frankly, it might be better to just kill me."

Chapter Fourteen

That next morning, I was sitting in my sewing room looking at the wall, thoughts churning, a piece of material forgotten in my hands.

Rene came in, her face breaking into a welcoming smile. "What are you making?" she asked curiously.

I looked at her, then away, my eyes filling with tears. "I'm not making anything," I whispered.

She came over and sat beside me. "Tell me what's happened," she murmured. "When I left a few days ago, all was well. Now I return to see Danial and his cat gone, Devlin walled off in his study, Lash gone away with Titus and you radiating pain and suffering."

So Danial was gone. Devlin had never come to bed last night, and hadn't talked to me this morning either. He'd missed having breakfast with Venus and me, something he'd never done since I'd Oathed to him last year, no matter how tired he was.

"Tell me what's wrong, Sister."

I related to her all of what happened. "I should've left it alone," I said wearily. "I should've told Danial to get out; that I had no idea what he was talking about."

"You loved him," she said, rubbing my shoulder. "And you're right in thinking he knew you enough to have found out if you lied to him. There wasn't another choice."

"But I can't do this," I said, furious and desperate. "I can't be with Theo again, I won't! I meant what I told them. I'll kill myself first."

"I will go in your stead," she said calmly, her green-blue eyes confident.

I gave her a confused look. "What?"

"You know I'm faerie. I can change my form. Even if Terian checks

154

me to make sure I am you, I used enough of your flesh and blood becoming human that there should be no problem."

I almost fell out of my chair; the relief pouring down on me was so overwhelming. I gave her a fierce hug. "Are you sure?" I said hesitantly, releasing her. I didn't want her to change her mind, but I also couldn't just dump this on her, and say, "Hey thanks!" as I walked out the door.

"You helped me escape Hell, regain my mortal form, and let me be with Devlin," she said, giving me a quirky smile. "There isn't much I wouldn't do for you. You are like a sister to me, Sar." Her smile broadened. "Literally, we are sisters, sharing the same DNA as we do." She hugged me back, and then released me. "Say nothing of this to anyone. The less who know, the better. That includes Devlin and Lash. Leave everything to me."

"What will you do if I'm pregnant by then?"

"It's a concern," she said musingly. "But again, there is enough of you in me to make a pregnancy possible. I am not human now, but neither am I faerie anymore. So my body harbors its own eggs as a human does."

Wait, female faeries didn't have their own eggs? How did they have children? Then it registered what she'd said. "You are going to get pregnant?" I couldn't keep the incredulousness out of my voice. "With who? And after that night is done, what will you do?"

"No, silly girl," Rene laughed. "There is an old spell that will mimic the signs of pregnancy. All that is needed is a human to cast it on, which will be me, and that she be fertile, which I am. I'll appear pregnant, though inside there will be no child. When the subterfuge is no longer needed, I will break the spell, and have my monthly curse."

I felt wild hope, and then a rock named Danial smashed down, crushing it. "Danial knows me too well," I said, shaking my head. "He'll know it isn't me at once, especially when you speak, but also by what is done in bed."

"I didn't say it would be easy," Rene said, rolling her eyes. "As for bedding Danial, that will have to be you. I could not stomach his touch, even if he somehow didn't realize it was you. But from what I know of him from Dev, he will not last long. All I can offer you is to take your place with Theo."

"How?"

"You will go. I will go with you, and watch you, unseen, so I know how to act. And when it's time for you to be with Theo, leave for the bathroom. I'll follow, assume your shape, and cloak you in invisibility. After, I'll leave you with them, and slip away, teleporting when I'm far enough away not to be noticed."

This might actually work. I nodded. "Ok."

* * * *

I got my period two days after that. I was upset, because I'd believed I was pregnant. What I'd thought would be so easy was going to be much harder than I expected. I was pushing forty hard, no matter that I still looked thirty-two or so.

There was also another complication. As usual, it was so obvious I completely missed it.

Devlin had resumed his normal loving persona with Venus and me a few hours after I spoke with Rene. He had presented me with flowers; we'd passed the night sipping wine and talking. I'd waited for the other shoe to drop, but he'd not brought up Danial at all.

Later that week, I was reclining with him on the loveseat in our room later that week, enjoying one of our monthly alone days. He was feeding me some grapes, the wood fire warming us and quoting me poetry. I was enjoying being adored, when he abruptly put aside the grapes, and took my hand.

"I asked you here for a reason, Oathed One," Devlin said formally.

I looked at him expectantly, figuring he had some gift to give me or wanted to act out a fantasy. A few hours ago, his fantasy had been the night we met, if things had gone as he hoped, and I'd liked him better than Danial. "Yes?"

"Will you not consider having another child with me?" he said cautiously.

I said nothing, but I was mentally kicking myself for not seeing it. "Now?"

"Love," he said, bringing my hand to his heart. "Michael may be right. We may not have many more chances. Whatever magic resides in your blood may fade with time, even as you remain relatively young.

You know as well as I do that this time it's taking you a lot longer to get pregnant."

"We don't know that he was right."

"We don't know he's wrong, either," he said firmly. "Do you not love me anymore?"

"I love you, it's not that."

"Then what? Because the first time it was not a request? I'm asking you this time."

"No, I—"

"Please, Sar. I want a son. Or another daughter. Or twins, whatever comes forth."

"Dev—"

"Please, Sar. Please?"

"I don't want The Lust again," I said flatly. "That's the real reason. I don't want to feel like I did. That's why I'm careful to always ask for your blood now, so it never gets to that point where I'm not in control."

"But Lash would be with you," he said in his best convincing voice. "He would sate it like last time. I could help him."

"Is some of the reason that you want to hurt me?" I said, giving him a penetrating look. "That you want me to ask you to?'

Devlin flushed, and then gave me guilty eyes. "You know I enjoyed what we did in those first months you had The Lust while pregnant with Venus. But the real reason is I love Venus. I'd like to have more with you, if you'll agree." He held me. "Lash's baby and mine could be twins, Sar. Real brothers, like Danial and I were. I'd love to share that with him, too."

"I'd have the heat, and the cooling problems."

"I'm here for cooling and Titus for heating. Last time worked okay. Besides, Lash's child will be cooler, being half weresnake. You may not need me to freeze myself."

I swallowed. "Rene loves you, Devlin. Could she—?"

"She would like to, but she cannot," Devlin said, pained. "She is not you: her blood is human with a hint of faerie, not summer-tasting. She has told me she would try if I asked it of her, but that most likely it would not work. I can't ask her to risk her life, not when a miscarriage could kill her."

"Dev—"

"I'm asking as your Oathed One, as your lover, and as a man that loves you. I'm asking on my knees. Please, just tell me you'll think on it?" he said, his golden eyes endearing, and winsome. "Please?"

"Agreed," I said. "But I want some time, okay? No pressuring."

"Take all the time you need," he said gratefully, enveloping me in a hug.

When I saw Titus later that day, I learned from him that Devlin had already asked him to begin assembling the necessary ingredients. *So much for no pressure.*

* * * *

A day later, Dev took the potion. Before, I had not been there to see it work its magic on him. Once I did, I got new appreciation for how much he wanted another child.

Devlin lay in bed, feverish, his body wracked with pain and heat, breathing hard. He snarled almost continuously, and sometimes screamed. I tried to remain with him, but within an hour, I left, unable to stand anymore. Lash was outside, guarding the door.

"Was it like this last time?" I whispered, worried. "He screamed like this when he was burned by sunlight."

"Exactly like this," Lash said, taking a drag on a cigarette. "It's going to last at least twenty-four hours. And I'm going to need to smoke constantly just to stand here and listen to him, because you know as well as I do that Dev's like me, that if there was any way he could hold it in and not scream, he would. But the pain's too bad for that." He took another drag. "Titus says that there's nothing he can do about the pain. It's a side effect of this version of the potion, and taking it away with another magic potion might screw up the results." He finished the cigarette and lit another. "My advice is go keep yourself busy elsewhere, and sleep in a guest room tonight. I'll let you know when it's time to come back."

Sickened, I went to my sewing room where I couldn't hear Dev's screams. As I lay in one of the guest rooms that night, a guard outside my door, I decided that if Devlin was willing to go through all this, then I was willing to try with him one more time.

* * * *

The next morning, an exhausted Lash shook me awake. "Go to him," he hissed tiredly. "He needs you."

I gave him an uncertain look. "You're sure? Shouldn't he get some sleep?"

"He needs to rest, not have sex," Lash hissed, irritated. "He'll rest best in your arms."

I got up, and went into Devlin's bedroom. The sheets were changed. Devlin had showered, and he lay in bed in an exhausted sleep. I went to him and maneuvered my body underneath his head. He didn't awake. Soon after, I slept as well.

Hours later, we awoke. I felt at once that his skin was warm. "It's worked again," he whispered wearily.

"Are you okay?" I asked.

"I'll be okay," he said, yawning. "I'll need to feed a lot today, but the hard part is over with. Keeping my body fertile isn't difficult, and from here on, there's no pain."

I hugged him, and he hugged me back. "Good."

"I need to sleep more. Hold me?"

"Sure."

* * * *

The rest of that week, Lash, Dev, and I made love as we had every night, the only change being that Devlin's skin was now as warm as Lash's. Devlin continued to take the potion, though as he'd said, there was no more pain for him after that first night. But in the end, it was for naught.

A month passed, and I got my period right on schedule. So under pressure from both Devlin and Lash, I enlisted Titus's help. Within a day, he gave me two potions to take. And when my period had gone, I took the first the next day.

Devlin came to me first, after an hour had passed, and the potion had taken effect. I shivered when I felt his warm skin. He was trembling, too.

For a while, we just held each other, and then he began to kiss me.

"I want the fantasy of reliving our second time together, Love. The way we were then and after, in the hotel room. Will you give it to me?"

I nodded, and he began to touch me as he had years ago, murmuring that he would show me what true intimacy was, and make my every wish a reality. Minutes became hours, as I lost myself in him.

"I'm afraid," he whispered to me, after he'd healed my bites, and my bruised flesh. "I'm afraid it won't work, that I missed my chance with you."

"Shh," I whispered back. "If it didn't work, we'll try again. It took Danial and I many months, Dev."

Devlin grumbled something but seemed reassured. We passed the rest of the day sleeping.

At dusk, I took the other potion, and then went in to wait for Lash.

He returned from one of his trips an hour later, saw me in his bed, and gave me a confused look. "Isn't this Dev's night? Are you fighting? Not that I mind you being here—"

I held his gaze. "I took a fertility potion. Actually, I took two today."

He stood there for a moment, watching me, and then strode fast for the bathroom. "I'll be right back, Sweetness. Don't go anywhere."

Five minutes later, he was back. By that time, I was nervous and trembling.

"Shh, Love, it's just me," Lash hissed soothingly, as he eased his body down on mine. "Relax and do what I ask you, ok?"

I made myself relax as he kissed me. "What do you want me to do?"

"Lie there for me and be still," he hissed. "I'm going to have you as I did that night on the truck, one right after the other. I'll stop for a little while, and then repeat it. Finally, I'll do it a third time. By the time I'm done, you'll be pregnant."

I gave him a skeptical look. We'd had a lot of marathon sex in the last two months, and it hadn't done any good. So what good would this do? The problem wasn't his. It was mine.

"I was always potent, before I took that potion of Titus's to extend my life," Lash hissed softly. "I should have done this the first time, but…well, never mind." Lash looked down at me, his eyes dark. "But are you sure you want me to? Because if I do this, there's no taking it back."

"Yes," I whispered tenderly, touching his cheek. "I want you to." I leaned closer, and embraced him. "Give me our child."

With a sigh, he slipped into me, and began moving.

There aren't words to describe what I felt, being there with him that night. He moved so gently and at times so urgently. When he grew soft that first time, I went to move, but he stopped me, whispering for me to lie still on my back, and just let him hold me. He held his hips to mine, staying inside me. In about ten minutes, he hardened again and began to move, groaning gently. When an hour had again gone by and he went soft, I just held him. Again, in ten minutes, he was hard, and for a third time, he exhausted himself in me.

By this time, I was exhausted, and so was he, the both of us dripping with sweat. And I was full of him, both his seed and his body, which was still inside mine.

"Could you go again?" I ventured, afraid of the answer.

"Technically, yes," Lash hissed, exhausted. "But even being weresnake, I'm a little abraded. It's getting very hard for me to climax, even though my body's making more seed every time I rest with you. And you must be sore, though I've tried to be gentle—"

"I meant, is this what a female weresnake would, um, ask of you?"

"I've never gone this long before with anyone," Lash hissed tenderly. "Not even half this long, or deliberately timed it to maximize the results, though I've always known the basics instinctively." He paused. "Sure, I've had sex before you. But I've never tried with a receptive woman to get her pregnant, Sar. You're the first." He stared into my eyes with his dark ones, raw with emotion. "No one ever wanted to have a child of mine. My world has changed so much, knowing you, Love. Part of me can't believe it, because I feel better with you than I ever had before in my life. And I'm scared to death of losing you, by asking you to do this, and wanting more than what we already have."

Lash eased his body down on mine, turning my hips so we were still joined. "I'd like to stay in you, fall asleep this way," he hissed. "Just this once?"

"Of course, Tryst. Whatever you want."

Lash handed me some water, as he had on and off all night. After we drank, we fell into a deep sleep.

When I woke up, I was sore all over. I shifted position, waking Lash. He separated from me with a sigh.

I moved to get up, but he pushed me back to the bed. "Lay there for a minute," he said quickly. "I'll get the shower ready. Then I'll carry you to the bathroom."

I nodded, thinking him sweet. A moment later, he carefully scooped me up in his arms. Once we were clean and dry, he helped me back into bed.

"Do you want me to help you get dressed? I'll stay near you the rest of today, but I want to check our perimeter first. Unless I check myself, I won't believe it. I'll be gone about an hour. But I'll take you downstairs, and put on a movie for you if you want to—"

"You don't have to," I said, touched. "I can get up myself, I'm sure if it's happened, it's already done."

"One might be, Sweetness, but I'm hoping for three or more," Lash hissed with love. "So you're going to stay on your back for a few more hours, okay?"

I did a double take, and my mouth fell open. "Three or more?"

"Relax," Lash hissed easily. "Weresnakes often have three or more at once. As these will be our only children, I want to have as many as we can. So I want you to stay off your feet as much as possible, to make sure all of the eggs you released get fertilized. Titus briefed me and Devlin days ago that you may release an additional two or three up to forty-eight hours after taking the potion." He grinned. "I'm nailing any that are there to be nailed, Sweetness."

His words brought a shiver of fear. "But can my body handle that many children? Your mother took a fertility potion and your sisters almost died—"

Lash was holding me tightly in an instant. "She was alone in a swamp more than eighty years ago, with only an inexperienced son to help her. My seven sisters still made it. This time, Titus will be there, plus Stephen, Devlin, and me with all of our resources. All of our children that you birth will live, Sar, I promise. Even with the potion, you may only have one, being human. Titus couldn't be sure." Lash kissed me. "But I'm holding out hope just the same."

Chapter Fifteen

I did as Lash requested. For the next three days, I got up only to use the bathroom. I didn't feel any differently. With a wry smile, I reminded myself that it would likely take at least a few weeks for any symptoms to begin. I wasn't looking forward any of them, especially The Lust. But I also preferred finding out that way than asking Titus or Rene to do any soul-checks on me.

* * * *

That following Wednesday, I lay in bed with Devlin, dozing. Lash was out, doing one last check of the guards. Even then, he would be going to his own room, not joining us. According to him, his nightmares were getting better, but they still woke him often. For some reason they had spiked in intensity after our last night together—the night of the potion—so much that he'd gotten little sleep in the last four days. *He looked so haggard earlier…*

"Love," Devlin murmured from my chest, fragmenting my worried thoughts. "I want to ask you something."

I braced myself. "Yes?"

"I want to go away with you for a week or so," he said. "I know we talked of going away for the winter. We never did, with everything that happened. It's true that Venus is too young to be left alone here, and now that you are pregnant again, it's better to stay here at Hayden where we can be protected. But I do want to get away with you as soon as possible."

"For how long?" His request wasn't one I'd expected, yet it was tempting. I hadn't travelled in years…*No, that's not true. You saw a lot of exotic locals, just as a prisoner…DON'T THINK ABOUT THAT.*

163

"And where?" I hurriedly added.

"For a week or so," Devlin replied. "Lash will come with us, and probably six of the bears. They can stay in rooms on either side of us, and Lash will stay in the room with us."

"Where?" I repeated.

"New Orleans," Devlin said enticingly. "I love the city, so many of the old places are still there, despite the storms and the years that have passed."

"I think this is a little cliché," I said, smiling. "You've been watching too many vampire movies—"

"I have just as good memories of other cities, like Petersburg, or Dublin," Devlin remarked, irritated. "We are not going to be roaming cemeteries, burning mansions, or expounding on what life as we know it means. Lash spent a lot of his youth there, and he would enjoy that destination most of all. We could show you some of the sites we remember. The night life in the French Quarter is spectacular."

I remembered Lash's comments about Lafitte's the morning of Sundown's wedding. Getting away next summer would be nice, especially just for pleasure with no vampire social engagements. "Would Venus come? You said no, but you know she'll want to."

"No, not until she is older," Devlin said regretfully. "I want very much to bring her, but The Quarter is not a place for a child who is young. There are many murders there, robbings, and assaults. I'll not have to look far to find blood every night that won't be missed."

Shudder.

"Besides, every so often parents need a vacation by themselves, without their children. So would you want to go?"

"Sure." I paused. "Will Rene come?"

Devlin gave me an unreadable look. "Would you want her to?"

"Yes," I said, nodding. "I think of her as a sister, Dev."

His face broke into a smile. "I'd hoped you'd say that. I didn't want to exclude her. But I did not know how you would feel if I asked her to join us."

"I have never been jealous of her, what she is to you," I said honestly. "She's a good friend, Dev. But the old rule applies here: we're not going to be with you at the same time. We're going for a chance to travel and have a good time, not for an orgy."

"Agreed," he said, his eyes laughing.

Say it and get it over with. "I have to ask: how is Danial? With the way he spoke, I expected him to have me chained to his desk by my collar weeks ago."

"Do not say such things," Devlin chided. "He loves you very much. He just needed some time to come to terms with everything. It would be like you thinking someone was dead and suddenly finding them alive in your arms. The sheer shock takes a while to recover from."

Like Darkness, I thought queasily, remembering the cross now lying beneath the bed. I fingered the one at my throat absently. "Yes."

"It will be Wintermas in another few days. Danial has requested your attendance to his house that night."

Danial must have moved back to his estate, taken residence there again with our son. Crap. I hadn't thought about Danial in terms of Christmas plans. "I need to go to my parents, Dev. They're expecting Lash, Venus, you, and me for Christmas dinner on the twenty-fifth—"

"Danial said he would abstain from that, saying your mother didn't like him anyway. But he expects you to see him at his home for Christmas Eve, no exceptions. Yes, he has moved back to his old estate."

"Will Emma be there?" I asked, cool as ice. "Danial spoke of Oathing her."

Devlin case a baleful glance at me, reproachful. "You know she will not be. Danial has never been unfaithful to you. He called her while I was looking for my copy of the lawbook that very night he came together with you, and told her he was unable to see her anymore. She was very upset, which is why it took us more than a few moments to return." Devlin gave me a grin. "Time you put to good use with Lash."

I retained my frosty demeanor. "Is Theo going to be there? I'm not going if he is."

"Danial said he will not be, that it will be just you, Elle, Theoron, and he. He has even asked that I not come."

"I don't want to go without you," I whispered softly. "I don't want to be alone with him."

"You can teleport, Love. There will be no danger. Danial is hurting inside; he's intensely jealous of Lash and upset that you're planning to have a weresnake baby, and not his. As for why, I'm not sure. This is the same sort of situation we had with Theo, and he handled that very well—"

"That 'situation' combusted after six months, Dev."

"Because of Theo and his jealousy. Lash has said he will not cause trouble, and besides, Rene is here to help you with my desires. I admit, I caused a good portion of the trouble, because I was jealous and have always disliked Theo. But I'll not fight over you with Danial, or Lash. Danial is reasonable, Love. He'll come round. It just may take a few months, or years."

"A few years? Dev—"

"No arguments, Love. Get some sleep."

I popped three valium and slipped off into dreams.

* * * *

The next few days were a whirlwind of preparation, and hurrying to finish last minute gifts. Rene was a great help to me as we wrapped and hung decorations, Venus helping with some of them. That Friday, we trimmed the tree, even Lash and Devlin, who demanded this time to be included. As I hadn't last Christmas, I told them my story of the Christmas Spiders, and we all made some and hung them on the tree.

As we did, I saw with a pang that Elle's spiders and Danial's from years ago were hung on our tree already. So before going to bed that night, I grabbed them, and put them in a bag to take with me, thinking they would be a kind of peace offering to Danial. At the very least, they belonged with Danial at his Christmas celebration, as a physical memory of happier times we had spent together.

That night, I teleported to Danial's house, arriving for the first time on the porch, something I'd tried so hard to do for years and failed. Taking that as a good omen, I knocked, praying that the rest of the night would go as smoothly.

Elle opened the door, and before I could say anything she was hugging me fiercely, and I was hugging her back, tears in my eyes. I came inside, and she helped me off with my jacket and boots.

"Is your dad here?" I asked.

She shook her head. "He's attending a party for an influential client.

But he said he'd return by ten."

Whew. Things are going well after all. "Do we have an itinerary? Is Theoron here?"

Elle looked upset. "Theoron is with him at the party. Dad made him go."

But he didn't make you go, or even ask if you wanted to. Thoughtless bastard. "Do we need to decorate here? Or would you like to make cookies?"

"I'd like baking," Elle said softly. "It's been a long time since you and I baked together."

"Come on, then." I threw my arm around her, as we headed to the kitchen.

"I don't bake as much as I used to," I said, shrugging as I pulled out bowls and flour. "But I do a lot more cooking, or at least it feels like it. I'm not sure where the time goes—"

"For Lash?"

I nodded. "And Devlin. He sometimes eats my cooking, with a little help from Titus."

"Are you pregnant yet?"

I dropped the baking sheet with a loud clang, and then bent to pick it up.

"I didn't mean to pry."

"It's okay, daughter dear," I said with a sigh. "We don't know yet. We've been trying and failing so far." I steeled myself. "You should know I'm trying with Devlin, too. That he asked me and I agreed."

Elle didn't reply, her face thoughtful. When I changed the subject, she let me.

For a while, we discussed what to make and ingredients. Before long, we were mixing and pouring, making both chocolate chip cookies, and cutout sugar cookies, which was my traditional holiday favorite. Soon the sugar cookies were done, cooling off on racks, and the first batch of chocolate chip was baking.

I poured us each a glass of wine. We sat at the kitchen table.

"Are you happy?" I said after a moment. "I don't talk to you every week, Elle. I hope you know that's from me not wanting to be in your face, not because I don't care about you."

"I know that. I'm okay, Mom. My courses are exciting, but they take up a lot of time."

"What are you taking?"

"Some science and some math. But my favorite is a course in philosophy, called 'The Wisdom of History'."

I was proud she was so intelligent. "What's it about?"

"Whether lessons that were learned by our ancestors and passed down through the years still have value for us today."

"Isn't that a forgone conclusion?" I asked, skeptical.

Elle smiled. "I thought so. Now I'm not sure. So many mistakes tend to be repeated hundreds of years after they didn't work the first time. The problem seems not to be that the lesson wasn't there, but instead that the people in charge didn't pay attention, or believe it could happen again."

I was familiar with that concept. *All too familiar.* "How's the house, and the barn? Devlin tells me you thought about having horses. Any yet?"

Elle shook her head. "None that are mine. Any one I'd get would have to have time to get used to my scent, or I'd panic it. But Dad did bring me both Poe and Annabelle Lee and I've been caring for them. They seem to like the barn and corrals, though Poe knocked down a lot of the fencing at first. It was my fault, for not seeing it had rotted—"

I let her talk, feeling sad. Danial had not only taken Briar, a cat I thought of as mine, he'd also taken the horses we'd rode together years ago. That made me angry at first, until I realized I hadn't ridden once since my return to Hayden. I'd gotten away from riding horses, as Lash hated them so much and they him. But I'd always enjoyed riding. I decided to talk to Dev about getting some horses for Rene and me. We could all go riding together.

"—so Dad's been riding with me every week, just around the fields mostly, though we've got permission to ride on the neighbors' land too. The crops are in, so we don't have to worry about them."

"How are the neighbors?" I posed.

"At first they thought I was a new tenant. No one believed I was your daughter because of my age, until I told them I was adopted. But everyone's been nice. I'm indebted to some of them for helping me settle in. Henry's son has been plowing the drive, though I'm getting better at working the tractor." She added prideful, blushing, "I'd never plowed before. But I'm pretty good."

"I'm sure you are," I said proudly. "There was never anything you tried to do you didn't do well."

"Sharon's staying with me for the winter," Elle said suddenly in an odd voice. "She's nice. The demon, Song, stays in the basement. I've set up a spare bedroom down there, like you had for Dad—"

"Tell me, why do they call her that? That can't be her real name."

"Short for Bloodsong. Her brother is Boneharp, or Harp. His is because he has a harp made of bones, human ones. He sometimes plays it for us at night, though he refuses to do it very often. But why she has her name, I have no idea."

Shiver. "That's okay, I just wondered."

There was the sound of a key in the lock, and then Theoron walked in, obviously pissed off in the extreme. "Hi, Sis, Mom."

He stalked by us into the dining room. I looked at Elle, and then we went after him, glasses in hand.

I went to Danial's old room, but Elle nudged me, whispering that Danial had that room again, that Theoron was in her old room. I followed her to it. Theoron was there, throwing clothes into a suitcase, muttering crude curses.

He sounded like Lash. Then it hit me that he had Lash's odd inflection for most of them, which meant he likely'd learned them from Lash. *Great.* "What is it?" I asked, worried I already knew.

Elle didn't mince words. "Theoron, where are you going? Don't leave; I'm sure Dad didn't mean whatever he said—"

"He meant it," Theoron hissed, his eyes reddening. "I'm to go to Europe. Samuel's asked for help, and Dad volunteered me." He looked at us with bitter eyes. "I'll be gone at least six months."

Six months? "Why so long? No case could take that long!"

"This one will, mostly because it's going to take a lot of legwork, a lot of hours sifting through old files."

"Send Theo or Terian," I said, feeling evil. "They can do the leg work for you. You're needed here—"

"I'm 'needed there'," Theoron sneered. "Theo is 'too valuable' to be gone that long. Terian is 'needed to watch Dad's back'."

169

"You aren't going," I said flatly, my words razor sharp. "I'm your mother, and I'll not allow it. You could be killed with no backup."

"Samuel's vouched for my safety. I'll be working closely with him. The work will be done at his estate, most of it—"

"I'm telling you, you aren't going," I said again for emphasis. "Because you and I both know this has nothing to do with some old case. This is just another way Danial is trying to hurt Lash, because he knows how close you've become."

Theoron locked eyes with me. "I know. Samuel hates weres, all weres, but especially snakes. Dad outdid himself this time." He came over and hugged me. "But I do need to go. I've felt overwhelmed since I had to take over Solutions, Inc. Dad's made it clear I've fucked that all up, so I want to get away. I need to decide what I'm going to do for the rest of my life."

"You haven't fucked up anything," I murmured, hugging him hard. "You did the best you could, better than most could or would have done. But you're right; you need some time away, some time for yourself. Think of it as a working vacation. Call me every week. I'll make sure Lash is available when you call, so you can talk to him."

"Thanks, Mom," Theoron said in a cracked voice. He cleared his throat. "I need to leave tonight. But you'll get the wine gift basket I sent to you tomorrow. There's a present in there for Lash."

"What is it?"

Theoron cracked a smile. "He'll know what's his."

The front door slammed, Danial's voice immediately calling for Theoron. Theoron's face clouded over and he resumed packing. I motioned to Elle to please leave, and she shook her head no, that she was staying.

Danial came to the door. He stood staring at Theoron, his arms folded across his chest. "Good, you're packing. Brian is ready to take you to the airport. You should leave in another ten minutes."

"I'm set to," Theoron growled. "Why don't you let me pack?"

Danial gave him a cool look, nodded, and left.

I crossed to Theoron, and put my hand on his shoulder. "Can I help?"

Theoron nodded. Elle and I pitched in. Ten minutes later, we were hugging him goodbye at the door.

"Be safe," I said. "And remember, call me."

Theoron nodded, and hugged Elle. "'Bye, Sis. Be careful."

"I will be. You too, okay?"

Theoron released her, and focused on Danial, who had just come through from his bedroom. Theoron stood there defiantly, clearly bracing for a verbal fight. Instead, Danial just hugged him, and after a moment, Theoron hugged him back.

"Don't think of this as a punishment," Danial said gently. "You've done better with the company than I'd have done at three times your apparent age, son. There is much you can learn with Samuel." He drew back. "But do not learn his views on vampire superiority. They are wrong, and one day soon they'll likely lead him to grief."

Theoron drew back, visibly astonished as I was. Danial nodded once to him. "Go son. Have a safe flight. Call when you've arrived, and then again when you're reached Samuel's estate."

Theoron nodded, gave Elle and me a last smile, and drove away.

Danial turned to Elle and I. "Do I smell cookies? They smell overdone—"

Oh SHIT! I raced to the kitchen, and took out the smoking cookie pan. The cookies were blackened lumps, and the kitchen stank of burnt dough.

I took them outside on the off chance some forest animal could stomach them, and then came back in, replacing the burnt parchment paper with new, and reloading the pan with dough mounds. Elle had opened the windows, and the smell was already dissipating.

"May I have one, Love?" Danial asked, inspecting the sheet. "I have never seen you make this kind that is tree-shaped."

"Yes," I said coolly. "But they aren't ready. We didn't expect you until ten."

"It's Christmas," Danial said caressingly. "I should be with my family, and that means you. So I got away as early as I could."

I didn't reply. Elle was already getting out different sprinkles, and frosting ingredients. She and I made frosting, and by that time, most of the chocolate chip cookies had baked, and were cooling. We frosted cookies, Danial watching us from his seat at the table. And when we were done, we all sampled them.

"These are very good," Danial said, his usually cool tone molten with calorie fulfillment. "I like the sweetness of the frosting. You did a good job, Elle."

"That's all I'm good for, isn't it, Dad?" Elle growled. "Making frosting."

Danial gave her a shocked look. "You are good at many things, daughter."

"I wouldn't have guessed that from how you treat me, Dad."

I abruptly got up, and they both looked at me. "You need to speak about this, both of you." I said in explanation. "I'll give you some privacy."

"Do not leave," Danial said, his words edged with anger. "I expect you to stay the night."

I did a double take. "Dev didn't tell me that. I haven't brought any clothes—"

"You won't need clothes," Danial said arrogantly. "At least nightclothes."

I gave him a disgusted look, and walked out, putting on my boots and jacket. As I walked outside, I heard Elle's raised voice, and then Danial's, though I couldn't hear what they were saying.

I walked to the fox compound, thinking I'd been right to leave. If I'd stayed, I'd have joined Elle against Danial, and he needed to hear her and work this out, not try to either get back at me, or get into my good graces.

I got to the compound, and went inside, wondering what all the noise was about. Abruptly the loud talking stopped, as everyone turned to stare at me.

Shit. In my desire to escape, I'd forgotten it was Christmas Eve, and the weres would be having their annual Christmas party. They were all here, well, all but Brian. Most of the foxes were on the floor, in stages of unwrapping presents. Theo and Jenny were there too, both of them looking at me with yellow eyes.

"I thought I scented snake," Jenny growled.

"What are you doing here, Sarelle?" Cia said formally. "Does Danial need something?"

"No," I said just as formally. "Danial and Elle are having a discussion, and I wanted to give them privacy. But I wanted to let someone know I'd be walking to the cemetery, so Danial didn't worry."

"We'll tell him," Cia said in that same emotionless voice. "Have a good walk."

I nodded, and left, hearing the talking and laughing start as soon as I'd left.

I walked for a while, feeling awful that all those people I'd once counted my friends weren't anymore. But that was okay; I had new friends, like Rene and Serena. Maybe not as many as I'd had here, but they were good ones. I reminded myself right then to go and see Serena the moment I got back. I'd still had not spent time with her. *It's been more than a month since I'd meant to...*

I arrived in the cemetery, and walked to my son's grave. It was odd looking at the statue of him, knowing that I might be pregnant again. I lightly ran my hand over his sculpted head, rubbing gently the way he'd always liked me to pet him.

"He liked that," a low voice said from behind me.

I turned to see Theo leaning against a tree, watching me.

"I know he did," I whispered. "I should have made a point to do that to him every day of his life."

Theo didn't reply.

I turned and faced him. "Why are you here? Isn't Jenny going to be upset?"

"Danial called, and asked me to find you. When I told him I knew where you were, he demanded I come and bring you back."

I sat down on the ground. "Will you give me a minute? I'll go back in a little while. You don't have to stay." I left off that I had my own demon protection just a mental call away.

Theo sighed, and then he was easing down beside me. "I'll stay. You know he'll ream my ass if I don't, and something happens to you."

I laughed politely, knowing he expected it. He wasn't part of my life anymore, but that didn't mean we had to constantly be at war. "Thanks"

"So they were fighting? Elle and Danial?"

I nodded. "He favors her over Theoron." *Plus her real father ignores her as soon as he's got another cougar to pal around with...* I blushed in shame, glad I'd kept that nastiness to myself. "He's never asked her to be part of Solutions, Inc."

"As a favor to me. I don't want her in this business," Theo said flatly, picking up a rock and throwing it. "I want her to find someone who'll take care of her, and keep her safe, especially now that Solutions, Inc is back doing vengeance jobs. They're high risk."

The woman in me spoke up loudly that Elle was grown up, and was capable of taking care of herself; she didn't need a man to do it. But the mother in me did want someone strong helping Elle through the bad times in her life, and someone to share the good moments with, as well. "I agree."

We were both silent for a few minutes.

"We should go," Theo said, getting to his feet. "I've got to get back."

I nodded, and got to my feet. Together, we started back.

"I heard you got injured down south," I said casually.

Theo looked at me and snorted. "I was. It was just a scratch."

"A scratch that had you hospitalized for a day and in bed for a week."

Theo let out a growl. "Doctors are supposed to be confidential." He paused. "Why did you ask?"

I was going to say I hadn't, Stephen had volunteered that info, and then realized that hadn't been what Theo'd meant. But I'd be damned if I admitted I'd been worried about him. "I know you're skilled and fast. But it was bad. That made me think whomever you went against was dangerous. I was worried about them coming after me."

"They might be after you. After all, you are with Lash now—"

Oiy. "Just stop it."

"—and they seem to be targeting Devlin, your other lover," Theo finished smoothly. "I'd be careful, if I were you."

I shrugged. "I'm safe enough. I've got you here guarding me, haven't I?"

"Not anymore," Theo said, shaking his head. "You can make it from here on your own; we're in sight of the house. I've got to get back to Jenny."

"Thanks. Have a Merry Christmas."

Theo gave me a surprised look. "Merry Christmas, Sar." He turned away, and headed through the trees. I headed in the direction of the house.

Danial met me at the door. Elle was nowhere in evidence.

"Well?" I said, facing him.

"Elle said some things to me that have been festering for a long time. And I said some things I needed to say to her as well."

"Is she gone?"

Danial nodded. "But we did not part angry, Dearheart. Both of us have much to think on. And she goes to her friend who'll ease her mind, just as your company will ease mine." He came close, and carefully enfolded me in his arms. "Would you like to go to bed?"

"No," I said flatly. "Would you?"

"What I'd really like is another cookie," Danial said meaningfully. "But I cannot have another until almost a week." He ran his lips gently over my neck. "Isn't it funny how the things we love and enjoy most are rationed for us, or denied us utterly?"

I pushed away from him gently. "I never said I'd deny you myself."

"You didn't have to say the words to mean them."

Danial's cell phone rang, and he held up a finger, telling me to wait while he answered it.

I fumed, glaring at him.

When his face became stricken, I ran to him, suddenly scared of what he would tell me. "What is it?"

"That was Devlin," he said softly. "Cain is dead."

Chapter Sixteen

Oh God. "Is Devlin okay?" I asked.

"He's devastated. He's already sent Titus to investigate, to make sure it was really a car accident that killed him." Danial hugged me. "He asked I send you home to him now. The funeral will be Monday. He said he needed you beside him tonight."

That's a relief, I thought guiltily.

"Teleport now," Danial said softly. "Dev needs you. Our night together can wait."

Even though I had been eager to go, now that the pressure was off to stay, I worried about leaving Danial all alone here on Christmas Eve. "Do you want to come with me? Devlin said Cain was like a son to you. I don't want you to be here alone."

"He was for many years, but I have my own son, Love, our son. I want to be here when he calls to tell him of this, as I know he met Cain." He gave a wry smile. "Besides, I'll not stay here alone. I'll go and join the werefox party. I know there are several presents waiting for me there."

"I have one for you too," I said softly, handing him the bag with the spiders in it. "I thought they should be here on your tree, since you and I and Elle made them."

"I don't have a tree," Danial said gently, taking them from me. "I didn't have time to get one this year. But I'll put them on my dresser to celebrate, Love. I thank you." He gave me a chaste kiss. "I have something for you."

He handed me a box, a familiar one. Before I opened it, I knew what it was: my foxhead choker.

"Let me put it on you," he said seductively. "Devlin has agreed to trade off with me."

I didn't move. "I haven't agreed, Danial. I'm not ready to wear your symbol again."

"Don't balk, Sar. You know this is right."

"No, I don't. I was made to come here, Danial, made by you. And like I told you, I'm not doing anything I don't want to." I turned venomous. "The more you try to force me, the more I'll fight you."

"Don't make me break you," Danial replied coolly. "I just want what I have a right to."

"I wanted what I had a right to months ago," I said sarcastically. "You denied me both your body and your blood, to say nothing of your love. Technically, I believe that is grounds for Oathbreaking, isn't it?"

"Devlin," Danial hissed malevolently. "He put you up to this."

"No. But it's a measure of your estimation of me that you thought I didn't have the brains to think of it myself." I shook my head. "And you wonder why Elle is so pissed off."

Danial's eyes were now a dark reddish brown. His tone was sharp as knives. "You're right, Love. I have underestimated you. I promise, it's a mistake I'll not make again."

I teleported instantly, arriving in the kitchen at Hayden. To my happy surprise, Serena was there sipping some wine alone. She was dressed up for some reason.

"Hi," I said with a big smile. "Are you going out?"

"I was," she said grumpily. "But Theoron called and cancelled. He's on his way to Europe. And I'm suddenly dressed up with nowhere to go."

"Go to the fox party at Danial's," I said encouragingly. "It's still going on."

"Theoron told me to. But I'd feel weird, Sar, even being around my own kind."

I gave her an odd look. "You mean other weres?"

"Other foxes. I'm all fox now."

Her tone made me not ask when in hell that had happened, or how. "Go to the party," I said, getting to my feet. "You belong there having fun, not here alone."

I grabbed her hand and teleported her. We wound up outside the werecompound door. Even from here, there was the sound of loud, happy laughing.

"Go in," I said, giving her a push. "You're welcome there. I've got to get back to Devlin." No way was I seeing Danial again tonight.

"I'm sorry I've been busy," Serena said quietly. "But I've gotten to be friends with most of the foxes. Although Theoron and I aren't in love, we have a kind of understanding and we're close friends."

I held my tongue, reminding myself to be happy for her. Serena hadn't had a great life, and it was good that she had more friends now. But that she was welcome here and I wasn't made me a little bitter, anyway. "Have a fun night."

She walked in. I turned to go, and felt a hot arm grab me. I looked up in shock to see Terian. He fastened his cherrywood eyes on me, and teleported us.

We ended up in what had to be his and Sun's room.

I pulled away from him. "Why did you take me here to your room?"

"My house, Sar, mine and Sun's." Terian strode out of the room.

He came back with a cat carrier, which held a growling Asher. "Sunrise is allergic, and Sun said Asher had to go." He wiped away a streaming tear. "As much as I want her to stay, I admit it might be better for her. She's scared most of the time with all the loud noises, especially all the crying Sunrise does." He gave a halfhearted smile. "Sunrise screams a lot. She's just having fun and it's normal, or so Titus tells me, but it's still nerve-wracking. I'm getting appreciation for all my brother Keriam did for me."

I remembered Keriam, remembered the man he'd been, one Matt Mariek, whom Terian's mother Leri had bespelled into thinking he was Terian's brother, so he would take care of her half-demon child. "He was a good brother to you. Yes, Asher can come home with me." *God, that will make five cats.* That was a lot for one family, wasn't it?

"Thanks." He paused. "I appreciate you trusting me with her, these years she stayed with me. I'll miss her very much."

"Why did you bring me here, Tears? You could have sent Asher to me via teleporting, and skipped this whole scene."

"I know Theoron's going to be gone for a while. A lot of other things are changing too." He paused, and seemed to gather himself. "You

178

were right, I wasn't a good friend. I took advantage when I shouldn't have. But I wanted to tell you if you needed me, I'd be there for you."

"Are you splitting up with Sun?" I said bluntly. "And this is you 'putting out feelers'?"

"No. We've been working hard, and so far, we're closer than we've ever been," Terian said evenly. "I was honest with my therapist, and told him about how I felt for another woman, and what I'd done. He suggested I do this."

That sounded like bullshit to me, but also like something a therapist would say. " 'There for me' how, Tears?"

"Like a friend would be. Like Titus." He took a deep breath. "I'm like your kin now. And being intimate with you would be like you having sex with Rip or Shaker, completely wrong—"

"Enough," I said quickly, coated in uneasiness. "I've got to get going."

"Do you want to see Sunrise?" Terian said shyly. "I need to be going myself. We're supposed to meet Sundown there."

I nodded, and followed him into a nursery decorated in many stars, moons, and suns, but predominantly suns. And as I looked at the quiet blonde baby girl sleeping there amidst all those suns, I remembered Sundown and Devlin, and it hit me like a 4 x 4 metal bar: Sun was still afraid of him, after all this time. She'd done the best she could to protect her child from her own mistake, even naming the little girl with the one thing left in the world that Devlin still was truly respectful and afraid of.

I went close, and touched the sleeping infant. "You're safe," I whispered. "And both very beautiful and very loved."

"She is," Tears said softly. He picked her up, and she opened her eyes, eyes I was relieved to see were not red, but instead hazel and very curious. "Have a Merry Christmas, Sar."

He and Sunrise promptly disappeared.

I teleported myself immediately, feeling odd to be suddenly alone in Terian and Sun's house, and appeared again in the kitchen at Hayden. This time no one was there, and so I let Asher into the basement, the place I thought she'd feel safest, and then walked upstairs to find Devlin. He was lying on the bathroom floor passed out in nothing but underwear. And he'd clearly been sick by the mess all over the floor, on him, and partially on the toilet.

I took off my good clothes quickly, and threw on some worn ones. Then I got some cleaner and went in to help him.

Before too long, I'd gotten him clean, rolled his dead weight onto a towel, and cleaned up the bathroom. The mess was what looked like blood and alcohol, and something else that was almost black that I guessed was half-digested blood. *Ugh.*

I was just bringing out the garbage when Lash walked in, blood all down one side of him. I dropped my cleaning stuff and ran to him. "What happened?"

He held up his hands to stop me from touching him. "Stay away," he hissed painfully. "I've got poison residue on me, bad stuff, Sweetness. It's the kind of thing Theo was dosed with years ago, only this works on humans, too."

"Are you okay?"

"I started to bleed out, but I'm okay now. Titus stopped the bleeding by drawing out the poison. The pain's still pretty bad though, which is why my voice sounds like this. But I'll be okay after a night's sleep."

I pushed aside my relief. "Then can you shower, and help me? Devlin's passed out on the bathroom floor. I don't have the strength to get him to the bed."

Lash grimaced, and went to look. "He drank too much wine, that's all. It fucks up his digestive system every time. I'll shower in my room, and be right back. Stay with him."

He left, and was back in just jeans ten minutes later, his hair still wet. He easily shouldered Devlin, and put him down gently in bed. "Go clean off, Sar. Dev'll be okay, but I'll stay with him until you get back, anyway."

I put everything away downstairs, and tossed out the garbage, leaving two empty wine bottles in the sink, and just as I was going back upstairs, I found Ghost on the kitchen floor. He'd somehow tangled his legs, and was having trouble getting up with his advanced arthritis. He looked at me with such a pitiful expression that I bit down into my lip to stop from bursting into tears.

Devlin had said I had a year left with Ghost. *God, what if he's wrong?* I couldn't handle this, not on top of everything else!

"Come on," I said gently, lifting my dog's back end to help him stand. "You need to go out. Then I'll make you a fire, and you'll feel better."

I got Ghost up, and he went out and did his business. As we turned around to go upstairs, we met Venus, who looked as if she'd been crying all night.

Shit, I'd thought she'd been...I didn't know where, but with someone watching her. I hugged her. "I'm here. What is it?"

"Dad locked himself in his room, and wouldn't come out. I looked for you, and couldn't find you. Then I looked for Lash, Serena, and Titus. I couldn't find anybody!"

God Damn it, Devlin. "I'm sorry for that. No one meant to scare you. Your father lost a good friend tonight, Venus. You remember Cain? He looked like Danial, but had Devlin's eyes? Well, Cain died in a bad accident." I paused, thinking quickly. "Your father's asleep now. And I really need your help."

Venus straightened up visibly. "What do you need, Mom?"

"We have a new cat. Her name is Asher. She's kind of wild, what's called feral. She needs food, and water. Can you bring them to the basement, while I carry a litter box?"

Venus nodded. "I'll go get the food, I know where it is, and dishes too."

Good, because I didn't know where to get an extra litter box on Christmas Eve. Shit, why hadn't Terian given me his? *Damn him.*

I looked under the kitchen sink, and managed to find an old dishpan. That would have to do. I filled it halfway with cat litter, and was just in time to follow Venus down the cellar stairs.

Asher was nowhere to be seen, but when I called her, she answered me with a timid meow. So we left the food and water near Rene's worktable, and shut the upstairs door. After living without other animals the last few years, who knew how she'd react to seeing dogs again, or other cats?

By this time, I was utterly exhausted. It felt like morning, though the clock just said eleven-thirty. I walked with Venus upstairs, and Lash helped her into bed beside her father, and tucked her in as I started a fire.

Venus cast an anxious glance at her unconscious father. "Are you sure he's okay?"

"He's fine, Venus." Lash kissed her forehead gently. "He'll feel hungry tomorrow, but that's okay, his donors are coming. So get a good night's sleep, and don't worry."

"Okay," Venus said, "Want to say my prayers with me?"

Lash looked panicked, and then nodded. "You say them for both of us, Venus. But I'll be saying them inside."

Venus said them, Lash clasping his hands over hers. He covered her up, and she settled in the crook of Devlin's arm, making room for herself.

By this time, the fire was made and burning warmly and Ghost was in front of it, dozing. Phantom, Jessica, and Cavity were curled asleep near him, though not on him, as they'd used to lay on Darkness.

Lash and I took off my clothes, both of us in the bathroom so Venus wouldn't see. I washed up and put on a long nightgown.

Lash reluctantly put on a pair of Devlin's silk bottoms. "Don't tell I wore these," he hissed. "I feel like a poofter. At least they're black."

I gave him an odd look, not recognizing the word but guessing the meaning. Then we crawled into bed beside an already sleeping Venus and Devlin.

"How did seeing Danial go?" Lash said casually.

"It didn't, Tryst. He had words with and for everyone, including Elle, T, and me." I related to him the nights' events, all of them. "I'll let you know when Theoron calls."

"Good. I want to talk to him," Lash hissed sadly. "I'll miss him visiting me." His voice dropped an octave. "You should know too that Danial is petitioning the other Rulers, Devlin included, to be recognized as co-Ruler of North America. It will mean he'd have equal standing as Devlin. Dev has already agreed."

"Why is that bad? Dev said Danial's been a big help. It's got nothing to do with me."

"Because he's going to force that threesome night on you eventually. The only reason he hasn't yet is that I have it on good authority that Theo keeps refusing." His voice dropped even lower. "But there's a reason he sent Brian away now, Love: he doesn't want Dev or I to know what he's planning."

I looked over my shoulder at Lash. "Maybe he's just had enough of being spied on. Brian's been out of the closet as Dev's man since my first being with Devlin. Danial knows he's reporting to you. I'm surprised he wasn't fired for that years ago."

Lash let out a thoughtful hiss. "Maybe."

"Can you get info from someone else?"

Lash shook his head. "Those foxes hate me, all of them. So do the cougars. And Terian won't do something so *immoral...*" he made a face. "I'll have to see if Titus can use an owl or some animal. Otherwise we'll just have to operate blind." He repositioned himself. "But don't worry about it, Sweetness. I'll find a way."

I hugged him, popped two valium, and went to sleep.

* * * *

Morning dawned bright and early, as Venus was eager to open her presents. Devlin was indeed wasted, but he got up, and we all opened presents, Rene and Kyle joining us after a few loud shouts from Venus.

Venus had gotten some clothes, books, and a beautiful gold bracelet that said "Daughter" from Devlin and me. At her request, most of her presents from everyone else had been in the form of large donations to a few charities she'd selected. Her presents to us were all donations in our names to various charities, something we agreed we all appreciated.

Devlin, Lash and I'd mostly gotten each other baby items: playpens, children's clothes, blankets, toys, even a huge tank with a heated rock inside it from Lash to me. Premature maybe, but we were all hoping. It was hard not to hope.

Kyle had gotten us all gift certificates to various online stores, saying uncomfortably that he hated shopping. Everyone, myself included, had gotten him bullets, gun-cleaning supplies, and a huge box of assorted bandages, gauze, and tape, which Kyle tossed angrily at a manically laughing Lash, telling him that it wasn't funny.

Rene had made us all spells. Kyle's was for protection against Hellfire, Devlin's was for eating food—one that would give him ten minutes instead of five—Lash's was for some kind of warming that was supposed to feel like being in the sun, and Venus's was for changing her appearance for an hour. But mine was best, as it was a spell to stop magic from affecting me.

"It won't work on demon magic," she said to me telepathically as she handed it to me with a smile. "But all others it will. And it's permanent, Sar. I'll help you insert it tomorrow."

I nodded, a little wary. *Insert it where?*

Rene liked her presents of chocolate and wine from Devlin, Lash, and I. After her generous gift to me, I felt like I'd skimped, but she just said she was glad to be here with us, and that was enough of a present all by itself.

Serena did not show, but I didn't think much of it, sure she was bedding down with the foxes, so I put her gifts of chocolate and other food aside. Several boxes of gift baskets arrived from UPS: one from Theoron, one from Erik and Van, and one from Danial to Devlin, Venus, and me. Theoron's I opened and put out for everyone to enjoy the breads, jams, and scones, handing the large smoked salmon tin to Lash who immediately began scarfing them down. Erik's and Van's Godiva basket I hid, taking off the tag so Lash wouldn't melt it, and so I could remember to send them a formal thank you. Danial's box I put under the tree, figuring I needed more time to deal with whatever it was he'd sent to me before opening it.

Rene and I made everyone breakfast, including Devlin, who pleaded for just a little drink as he was dying of thirst. Between the both of us, we managed to feed him enough blood to mellow him out without either of us getting faint. His donors came about noon, soon enough so he looked a good deal better when he emerged around one.

We teleported to my parents about three p.m., Rene included. The visit was awkward, as my mother was clearly pissed to see Rene's familiarity with Devlin. But there were no scenes, for which I was grateful. I played some Ping Pong with Venus, and taught Rene, who enjoyed learning, even as I laughed a good deal at her. Lash drank my stepfather under the table, something my mother and I'd never thought was even possible, much less ever seen happen.

My mother asked me in the kitchen if anything was wrong. "You didn't call us for months last year. You used to call me a lot more. We hardly see you, Sar; this is the first time since you returned from your trip. And who is this new woman, Rene?"

I nodded, grimacing again at the lie that my imprisonment last year had been an extended overseas trip. "A good friend," I said, giving her a hug. "I'm fine, Mom. I'm just very busy."

"We just want you to be happy," she said softly. "I'm glad to hear that you are." She hugged me. "Call me more, please. I don't have to see you, so long as I know you're okay."

I hugged her hard. "I'll call you every week, Mom. I promise."

* * * *

The rest of the day was spent watching old movies, including a funny one from the twenties that was silent called "The Navigator" with Buster Keaton. I found it hilarious along with Lash, Rene and Dev, but Kyle was under-wowed, saying this was pure slapstick, and he didn't get why we thought it was so funny.

"It was cutting edge to me when I was sixteen," Lash said jovially. "Pictures that moved. God, I thought it didn't get any better."

"Then color came, and sound," Devlin said, grinning. "We were in Heaven."

Lash and Devlin began to talk back and forth, recalling old movies, and comparing them to some present ones. Rene and I dozed, half-listening, Venus busy on the floor with her new laptop. Before I knew it, I was waking up and it was Monday, the day of Cain's funeral.

Chapter Seventeen

It was a cold day for Georgia, or so the funeral director hosting Cain's funeral mass told us. We'd arrived to pouring rain that showed no sign of letting up anytime soon. Devlin was white as a ghost, despite having fed heavily earlier that morning.

Lash and I'd teleported via Rip to a nearby town, then driven my old truck to the funeral home to make sure there was no one lying in wait. After Lash's check of the facility and Rip's laying down of a "teleportation-free" spell that would admit only myself and he, I'd gone into the woman's bathroom and fetched both Devlin and Venus, teleporting them in. Together, we then joined the line of mourners. I tried hard not to look at Cain in his coffin, unwilling to see his laughing golden eyes that were now closed forever.

Devlin introduced me as his wife, and Venus as our child. Lash hovered near the door, wearing his customary black.

"You must be a long lost relative," Cain's mother said gently to Devlin. "You and your daughter have his eyes."

"I am," Devlin said smoothly. "A distant relation. We met years ago, when he was in school. He was a good friend to me, one I'll miss dearly."

"After a short intro, please feel free to speak at the podium, if you have any stories or memories you would like to share. Your name?"

"Devlin Dalcon. I understand Cain was named for his grandfather?"

Devlin talked for a while about Cain and their shared times together, not caring that he was holding up the line of mourners. But Cain's mother didn't seem to mind, and she gave him a big hug at the end of their talk. With Lash glaring at everyone who looked askance at Devlin, there was no trouble.

Then we were before the casket, which was open. It was odd to see him there, looking for all the world like Danial had in his coma, save he was a little older and didn't have luminous skin. *But he isn't just sleeping; Cain is dead. He'll never get the chance to get up out of that coffin. He'll never get the chance to do anything again.*

"Be at peace," Devlin rasped out finally. "I'll miss you very much, my friend."

Venus put down the single red rose she'd carried until now, leaving it on Cain's chest. I said a silent prayer asking God to watch over Cain, and left it at that.

We walked to the back and sat down in the last row of assembled chairs. Devlin didn't speak; he just clutched Venus close, and wiped his eyes. I held his hand, and contented myself with looking around as the service began. After his mother shared a tearful brief prayer for her son, she left the podium and others began to speak of Cain, and what they had meant to him.

There were a lot of comely women here, most of them Cain's age, or younger. But there were friends here, too, and family, not just old and current lovers. I felt another pang that Cain was dead. Sure, he'd been a womanizer, but he'd been kind at heart, or at least appeared to be with all the good things being said about him by those who spoke at the podium. Hell, he'd even planned or asked for a night burial, so Devlin could attend. Now he was just dead.

I noticed that one dark haired, brown-eyed man kept staring at me a lot. Instead of looking away when I looked steadily back at him, he just glared back at me.

The actual religious eulogy was brief, taking place after everyone who wanted to speak had spoken. Then we were in the line of cars to attend the burial, the night already deepening around us, making the few stars shining down through the many clouds seem all the brighter.

The gravesite memorial was ephemeral, as the rain was still coming down hard. Most of the mourners had skipped this, not wanting to get wet. I didn't mind. It had been easy to see Devlin wanted and needed to be here. The preacher said a short paragraph about death and life, the normal ashes to ashes stuff. Soon we were filing away with the rest of the bunch toward my truck.

We'd gotten a few steps when I heard an angry voice hiss, "Leaving so soon?"

I whipped around to see the man who'd been staring at me, but before he could do anything, Lash had hold of him, and had thrown him up against a tree, and driven his knife into his tie, pinning him to the tree as the man struggled hard.

"Who are you?" he hissed angrily. "Tell me, or you'll be resting forever in that grave with the departed."

"You've got his eyes," the man said angrily to Devlin. "My brother's eyes! No one had them, except my father and grandfather! Who are you?"

"A distant relation," Devlin said in an old tone filled with too-much sorrow. "What concern is it of yours?"

"You're lying," the man hissed. "You're my father's bastard! We knew he cheated on Mom, and you're the proof!"

Devlin eyed him. "I'm no bastard. I just wish that this age was still a time I could duel with you over that insult to see what you're made of. But I'll not kill any brother of Cain's. What's your name?"

"Fuck you," the man answered defiantly. "That's my name."

"Answer him," Lash hissed in a low voice. "I've got no problem killing you."

"Fuck you, too!"

"He's my descendant," Devlin said with a trace of pride. "Let him go, Lash, if he answers me this: who was the woman your father dallied with? I want her name and current address."

"I can't be your descendant; you're at least ten years younger than I—"

"Answer me," Devlin growled, his eyes bleeding to red. "Now." He bared his fangs.

Cain's brother recoiled visibly, and said in a small voice, "Our chef." The man gave a name and an address, which Lash wrote on a piece of paper and handed to Devlin. "But that was over thirty years ago, after she was fired by my mother. She could be anywhere now."

Devlin nodded and walked away. I followed him with Venus, watching Lash give Cain's brother a solid punch before leaving him there out cold, propped up against the tree.

"I'll get Danial on it," Devlin said as we drove away. "He'll find out if Cain had an illegitimate brother."

I teleported us home, once we were a safe distance away from the cemetery. Lash left us to sleep in his own room, saying to call if we needed something. Devlin tucked in Venus while I made Ghost a fire. Soon after we were snuggling together in bed, Phantom on the bottom end, sprawled out snoozing.

"Cain asked me to make him vampire the last time he visited," Devlin said brokenly. "He said he was getting older, and he wanted to join my world. I told him it was a hard one, that he'd have to start at the bottom, that I'd not be able to watch out for him, that others would target him for knowing me. He said he didn't care. I said I did, and refused—"

"You couldn't know what would happen."

"I could've saved him and I didn't."

"Dev, rest. Tomorrow is another day."

"Not for Cain," he said brokenly, and he began to cry again, great heaving sobs. And I held him, and didn't say anything, telling myself there was nothing to say that was going to help, because he was right.

* * * *

The next few days passed solemnly. Many flowers and sympathy cards arrived for Devlin from various vampires across the United States, including all State Rulers. There were so many that I didn't know what to do with them, so I set up one of the party tables in the ballroom, and put most of them there. Venus took a few flowers for herself, and I put some on various tables around the house, telling myself they should be viewed and enjoyed, even if their reason for being here was a grim one.

Samuel and the other Continental Vampire Rulers also sent sympathy cards. I spent a day writing letters, and thanking everyone on Dev's behalf for their thoughts and good wishes. Rene helped me, writing out at least half in her elegant hand. I also wrote a letter to Theoron, and sent it by airmail, as I'd not heard from him, and was damned if I would ask Danial.

Devlin kept to himself, though he didn't do anything self-destructive again. I gave him space, asking him to tell me if he needed me. He cried every night, but after a few days, he seemed to be healing, especially after Titus's report that Cain's death truly had been just an accident, not a murder. That was a relief, because a lot was happening.

Danial's petition was granted, and he became co-Ruler with Devlin of North America, by unanimous approval of the other Rulers. I also heard from Lash that Danial was very busy with Solutions, Inc., that business had increased by a third after word got out he was back at the helm. My email work increased in turn, and I did it almost every other day. Though Danial emailed me a good deal about the business, he never wrote a word about anything personal. Lash was still bent, grumbling one night that he'd been stymied so far in getting any information on Danial's doings, despite Titus having put several owls in place in Danial's woods to watch the comings and goings.

I didn't pay much attention to this, as I had my hands full. Venus was fast going from tween to teen, and she'd discovered boys. We had the uncomfortable talk about where babies came from, and how to be careful around males, and what not to do. Even though I worried at the correctness of it, I told Venus of what had happened to Elle. She was upset to hear it, but I could see it had an effect on her that my words of general warning hadn't. I told myself that was what mattered, and left it at that.

Venus had been very interested in charities since that day I had spent with her in town. She'd done a lot of emailing on behalf of one group or another, hence our gift to her of her own laptop. I encouraged this, thinking it was a safe outlet for her growing energy. I tried to keep track of her, making sure I knew how she spent her time, both online and at Hayden.

Shaker had recovered his full strength. What he did most of the time I didn't ask, and he didn't volunteer. But I set up some parameters with him on what thoughts and actions of mine he was allowed to listen in on, and he adhered to them, even if he was mockingly formal with me sometimes.

Asher was still in the basement, acting antisocial, scared of all animals, people, and even the house ceiling fans. She and Moonshadow took an immediate dislike to one another, resulting in wads of black fur left daily from their fighting until I banned Moonshadow from the basement. Part of me wanted to ream out Terian, telling him he'd made her worse than she'd been years ago with me. Luckily, Rene took an immediate liking to her, and in what seemed like a night, Asher took to sleeping in her room. I breathed a sigh of relief, glad that the cat fighting was alleviated, at least most of it.

Asher's affection for Rene made me trust Rene more. And so the day before New Year's, I let Rene insert the stone-like lump into my left arm to protect me against most magical spells. It didn't hurt much, though I was conscious of it at all times, feeling the hard mound shift beneath my skin every time I used my arm or hand.

That same day, Rene also began to teach me healing. It wasn't hard, mostly involving a lot of willpower, and using your mind to reach for the thing you wanted to happen. I found it similar to teleporting, something I had become very good at now. By the end of the first day, I was able to heal a simple scratch, though all I could manage to do was close the wound. It was still red, raised, and stung like the paper cut it was.

"I'll teach you how to take away pain, and ease infection and scarring later," Rene said in approval. "You'll need to get better at closing larger wounds first. But you did well, Sister, for your first attempt."

"Will you teach me to draw out poison?" I said tentatively. "Lash was dosed with some a few days ago, and Titus got it out. But he was hurt bad."

"Yes," Rene nodded. "But that's last on the list. And you've got to remember that poison aimed for him can easily kill you, even his own. Your immunity to spells won't protect you."

"How do I heal him if I can't touch him?"

"You'll need to protect your hands. There are barriers that can be invoked that magic can pass through but poison cannot. I'll look into it."

"Thanks," I said gratefully. "I appreciate this, Sister."

"It feels good to help you," she said, laughing. "I never had an apprentice before." A shadow passed over her face. "It's good to do good. There was much I did in my life that was not."

Her tone was both sad and unsettling. I changed the subject. "Want to go for a walk?"

"Sure," she said, her beautiful face breaking into a smile. "We could use some fresh air."

We got on our clothes, and boots, and headed out. V was at her lessons with Caitlyn, so I didn't worry about her, though Ghost came with us.

We headed to the stables first. Gestapo was there, and so was another horse, a palomino mare.

"Who's this?"

"Morgana," Rene said with a little shyness. "Dev bought her for me. We've only ridden twice so far though."

I felt annoyed at not being included, but pushed it aside. "Should we go for a ride? I can handle Gestapo well enough—"

"Do you want me to saddle them?" a rough voice asked.

We both started, to find Bobby the werewolverine standing there beside us, a pitchfork in one hand.

"No, I can saddle them," I said confidently. "How've you been? I never thanked you for warning us, God, it's been over a year." I turned redder and redder as Rene chuckled.

"It's my duty, ma'am," Bobby said, nodding once. "I still patrol at night, even in the snow. I like the rabbit hunting. They're always nice and plump. I like that shriek they make when I sink my teeth in."

Yuck. I tried to smile and not grimace. "I'm glad you're happy here."

"Call out when you come back, and I'll take care of the horses," Bobby said, moving off. "I've got a lot to do. The tack is in the usual place."

I thanked him and got busy. A half hour later, Rene and I were slowly riding through the woods, following a deer trail, Ghost trailing us. We spoke about various topics, and then abruptly, Rene asked me if I was going to go see Rosalyn.

"Not you, too," I said irritably. "I don't need to see anyone, Rene."

"Okay, Sister."

"She's going to tell me what happened wasn't my fault, and I know that already. It was Michael's fault and Cyrus's." *And Terian's.* "I'd go if there was a benefit, but there isn't one, not in dragging that all up again."

Rene said okay again, and changed the topic. "Devlin told me Hector's daughter got killed. She was out with some vampire friends, and somehow forgot to come home by sunrise, and was killed in sunlight. Hector's angry, though so far Mad's got him channeling his anger into going after the vampire friends, and not Devlin."

It took me a while to remember who she was talking about, and process that. *Madeline was the leader whom Devlin put in place to liaison with the vampire hunters Hector and Peter, who had attacked Hayden, leading to my capture by Michael. Hector was the vampire hunter leader whom Devlin and Nate went after, and Nate turned Hector's daughter, making her a vampire.* "Does she seem good? Mad, I mean. Devlin hasn't said much."

"From what I've heard, she's doing a good job, though I admit I've not heard a lot. Devlin did say that vampire deaths as a whole are down by a tenth of what they were. He credits the vampires working with the hunters for the improvement, including turned former hunters like Peter. They step in and can help in situations where killing can be alleviated. Peter and Mad are losing a lot fewer human hunters, too."

That was good news. But I had a new topic of my own to raise. "Rene, what about Kyle? What does he remember about his battle with Shaker? He seems to have selective memory."

Rene was silent for a while. "I couldn't have Lash going after Shaker for revenge," she said finally. "Besides, Kyle saw Shaker and would be able to identify him. So this was easiest."

It bothered me that she'd changed his memories so straightforwardly, but I told myself it was what was best, and to just let it go. "And the stuff you set up to help me deal with Shakers 'needs'?"

"Working fine," Rene said pleasantly. "And hopefully keeping you pure while not impacting Shaker's strength."

People are dying to feed a demon; does it matter that my hands aren't the ones doing the killing? Just leave that completely alone. Don't think about it. So I changed the topic instead to Devlin's odd desire to try potato salad. Rene and I were soon laughing as we rode though the forest.

* * * *

When we got back a little before dusk, Rene and I walked into Hayden to find Devlin waiting for us.

"Get packed," he said seriously. "We are leaving tonight for New Orleans."

Chapter Eighteen

Rene and I looked at each other. "Now?" I said. "You talked about in a year or two."

"I'm not going to put it off," Devlin said flatly. "Cain's death brought home to me how easily things change. I've already arranged for the rooms and chartered a flight. Please pack, Loves."

"Did you tell Venus?"

Devlin nodded. "She will be staying with Danial while we are gone, as will Ghost. Rip teleported them plus himself there a few minutes ago. Lash is already packed, and going over procedures with Kyle, who'll take over for him while we're gone."

I gave him a shocked look. "But I should have said good-bye to her, Dev. Venus is going to be upset."

"On the contrary, she was very excited, having not spent time with Danial since he moved out. I understand he had some presents for her. He's off from Solutions, Inc. for the next week anyway for the holidays, so this works out best. They'll have time together as uncle and niece."

That took care of my email work, too. Devlin had arranged for everything.

Rene took my hand, and guided me upstairs. "Do you not want to go?" she said curiously to me when we were alone. "You seem upset."

I got down my suitcase and reluctantly began packing, trying to sort out my feelings. "It's not that, Sister. I just don't handle spontaneous trips well. But maybe this is just what we need. God knows, I'd welcome some warm weather and good times. I'm already sick of winter."

"Then I'll go pack and meet you here in a few moments," she said excitedly.

I paused briefly to call my parents, and let them know that I was leaving town. They wished me a good vacation, and I promised to visit when I returned. I thought my mom could sense I didn't really want to go, but she didn't say anything. I continued packing, telling myself that a change of scenery was a good thing. Change was inevitable, like life; it was better to embrace it, and make every day count.

* * * *

To say we had fun on our first night in New Orleans would not be strong enough words for the experience. We had an absolute blast.

We arrived by private plane, and were driven by limo to our hotel, the Bourbon Orleans. It was absolutely beautiful, taking up almost an entire block of the French Quarter. And I was pleased to see our room had a view of Bourbon Street, which was already hopping at nine p.m.

I went to grab the bags, but Devlin motioned to Seth, and to Keith, and they took them, to the dismay of the bellboy. Devlin put one arm around me, and the other around Rene, and Lash trailed in last, looking around alertly.

"God, it's so beautiful," I whispered.

There were paintings of angels and clouds on the ceiling more than thirty feet above us. Everything was absolutely elegant, and beautiful. It reminded me strongly of that hotel in Switzerland where I'd stayed with Danial years ago.

"You'll find it under 'Dalcon', I believe," Devlin said, grinning at the hotel manager, even as he rubbed my shoulder.

"Yes," the manager fawned. "Please come this way."

We followed him to the room, which was really more a set of three suites, complete with balconies and sitting rooms.

I looked over at him, once we were all inside. "Devlin, how's this going to work?"

"Keith's team is to our left, and Seth's is to our right. We won't leave tonight until the other bears arrive." Seth and Keith grabbed their bags and left, the sound of their footsteps receding down the hall.

"Who else is coming?" Rene said liltingly, sitting on the edge of one of the beds.

Devlin was hanging up his clothes and didn't answer.

Lash was peering out the window toward Bourbon St. through a gap in the curtains "Ranger," he hissed to her. "Jazz. Jordan. Brett."

Rene seemed to be considering something. "Okay."

"Unpack, Loves," Devlin said as he continued to hang up suits, and shirts, not looking at us. "We have much to enjoy, and a good part of it will not be with wrinkled clothes."

I shrugged, but both Rene and I did as he said. I was a little worried to see that both Dev and Rene had brought many more dressy clothing than I had.

Lash had brought only one black suit, along with more than a few pairs of his normal black cotton shirts and jeans. "Aren't you going to be too hot, wearing all black?" I said, looking at him out of the corner of my eye. "Remember the Everglades?"

Lash snickered. "These are light shirts, Sweetness. I have a tank top or two, and some lightweight black pants. You forget; we won't be going out in the daytime for the most part."

I was dismayed to realize that, but didn't say anything, as it was too cruel to Devlin. "You're right. I didn't think."

"Don't worry about it, Sar," Devlin purred, sensing my mood. "Lash will likely want to take you by day to see some of what he remembers. So it's good you packed comfortable clothes, as that most likely means swamps and dives."

Lash shot him a reproachful glare. Dev smirked at him. Lash looked back at the street.

"Should we get dressed?" Rene offered. "I'm okay in here, but the air conditioning is on full blast. We need to put on lighter clothes if we are going out."

"Just to Bourbon Street tonight," Lash hissed, turning away from the blinds. "Tomorrow night we can explore further, but I want to walk around first and get an idea of how much has changed. I was last here decades ago."

"I'm already tired," I said, yawning. "I'm not going to last very long tonight. Be prepared to carry me home to bed, Tryst."

I expected Lash to say something sexual, but he didn't. I looked over to see why, and found him looking hard at Devlin, Devlin looking back in an arrogant way.

"What are the sleeping arrangements?" Lash hissed in a deadly voice. "I see one king size bed here, Dev."

"That is big enough for the four of us," Devlin said with a grin.

Lash swore angrily. "I asked you not to do this," he hissed flatly. "I told you, I can't sleep with that witch in the bed. I won't!"

"You can for a few days," Devlin said stubbornly. "And you will."

"I won't!"

"Stop, please," Rene said gently. "With money, all is possible. We'll just request another bed be brought in—"

"You'll still be right here next to me, Witch!" Lash hissed violently at her, his lips wrinkling back to bare his snake fangs. "Fuck, I'm going to have to sleep on the floor on the lower level to feel safe."

"Lash, enough!" Devlin said loudly. "Rene can be trusted, you know that. What is the problem?"

"I didn't come here for an orgy," Lash hissed angrily. "I have to be on my toes to watch our asses."

"Neither did we," Rene and I said in chorus. I looked over at her, and she at me. "But it makes sense," I continued, turning my attention back to Lash. "We're all together. I didn't think too much of it, but Rene's right, we're a lot more vulnerable here than we are at Hayden. If something were to happen, we'd be safest together, right?"

Lash looked at me for a split second, then back at Rene. He hissed again, baring his snake fangs. "I don't trust witches, I never have. I'm alive today because of that."

"You can trust me," Rene said calmly. "You know what I did for Devlin, that my brother was just as loyal, dying in his service. Nothing has changed." She gave him a questioning look. "Do you really think I mean to do something bad to you as you sleep?"

Lash gave her a long look. "I know of all that, your history with Devlin," he said more quietly, turning back to look outside again. "I'm not saying you aren't loyal to him. I'm saying I don't want to be in bed with you."

"Not even if we're just sleeping?"

"Not even if we're just sleeping. I nightmare sometimes and I'm not a heavy sleeper. You'll be going at it all hours with Dev, and I need my sleep."

"I'm not a heavy sleeper, either," Rene said apologetically, looking from Devlin to me to Lash. "Maybe I should sleep in another bed?"

"Enough already," I said, rubbing my eyes. God, we hadn't even fully unpacked, and we were already having trouble. "I'll sleep with Lash downstairs, after we request another bed. Rene and Devlin can sleep up here."

"I want to sleep with you, Oathed One," Devlin said stubbornly. "I want you and Rene near me. It will just be sleep, I promise—"

Yeah, right, like I believe that after seeing the bed. "Look, let's just try it tonight," I said flatly. "Please? We're all tired out from traveling. I'm exhausted."

"For tonight only," Devlin said grumpily.

I called the front desk, and they happily delivered us another bed, a blow-up type one. By the time it was made up and readied for us, we were all strained and on edge.

I was maybe pregnant, but I needed a glass of wine and to blow off some stress before trying to sleep. Therefore, Rene and I put on some lighter clothes, and together with Lash and Dev, we went down to Bourbon St.

It was loud, gaudy, and absolutely wonderful. The neon lights were flashing, tourists and locals were walking and drinking, and there were people in elaborate costumes, some hawking drinks, but others for no apparent reason. As we strolled, I saw there were stores that just sold condoms and others where dancers were just walking on the bars in their underwear. I was aroused to see in some of the bars, the dancers were all men.

Rene noticed too. "Come on," she said, beckoning. Devlin and I followed her in.

We had a drink, watching the dancers stroll back and forth, but didn't stay long. The male flesh was enticing, but Devlin was more attractive by far than these men in their underwear, even if they were younger. Besides Lash was sipping his drink leaning against the farthest wall nearest the door, he was so ill at ease.

By now, we'd all woken up a little, so nobody protested when Dev suggested we head down the street a little farther. We walked all the way down Bourbon to Jackson Square, and then on to Decatur. There was another bar there, a more upscale one. Though we got looks for Lash's untucked shirt and my handmade simple cotton dress, they let us in, and got us a seat at the bar.

"We'll have dinner tomorrow in the restaurant upstairs," Devlin said excitedly. "You can see the Mississippi from there, Loves." He kissed Rene's hand. "After, we'll go for a walk along the waterfront, and maybe take a ride on one of the riverboats."

"It will be good to smell the water again," Lash said sadly. "It's been many, many years since I have."

I took his hand, and kissed it gently. "Why so long?"

"I first got into my trade here," Lash hissed. "I had a good friend for many years when I lived here. He died."

"I'm sorry, Tryst."

Lash shook himself, and then kissed my hand, which still gripped his. "No, I'm sorry, Sweetness. I should be thinking of the future and our children, and instead I'm dwelling on shit that should be left in the past." He downed his drink. "Let the good times roll."

"Amen to that!" Devlin said, raising another glass. "To us, Lash and my Loves. To us being Oathed, and loving one another. To Sar and me, that we have another child on the way, or will soon. And to Lash and his mate, that they have one as well."

Was he saying it like that in case someone was listening? *Must be.* "To us!"

"To us," Rene said lovingly. "To Dev and I being together, when it seemed there was no chance of it happening. To Sar, who has become my sister. And to you and Dev, Lash, for you are brothers, even if you were born centuries apart."

We clinked our glasses together and drank.

I can't remember what we talked about. Lash told a few off-color jokes, and Rene did, too. We watched some of the people, guessing to each other who they were and how they'd come to be at this bar this night with us. We were all happy to be out in this exotic place that was so much different than home, to be smelling the scent of the river wafting through the open doors and windows on the night breeze. In a few hours, we'd drunk the two bottles of wine, most of the first bottle going to Rene.

It was one a.m. when we staggered home. Dev helped Rene upstairs after kissing me good night.

"Think they're going to have sex?" Lash hissed to me as we undressed.

"Are you saying that because you want us to?" I offered.

"I always want to," Lash hissed amorously. "But you're tired, so I'll wait until morning." He lay down near me, and I went to move closer. Then I stiffened, to see him laying his knife and whip beside the bed.

"Should I go upstairs?" I said pointedly. "I don't want to be injured my first night here."

"No," he murmured softly, kissing my forehead. "I haven't nightmared in weeks, Sweetness, that was just so I didn't have to sleep with Rene. I'm putting the whip before the knife, so I'd touch it first, if I reached for it in my sleep. Good as I might be with it, I couldn't use it with my eyes closed, especially not so close to you."

I looked at him dubiously. "You're sure?"

"Trust me," he hissed, cradling me close. "I won't hurt you."

* * * *

I awoke to realize I'd heard something. Then I remembered where I was, and decided it had just been a sound from outside on Bourbon, where the party was still going strong. I made my way to the bathroom in darkness, leaving Lash asleep.

I was just washing my hands when I heard a crash, then the sharp crack of a whip.

I ran frantically into the other room, and turned the light on. Lash was fighting with a large man, his knife at his feet. Another man was on the ground, but he was healing. He got to his feet, baring his fangs before he quickly attacked again.

I took a breath to scream for Dev, and a hand closed over my mouth, stifling it.

"Shh, little one," a gruff voice said. "Be quiet and watch."

I struggled hard, but the man held me easily. When I felt the prick of fangs against my throat, I went utterly motionless. "God, I'd love a taste of your blood," the vampire holding me hissed in longing, cool breath on my throat. "But it's my head if I take any. My master wants it all to himself."

201

Lash was opening wound after wound on his attacking vampire with every stroke of his whip, but it was still on its feet, darting after him, hissing, its fangs bared, healing almost as fast as he hurt it. The other vampire was circling him, Lash's knife clutched in one hand, ready to strike at the first opening.

Suddenly, Lash wrapped his whip around a huge painting with a snap of his wrist, and pulled it down. It splintered over the armed vampire's head, knocking him down, though it didn't let go of the knife. Lash was on him, a shattered table leg in his hand. With a snarling hiss, he drove it into the vampire's chest, even as the other grabbed hold of him. The staked vampire let out a breath to scream and dropped the knife, even as Lash turned to punch the other vampire in the teeth, breaking one of his fangs.

The staked vampire was trying with blood-slick hands to pull out the stake, but Lash decapitated him with a blow to the throat with his blade, severing his head, blood spurting out. Lash cleaned his knife on the dead vampire's clothes, and got to his feet, still only in his underwear. The broken fang vampire backed away, until he was in front of the one holding me.

Lash advanced slowly. "You bastards," he hissed menacingly. "Come over here."

"Come and get me, Lash," the vampire holding me hissed. "And see what happens!"

Lash started for us, but another vampire erupted from the shadows, grabbing hold of him. I watched in fear as it sank its fangs into his neck and began to drink. Lash snarled in pain, bared his own fangs, and sank them into the vampire's hand. The feeding vampire tore his fangs out of Lash with a scream and tried to pull away, fighting hard as he began to shake. Lash shoved backward into him, knocking them both to the floor and kept biting for another few seconds before he abruptly let go.

Lash sprang to his feet and stalked toward us. The bitten vampire stayed down, now convulsing.

"So it's true!" the vampire in front of me said incredulously. "Your poison can affect our kind."

"You want some of that?" Lash hissed in fury. "You're getting some either way, Fuckface. Let her go. I'll give you a head start, if you let her go now."

The vampires both hissed, backing away with me towards the door as Lash advanced. Abruptly, the vampire holding me let go and began convulsing. He fell to the floor, his back bent almost double as he screeched his lungs out. With a deafening crackle of energy, the vampire in front of us also went to his knees, his hair alight at the ends, his eyes melting as he scrabbled at them with his fingers, unseeing.

Rene was behind me, sparks of energy still running through her hands. "He's dead," she said calmly. "They both are. A few more jerks, and that'll be it. Are you okay, Sister?"

"She's fine. Is Devlin safe?" Lash hissed, coiling his whip.

"Sure," Rene said sarcastically, releasing her magical power and folding her arms across her chest. "But only because I killed the three vampires that came for him, with his help on the last one."

Lash looked at her, then away. "Son of a bitch. Thanks," he said gruffly.

"You're welcome," Rene said genteelly. "But I think this has demonstrated that we need to rest together after the sex is done each day."

"It did," Lash said curtly. "But it also demonstrated our guards are useless! Where the fuck were the bears?"

"I'll go and see." Rene disappeared.

Lash and I walked up to a pacing Devlin, who was already on his phone.

"I was attacked here, Jake," Devlin shouted. "I've been here less than a night in your territory and been attacked! By vampires, no less!" He paused. "Don't give me shit that these were young ones newly turned. They were over fifty years, all of them!"

"They weren't mine!" a sturdy Southern voice yelled from the receiver. "I tell you—"

"I don't care if they were yours!" Dev continued. "I'm here on vacation, and I'll hold you responsible if I am disturbed again. Find out whose they were, and where they came from! Or you'll be replaced as head of this state!"

He threw down his phone, grating his fangs, and saw me. A moment later, I was in his arms. "Are you okay?" he said urgently. "Where is

Rene? I sent her to see if you were okay."

"The bears were not aware anything had happened," Rene said, appearing in our midst. "No one is. No one heard anything."

"Sound like a dampening spell?" Lash asked her.

Rene nodded. "I'd bet yes. That means these weren't just vampires out for a feeding on tourists. They had magical help, Dev."

"Tell me you don't believe that random feeding was even an option?" Lash said sarcastically. "This was an assassination attempt, pure and simple."

"They were here for me and for Sar," Devlin said angrily, throwing the body of a partly charred dead vampire against the wall to land on the floor. "They knew we were here. They even knew we'd be sleeping separately."

"Spies in the hotel," Rene said musingly.

"Or on the streets or in a lot of other places," Lash hissed reluctantly. "There's always someone willing to sell out for money."

"Titus will be here shortly to collect the bodies," Rene said. "He has use for them."

Don't think about what use, Sar. "Listen, I'm exhausted. I'm going back to sleep. As long as we're all safe, we can talk about all this tomorrow night." I lay down in the big bed, and before long, the others had all lain down, too. Devlin was near me, with Rene on his other side, and Lash on my other side. We were all tense at first, but eventually we slept. I didn't hear Titus come for the bodies at all.

When I awoke, it was early afternoon. A shattered lamp confirmed that last night had happened, but that all the actual blood and other nastiness was no longer present. *Whew.*

Devlin was on my chest sleeping. I shook him awake. "Where are Lash and Rene?"

"Lash is out looking around," Devlin said, stifling a yawn. "He wanted to walk the nearby streets. Some of it is to make sure we have escape routes, and some to make sure things are where he remembers them. But more than a little is because he is remembering being here long ago, and he needs some time to be alone with those memories, to work through them."

"Who was the friend of his that died?" I asked.

"His name was Abraham," Devlin said, after a moment. "He was a good vampire and a good man, one of the rare beings that can be both. His only fault was he had no ambition, and couldn't understand that desire in others. A hunter killed him long ago."

One of Peter's family, probably, or Hector's. "Was he Lash's best friend? I saw his headstone in your cemetery."

"Abraham's remains are not there, but in another spot here that Lash alone knows the location of. I put the marker in my cemetery long ago for him, as Lash couldn't come here himself for a long time."

"Why not?" Something was making me uneasy about this.

"He had enemies," Devlin said shortly. "Leave it at that, Love. This is disagreeable business to speak of in the morning. We are on vacation."

He has a point. "So what are the plans for this evening?"

"Rene is visiting a few local witches for magical supplies, as she said she wants to be ready for anything. She said she'll be back a little before dark at the latest. Our bears are here in force now, twelve of them. Four are below in this room, keeping watch, with the other four on either side in their rooms resting. Some will go out with us tonight when we go, and some will stay here in our room on the lower level."

"That's a relief."

"The state Ruler, Jake, has said he will put some guards of his own here for the duration of our stay. They are jaguar and will not get along with Lash, so be prepared."

I made a face. "Are we going out tonight?"

"Dinner reservations have been made, yes. We will see some of the sights and visit the local famous spots."

"Are you going to take me for a carriage ride?" I'd seen the carriages last night waiting for passengers in a line in front of Jackson square. "I'd like that."

Devlin nodded. "Of course, though Lash will have to stay behind. You know his feelings on horses."

"I know," I acquiesced, yawning.

"So are you in the mood?" Devlin said lightly, running his fangs over me. "You know I am."

I hadn't been, but it was remarkable how quickly perception could change in the space of a few touches. And some was I wanted sheer escape from everything. "Maybe. I might need a little persuasion."

"I'm a master of persuasion," Devlin purred, moving me beneath him. "And here's my first large motivating reason for your cooperation."

Chapter Nineteen

We lay entwined after, tangled in the sheets, breathing hard.

"That was great." Devlin sighed. He gave me a kiss, and then propped himself up on one arm to look at me. "I need to ask you something, Oathed One."

There was an odd note in his words. *He doesn't want to say whatever he's going to tell me.* "What is it?"

"I think we should not be intimate again this vacation," Devlin said regretfully. "As we just were, I mean. I do not want to risk the children, Love, just in case there are any. I remember what Camlyn said last time, that it was me who caused trouble."

I looked at him in shock, then resentment flooded me. "Why didn't we wait to go away together then?" I said abruptly. "You told me the point of taking this trip was you wanted time for you and me. If we're only going to have sex with other people during it, we should've waited, Devlin."

"I wanted to be here with you in this city," Devlin said seriously. "To see your face as I show you its beauty and charm. Do not confuse sex with love, Sar. Do not think I want or love you any less because I'm intimate with Rene. I believe you love me despite you are mated to Lash and having his child. It is my love for you and our child that is making me put your safety and wellbeing in front of my desire for you. Tell me you understand that."

What he said made sense from his actions and what I knew of his personal beliefs. However, the values and logic of human world I'd lived in most of my life contrasted sharply. I told myself that I'd bought into being with both he and Lash, that it could work if we all tried hard. If he, Rene, Lash and I were okay with the terms of our relationship and the

Oaths we'd said, wasn't that all that mattered?

Normal human ethics had only one answer to that question, a resounding no. But this was my relationship. The decisions of what was acceptable and not acceptable was up to me, not anyone else. Here and now, I told myself the answer was yes.

"I know that," I answered him. "It's just my sense of morality telling me this is wrong. And yes, I agree that this is the best decision, Dev."

Devlin laughed. "It's immoral to be happy? To be with men that love you, just because there are two of them and not one? To be having children that you and they want very much?"

"All that, and to have another woman being intimate also with one of the men."

Devlin laughed again. "Why? No one is sneaking around, Sar."

"But is Rene as happy about all this as she says she is?" I asked him bluntly. "Sometimes she seems too good to be true." *And the bigger question: can I trust her to help me with Danial and Theo, if Danial does force us to comply with his wishes for a threesome?*

"Her actions are altruistic," Devlin replied. "I myself have never understood that about her. She was the same with Anna and I all those years ago; not acting as more than my friend until I offered more than friendship, even though she'd loved me all along." He pushed golden hair out of his shining eyes. "But she isn't missing out, Love. She has my love, my Oath, and anything she asks me for within reason is hers. What more could any woman desire?"

What indeed. I held in my snort, but just barely. "To be the only one that has those things, Dev. To not have to share you."

"She is not from your time, Love," Devlin answered, kissing my forehead gently. "She is not even of your race. You must have deduced by now that she does not have your morality, or your ethics, just as Lash and I do not."

Now was not the time to tell him how much that fact sometimes bothered me. "I have."

"Then logically you can't judge her by human standards. Know this: of all the men and women that have ever served me, she could be called the most loyal, save Lash. Even then, I have to admit it would be a tie. She means none of us any harm. She protected us all last night."

Hmm. True. "So are you saying that faeries are loyal, but loose?"

Devlin looked at me aghast, and then burst out laughing. "Well put!" he said, baring his fangs. "Yes, that is fair to say. But the truth is most faeries are not loyal either, save to themselves. You saw firsthand what Leri did: try to kill her own child when it interfered with her plans. That is often the norm, and the reason why faeries are rare. Rene is more the exception than the rule, just as Titus is for demonkind."

"His brothers don't seem that bad." Shit, why had I gone and said that?

"Don't be fooled," Devlin said, his smile fading. "Shaker is pure demon. He would've taken Rene to Hell, and torn her soul to shreds. He'd do the same to you, if he had your soul."

Shiver. "What makes Titus and Rip different?" I said quickly, trying to get off the subject of Shaker before he heard me thinking of him and broke into my mind.

"They just are, Love. But enough talk. Let's shower and get dressed. Rene and Lash will both be back shortly.

I shrugged, and got up.

We were just getting out of the shower when Lash came in. He was dusty and soaked in sweat, carrying extremely muddy shoes in one hand.

"Were you catching fish?" Devlin asked, throwing him a towel.

"No," Lash said as he deftly caught it in his free hand. "I was looking at the levees that were built after Katrina, specifically the one closest to us."

"And?"

"And it looks okay, but only if a strong hurricane doesn't come up against it," he muttered, stripping off his shirt. "Fucking government. You wouldn't believe how much is still devastated, Dev."

"I'd believe it," Devlin said in an old voice. "Bonaparte left wreckage behind him after his wars in France that was being cleaned up over a decade later. The World Wars were even worse."

"I know, I was there the second time around," Lash hissed irritably, stripping off the rest of his clothes, and putting them into a bag. Rene now teleported them home daily for washing, as Lash was worried about someone dosing the material with poison.

Watching him, I thought again how dumb it was that we'd bothered packing so much if Rene was going to make daily trips home. Then it clicked in my brain what Lash had said. "You fought in World War II?"

"Yes," Lash said curtly. "It wasn't a good time, Mate."

He's using official titles. Cue to drop it. "Did you have a good day checking out the sights?"

"No," Lash hissed curtly. "I need to shower." He went in and slammed the door hard. A second later, water began to run.

"Make it a fast one," Devlin called.

I looked over at Devlin. "What's wrong now?"

"Things he cared about and remembered are likely gone," Dev whispered. "The Quarter is a lot more commercial than it was in his time, and much has changed no doubt on Canal St., and also in the surrounding areas. The hurricane here just added to that. It upsets him."

"Then why did we come?" I whispered back. "This was supposed to be partly for him, so he could be happy."

"He will be, once we are out drinking," Dev said reassuringly. "And once he takes you by day to the swamp. The changes there have been small next to the changes to this city."

I tried not to cringe. Seeing pictures of huge trees sunken in water and lush moss was one thing. Being ankle deep in brackish water was another. "When are we going?"

"Tomorrow," Lash hissed, coming out of the bathroom with a towel around his waist, dripping water. "I arranged a guide for us to take us out in a boat to some land. We'll have a picnic." He began to towel himself dry.

"Am I invited?" Rene quipped, walking into the room. She had on a long pink dress of some light material. The scoop neck was so low I expected to see her breasts pop out of it.

Lash's eyes weren't on her face as he made his reply. "Why would you want to go?" he hissed curiously.

"I don't," she said kindly. "I was just seeing what you'd say."

"Good, because you aren't invited," Lash said with a sneer. "I need time alone with my mate."

"And I with my Oathed One," Rene said lustily. She gave Dev a big kiss.

He kissed her, and then pushed her gently away. "We have to get going, or we'll be late," Devlin said apologetically. "But we'll pick this up later, Love."

"It's a plan," Rene said, winking.

By this time, Lash had on his black clothes, and I'd donned a low cut billowy dress of a sea green color with a wide skirt.

Lash leaned over and kissed the tops of my breasts. "I'll see you both later," he hissed lustily. I gave him a shove, and he laughed.

That night was wonderful. We had a gourmet dinner with a few bottles of wine. After a scrumptious dessert, we walked along the riverbank. The night was balmy, and the Riverwalk was crowded enough I wasn't worried about Lash killing any would-be muggers.

We got on a riverboat near Canal. For a while, we drifted up the river, looking at the lights of the city and the black moving water of the Mississippi.

By the time we got back to the hotel, it was three a.m. Despite Lash's ardor-filled looks, I told him he had to wait until tomorrow.

* * * *

Our picnic the next day was better than I'd hoped. The sky was blue, the air was fresh, and the swamp smelled green and mossy.

Our guide was a middle-aged man in a funny looking hat with fish jigs hooked in it. He had a small dog with him who yapped a lot called Bruiser. Within ten minutes, we'd arrived at a nice sunny spot of dry land within the swamp. He dropped us off, saying he'd return in five hours. For the next three hours, we lay there sunbathing as snakes, dozing in the stillness of the swamp, swatting at the occasional mosquito with our tails.

The only bad point was that Lash insisted on going hunting. He changed back to human form, dressed and headed off with his knife. When he came back fifteen minutes later with a dead alligator, I was more sickened than proud of him. But I was a lot sicker when he told me he wanted me to eat some with him.

"Now? I'm um, back in human form." Plus the mosquitoes were really beginning to bother me.

"No, Sweetness, we'll eat it later. You can teleport it home. Skinning and dressing should only take a few moments. Just take it to

Titus; he's expecting it. I'll cut it up later."

I didn't want to touch it, much less consume or wear it. "Why?"

"I want my child to eat some of this, like I did when I was young. We can have it as our first meal as a family. I think I remember the recipe well enough. I'll make him some boots or something out of the skin, when he gets older."

Telling him I didn't want to seemed wrong. He was clearly excited about this. Maybe it was some weresnake ritual. "Okay. But you have to leave the head and feet here and roll up the skin gross side in."

Lash gave me an odd look as he began to skin it. "It died fast," he said seriously. "I stabbed it in the heart, Sar. It didn't suffer. It's a male, it had no young."

"Okay," I said, trying to make the best of it. "I'm sure our baby will appreciate it."

"He'll be snake, he'll like it." Lash cut up the carcass in record time, and then packaged the chunks in large plastic bags he'd brought with him. Then he rolled up the skin. "Here. It will be good to taste gator again. Leave it with Titus; he can finish the skin for us."

I nodded, trying hard to look like I was eager to try it. I teleported fast to Titus's home, where he was playing with Sunrise.

"I know," he rumbled before I had a chance to speak. "I've been expecting this. I'll take care of it, Sar."

With a grateful look, I hand the alligator parts to him and disappeared.

Later that night, the four of us again went out to dinner, enjoying some very spicy pasta. It was a great night, if an early one. Rene and Devlin had been awake the whole day, and they were as tired as we were. We were all sleeping by ten p.m.

The next morning, Devlin shook me awake. "Wake up, Loves."

"What is it?" Rene said, her eyes bleary.

"I must go speak with Jake," Devlin said, annoyed. "He caught a vampire who says he knows who behind the attack two nights ago."

"I should go," Rene said, trying to get to her feet and still yawn. "Lash should stay here with Sar."

I looked over to see Lash sitting in a hotel robe in the chair, looking at a few maps of Louisiana

"Titus is going with me," Devlin said, gently pushing Rene back down. "Sleep, Love. Lash will stay here, and watch over you both. Tonight we'll go out for New Year's Eve."

"Aren't you worried about more attacks?" I said, shaking my head as I tried to get the sleep out of it.

"No," Devlin said, grinning. "Titus has all defenses maxed to the limit of what can be done. Besides, the bears and Lash will be enough to defend you and Rene."

"As if I needed defense," Rene said, and then colored, shooting me a guilty look.

"It's okay," I said, very offended. "You're right; I'm the one liability here."

"You're my Mate," Lash hissed proudly. "It's my privilege to defend you and our young. I'll be right back, I need a quick shower. I didn't get more than a quick rinse yesterday."

He shed his robe right there and walked off into the bathroom in the nude, the snake on his back seeming to slither as his back muscles knotted and released. I admired his form until he shut the door, and then turned my attention back to Devlin, who was making irritated noises as he viewed his emails on his phone.

"I'll be back at dusk or so," Devlin said, as Titus appeared. "Don't go anywhere without Lash, either of you." He blew me a kiss, and then they disappeared.

Rene excused herself to go shower in the bears' quarters. I gave a passing thought to whether she would be showering with some of them, then told myself I was being ridiculous and went in to shower with Lash. By the time I got in there, he was done and I ended up showering alone. When I came out dressed, Lash was laying on the bed looking at me with a big grin.

"We got new sheets, I see."

"The maid got here just in time," he hissed meaningfully.

"Something on your mind?" I said teasingly

"You know what on my mind." His grin widened. "It's been days, Sweetness."

I let out a laugh at his eagerness. "Now? What if Rene comes back?"

"She can watch," he said, baring his fangs. "I don't care."

213

I cared, at least I thought I did. "I could teleport us home, if you wanted some privacy."

"What I want is you," Lash hissed hungrily. "Come here, Love. I can't wait any longer."

"Can't wait for what?" Rene said from downstairs. She walked up the stairs, saw us, and laughed a little. "Ah. I see what."

I blushed, but Lash answered her. "To be in her, Witch. That blunt enough for you?"

"Do you want me to leave?" Rene said, looking at him steadily.

"I don't know," Lash hissed dangerously, sliding to his feet in a sinuous motion. "Are you the voyeur Dev is? I wouldn't want you to miss getting off by watching us."

"I don't get off by watching," she answered coolly. "I get off by having someone get me off."

"Then sadly you're out of luck," Lash hissed, as he placed his whip and knife beside the bed and begin to undo his belt. "I'm mated."

"I'm part of that," Rene said evocatively.

The first real stirrings of jealousy ran through me. *Is this why she'd wanted to share the same Oath? Was this about him, and not Theo?*

"No, you aren't," Lash hissed. "Dev can do what he likes with you, you're his Oathed One. I gave my word to Sar." He pulled off his shirt. "And that's that."

Not for me it wasn't. "Why do you want to be with him, Rene?" I said pointedly, my tone razor sharp. "Because you know how good he is?"

"With all respect to you, Lash, no," Rene said, sitting on the bed. "But I thought about what happened with the vampires that went for Devlin last night. He thinks they came for him." She paused. "But I think they came for Lash."

Lash whipped his head around and looked at her. "Why would you think that?"

"Because Devlin was right, they knew our sleeping arrangements. There were only three that came for Devlin, and four at least that came for Lash. They didn't expect me to be there, which is why I overwhelmed them so easily."

"More always come for me, that's normal," Lash hissed flatly. "I fall, Devlin's a much easier target, so—"

"But they knew where to find Sar, that she'd be with you and not Dev. So someone knows what she means to you, Lash. That means someone suspects she's your mate. So they might know she's possibly pregnant."

"That they knew she was with me doesn't mean anyone knows anything. I could've been guarding her for Dev while he got it on with you."

"They meant to take her with them last night, Lash, and it had nothing to do with Devlin. It had to do with you."

"Did you foresee something?" Lash hissed in a deadly voice. "Say right now if you did. Because unless you have more to go on, there isn't enough for me to believe this was anything more than an assassination attempt."

Rene looked away. "I see them trying again before we leave, Lash, though I don't recognize the place I see. But it is you being attacked, not Devlin."

"Is he hurt?" I said quickly. "Tell me!"

"He's hurt, but he lives," Rene said darkly. "I don't see if someone comes for you, Sar. I'd rather do what we could to make whoever comes for Lash's mate come for me instead."

Lash was eyeing her. "If we can trust your vision, you have a point," he said finally. "But that makes no sense. No one comes after me anymore, Rene. No one."

"Someone does now," she said, not backing down. "And they also come after those you love. Do you want Sar in their crosshairs or me?"

"You," Lash hissed emphatically, his eyes boring into hers. "I want her safe, Rene, no matter what I have to do. No matter who else has to get hurt, even if it's you."

Okay, this has gone on long enough. "How are you going to make this believable?"

"If I go out tonight smelling of sex with Lash, it will be believed," Rene said. "So do we have your permission, Sister?"

Chapter Twenty

I stared at her, a flush suffusing my face. "Answer me, is this really about deceiving attackers, Rene? Because I have a problem if you are going to—"

I cut off abruptly, unwilling to speak "share all of my lovers," as that was exactly what she might have to do with Theo and Danial. For them, I'd been willing enough to let her go in my place. But this was different: this was Lash. I didn't want to share him with anyone, ever.

Rene gave me an odd look. "This is not about anything but protecting you for Devlin and keeping you alive and healthy."

"Thanks for making me feel fucking wanted," Lash hissed sarcastically at her. He folded his arms across his chest and looked over to me. "Finish your thought, Sweetness. You have a problem if Rene is going to what? Enjoy me?"

"Going to be with you on a regular basis."

"I'm not," Rene said, just as Lash spat out the words, "She's not."

Convincing. Sure. "Give me your word, both of you."

"You have it," Lash hissed.

"No," Rene said.

We both gaped at her.

"I don't give my word if I can't keep it," Rene said coolly. "This isn't about emotions. There may come a time this might be necessary to do again, before you give birth or after."

"My word will be enough," Lash hissed, coming over and hugging me. "Because this is the last trip we're taking, Sweetness, until you have our child. No more deception will be necessary. And if we need this kind of deception again, we'll find another way with magic." He turned to Rene. "Speaking of that, are you sure there isn't another way to fake this with magic right now?"

"Not likely," Rene said, laughing. "We faeries invented magic, at least, the first pure form of it. As a rule, we never use magic to forgo sex when there's another more enjoyable option."

Her lust for him was unmistakable. My jealousy thickened into heavy clay. "Then go ahead," I said stiffly. "I'll leave."

"Stay, please, Mate," Lash hissed quickly. "I wanted to bed you and I still want to."

"Sar, please stay," Rene said apologetically. "Know that I'd try to fake it, if there was another way that'd get the job done. But there isn't, and we can't risk your life on a cheap trick."

She's right. I remembered the sound dampening spell that had been put on the room. Even if there was some way to fake the scent of Lash on her skin, that deception might be uncovered easily if our enemies had someone as knowledgeable as she was working for them. The real thing couldn't be anything but what it was.

Shit, this is exactly what I'd told Devlin wasn't going to happen with him. But this wouldn't be an orgy: Lash wasn't going to do exotic stuff; he never went in for that. I'd been in bed with two men before. Was it so different, being in bed with a woman and a man? My moral code was saying it was a lot different. But the voyeur part of me was excited, too. "Okay."

Rene was already naked by this time. She waited for us, reclining on the bed. I was a little jealous of her curvaceous yet still slender form, but not like I had been in September. Some of that was because in the last few months she'd put on weight, and we weren't that different now. *Has to be all that Godiva chocolate Dev was always buying for us...*

I got out of my clothes, and lay down beside her, giving her an uneasy look.

She looked back at me curiously. "What?"

"I'm not a lesbian," I said awkwardly. "I like you, but—"

"I'm not going to do to you anything Devlin and Lash don't do to one another," Rene said, stifling a giggle. "Fair?"

"Super," I said in relief.

Lash had pulled off his shoes and socks, and was standing at the foot of the bed, stripping off his jeans. "So what do you like, Rene?"

If it'd been just he and I, I'd have been reaching for him or saying provocative things. Instead, I was embarrassed and self-conscious.

"I like most anything," Rene said easily, watching him lustily. "I don't like a lot of pain, but anything else is okay."

"I'm not into giving pain." He rearranged his weapons beside the bed. "You mind if I bite you, and drink your blood? It'll be during the sex."

Rene laughed, and then choked off when she saw he was serious. "I guess not," she said cautiously. "Will it hurt?"

"Sar says it doesn't, as my fangs are smaller than a vampire's," Lash said, slipping off his underwear. "But tell me if it does, and I'll stop. Same goes for anything else I do to you. Okay?"

"Okay."

"Good. Join in when you're ready." Lash crawled onto the bed, and took me in his arms, his tongue winding around mine as he kissed me passionately. Abruptly he arched his back and jerked, letting out a cry.

I looked down to see Rene moving on him, her mouth wrapped around his cock as she massaged his balls in her hand.

"Oh fuck!" Lash moaned. "Oh God. Oh damn, that feels so good! Ahh!"

Rene moved on him faster, and he began to let out cry after cry, grabbing hold of the bedcovers with his clenched hands. Seeing him so aroused, I switched from feeling weird to being completely into it.

"How does that feel, lover?" I said, kissing up Lash's neck, feeling his heart racing under my hands. "It feels good, doesn't?"

"Fuck, yes!" Lash shouted. "Suck me, suck me! Oh! Oh Fuck! Fuck!"

Lash shoved up as he came and Rene swallowed him down.

He pushed her back from him gently as he finished, and then lifted me to straddle him, letting out a grunt of pleasure as he slid inside. He kissed me over and over as he moved in me, going as deep as he could.

"Take me," I whispered greedily. God, he felt so good, his hard chest beneath my fingers, his strong hands gripping my hips as he rocked me on him, his swollen shaft inside me to the quick.

Lash smirked up at me, and thrust harder, even as his form shifted, his scales rippling out of him to cover his chest, his teeth melting away to be replaced by his hooked fangs. He pulled me closer to him, his arms holding me tight, one hand still moving my hips skillfully on his. "Sar," he hissed lustily in my ear. "Ride me, Sar."

I leaned in and whispered "Bite me."

Lash kissed my neck, and then sank his fangs in, sucking at the wound. I rocked harder on him, reaching for my orgasm that was building beneath me like a bonfire.

I came in moments, gasping, and then Lash lifted me off him gently, to lay me beside him. Rene moved to climb on him, but he sat up, grabbed her legs, and flipped her onto her back, flattening her down to the bed with one hand. Then I saw him part her legs and dip his head.

Rene got a look of fear on her face when she felt the brush of his fangs on her inner thighs. Then her features went slack with pleasure when he began moving in rhythm. Soon she was groaning, moaning loudly as he stroked her with his dexterous tongue. She came screaming a few moments later, her hands pulling his hair.

Lash eased her limp body back on the bed, and then came to me. With eagerness I felt him begin to stroke me with his tongue, slipping inside to touch me as only he could. When I came moments later, I was shouting and screaming, too.

As I lay gasping, Lash gave my belly a final kiss, and then crawled up to Rene, thrusting into her on one motion that brought a sharp cry from her throat. She wrapped her legs around him, groaning as he began to move in rhythm.

"Stroke me," she whispered. "God, you're big!"

"I am, for a snake," Lash hissed lustily. "But you'll adjust."

"God, you feel good, Lash… Ah!"

"Shh," he hissed, thrusting into her very hard, so she let out another sharp cry. "Less talking and more moaning." He began to thrust into her deeply, bringing groans of ecstasy from her throat.

"Let me ride you," she moaned, full of need. "Please, I want to—"

Lash wrapped his arms around her, and sinuously rolled onto his back, still thrusting. Rene groaned as she began riding him, and Lash let out a sharp hiss, arching beneath her as she squeezed him. He reached up and grabbed her breasts, bringing the left one to his mouth, and Rene let out a cry, her hands cradling his head as her movements became more frenzied. Lash hissed excitedly, clamped his hands on her hips, and began moving her on him vigorously; letting out grunts of pleasure every time he slid home. In a minute, Rene let out a long scream of pleasure as she came, begging Lash not to stop, and yelling for her Goddess. As her orgasm ebbed, Lash let out another hiss, flipped her over on her stomach, and then he covered her body with his, pushing into her as fast and deep as he could. He quickened his movements, and a few moments later, he came again, sinking his fangs into her shoulder as she let out a jagged cry. He held her struggling form tightly as he finished coming, sucking gently. After, he took his mouth off her, and leaned in close to whisper, "You okay?"

"Yes," she said, her breath coming in gasps. "That was great."

He moved off her. "Get your breath." He rolled onto his back, and beckoned to me. "Come here, Sweetness."

The afternoon moved on deliciously. Lash alternated being with one of us to the other, over and over. But though he pleasured us the same, he made sure to come only in her. He also showed no signs of getting soft.

After two hours, even with taking turns, I was a little scared, slightly abraded, and utterly exhausted. "I'm used up," I said gently, stopping him from entering me. "I need to rest."

Lash gave me a gentle kiss on the cheek. "Rest then, Sweetness. I love you." He turned to Rene. "Do you want me to stop?"

"No," Rene said hoarsely, her chest still heaving from her last orgasm. "But you can if you want to. I wouldn't want to tire you out."

"Do I look like I'm tired?" Lash hissed raucously and laughed. "Lie back and spread 'em, Woman."

I dozed off as he began to move again on her.

I awoke, feeling someone gently hugging me in strong arms. I looked up with sleep-filled eyes to see it was Lash.

"Were you dreaming good dreams?" he said, very sated. "You looked incredibly peaceful."

"I'm feeling rested. And you?"

"Satiated," he hissed happily. "Are you? It's been a long while since I had two women at once. I think I performed well for not being in practice."

"I thought you might have done this before," I said hesitantly. "You made me feel, um…you made sure…"

"That through it all you felt involved and appreciated," Lash finished for me, giving me a squeeze. "There's no point to trying something like this if someone feels excluded or less important." He paused. "I'm glad you liked it, Sweetness. Rene seemed to as well, before she passed out."

I looked over to see Rene laying on the other side of Lash's chest, dead to the world, her head lying on his shoulder.

"She just went limp," Lash said, pride dripping from his words. "I told her we should stop after twenty, but she was having too much fun."

I gave him a look of reproach.

"She's lover to Devlin," Lash said defensively. "I thought she could take it, when she said she could. Besides," he added, "A man likes to be remembered. Stamina might be the only thing I have over Devlin. Well, that and my nimble tongue."

I snickered, enjoying the naughtiness in discussing this. "Will she be able to walk?"

"Can't say," Lash said, grinning widely.

"You're bad," I said, nestling down into his chest. "Bad to the bone."

"I'm good," he said proudly. "She said I was. And if I remember right, you did, too. I—"

I fell asleep before he finished his thought.

I awoke to a gentle kiss. Again, I looked up to see Lash.

"Good night," he hissed. "We should get up and get dressed. I'm starving. Can you move?"

"Can you?" I teased.

"I awoke with two warm gorgeous females asleep on my chest smelling of me," Lash hissed in utter happiness. "I can do anything, because I've died and gone to Heaven."

Seeing him so utterly happy, I made a snap decision. "Sweetness, if you want, we can do this again. I won't be angry, if—"

"No," he hissed softly. "This was a one time thing. I enjoyed it, Mate, and I'm glad you liked it. I'm not Devlin, to want more than one female at a time. Besides, I'd rather have sex with just you."

My jealousy disappeared as if it had never been. "You're sure?"

"I'm sure," he said, kissing me on the cheek. "I've had many women, Sar. Too many to remember even half their names, or even accurately count. And it was fun. But it was never what I wanted." He gave me a tender look. "Believe me when I say that I'd have been happy meeting you when I was young, getting mated, and never being with anyone else. If I wanted any more of that shit, or thought I couldn't do without it, I'd never have told you I'd be your mate. You get that, don't you?"

"I do." I gave him a gentle kiss.

Devlin opened the door and came in, Titus behind him.

"Hi," Lash hissed slyly, folding his arms behind his head, looking like the cat that ate the cream. "And how was *your* day?"

"You snake in the grass!" Devlin said jealously. "Here I am, working hard to find out who's behind the attack last night, and you're here enjoying yourself!"

"I've got to go," Titus said, trying hard not to look at Rene, who was just blinking her eyes in wakefulness. "Bye, Sar."

I had the good moral sense to feel appalled. "Goodbye, Titus—"

The door closed before I finished saying his name.

Devlin rolled his eyes. "You wouldn't think he was a demon," he muttered. "If I didn't know Leri's appetites firsthand, I'd think he was celibate."

Rene shot him a mortified look, and then just rolled her eyes.

"So tell me what you learned," Lash said, already buckling on his weapons. Somehow, he already had his jeans on, too.

"Jake did catch a vampire, but he knew almost nothing. He was paid to keep watch for the vampires who attacked last night. He says he was the only one who got away. From the descriptions and other information he gave, I believe him. He said one of the ones we killed arranged everything, so he had no idea who was behind it."

"Did Jake agree to give him over?" Lash hissed, buttoning his shirt. "I may be able to persuade him to remember more."

"Titus did a truth spell," Devlin said dejectedly, flinging himself down in a chair. "He was telling the truth, Lash. Jake disposed of him. So we're back to square one."

"Not entirely," Rene said as she finished buttoning her dress. "We made a plan."

I realized I was the only one still undressed. Blushing, I grabbed for my discarded clothes. I finished dressing as Rene explained to Devlin our plan to make whomever was after Lash think she was his mate.

"It's a good plan," Devlin said slowly, his golden eyes focused on her. "But tell me the truth right now, Oathed One: did you foresee this attack? Is this why you made me ask the same Oath of you that I made with Sar, to ensure you'd be able to divert our pursuers in just this way?"

"I didn't need to foresee anything!" Rene said scathingly. "It was sound reason that once it was known you loved someone, people would target that woman. That the woman also happens to be Lash's mate just makes Sarelle that much more in danger. To have another woman who looks similar who is also intimate with you gives them two targets instead of one." Rene held up her hand, and blue fire ignited from her palm, burning furiously. "And a place for a guard to hide in plain sight."

Devlin grabbed hold of Rene forcefully. There was nothing of anger in his touch, more desperation. "Why do you help me?" he whispered to her, his eyes tortured. "Why are you so loyal? I know I'm not a good man. Hell, maybe not even what most would call a good vampire. You say you love me. If you love me, tell me, Rene."

Rene arched one delicate brow. "Lash helps you, and is loyal."

"I know his reasons," Devlin said, deadly serious. "I understand them, all of them. I don't understand yours. I never have, Rene."

"That's because I have only the one: I love you," Rene said chidingly. "For one who's professed his love in verse a billion times, your understanding of the concept seems very limited."

Lash let out a snicker, and then cleared his throat when Devlin shot him a nasty look.

"You've killed people for me," Devlin said brutally. "You've let me kill people, innocent people! Is that love—?"

"Stop!" Rene said harshly, shooting a worried look at me. "Leave the past in the past, Dev. And stop trying to make me into some kind of saint, because I'm not. You'd better believe that if I didn't love you, I'd never have given you so much as the time of day, much less everything I have. If I hadn't dreamed of you, I'd have sent you away the first time you asked for my help." She traced his cheek gently. "But I did and we're here together. Now let's get back to figuring out a plan. We're wasting night."

"She's right," Lash hissed. He was fully dressed, his arms folded across his chest. "It's pointless for me to have done all that hard work today with Rene if we aren't going to make use of the result."

Rene shot him a look, and he grinned lecherously at her. But to my surprise, she gave him a leer back, and it was Lash who rolled his eyes and looked away.

"So where should we go?" I said, fastening on my bear head earrings. "Dinner? I'm hungry, I admit."

"So am I," Rene said, applying a dab of makeup. "I want some steak."

"You never order steak," Devlin said, shooting her an odd glance.

"Who gives a fuck what she orders?" Lash hissed, annoyed. "Let's get going!" He slung his arm around Rene's shoulders, and walked her out of the room.

Devlin took my hand, and laughing, we followed.

If I was worried that somehow our plan wasn't going to be effective, I was disabused of that right off. No sooner had we gotten off the elevator than we passed one of the bellhops. He had a slightly bored look to his face, but when Rene and Lash sauntered past, his eyes abruptly snapped open. He sniffed again rapidly twice, looked at Rene, and then back towards me, giving me a sickly smile as he met Devlin's red-cast staring eyes.

"Sorry, sir," he said, cowed.

"Do not be sorry for looking at my lover," Devlin said, proud yet also playboyish. "She's lovely, as is my other one."

"That she is," the bellhop said, nodding energetically. "If you'll excuse me." He walked away down the hall.

"Our security leak?" I said as we walked outside following Lash and Rene, who were making a big production of strolling together down Bourbon. Jake's jaguar guards had been waiting for us outside the door of the hotel, a sullen but sturdy pair of men who gave Lash looks of disgust and fear, which he ignored. They fell into step behind Devlin and me.

"Yes, but not the only one for certain," Devlin said, putting his arm around me. "He is off to make his report to someone, be it Jake, the vampire who is after Lash, or maybe someone else. This is good. Rene's idea worked."

"Does this ever get easier?" I said, leaning into him. "Am I going to have to worry forever?"

"I'd like to lie and say no," Devlin whispered, his beautiful voice sad. "The truth is the answer is yes, Love. But you have people watching your back and they're all immortal, or as close to it as you are. That should ease your mind somewhat."

We walked for a little while, and finally arrived at the Court of the Two Sisters. Lash said he'd been there long ago, and Devlin also admitted to being there years before, though he said much had changed.

We had a wonderful salad prepared at our table, and then some turtle soup, which I felt very guilty about but salivated over, and then some steak. Devlin abstained from eating, sipping a glass of red wine as we talked. For dessert, Rene and I had cheesecake. By the time we left, we were full and feeling good.

It was just at that moment, when I was most relaxed and happiest, that we were once again attacked.

Chapter Twenty-One

It happened only a block from the Bourbon Orleans, in an alleyway near the church. Lash and Rene were in front of us, his arm around her, kissing now and again. Suddenly they were fighting hard, surrounded by figures.

Devlin put me behind him immediately, scenting the air and looking around. The jaguar guards drew their guns, taking up positions on either side of Dev and me.

A lone man walked up to us. "Please stay out of it," he warned, baring fangs. "We want no trouble with you or your Oathed One, Dalcon."

"I beg to differ," Devlin said, and suddenly grabbed him, throwing him hard against the brick. I heard the snap of breaking bone as the man hit the wall, and then he was lying on the ground twitching. Devlin knelt quickly and snapped his neck.

"Is he were?" I asked.

"Yes, but not one I'm familiar with. Maybe a marshhawk." He hugged me quickly. "Teleport back to the hotel," he said urgently. "I have to help them. There has to be thirty vampires and weremen there and that's more than they can handle alone. Go!"

I teleported to the hotel and sagged into a chair immediately, worried and relieved. I debated calling Shaker to help, but didn't know if he was really needed. Titus would have already been in the fighting if the situation was dire.

"Here all alone, my sweet?" a beautiful voice said.

I turned to see a male standing there in the shadows, his arms crossed over his chest, his red eyes shining.

"Shaker!" I shouted, and backed away, concentrating to teleport myself home.

Nothing happened.

"Shaker!" I screamed again, feeling desperately with my mind for my demon. But Shaker wasn't there.

"Your demon can't help you," the man said in glee. "My demon is blocking you from teleporting." He advanced toward me. "Shaker is not the evilest being in the pit. Azaroth is easily his match."

I turned and ran. Suddenly the vampire was before me, his cold hands grasping my wrists.

"Please don't hurt me!" I said desperately. "I might be pregnant!"

The vampire smiled, and then bit down hard into my shoulder. I shrieked, and struggled, but he held me easily, making soft sucking noises punctuated by an occasional moan of fulfilled lust.

Enraged, I bit down into his neck. His flesh resisted, and then parted. Instead of pushing me away, he squeezed my head down into his neck, making his blood pump into me.

I choked, and swallowed his blood as I tried to breathe. God, it tasted like thick white chocolate, so sweet it was sickening!

I struggled frantically to get away, but he held me tightly, making me drink him as he was drinking me. Suddenly I felt so sick I swooned.

He slid his fangs out of me and let me collapse to the floor, stepping away. "So it's true," he said musingly. "You can't be turned the normal way."

"Who are you?" I whispered my eyes wide with fear.

The man leaned forward into the light, and I got my first good look at him. He was handsome, his face almost noble and yet savage in its severity. His eyes were black, his long straight hair was dark, and his skin was tanned.

"Ask your snake lover," he said, a faint smile on his lips. "Ask Devlin's witch. Ask Devlin himself."

"Stop being so Goddamned cryptic," I rasped. "Tell me!"

"I'm your master," he said. "Or I will be, as soon as the blood you drank takes effect."

"Devlin will kill you for this," I said hatefully. "If you've harmed our child—"

"It is Lash's child, not Dalcon's. Your collar is a lie."

227

"The child is Devlin's," I said triumphantly. "His son! You've sealed your fate by trying to drink from a Ruler's Oathed One! He'll burn you alive for this!"

The vampire got a look of horror on his face. I tried to take the opening and move, but he grabbed me, holding me down. "No, you're lying!"

He arched his back with a gasp of pain as Shaker appeared with a guttural roar, his blackness engulfing me, his eyes red glowing holes, his razor sharp teeth dripping black blood.

The vampire released me, quickly ducking as Shaker threw red fire at him that scorched the floor and vaporized a lamp. The vampire ran downstairs, snarling, as a bellowing Shaker pursued him, blasting the bedroom door to shards.

I tried to get up, because I wanted to follow. *I have to follow my master, I have to—!*

I went to my knees and stuck my finger down my throat. In a sickening gout, I threw up the blood I'd drunk, and my dinner. Immediately my body was wracked with pain, and I collapsed, screaming. Ranger grabbed me just as my eyes rolled up and I fainted.

* * * *

I awoke in Devlin's arms in our bedroom at Hayden. Immediately I began shaking, waking Devlin, his golden eyes already frantic. When I bit him weakly, he cut himself on his wrist and murmured for me to drink. I bit into him gratefully, hearing him sigh in pleasure as I swallowed him down, his hand massaging my back in a gentle circular motion. After about ten swallows, I drew back, his flesh already knitting together.

"You were burning up, but you're cooler now. Is the pain gone?" he said worriedly.

"I'm okay. He tried to turn me, and when that wouldn't work, he tried to get me in thrall to him. It was pure agony."

Devlin had already dialed Lash. "Come. She's awake." He turned to me. "It was likely because of a different strain of vampire virus."

"What—?"

My thought was cut off as Lash came through the door followed by

228

Rene. "Who attacked you? Did you see?" Lash asked.

I gave them a description. "He said you would know him, Lash. That Devlin would, and also Leri."

"Leri?" Devlin and Lash looked at one another.

Another call was made, and soon Leri was there, too, Rene glaring at her.

I gave her the description. "Who is he?"

"You don't need me to tell you," Leri said, looking balefully at Lash and Dev. "You know it was Valerian."

Chapter Twenty-Two

This wasn't a name I'd ever heard before. "Who is Valerian?"

"An old enemy, one we thought long dead," Devlin mused.

"Why are you involved?" Rene said suspiciously. "Did you help him, Leri?"

Leri shook her head. "He's acting on his own. The reason he said what he did was because I knew he was alive."

Lash strode to her and backhanded her across the face. Leri fell against the door. Lash kicked her hard in the side and she flew through the air to crumple against the far wall. Titus appeared and started for Lash, but Devlin grabbed him, holding him back.

"You never said a word, you fucking bitch!" Lash hissed, livid as he advanced on her. "For more than half a century, you let me believe he was dead!"

"He's my nephew," Leri said gasping, her hand to her face. "My only living blood relative, next to Terian and Sunrise. I had to protect him. I swore to my sister Vera on her deathbed that I would." She looked up at him with pleading eyes. "That's why Vera gave him my name, with just the V from hers. I've always thought of him as a son, even after he was turned."

Lash pulled her to her feet, and threw her into the wall hard enough to break it. She lay there moaning, chest heaving, half inside the lathe and plaster.

"Stop, Lash," Devlin commanded. "We need more information from her before you kill her."

Another enemy. There's going to be another war, and more bloodshed. It's never going to end, never. "I thought faeries couldn't be vampires," I murmured, feeling hopeless.

230

"Half human ones can be," Leri said miserably. "Valerian's father was human."

"I told you if you lied to me again, we were through," Titus rumbled. "And you have."

Leri turned pleading eyes to her demon lover. "I couldn't say anything, Titus! I promised my sister! Val gave me his promise he would never come back! He stayed with Michael as he said he would!"

Devlin's eyes about popped out. "He's been with Michael these past seventy years?"

Leri nodded. "Valerian has been happy to be second in command, as well as Michael's lover. Michael lied and told everyone he'd killed Valerian, as he desired him."

"What changed, to make him come back after all this time?" I said to Leri. "Why would anyone want revenge after seventy years?"

Her eyes looked up from the floor, and met mine. "You. You could give Michael what he's wanted his whole vampire existence. You turned his focus from Valerian to a child. Michael knew well Valerian's tastes in children's blood, and would never have risked his child's life. And so Michael arranged with Cyrus to have Valerian killed as soon as you were pregnant."

Devlin eased me down to his lap. "If only he had succeeded. We'd have been saved a lot of grief."

Lash looked thoughtful, but still very pissed. "Val must have discovered his plot."

"Tell us what you know, Leri," Titus rumbled.

"Valerian came to see me last spring for the first time since he left. He was happy, told me soon everything was going to be perfect. I thought Michael and he were finally going to be Oathed, that he was going to come out of hiding. But now I think he was referring to Michael's plan to have a child."

"That fuck probably couldn't wait to drink its blood," Lash hissed angrily. "Do you know what went wrong? Why didn't Michael succeed in killing Val? Why did Cyrus try to kill Michael instead?"

"I can't tell you the how, just the why. The oldest reason there is for murder: love. Valerian loved Michael, and Michael tried to have him killed. Valerian must have found out about it, gone crazy, and done

231

something—"

Fuck me, this was complex. *Why hadn't Shaker mentioned any of this?* I'd be talking to that damn demon shortly.

"——put that together with his old hatred of Lash, and he's here for vengeance."

"You dared to keep this from me," Devlin hissed at Leri. "You knew the consequences, yet you still dared."

She looked back at him, defiant. "I had my reasons."

"They were not good enough," Titus rumbled sadly. He raised his hands, and black fire erupted, engulfing Leri. She screamed horribly, writhing, but it consumed her in moments, until she was nothing but a pile of blackened scorched bones smoking on the stone floor.

We all looked at Titus, shocked.

"I forgave her so many times," Titus said, his rumbling voice cracking. "I told myself she loved me, that nothing else mattered. But it was never going to stop, the lies and the betrayal."

"I was going to order you to do it," Devlin said comfortingly. "It had to be done."

"Shit, I'd have done it gladly," Lash hissed flatly. "Are you sure she's gone?"

"Shaker," I said in my mind. "Titus just killed Leri. Make sure this wasn't an act: something to save her from being killed for real by us. Report to me when you have proof."

Shaker nodded mentally, and broke the connection.

"Yes, she's gone," Titus said. He went to his knees, suddenly sobbing, his tears splashing to smoke on the floor.

I crouched down and hugged him, and he held onto me as if his life depended on it, bathing me in tears like bathwater. The others left. I held Titus until he stopped crying about ten minutes later.

"I'm sorry," he rumbled finally. "I feel like a fool for not doing this sooner. I knew she was evil, more evil than I was, always in pursuit of what she wanted at the expense of everything and everyone around her. But I loved her."

I hugged him and said nothing. Then I helped him get to his feet, and Rip appeared, saying he would stay with him. They winked out of sight, teleporting.

I went downstairs to find Lash and Devlin drinking, Rene hovering with a glass of wine in her hand.

"What's the plan?"

Everyone looked at me. "We wait," Lash hissed, furious. "Devlin has put every vampire in a position of power on alert all over the world, and also put out the word that we'll pay ten million for Valerian dead. It's the biggest offer to hit the merc world in years."

"You aren't going after him?" I said in surprise.

"My place is here with you, making sure you're safe," Lash hissed tenderly. "He wants me to go after him, I'm sure that was his plan all along. So you and Dev are staying here, where you're safe, and so am I. We have enough money to last forever, and I have enough for our child, Sweetness. Valerian will play his hand before too long, or else one of the mercs will get him. Either way, it's the best thing to do." He got up. "Go and rest, we have an appointment with Camlyn the day after tomorrow."

Rene walked me upstairs and helped me get into bed. After she left, Shaker contacted me.

"He really did it," he said, amazed. "Leri's in hell now, I have it on good authority."

"Prove it."

"Come to me and I will. Anna's grave is safe. Meet me there."

I teleported, and in a second, Shaker shimmered into view. He offered me a glass orb. I took it, giving him a questioning look.

"Look into it, Mistress."

I looked into it, and soon a swirling mist revealed a burning landscape, the ground pitted and black, steaming. Writhing upon the ground were figures, most of them burnt, all of them screaming.

"The newly arrived," Shaker said in relish. "They still have lungs to scream."

I felt my stomach flip-flop. "Is she there?"

"Look in the middle of the picture."

I looked closer, and there indeed was Leri, her long brown hair a snarled, half burnt blackened mat, her beautiful face raw, her left brown eye wild, and her right one hanging by a tendril on the outside of her face as she screamed, and tried to crawl...

I dropped the orb, swooning, and Shaker grabbed it in one hand and me in the other, easing me down to sit on the ground.

"Shh," he said, hugging me. "You are safe, Mistress. Rest assured, Leri is out of the action for now."

I gave him a look. "For *now*?"

"Titus will likely reconsider and try to save her. This isn't the first time he's sent her to Hell. Leri usually benefits from time spent there. At the least, it will make her more truthful."

"Did you kill Valerian?"

"No," Shaker said reluctantly. "I came back for you, when I felt your pain. Devlin's bears were there taking care of you, so I went back out after him. By then he'd vanished."

"Tell me what happened with Valerian and Michael."

"Val had been Michael's lover. They were together for a long time, by my guess. And then Michael ordered Cyrus to kill him."

"Tell me everything of what happened. On our bond, Shaker, the truth."

He scowled at me. "I don't know everything; I'm a demon, not the Devil. I know Valerian found out, used some kind of leverage over someone, and got wind of the plan. He made a pact with Cyrus to end you, so he could be with Michael again. But why Cyrus went along with that, I can't answer."

I remembered Cyrus's speech about how I was the cause of all vampire monarchy strife. "I think I know Cyrus's reasons. Anything else?"

"I didn't know of Cyrus's deal with Valerian. I do now, Mistress. I will stay near you at all times until he is killed."

"No. You are to hunt Valerian, Shaker. You are to hunt him until you find him. And then you are to bring me his head, and torch the rest of him."

"Understood. I'll need to have sustenance, before I began."

"See Rene."

Shaker nodded, and vanished.

I sat thinking for a long while in silence at Anna's grave. How close was I to screaming in that burning plain? And would there be anyone who loved me enough that was not already there in Hell with me that wanted to get me out before my lungs became nothing but ashes?

Chapter Twenty-Three

It was a somber New Year's Eve. Rene had retired to her room in an attempt to foresee all she could. Venus was still with Danial at his house. Lash was with Kyle and most of the bears, making sure everyone was on high alert. Titus and Rip were monitoring all of Hayden, watching for an attack. I understood from Titus's remarks that Valerian usually attacked right away if he was going to attack at all, so that made sense.

I wasn't sure what to do with myself. So I went through the mail. In the midst of bills and junk mail, I saw a thank you postmarked out west. Thinking crazily it had to be from my first mother in law, I opened it, but it was just a card from Amber and Drake, the werebat couple we'd attended the wedding of seven months or so ago.

God, had so little time passed? I sat for a moment and thought of all that had happened to me in the last five years. God, how could it have only been five years since I'd met Danial, and Oathed to him? I felt like I'd aged twenty in that time.

Moved, I went to Danial's basket and opened it. He'd gotten me the kind of chocolate I liked with creamy centers, chocolate covered pretzels, and even some kind of chocolate liqueur. I left the basket on the table with a sign for everyone to help themselves. I also opened up Erik and Van's basket and left it there, after writing a quick thank you to them for their thoughtfulness and putting it in the pile of outgoing mail on the hall table. *At least they'll know for sure I got their present, this time.*

I heard some music, and wandered into the ballroom. Devlin was there, playing the piano.

"What is this?" I called gently.

"Blood Music." Devlin didn't miss a note. "Circa 1992. I admit, I like it for its name more than anything. It doesn't particularly move me.

235

But some of my donors find it appealing."

I tried not to be grumpy. "I didn't know you played for your donors."

"Sometimes," Devlin said without turning. "Sometimes I sing to them. Women have to be finessed, Sar. Two of mine used to be lovers as well as donors, and they are not anymore, something they are not happy about. Playing for them makes them feel closer to me, or so they tell me. Whatever they need to feel to make them keep giving me their blood is what I must do."

"Did you sing for Monica and Angelica?" I asked nonchalantly.

He glanced over at me, his fingers not missing a key. "Never. The latter only needed a crooked finger to share my bed, and the former had no love for music. Both were a disappointment."

Hearing him be so methodical about it, I stifled my jealousy. "Tell me about the virus. Why did drinking Valerian's blood cause me pain?"

"You know viruses mutate, Love, from modern science. Each vampire has a slightly different version of the virus. For the most part in my experience anyway, that strain doesn't constantly change as human viruses do. But over hundreds of years it does."

"I don't follow you."

"Valerian is old. He was about a hundred seventy years ago, so now he is close to two hundred. Odds are that knowing what he was to Michael, it was his blood that was in Cyrus's lab, though I have no idea why he'd donate so much. But what I'm getting at is that the virus in Valerian's veins is different from mine, enough so it fought with mine. That may have caused the pain."

"I didn't have pain until I threw up his blood," I said queasily. "But he tasted different."

"All vampires will, at least to one such as you. All viruses, be they human or vampire, try to replicate themselves in whatever body they are inside. The older the vampire blood, the more concentrated the virus is within it and the quicker it will take over a being. Val's blood was trying to colonize you. Your body resisted under command from the virus already in it from me. It gave you the strength to resist him, in addition to your natural resistance."

"Danial and you taste different. But there was never any pain."

"Danial and I've shared a lot of blood in the last few years, Love. He drank a good deal from me the night he became Ruler of the States, then Ulysses drained him years later, and he and I drained Ulysses, not to mention the other times we've donated to one another on a smaller basis. Or for another example, I drained Ebediah. His blood was so bitter with virus it was all I could do to not throw up."

"I'm still not following you, Dev."

He stopped playing, and turned to face me. "Look, Danial and I have shared a lot of blood. We can handle drinking older vampire blood of a different strain and process it, being as old as we are. We also were made by the same vampire. So the virus in our blood is not dissimilar, despite how we taste to you. Valerian's is very different." He made me look at him. "Pay attention, this is important. You would likely be in no danger from drinking a little of his blood; in fact, it was probable that your body was already processing it, as the virus in you from me is much more powerful. It just needed time to get the job done. But when you vomited it up, the sudden loss of so much of the virus from me that was utilizing the blood you'd drunk from him was too much of a shock for your system to handle, hence the pain. Is that a better explanation?"

Ah. "Much better…" I trailed off, thinking hard on his explanation, and the sudden ramifications.

Devlin put his hand on mine. "What is it, Love?"

"I have another question," I said, "Well, um, several."

"There is weight to your words," Devlin said, concerned. "Tell me your questions."

"I looked online some time ago, when I was trying to research what makes my blood different than other women's, and why. There was a lot of information on vampires, and most of it was false."

"Deliberately so," Devlin said, nodding. "We do not want human attention, other than that of the young." He flashed an evil smile. "Makes it so much easier to feed on them."

"There was a good deal about blood, how it's not very nutritious."

"Talk plainly, Love. We are past the shy point of our relationship."

"What is it that makes you a vampire, that makes it possible for you to drink blood and not only survive, but also remain ageless? Yes, I know it's caused by a virus, and all the usual signs and symptoms. But what is actually happening on the inside? Something must be on a drastic level."

Devlin looked at me for a long moment, weighing his words. "I cannot tell you the particulars, Love," he said finally. "It is a secret kept by the Ruling Class exclusively. Much as I enjoy breaking the rules, I cannot break this one, even for you."

"So it is known?" I said, surprised.

Devlin nodded. "We used modern science, and found the answers. It was simple enough, really. I can tell you that the virus mutates our digestive system so that the various proteins found in the blood satisfy our needs completely. Moreover, the DNA in our systems are not just altered, the way they replicate is altered. Much as a stem cell can be used to grow a new muscle, our bodies can use various cells to regrow any damaged tissue. Our youth, at least back to when the virus hit our systems, is due to this constant exact replication and replacement of our existing cells." He made a face. "Sunlight, or other UV rays of certain frequencies not only impede this reconstruction, they cause the virus to disintegrate. Our core temperature elevates by an increasing magnitude every second we're exposed. The continuous replication and replacement is interrupted, and our cells break up, their core temperatures baking to the point where it appears we spontaneously combust." He gave a wry smile. "Hence the smoke and flame."

"Is it known why those vampires with the older blood can make others, and the young ones can't?"

"There are theories," Devlin replied, closing the piano keyboard cover. "The most likely one is that it takes a powerful dose of virus to colonize the human body, which has a dearth of defenses. The newly made have tiny quantities of vampire virus in their entire bodies; I have that much in a few drops of my blood. Human immune systems are strong; they repel the virus, unless it attacks repeatedly, as when the same person is bitten over and over. When that happens and a virus is potent enough, the human becomes vampire. When the virus is weak and the human's systems are too compromised by repeated exposure, the human dies." He paused. "This theory also fits with why weres can't become vampire: their immune systems are just too strong."

"Is this known by doctors? Camlyn never told me any of this, yet he must know it."

"Part of Camlyn's oath to do no harm includes keeping this secret. Youth or at least immortality is obtainable for most creatures in our world, Sar. But how much would human pharmaceutical companies give to synthesize a copy of the virus for profit? Also, we don't want anyone developing a vaccine against the virus; a little research and soon there would be an injection that would kill us Rulers easily. There is our existence hanging in the balance. Camlyn respects that. He doesn't want a vampire-ridden world anymore than we do, but nor does he want one with supernatural beings running amok without rules."

"It does fit, I said, musing. "I'm surprised that you did all this research."

"I've always wanted to know," Devlin said, clasping my hands in his. "Superstition and legend is entertaining until you have become it yourself. Then all the half-truths and myths are just frustrating." He kissed my hand. "Any more questions?"

"No. Thank you for telling me what you knew."

"Good. Come. I'd like to bed you." He brought me into his arms. "I know your doctor's appointment is tomorrow, and I want to make sure that Stephen finds my DNA in your bloodstream when he tests you." He nibbled my ear. "I'll be very gentle."

So much for his big speech about abstaining from sex with me. I cracked a smile. "You know tonight won't make a difference, Dev. If I didn't conceive almost a month ago, it won't show up on the test." I took a breath. "It's likely he won't find anything."

"Then I just want to make love with you because I love you. Is that reason enough?"

"You don't need a reason, Love," I said tenderly. "Come to bed."

* * * *

The next morning was a surprise. Stephen was indeed going to do a blood test, but on Lash and I both, as well as a sample of Lash's semen in terms of testing for fertility. So he took samples, and told us to come back at the end of the week. We left disgruntled, but also relieved. At least if there was bad news, it could be put off a little longer.

There was enough bad news waiting for us at home. Lash and I returned to find Serena waiting for us, suitcase in hand.

"I'm giving you my notice, Lash," Serena said softly. "I've told Devlin, and he asked that I not wait the normal two weeks to leave. I just wanted to say goodbye to Sar."

Lash swore loudly, and stalked upstairs.

I walked over and gave Serena a hug. "I'll miss you," I said, choked up. "I'm sorry we didn't get to do very much together in the last few months."

"Sar, we haven't done anything together in almost a year," Serena replied bitterly. "Rene's always with you. Even when she isn't, you don't have time for me." She swallowed whatever else she was going to say. "I'm glad you were my friend, but you aren't anymore. It's okay, because I have a place I belong now."

It hit me suddenly: she was going to Danial's. "Are you going to be a guard for him?"

Serena broke into a smile. "I'm going to cook for him and clean house. A few of the single male foxes there have told me they'd like to date me, if I'd come live there." She smiled wider. "It'll be a good life, hopefully a quiet one."

I wanted to ask a lot of questions about what Jenny was going to do if Serena was going to do the housework. I'd already gotten the email work back, so how was she filling her days? Then it dawned on me that Theo could support Jenny, she didn't need to work at all if she didn't want to. I swallowed hard, thinking that maybe she'd gotten pregnant in the last few months. I hadn't looked at her belly closely on Christmas Eve; I hadn't thought to. Maybe that was why Serena was leaving, because Jenny was going to be busy raising Theo's children.

I abruptly noticed Serena had stopped speaking. I'd missed whatever else she'd said. *Sar, you are an ass. Cringe.* "Take care of yourself," I said sadly. "Please send me an email now and again."

She was facing me but didn't hear me, her eyes on something unseen. "I thought I wanted excitement when I went to work for Devlin two years ago," she murmured. "I wanted to be desired, to live in a great house. But I've seen too many of my lovers die, too much pain and suffering, even if most of it wasn't mine." She swallowed hard. "I'll be twenty-one soon but I feel twice that. Whatever time I have left isn't going to be spent like this."

"You'll have a good life at Danial's house." I hugged her. "He'll be good to you."

"I'll keep in touch," Serena said kindly. "Take care of yourself, Sar."

She walked out. A moment later a black Expedition headed down Hayden's drive.

I walked upstairs to find Rene and Devlin fighting, though it didn't get loud until I opened our bedroom door. Guess I'd never noticed before how soundproofed the room was.

"You are not bringing that harlot here!" Rene shouted. "I'm telling you I won't stand for it, Devlin!"

"I'm not going to be laying her," Devlin said patiently. "Jezebel is going to be for the men. She is goblin, and can change shape easily. It will save on potions."

"No. You bring her here, and I'll kill her," Rene said flatly. She stalked out, slamming the door to her room with a crash.

Devlin muttered something in French, and shook his head.

"So you've already got another woman lined up for the bears?"

Devlin rolled his eyes. "I thought I had. But maybe not."

"Tell me the truth: do you want her? Jezebel?"

Devlin colored slightly. "I've always desired her, yes. But we've not been lovers for a while, Love."

His words on reunions with old lovers came back in a rush. "How long is 'a while'?"

"I last saw her years ago."

"How many years ago, Oathed One?"

Devlin sighed. "I saw her in Rio. We spent a few nights together. I've not seen her since."

"Don't bring her here," I said flatly. "I'm with Rene on this." I stalked out, too, and spent that night in Lash's room.

* * * *

Jezebel arrived the next evening by limo, looking like a black haired Spanish version of Angelina Jolie. She had time to smile and put her hand out for me before Rene hit her with a burst of blue fire that knocked

241

her off the porch, sizzling all her black hair into ashes.

"Leave," Rene hissed, lightning cracking from her hands. "I'll kill you before I let you set foot inside this door, goblin."

Jezebel's new black hair slid forth from her skull in a rippling motion as her features shifted, and I got a glimpse of some wizened gnarled creature beneath the beauty before they smoothed again. "Dev hasn't said that. Until he does, honey child, I'm staying."

Shaker, I called in my mind. *Come and get her. Take her somewhere else.*

Shaker appeared, grabbed a struggling Jezebel, and disappeared. *What do you want me to do with her?* he rumbled in my mind. *Once I release her, she'll come back there, Mistress.*

Something to ensure she never comes back then, I said mentally. *Whatever you want to do to make that happen, do it. I never want to see even one hair of hers again.*

Yes, Mistress! Shaker said in absolute maniacal joy, and then he severed the mental connection.

I turned to Rene. "That's solved." I smiled feebly. "Shaker will take care of her. I guess my soul's getting dark now."

"It's okay," Rene said, hugging me with one arm. "Join the club, Sister. We do the best we can."

We walked upstairs to find Devlin looking resigned. "I take it you sent her away?"

"In a fashion," Rene said gleefully. "She won't ever be coming back."

Devlin glowered. "Fine. Then I leave it up to you to arrange a new woman for the bears, one that can be trusted, Rene. You have one week."

"I'll only need a day," she said arrogantly, and headed into her room.

* * * *

That Friday at eight, I arrived at Camlyn's with Lash. To my surprise, Brenda, the female doctor I'd last seen years ago in Pennsylvania was there with him.

I welcomed her, while looking around discreetly for her former assistant, Bitch Woman. With relief, I saw no sign of her.

"It's good to see you," Dr. Brenda said pleasantly. "I understand you're pregnant, congratulations. And where's your handsome husband this morning?"

"I'm her mate, and the father," Lash hissed loudly. "Well, one of them, anyway. Her husband was an asshole."

"This is Lash," I said loudly over him. "I'm divorced, Brenda. We're not sure I'm pregnant, which is why we're here."

"Come in, Sar," Stephen said jovially. "We'll get started. We have a lot to discuss and Devlin's already on the line, waiting for news."

Brenda looked at me, then Stephen, and then at Lash. "I can see I have a lot to catch up on. I'll just listen, and be quiet."

We all went into exam room one. I sat on the table.

"Good morning, Dr. Brenda," Devlin said melodiously over the intercom. "It's good to speak to you again. That you are taking over for Camlyn eases my mind, after seeing firsthand your eagerness to help Sar."

"Have we met?" Brenda said curiously.

"Yes, some years ago. I brought Sar to your emergency ward."

Brenda looked incredulous. "Yes, you said you were her husband. But you were really his brother, am I right?"

"Not exactly," Devlin laughed. "But I'm her man now."

"Enough," Lash hissed, baring fangs. "I want to know test results. Talk, Stephen."

"First off, Lash, there is something very unusual in your semen," Steven said delicately. "I wanted to talk to you about it."

I gave Stephen 100% of my attention. "What did you find?"

"Vampire DNA?" Lash hissed irritably. "Demon DNA? That's to be expected."

"No, none of that is present, that I saw," Stephen said, rolling his eyes. "But I wasn't looking for that. I'm talking about something I've never seen before, not in any were, or human for that matter. It seems to be a hormone, something that acts on a female, any species of female to release an egg, at least, that's what it did to both a snake, and a mouse, when I isolated it, and tested it in them—"

"What the hell are you shooting bits of me into a mouse for?" Lash hissed angrily. "Don't be doing that! You fucking know pure animal

243

tests don't always adequately reflect on what happens in humans, weres, or vampires."

"Calm down, please. My point is, between this, and that your sperm is also long lived, lasting ninety-six hours instead of seventy-two, I'm surprised that the birth control pills even worked for Sar for those few months."

"They were not human ones; they were for weremen and human, the strongest available."

"I know, Lash, Sar told me. I'm telling you that given enough time and sex with you, even the ones you got for her that were made for human women having intercourse with weremen would not have prevented a pregnancy."

I let out a gasp, and Lash looked very proud of himself.

"How is it you didn't have children, when you were young?" Stephen continued. "I know several male weres in their later years, that they don't usually abstain, not until they are no longer capable of fathering children or their mate is too old. These pills didn't exist back then—"

"No one I was with wanted to be pregnant," Lash hissed icily. "And I took some precautions myself. That's the end of it, Camlyn."

Stephen nodded. "Well, my point is that it's good you both wanted a child. Because with this kind of test result, Sar, without even testing you at all, I'm betting you are already pregnant. Go ahead, and take what you like, or be with Lash, but given that you've been trying as much as Lash said you've been, I'm guessing that the deed is done."

"When can we make sure?" Devlin asked. "I'm still on the potion, and we're intimate. I don't want to cause trouble, as I did before. But I don't want to stop being intimate if she isn't pregnant."

"Keep taking the drug, and continue trying, just be gentle and use common sense. I don't need to spell it out for you, Devlin."

Devlin grumbled something.

"Come back in a month, Sar, if you miss your period. We'll go from there. All your tests look good, so keep doing what you have been."

I shrugged. "Okay."

When we arrived home, Rene brought a woman in to meet us. She was beautiful, almost ethereal looking as Rene was.

"Enchante," Devlin said, kissing her hand. "And who is this?"

"A construct spell," Rene said sharply. "One who looks as the man beholding her would wish her to in his wildest fantasies. She can respond as a woman in the flesh, though she can't speak. But your men may find that an asset."

"Likely," Devlin said, looking the construct over. "Put her in Serena's room. I'll send up a few men to try her out tonight."

Rene nodded. "I'll need to recast the spell weekly. Constructs wear out fast. But there is no security risk this way. And I can create any form, so female bears can also be made, as needed."

"It's a good plan," Lash said, nodding. "I much prefer this to that slut Jezebel." He gave me a hug. "I'll see you later, Sar." He left, closing the door behind him.

"I'm sorry, my Oathed Ones," Devlin said suddenly. "I meant no insult with Jezebel to either of you. You are right, this way is much better. I should have gone to Titus, asked him for a spell."

"Titus would not have done this," Rene said angrily. "He would think it was immoral, to use magic this way. But Leri would have done it."

"Don't speak of her," Devlin said angrily. "I'm still irritated over her keeping secrets from me, after all I did for her over the years."

"When were you intimate?" Rene said sharply. "I've been meaning to ask you, Dev."

"Now you are going to be jealous?" Devlin growled. "Just what I need."

She glared at him. "Answer me, vampire."

"When she was on the outs with Titus, in 1901 or thereabouts. It didn't last long, as they got back together, not that I wanted it to in any case. Satisfied?"

"As you've said, past is past," I said calmly. "I don't care what you did a hundred years ago, Dev. I care what you do now, as Rene does."

"Then ease your mind, Loves. I've no desire for anyone but the two of you."

"Sadly, you'll have to pine away by yourself tonight," Rene said, heading to her room. "I have matters to attend to." She slammed her door.

"What was that about?"

"Leri and she had a longstanding feud of some kind," Devlin said, leading me into his room. "She's angry we were intimate, no matter it was a hundred years ago. Leave her be for tonight."

I turned on the shower and we took off out clothes. "Will Lash be back tonight?" I asked as I got in.

"No," Devlin said, coming in right after me. "He has a job that will take the next few days. Plus he's going to meet with Akira and Van regarding the missing children matter on my behalf, and also Mad. So you should sleep here, unless you'd rather be alone like Rene."

I ignored the barb. "Any news on Valerian?"

"No. He did always have a taste for children's blood, so I'm guessing he was behind the rash of disappearances months ago. Children are still being reported missing, but the numbers are much closer to normal now." He hugged me under the spray. "Lash will find him, Sar. It just may take more time."

He moved to embrace me, and I stopped him. He drew back, looking put out. "What is the matter?"

"Can we talk?" I said. "I do want you, but I need to talk to you first. It's important."

"Then I'll listen. Let us get clean, Love."

A little while later, we sat before the woodstove in our towels, sipping wine as we watched the flames dance.

"What is it, Sarelle?" he asked finally.

"How is Theoron? I wrote a letter and heard nothing. I'm worried."

"He is fine. Airmail is slow. Samuel blamed email for Sharon's rebellion, and apparently destroyed his home computer in a rage. He relented and is getting a new system installed soon. Theoron should be able to email us within a week."

One down. "May we visit Van and Erik? They invited us."

Devlin considered that for a moment. "Likely not, Love. Other state Rulers would cry favoritism, and use it against me to make us visit them all, something I wouldn't do. I would like to visit Van and Erik, but I'd have to create a reason for a visit outside liking them more than others. Let me think on it."

Two down. "Are there any threats, bounties on anyone's head? It's been a while since I heard anything."

Devlin mused for a moment, petting Ghost. "Not that I know of. Danial will likely have one before the year is out, but Terian and Theo will deal with it. Don't worry."

Well, that couldn't be crossed off the list, then...*sigh. Next.* "The werebats, you mentioned they were your allies. Why not hire some to work here with us?"

Devlin looked dumbfounded. "Is there a reason you want werebat guards?"

"You're always telling me to spend your money. So why not, if you trust them? I think it would be neat. Do they really become large bats, or normal sized ones?"

"They are large enough to ride on. Hmm. I'll have Lash check into it. Is that all?"

"No. How are David and Krystin? You didn't get a sympathy card from them. Was she staked or something, after you turned her?"

Devlin made a face. "No. But she had a kind of breakdown after becoming vampire, due to the events that happened at their wedding when the hunters attacked. She is under treatment for post-traumatic shock at David's estate. He has resigned his position as Ruler temporarily, in order to take care of her. It's a mess, to put it lightly. But she is recovering, or so his last email a week ago said. In regards to the missing card, David is one of the tech-savvy vampires, who embrace email. I got a great many sympathy cards online instead of via regular post, such as the one from Nate."

Relief for him bringing up the subject of Cain swamped me. I hadn't known how to broach that myself. "Have you located Cain's brother?"

Devlin nodded. "Yes. He is a man located in Montana by the name of West. By his picture, he is a dead ringer for Cain, though he is blond like me. But I have not contacted him yet." He sipped his wine. "I wonder that maybe it's better not to befriend him, to let him live his mortal life without interference. I'm thinking about it."

That was good; there would be no pressure to "share" in bed anytime soon. "Is Kyle still talking of leaving? I saw him using my treadmill the other day. He looked fully healed."

"He is better, yes. He will always have scarring, but he's regained full use of his limbs. No, he is not leaving anytime soon. Lash asked him to stay until Valerian is dead, and he agreed. Rest easy."

Before I spoke, he changed topic. "How are your bad dreams? Lash says they are bad, yet I've never woken you from any nightmares. Did you have any lately?"

"I've been using valium, Dev. But no, I haven't."

"Good. Likely they'll clear up with time." He hugged me gently. "Anything else?"

"Would you mind if I painted the barn, after I give birth?" I said hesitantly. "I'll want to get into shape, and I notice it needs painting."

"No, I'd rather you didn't. Bobby is attending to that, as soon as the weather gets warmer. But why don't you ride with Rene and me? She mentioned that you and she went out recently. It's good exercise. I've been looking at horses for you, and have found several that are similar to Annabelle Lee."

"Then that sounds fine to me. And yes, that is the last thing."

"Good," Devlin said, putting aside his wine. "I was hoping you'd say that. Come here."

Chapter Twenty-Four

A month later, Stephen confirmed I was pregnant. He also said that there was both vampire DNA and weresnake DNA in my system. I was worried and excited at the news. Lash and Devlin were so ecstatic they went a little nuts. In short, they went to Davy's again, and got their werebear guards trashed. They came home utterly trashed, too, and I made them sleep in Lash's room, because I was having morning sickness by then, and they reeked of alcohol.

Rene helped get them settled, and then came in to me. "Remember our plan," she said softly. "Tell me at once if you hear anything from Danial. My spell is prepared, and I'll complete the last steps to put it into effect tonight."

I gave her an odd look. I hadn't forgotten the plan, but Danial had been silent now for going on almost three months about anything to do with me. Venus had had a good time over New Years with him, but that had been the last I'd heard about him. Personally, I hadn't heard from him since his gift basket. Given all that, I had been sure there wouldn't be a need for us to go through with "our plan." Maybe she had foreseen something? "Of course, Sister."

Rene walked out, leaving me alone with my thoughts.

* * * *

That next night, Devlin and Lash celebrated with me.

"Sar," Devlin crooned gently, as I came into bed. "Tonight will be our last time together, now that we know you're with child. So I want you to do something special for me."

Okay, he had all my attention. "What?"

"I want to be in you with Lash."

I did a double take, then blinked. "I don't think that's a good idea."

"Not as Danial and I were with you," Devlin said quickly. "Lash doesn't like that."

"Don't even fucking talk about it in front of me," Lash hissed with a grimace. "Please."

"Anyway," Devlin said with a nasty look at Lash. "I didn't mean that. I want you to fellate Lash as I make love to you."

It took me a minute to understand what he was saying. Once I did, I flushed red.

"You don't have to, Sar," Lash hissed quickly.

"I'm surprised, that's all," I said quickly, laying my hand on Lash's as a comfort. "Dev, why would you want to watch me do that?"

"Because I like to see you make love to each other," Devlin said lovingly. "And I've never seen you do that with him, though I'm guessing you have."

"We have," Lash hissed affectionately. "But only twice."

"Only once, really," I said with a soft smile. "You didn't want me to, at first."

Lash got an uncomfortable look as Devlin laughed. "That's a new one," he said melodiously. "Shall we begin?"

Lash lay back against the mound of pillows. He was already stiff for me, a drop of fluid glistening on the tip of his penis. I ran my hand over the head of him, and he let out a long hiss. I kissed the tip of him, and then slid him into my mouth. Lash was already hissing continuously, and thrusting gently into me. As I moved on him, I felt Devlin kissing down my back, and then he reached his hand between my legs, and stroked me. I gasped a little, and Lash jerked, as I ran my teeth over him. But I kept moving on him.

Devlin moved into position behind me, and slipped the huge thickness of himself between my thighs, to rub on me. "God, you're dripping with excitement," he said lustily. "I'm going to love this."

He pushed in very slowly. I was so wet, I accepted him easily. Then he began to move, taking up the same rhythm of my mouth on Lash.

"Sar," Lash hissed eagerly. "Oh, Sweetness, please, take me just a little deeper inside…ahh…"

I put my lips down to the root of him, and he let out a sharp cry. He began to work himself in and out of me on his own, no longer content to have me move on him. Devlin also speeded up, stroking me all over inside as only he could, and making sure now to sink himself completely into me with each movement of his hips.

"I'm going to come!" Lash hissed suddenly, "Please don't stop, Sar, please!"

I swallowed him all the way, massaging the tip of him with the back of my throat, and he began to come, moaning loudly as he ejaculated into me in long spurts. Devlin continued to move in me rhythmically.

Lash came for several seconds. When I slipped his organ out, he was spent and sated. He lay there with his eyes closed, hissing in utter contentment.

It was at that moment Devlin began to whisper in my ear. "See how good you made him feel?" He bit my earlobe gently. "God the love coming off you both is so strong it's like a bolt of lightning."

Devlin paused. "Look at him," he whispered seductively.

He bore down, moving gently as he began rubbing me with his hand. I cried out as my climax began to build, and my head sought his, wanting badly to kiss him, my breath coming in ragged pants.

"Please, Dev! Please!"

"No, look at him," Devlin said lustily, still moving purposefully. "Tell him you love him. Tell him now!"

Lash's eyes snapped open, shocked, and appalled. But I was climaxing, and didn't care.

I looked into his eyes as I came, screaming, "I love you, Trystan! I love you!"

Devlin roared out his orgasm in a guttural scream. I squeezed him inside me as hard as I could, making him jerk several times in pure pleasure as I wrung out every last drop of his semen. Slowly our breathing quieted. When he slipped out of me, he was no longer erect. Devlin eased me down between Lash and he. For a while, we just held each other.

I was just drifting off, when Devlin sighed in utter contentment. "God, that was great."

"Why'd you fucking do that?" Lash hissed angrily, barely audible.

I roused myself, but didn't move.

"Tell me you didn't like it." Devlin's voice was arrogant, and blatant.

"Don't fucking play, Dev. That was weird."

"No, it wasn't," Devlin said, and now he was angry too. "I wanted to see her love you like that. That's all I wanted."

"Bullshit. That was weird, you having her and asking her to profess love to me as she came."

"Look, we make love to her most every night," Devlin sighed. "I've made love to her with Danial. But I have never seen her make love to anyone but me. I wanted to see her make love to you. I loved watching her touch you."

"Why? I've never understood why watching other people fuck makes you so damned excited."

"Isn't it obvious how much she cares for you?" Devlin said. "I wanted to see if she could tell you she loved you in the midst of climax with me and mean it."

"She meant it," Lash said finally, still barely audible. "I saw it in her eyes."

"I know," Devlin said jealously. "I heard it in her voice."

Lash shifted uncomfortably. "Why do it, if it made you jealous?"

"Because I can deal with being a little jealous. It was worth it, to see the look on your face as you watched her and saw that she meant it. That even with me inside her, bringing her, she still loved you." He paused. "To know she has never been with you and wanted you to be anyone but yourself. I wanted to give that to you, my friend."

"I still think it was weird of you to do," Lash whispered, an odd note in his words.

"You're welcome," Devlin said softly.

"After all these years with me, why not be honest? You could have just said—"

"Talk about honest! I know you would have killed for some oral sex from her from the first! So why did you tell her you didn't want that?"

"Because I thought you and she...I thought you'd for sure made her do that for you, the way you like it, after all those months you were together," Lash said very, very quietly. "And I didn't want her to think of you when she was with me and get scared or turned off, or even see in her eyes she was thinking of you, imagining me to be you. It was enough to have regular sex with her, that she wanted that with me. I wasn't going to risk asking for more."

"I'm not enough of a deviant to ask Sar to do what would for sure hurt her."

Lash snorted. "Yes, you are."

"Talk about deviant! Who tells someone they are coming during sex, like an announcement, before they come?"

"I usually try to remember to during oral, because I'm polite," Lash hissed with pride. "If I was the one on the receiving end, I would want some warning before it happened to prepare myself. My mate's to be handled gently. She's not like Rene, who can take whatever she's given."

"Experienced women know without you telling them!" Devlin laughed richly, his body vibrating next to me. "I forgot you haven't had fellatio often. With practice, women can tell from a man's body when it's time. Sar's had a lot of practice, the way she's so good at swallowing—"

"Don't be talking about her like that," Lash hissed meaningfully. "Or I'll have to hit you."

"I'm being honest," Devlin said, miffed. "I'm happy she's had practice, and you should be, too. Most women are horrible at it, until a man takes the time to teach them. But others are a natural at it, like Sar—"

"Dev," Lash hissed menacingly. "Watch it."

"Fine," Devlin said in annoyance. "Let's get some sleep."

I bit my lip to stifle my laughter, letting out a sigh of contentment myself.

* * * *

The next night, I was reading when I heard the phone ring. Thinking it was Lash, I picked up. "Hello?"

"Sar?" a slurred voice asked.

"Hello?" I repeated. "Who is this?"

"Theo."

Ah shit. "What is it? Did something happen to Danial?"

"No. Can you send Terian for me? I need a ride home. The bartender took my keys. Danial's overseas with Rip, and Terian's not answering his cell." He cleared his throat. "I didn't know who else to call. I don't want the foxes to see me like this."

This was way out of character. I got a hold of Demi finally at the werefox compound, who said Theoron and Terian were out at a meeting. *Great.*

I got back on the phone with Theo. "Where are you?"

"Davy's."

Shit, who could I send for him? Titus was visiting with Sunrise. Venus was in her room, talking to Sharon at Elle's house. Lash and Dev were at a meeting with Tony and Thane. Rene was also out, doing who knew what. There was only one other who could help.

"I'll send someone for you. Sit tight."

I hung up, and thought of Shaker. Immediately, I felt him in my mind.

Mistress?

Come to me at Hayden. Now.

Shaker appeared before me an instant later. He was just as I remembered, though I hadn't seen him for almost a month. I was both uneasy, and also...really uneasy.

He went to one knee before me. It was odd, his lower half being animal. "What is your command?"

"I need you to teleport to Davy's, and take Theo back to Danial's house."

"I cannot," he said apologetically. "I have never been to the current Davy's."

Could this be any harder? *Shit.* "Come with me, then, and guard me, ok?"

"Your wish is—"

"And stop being so formal already!"

"Of course."

I took his hand, and teleported to Davy's. We arrived in the parking lot, by chance next to Theo's Silverado truck.

So he is here. I went in, Shaker beside me, apparently unconcerned that he might be seen as less than human with his hooves and horns. We got to the bar and found Theo snoring on it.

Gary handed me Theo's keys, looking apologetic. "Sorry. He was ready to pass out and I knew he shouldn't drive."

"Thanks," I said. "We'll take him home."

Shaker grabbed Theo easily, and carried him out to his truck. He put him in the backseat, and then he teleported everything to Danial's house. I parked Theo's truck in the garage, and Shaker carried him to the werecompound. I had Shaker cloak us in a spell of shadow, but during the walk and even getting inside, we saw no one.

That set off alarms all over the place for me. Hell, it was the middle of the night. Where were the guards?

"Mistress, where to from here?" Shaker said, startling me.

Shit, I am going to have to face Jenny. Maybe I could just have Shaker do that, and watch invisible from a distance. *Sounds good to me.* "Can you find his room?"

"By scent, yes," Shaker said. Within a few minutes, we'd found it. I made him become visible and he knocked, but no one answered.

Theo began to stir at the noise, so Shaker took him off his shoulder and leaned him up against the wall. Blearily, Theo opened his eyes.

"Are you okay?" I said gently, holding on to his arm so he didn't fall over.

"Now that you're here," he said, giving me a sad smile. "Thanks for coming to get me."

Shaker went to open the door, but it was locked. He cursed, and began trying Theo's keys.

Theo in the meantime used the opportunity. He tilted my head up. A second later, he was kissing me gently.

"Stop it," I said angrily, breaking away from him. "You want your mate to see you kissing me?"

"Jenny's dead," Theo said sadly, his eyes filled with grief.

Suddenly, the missing guards, the being drunk, him not calling her, it all made sense.

"I'm sorry, Theo. What happened?"

"The cancer came back," Theo said emptily. "It was quick, Sar. We only found out a month back. She died a couple days ago."

So Jenny had been diagnosed about the time Serena had left. That had been the real reason she'd been taking over for Jenny. I hugged him, stroking his hair. "I'm sorry. I thought you turning her cured her."

"Sometimes it happens, the doctor said," Theo said. "Stephen said she waited too long to try to turn. The werecougar virus saved her temporarily, putting her in remission, but the cancer wasn't gone. And the virus strengthened the cancer, so when it came back, radiation didn't even hurt it, no matter how much they gave her." He laughed bitterly. "If she'd become vampire, she'd be alive right now. Guess it's just another reason vampires tend to always get the best girls—"

"I'm so sorry, Theo."

He hugged me tightly. "She wanted to have my baby. We were trying, but it's much harder for two weres—"

"Shh," I said softly, kissing his cheek. "You gave her a new life, even if it was only for a short time. You made her happy. That's what counts."

"I'm sorry," Theo said, burrowing his face in my neck. "I should have appreciated you when I had you. I drove you away from me."

"It's old news, Theo. Leave it."

"Danial still wants us to be with him. He's been talking about it, Sar."

Foreboding flooded me, because now that Jenny was dead, Theo wouldn't be so quick to say no. In fact, it was in his tone that he was going to say yes.

I pulled away. "And?"

"I'm still worried about it. I don't like other men in bed with me. But I'll agree if he asks me again, because I'm not mated now and it'd be worth it to be with you. I think he's going to ask Devlin about it in the next month." His storm cloud eyes looked deep into mine. "I didn't want you to be blindsided. I know Brian's with Theoron now, so you probably had no idea."

"Thanks for warning me," I said casually, my mind racing. *Rene said she would help. I have to trust her.* "But it's moot. I said I'd do it."

Theo said nothing, he just let me go, his blue eyes unreadable. He walked into his bedroom and closed the door.

"Mistress, shall we return?"

I nodded and teleported home, wishing instead to go to Davy's and have a glass of wine to think things over. But I was pregnant, so I couldn't risk it. Shaker and I appeared in the kitchen, where he pulled out a chair for me. I sat, and he got down a bottle of some reddish scotch from a top cabinet and a glass.

"I think Titus will mind you Bogarting his Black Arts," I said with a forced smile. "That's expensive scotch."

"You can't drink, so I'm drinking for you," Shaker said with a shark's grin as he took out the cork and poured a shot into a glass. He sipped the liquid, then sighed happily. "Good stuff."

"You don't have to stay," I said, debating inwardly if having him to talk to would help me work out my feelings, or just annoy me further.

"You forget, I see your thoughts," Shaker said, studying me with his red eyes. "You can lie to me all you want, Mistress. But I will always know the truth."

"If you know how I feel, you don't need me to tell you," I replied evenly. "Tell me instead what to do."

Shaker chuckled. "Sorry, my guest column at Hell's Ask The Demon blog isn't due until next month." He softened his words with a non-toothy smile. "Besides, you're doing okay on your own."

"I always thought I did," I said, blinking back sudden tears. "Now I'm doubting every step I'm taking. Yet standing still isn't an option for me, either."

"You're moving forward," Shaker offered, sipping most of his scotch. "That's more than a lot of humans do, Mistress."

I snorted bitterly. "That's enlightening, Shaker. Hell's font of knowledge, that's you."

His red eyes narrowed. "Then how's this? You're preggers again, and not sure you want to be, because you're feeling like there's no end to the dangers in your life. But you had kids before while you were in the same kind of danger, and they survived. Yes, you're with three lovers again, but that sorted itself out before, and it will this time too, most likely. Sure, Serena left, but you have Rene now. That witch is loyal to a fault for those she loves and she's very powerful, so you seem to have actually traded up in the friend department. Your daughters and son are growing up, but they'll still need you, just as Dev and Danial will need you, when the latter calms down his ruffled ass-feathers." He threw back the last of his scotch, and then stood. "And our arrangement is working out decently, even given the near miss we suffered."

"He's alive," I murmured. "He'll try again." *For both of us, Shaker.*

Kyle is not going to tangle with me until he heals, Mistress, he answered mentally. *When he does begin hunting again, I can simply evade him. He's gotten a taste of death, and discovered he is not immortal. He may decide to give up hunting and go on working for Devlin.*

"Maybe," I said aloud. "But what about Valerian? He's my chief worry. What do you know of him, Shaker?"

"That you're right to be afraid," Shaker said, finishing his scotch in one long swallow. He held the empty glass, tilting it slightly in one clawed hand back and forth. "You already know of Valerian's involvement with Michael, and that he may be here this time seeking revenge."

"I understand he's not completely sane, just from speaking to him a few minutes. Yes, he's bent on revenge, but it seemed like that was to do with hatred for Devlin and Lash, not his love for Michael."

"Valerian had been an enemy of Lash's and Devlin's in their early days together, back around the time of the Great Depression. Lash and he traded blows back and forth, both of them losing loved ones and sustaining crippling injuries, until Valerian disappeared. That vampire is as ruthless as they come, Sar. Worse, he's very intelligent."

"Why did Valerian disappear years ago, if he gave as good as he got?"

"The short story is that in his coup de grace, Valerian tried for Devlin's throne with the help of the best assassin of the time. I can't remember his name, but he was a huge werebear, carried an oversize axe. Devlin and Lash killed him together, though Lash nearly died saving Devlin's life. Lash took a stake in the heart for him."

I nodded, remembering the story both Lash and Devlin had referred to before. *I think Ramirez was his name?* "And Valerian fled?"

Shaker nodded. *Yes, you're right. Ramirez was the bear I spoke of.* "A vampire fitting Valerian's description was sighted some months ago, and children went missing for a while south of here. Do you remember? Lash went to investigate."

I nodded again. "Was it Valerian?"

"Lash found nothing conclusive, but I think that it was," Shaker said solemnly. "Valerian always had a taste for children's blood, as well as torture. That was the reason Lash began their feud; he found out about it, and laid a trap for Valerian with some mystical fire. Valerian was burned and unable to heal for years. He never forgave Lash that injury." His eyes met mine. "Memory is a spider's web, Sar. Don't get trapped always looking back, or you'll never free yourself."

"We were talking about Valerian," I replied. "Not me."

"In the end, its always about you, and your choices," Shaker said, getting to his feet. "You write your own story with your actions, be they reactions or proactive assaults."

I got to my feet, facing him. "You're saying I should be decisive, and make my own path. I've been doing that, Shaker. And I think I'm doing a good job, all things considered."

He put a clawed hand on my right shoulder. "Don't doubt yourself." He smiled suddenly, humor in his red eyes. "With me on your team, you'll be okay."

"As long as I provide for you," I added sarcastically.

Shaker let out a low laugh. The evil in it registered, but I didn't shudder. "Yes, good human." He smiled widely. "It's so good to work with someone reasonable." He squeezed my shoulder. "Call if you should need anything, be it another pep talk or more licentious conversation." He disappeared.

I sat at the table, thinking on his words. *He's right. It's not a wonder I've been losing it, with all the things that have happened to me. But that's life for everyone, be they supernatural, mortal, or something in between. Yes, bad times are probably coming, but so are good times. I need to squeeze every drop of happiness from the latter, they won't last forever. The bad times I'll weather somehow, with support from my loved ones. Valerian... There'd be some kind of reckoning coming. There always is.*

He'll want a fight, Shaker intoned in my mind. *And he has a talent for plotting. It's his way to feint and vanish for months, only to reappear suddenly with the weight of all his men behind him. If Valerian ever truly comes out of hiding, he'll make Ulysses seem like an incompetent kid brother.*

He has a demon, too, I replied telepathically. *Azaroth. Valerian said you were no match for him.*

We are evenly matched, Shaker replied, obviously miffed. *But it's not just me, Mistress. You're loved ones will fight for you. Be warned though, Valerian will have formidable allies, too.*

Can we win? I wanted to snatch the thought back as soon as I felt it escape, not wanting to hear if the answer was no.

Do you believe we can? he answered.

Of course! It's not me to give up, I thought indignantly. *I'm going to battle with everything I have for my family, for my happiness, for my future. I want to be here, with my loved ones. My life's a good one. It's worth fighting for.*

Then you have your answer, Mistress, Shaker said, an almost proud note in his mental voice. *You are not afraid. Now get some rest.*

I stood up and went to the kitchen sink. Turning on the tap, I poured a glass of water. *Why didn't you just tell me we could do it?*

I already believed. It was you who needed to believe, Mistress. Rest, please. The battle looms on the horizon for us both.

I looked out into the night, my last shreds of sadness and despair solidifying into surety as Shaker severed our link. "You want a fight, Valerian," I murmured under my breath, resolute. "You're going to get one."

About the Author

Tara Fox Hall's writing credits include nonfiction, horror, suspense, action-adventure, erotica, and contemporary and historical paranormal romance. She is the author of the paranormal action-adventure *Lash* series and the vampire romantic suspense *Promise Me* series. Tara divides her free time unequally between writing novels and short stories, chainsawing firewood, caring for stray animals, sewing cat and dog beds for donation to animal shelters, and target practice.

www.tarafoxhall.com

Other works by the author with Melange Books, LLC

Return To Me
Surrender to Me
The Origin of Fear in Spellbound 2011 Anthology
Night Music in Midnight Thirsts II Anthology
Partners in Midnight Thirsts II Anthology
Kink in Wicked Christmas Wishes Anthology
The Oath in Wicked Christmas Wishes Anthology
Bedtime Shadows Anthology
Make Me Behave Anthology
Latham's Landing, An Anthology
The Oath
Her Frozen Heart, in Frozen Anthology
Night Music, a Novella

The Promise Me Series
Promise Me, Book 1
Broken Promise, Book 2
Taken in the Night, Book 3
Taken for his Own, Book 4
Promise Me Anthology, Book 4.5
Immortal Confessions, Book 5
Her Secret, Book 6
Point of No Return, Book 7
Lost Paradise, Book 8
Dark Solace, Book 9
Eye of the Storm, Book 10
Tempest of Vengeance, Book 11

Tara Fox Hall

Sundown-Serena, Book 12
Hope's Return, Book 13
Fate's Prison, Book 14

Coming Soon*!*
A Good Year
Forever, Forever, Promise Me, Book 16